ONE TRUE MATE

ONE TRUE MATE

A Westin Pack Novel

By

Julie Trettel

One True Mate

A Westin Pack Novel: Book One

Copyright ©2017, Julie Trettel. All rights reserved.

Cover Art by, Desiree Deorto Designs

Thanks and Acknowledgments

I am blessed with a great many people in my life who champion behind me in everything I do. Writing is no exception. To my family, both the one I was born into and the one I married into, thank you. Your continued support, encouragement, and love strengths me. Without you all, I would never have published my first book and would certainly never have had the courage to step out of my comfort zone and into the world of Indie Publishing.

To my amazing husband, James - yeah, I'm probably going to have to dedicate every book I write to some extent to this man - even knowing you have absolutely no interest in paranormal romance and wolf shifters, your insistence and time spent reading, critiquing, and praising my work spurs me on to success.

To my kids, Roman, Hope, Bethany, and Katy, you guys are growing up far too quickly on me. Writing has been both an outlet from the daily stress and grey hairs you cause, as well as a drive to show you that your dreams are always achievable with hard work, persistence, and a lot of prayer!

To the many authors and bookies I interact with daily, but most notably my dear friend, Heather Karn, thank you for your support and willingness to answer questions, back new releases, and offer encouragement through this crazy world of self-publishing. I certainly would not have made it this far without you.

And finally, to my readers and awesome new Elite Review team. Thank you for taking a chance on a new idea. You humble me with your encouraging words.

Kelsey

Chapter 1

"Mama," I cried, laying my head on her lap. Blood was everywhere, and I could hear the snarls and growls outside as my father fought valiantly against the rabid wolves attacking the house. "Mama, please don't go. Stay with me, mama."

The howl from outside the house nearly caused my heart to stop.

"Kelsey, run. Run, baby, and don't look back. Don't ever look back...."

I woke with a start, a cold sweat giving me goose bumps all over.

"Mama," I said aloud, letting it sink into the night air.

It was only a dream. The nightmare that still haunted my every sleep. It had been worse since coming to San Marco, since I finally stopped running away.

For six years, I ran from foster home to foster home, never allowing anyone to get close enough to know what had happened to me that same night, the night the wolves attacked and killed my parents, leaving me with a ragged scar across my upper thigh. Werewolves, not wolves, I corrected my memories. I knew they were werewolves, because that very night I changed into one too.

I was so numb from the pain of watching my parents die before my eyes that I don't remember the feelings or the pain of that first change, but I remember running through the woods with the wind in my face. I remember cowering under a fallen tree while the rain beat down on me, and I remember waking up one morning, naked at the edge of the woods where I was found. I was twelve years old.

Before the next full moon, I ran away from the home for girls they had put me in, terrified I would change again with the moon. That's what they tell you in the movies, but the movies are wrong. I didn't change that night or again for a long time, but after several months in human form, I grew impatient and short tempered and my skin itched all over. I knew something terrible was wrong. I've since learned that's the sign that I've been in human form for too long. That's when I would run away into the woods and never return to the home I had been in. I would always wake up naked and alone and they'd always find me and put me in another new home. That was the cycle of my life for six years until I finally turned eighteen and they could no longer hold me prisoner.

My parents hadn't had much, but on my eighteenth birthday I was handed documents upon my release from the foster care system that contained a small trust fund they had left me. It was enough to get by for a few years, but not enough to pay for college and a place of my own to live, and I couldn't risk being stuck with humans all the time. It was too dangerous. I was too dangerous.

I wandered around searching for just the right place, finally stumbling into San Marco, nestled deep in the mountains. I felt at peace for the first time since before my parents died and as luck would have it, a small one bedroom cottage sat on the edge of a large forest for rent. And the best part of all, the house had an unfinished basement that the owner said I could do whatever I wanted with. I immediately set to work fortifying a safe room where I could change without worrying about what I did in wolf form or who I came across. I never wanted to turn anyone into the beast that I had become that awful night.

It didn't take me long to figure out that most of San Marco was owned by the Westin family, including the property behind my home that I had planned to occasionally allow my wolf to run in. I wasn't as scared of my wolf as I had been as a child. She gave me a sense of peace.

I felt optimistic about this new venture, and as soon as I was settled, I began searching for work in the area. I wasn't very comfortable around people, and at first no one in town seemed all that comfortable around me either, but still, I knew I was different and an outsider. I had always been, so I didn't let it get to me and kept my head up and continued searching for work.

No one seemed to want to hire me. I was turned down more times than I could count and worried that if something didn't come up soon, I'd have to leave the little house that felt like home. Desperate not to let that happen, I applied to everything and anything in the area I could find and one day my phone finally rang.

"Hello," I said hesitantly.

"Hello, is this Kelsey Adams?" a bubbly voice returned on the other end.

"It is." I was still hesitant, but something about the friendly voice put my anxiety at ease.

"Hi, Kelsey, this is Elise Westin from the Westin Foundation. I was just going over your application, and see that you are currently studying business online and looking for full-time work. It doesn't really tell me what kind of work you're looking for, but we have several openings. Would you be available this afternoon to come by our testing center for some placement tests, and we'll see what you could be a fit for?"

I couldn't believe my ears. They were going to give me a chance!

"Yes, yes of course. What time?"

I tried to reign in my enthusiasm, but I could hear the smile in her voice as she relayed the information.

"I'll be there. Thank you so much, Ms. Westin."

I could barely contain my excitement as I quickly dressed in a conservative business suit I had bought just for interviews. It was dark brown and looked great with my long blonde hair, which I left down, and accentuated my brown eyes. It also highlighted my long legs perhaps a little too much. I looked down and frowned.

All I saw were chicken legs. That's what the other kids in several homes had called them. I couldn't help that I had long, thin legs. Maybe it was a werewolf thing. I didn't seem to ever put on weight, no matter what or how much I ate, and I knew I ate more than most because every foster family I'd ever lived with had complained about it. Still I was long and lean and muscular. The long runs in wolf form seemed to have made that come naturally. I wasn't exactly flat chested, I did have a figure, but it would never be considered curvy or voluptuous. I didn't mind my appearance except for those long chicken legs. I frowned in the mirror and shrugged. Oh well, nothing I could really do about it.

The moment I walked into Westin Foundation headquarters, I knew I had to work there. I felt an immediate connection in the same way I felt when I had first found the little cottage that was now my home. It wasn't sterile and impersonal like most offices. No, when you walked through the door you were met with warm browns and blues and greens. There were potted trees everywhere, and it smelled of pine.

I walked to the front desk and told them I was there to see Elise Westin. At first the receptionist looked strangely at me. I even thought for a minute she sniffed the air like I smelled funny or something, but then she moved on as if nothing had happened and I guessed I had just imagined it. I tried to discreetly smell my pits, trying to remember if I had put on deodorant.

Elise Westin was the friendliest person I had ever met. She hugged me immediately and welcomed me with open arms to the Westin Foundation. She seemed positive that the perfect job would be found for me there. As she led me to a small room with various office equipment, she explained the process. I would be given several tasks and asked to complete them.

"Don't worry if there's something you don't know or understand," she assured me.

I didn't usually feel comfortable around new people, but I immediately felt at ease with Elise Westin, and set to work doing the best I could on each task she asked of me. In the end, she seemed pleased with my work and optimistic we'd find a match.

Two days later I received a call back. I had a personal interview with the CEO of Westin Foundation, who was interviewing personally for a new administrative assistant. When she told me the pay grade, I nearly had a heart attack. I had to have this job.

KYLE
Chapter 2

My wolf had been restless for weeks. I had taken off more work than ever letting him run, and every time he headed to the little cottage that butted up to the south property line. The pack had all been abuzz about the new little she-wolf that had moved in. Why hadn't she come to me or my father already and make her presence known?

She had to know she was in Westin territory, and proper protocol for an outside wolf would be to meet with the alpha immediately and state her business in the area. Yet rumors said she mostly kept to herself, roaming around town, barely talking to anyone, and showing no signs of aggression nor submission. If it wasn't for the obvious scent her wolf put off, it was largely agreed that no one would even suspect she was a shifter.

My sister, Elise, had even reached out to her, and upon meeting, said there were no formalities or any signs whatsoever of acknowledgment. It was the oddest thing I'd ever heard, and now my evil sister had manipulated the situation to ensure we met by offering her an interview for my much-needed new admin position.

My wolf was restless and wanted out again. I had just spent the night letting him run. I didn't understand why he was feeling so aggressive when we were usually at peace with one another. Perhaps it was the scent of the new wolf in town. I wasn't exactly thrilled with the situation myself. How could any wolf be so blatantly disrespectful of territory lines? And why was a young she-wolf even here unprotected and alone? Where was her pack?

"Kyle." Elise peeked her head in without even knocking and

before I saw who was with her, her scent hit me like a ton of bricks. It literally knocked the breath out of me and I had to sit down. My heart was racing in my chest, and I imagined my wolf jumping for joy and running in circles. "I have Kelsey Adams here for her interview, are you ready?"

I must have looked as shocked as I felt because the smell of worry immediately flooded my senses, pouring off my sister, but also taming the smell of the young she-wolf in the next room, and allowing me to return to my senses.

"Are you okay?"

"Yeah, um, just give me a minute, okay? Have her wait out there. I just need a minute."

I could tell Elise was still frantic with worry, but she nodded and closed the door. My wolf ears noted she did not leave, but stayed with this Kelsey Adams, the lone she-wolf who had strolled into my town. Who dared to live in my territory without the proper respect given to be here? The woman whose smell alone assaulted all my senses and raised me to a new level of awareness. My mate. My wolf howled his approval in my head as I made the acknowledgment. My mate was standing just on the other side of this door. I had never laid eyes on her, but I knew she was mine just from one whiff of her scent.

Bracing myself for what I knew would be the full impact of my mate's scent, I took a deep breath and opened the door to the reception area outside my office. Her scent struck me, but I was more prepared this time. Big brown eyes met mine and showed no signs of recognition. Nothing. My wolf growled in my head and I fought to keep from letting it escape me.

"Kyle," Elise said, eyeballing me with open curiosity and still scenting of worry, "this is Kelsey Adams here to interview for the position of your new assistant. Kelsey, this is my brother and CEO of Westin Foundation, Kyle Westin."

She stood and walked over to shake my hand. The first thing I noticed was how tall she was. She had to be at least 5 foot 10 inches, taller still in heels, and nearly looked me in the eyes. Standing at 6 foot 4 inches, it was rare to find a woman that could match my height. I liked it immensely. Second, her handshake was firm and professional, but the touch of her skin sent shockwaves through my arms, nearly taking me to my knees from the impact. Yet the only indication she felt anything at all was a slight dilation of her pupils.

She eyed me curiously but said nothing about it, and while professional and respectful in every human manner, my wolf was put off at the blatant disregard she showed him. He tried to reach out to her wolf, but it was like she wasn't really there. It was very unsettling.

"Hello, Mr. Westin, it's a pleasure to meet you." Her voice was like the sweetest of chimes on the wind, and I couldn't help but smile back, and hearing it set my wolf's agitation at ease some.

"Please come in." I held open the door to my office and allowed her to walk in first. It was a human respect. An alpha wolf would never allow anyone to enter ahead of him, anyone except his mate, and the gesture immediately piqued curiosity from my nosey sister. I knew an ambush of questions would ensue later tonight.

"Do you want me to stay?" she asked with unease and anxiety still wafting off her.

"No, thanks. I've got this," I told her, trying to be cool and not alert her to the fact that my mate had just walked into the room. My one true mate.

As I turned to enter my office, closing the door behind me, it dawned on me that we were truly alone for the first time. My wolf howled in approval, begging me to take her right there on my desk and stake my rightful claim, but she hadn't even acknowledged my wolf. It was as though she didn't even know I was a wolf shifter too.

"Please, have a seat," I told her politely.

I had to find out her story. Who was she? Where had she come from? And why was she here? The slight sting of rejection from not recognizing and acknowledging me as her true mate made me angry and upset at the same time, and I set out to learn everything I could about Ms. Kelsey Adams.

"So, Kelsey, please tell me a little about yourself. I understand you're new in town. What brings you to San Marco?"

She did waiver a bit, but it was like she had rehearsed for just this question.

"I love the outdoors and wanted a place I could afford on my own, with opportunity to work while I finish my degree."

"What's your degree in?"

"Business Management."

"And what college do you plan to attend out here in the middle of nowhere San Marco?"

She smiled like she was expecting that one too.

"I'm doing college online. As long as I have internet connection, the location doesn't matter, so I was free to find some place I enjoy, someplace to call home, and San Marco is it."

I considered that for second.

"No friends or family in the area drawing you here?"

"No. No family. No friends really."

"But." I almost said, 'what about your pack?' but caught myself first. Something seemed off. My wolf recognized her as our mate. Heck, I recognized her before even setting eyes on her, but she didn't seem to give any inclination that she was a wolf at all.

"But," I started again, "how can someone as lovely as you be such a lone-er?"

I had to catch myself because I almost said, 'lone wolf'. Since she seemed so determined to ignore pack protocol and try and hide the fact that she was in fact a wolf, then I would wait her out until I discovered the reason behind it.

She shrugged, "When you have no one, you have no one to worry about. I don't really think about it. It's just the way it is."

It doesn't have to be. I'm here. I'm right here. I wanted to yell, but I held back.

"So, no friends, no family. Tell me, what do you do for fun?"

"For fun? What does that have to do with the job?"

"I just like to get to know my employees, or potential employees, first." I gave her a huge smile and even leaned in when I said it. Nothing. I gave her the lean. Even as just a woman, she should have recognized my interest. But nothing.

I sat back and cleared my throat. Fine. She wants to be professional, then that's what I'll give her.

"Ms. Adams, what is it you like to do for fun?"

"Well, I suppose I like to read. Oh, and run."

"Okay, read and run. Got it. Well, looking over your paperwork everything seems in order. Your evaluation went great. How soon can you start?"

This was the first sign of interest in anything that I had received. Her poise of perfection finally slipped as she lightly bounced in the seat.

"Really? Sorry, I'm a little excited to get this job. I can start immediately, today even, or whenever you want."

She was genuinely happy, and that made my wolf very happy and gave me a peace I hadn't realized I was missing.

"How about I call Elise back in here and she'll go over the contract and paperwork with you and you can start first thing tomorrow. Eight, okay?"

"Eight AM, is perfect!"

She stood and crossed the distance quickly before I could brace myself for the full force of her smell that came with the sudden movement. I couldn't help myself. I took a deep breath and let her scent fill me. I slowly met her outstretched hand and welcomed her to the team.

"Thank you for this opportunity, Mr. Westin. I promise you won't regret it."

"Kyle, please."

"Oh, I couldn't possibly." She brushed me off. "I'll see you tomorrow morning bright and early, Mr. Westin."

Kelsey

Chapter 3

I sat in the car outside the Westin Foundation and stared back at the building in shock. Oh my gosh, I got the job! It wasn't a hand out for once in my life. It was all me. I did it and it felt great. Then fear crept back in as I remembered the brief meeting with one Kyle Westin.

I really hoped he didn't notice me staring too much. But oh my gosh, how could I not? I had never seen such an incredible man in person. And his smell. Oh, I could die happy surrounded by that smell.

Normally I have an aversion to smells due to my heightened wolf senses. They're always there even when she isn't present. But not Kyle Westin. He smelled of pines and comfort and home. His smell was exactly the smell that caused me to stop here while driving through this small town of San Marco. It's the smell of the woods near my house and what makes me feel so secure and at peace. I couldn't ever remember feeling like that anywhere else and I would have been heartbroken not to have gotten the job and have to leave in a few months when I could no longer afford both school and the house.

But it wasn't just the smell of the man who was now my new boss. It was everything. He carried himself with such authority even my wolf was cowering at times. However, he also seemed kind and maybe a little too interested in getting to know me. Whatever happened, I could not let him in. I had to stay strong. I've never needed anyone. Just me and my wolf and that's the way it always had to be, because I couldn't bear the thought of him knowing I was truly a monster.

I backed the car up and quickly headed home. My skin was itching all over, which was a clear sign my wolf wanted out. I couldn't let her just run off in the woods though. We did that a few times when we first arrived, but it was a such a small town I was afraid someone would learn my secret. I made a promise to myself to lay low and not let that happen. I wanted to be here for more than a few months.

As I pulled up to my house, my wolf surged forward trying to take control. She hadn't done that since my earliest transformations.

"What is wrong with you? Calm down!" I said out loud, thankful once again for the lack of neighbors around.

As I was turning the key in the door, I heard a howl and froze. I looked around and was startled to see a very large brown wolf standing at the edge of the woods. He sorta bowed, or at least that's what it reminded me of, and then sat up and howled once again. It seemed to speak to my wolf in a primal way that I didn't understand, and it scared me. I quickly ran inside and shut the door. Why had I taken so long to do that to begin with? I knew better than anyone how dangerous a creature like that was. Sure, he was just an ordinary wolf, but still.

My wolf surged again, trying to gain control.

"Stop that," I fussed. "Let me change first. You aren't messing up this suit."

I quickly changed not bothering to put anything on, then gave one last look out the big picture window facing the woods only to find the wolf still standing guard.

"Standing guard?" I laughed to myself. "Where on earth did that come from?"

I headed down to the basement, locking the door behind me and inhaling the pine scent. It was missing something today. It was missing something uniquely him that I couldn't quite place, but for now, this would have to do. Looking around at the new den I had created for us, I gave into the shiver and let my wolf take control.

Shifting had never really hurt me. I didn't understand why or how, but I was thankful for it, and I was still coherent even when she took over. I saw everything and heard everything and felt everything. It was still me, only it wasn't. Or at least I had always needed to keep the two of us separate in my mind. It also allowed me to talk to her, and while some people would think that insane, it comforted me.

When I had first changed, I was scared to death of my wolf. I was scared of me and what I might do to someone, but as time went on, I found comfort in her instead. After all, she was the only one who could ever know our secret. Her constant presence gave me comfort and companionship where I hadn't found, or allowed myself, with humans.

My wolf tried to run for the door. I knew she wanted to just run. So did I. I was sad for her and for me, but for now, this was just the way it had to be. She paced restlessly around the room for quite a while before settling down with a sad whimper.

When I awoke the next morning, naked and back in human form, it took me a few minutes to get my bearings straight. The den. I was down in the wolf den. Sunlight was creeping through the tiny window I had carefully covered to allow light through but make it impossible for someone to really see in. Groggily, I looked around and spotted the wall clock I had put up just for times like this. It read 6:00.

Six am? I bolted upright and ran up the stairs, unlocking the door and slamming it shut behind me. I headed straight for the shower. Even coffee would have to wait. I was not going to be late for my first day of work.

Dressing in a short navy pencil skirt and cream colored blouse, I threw on a pair of cute strappy heels and carefully applied my makeup. I had never really needed much in the makeup department, but I made the extra effort for my first day on the job. Nerves and excitement coexisted the entire drive over, but when I reached what was to be my new office, I took a deep breath and was instantly calmed.

Two minutes later, Kyle Westin strolled into his reception area. He froze and appeared to breathe deeply before looking around.

"Good morning, Mr. Westin," I said trying to keep the nerves out of my voice.

When our eyes met, I felt a weird slam of recognition. The same thing had happened the first time I had met him. It was sort of a déjà vu feeling. Can you déjà vu a déjà vu incident?

He looked at his watch and frowned before looking back at me.

"Ms. Adams, I wasn't expecting you for another half hour."

"I know you said 8am sharp, but I like to be early. It gives me time to settle in and sip my coffee before the craziness of the day begins."

I smiled sweetly and hoped he didn't think I was weird. I really wanted Kyle Westin to like me and approve of my work. I've never really cared much what anyone thought of me as long as my secret stayed safe, but for some reason, it mattered to me now.

"Did you find the coffee maker and everything to your satisfaction? I can call Lily in here to show you around and how to use the thing if you want. Heck if I could ever figure it out myself."

He gave me a big smile that nearly melted my panties off. I hadn't even thought about the need to make him coffee, but of course that would likely fall under an assistant's responsibility.

"Of course, that would be great."

I expected him to walk into his office and perhaps place a phone call. I was more than a little surprised when, instead, he poked his head out into the hallway and yelled.

"Lil, get in here."

A petite brunette with similar hazel brown-green eyes to Kyle bounced into the room.

"Morning," she said as she stood on her tippy toes and gave him a kiss on the cheek.

It shouldn't have mattered to me one bit, but for some reason, my wolf surged and I was flooded with anxiety. I had had strong reactions and similar battles the previous day during my interview with Mr. Westin. I hoped it would stop soon. I had to get my wolf under control, and I was thankful they were distracted long enough for me to gain some semblance of control.

"Lily, this is Kelsey Adams, my new assistant. Kelsey, this is Lily Westin, my youngest sister. She's agreed to take today to show you the ropes and expectations of the job."

Sister? I should have seen it in the eyes. Still it shouldn't have mattered. So why was I overwhelmed with relief?

"Hi, Lily, it's nice to meet you."

I rose and shook her hand, but not before noticing the frown and small head shake Kyle gave. Still frowning, he said goodbye and walked into his office, closing the door behind him.

"He's not much of a morning person. You'll get used to steering clear of him until at least his third cup of coffee. We all do."

I snorted a little trying not to laugh. I liked Lily Westin immediately. I thought briefly that she might even be a friend. I had never really allowed myself to have a friend. I didn't let people close enough to form actual relationships with anyone, but Lily Westin I might consider taking a chance on. The thought was more than a little shocking.

As the day wore on and she explained the much too complicated coffee maker and showed me the copy room and some brief tutorials on some of the software and where to find Kyle's calendar, I realized I felt completely comfortable with this woman. My initial reaction, okay, after I found out she was his sister – I was choosing to forget that little jealous moment before then – of thinking of her as a possible friend, only grew stronger the more we talked. She was spirited and funny with a hint of sarcasm that I could absolutely appreciate.

As lunch approached, she informed me that Mr. Westin often took lunch alone in his office, continuing to work while he ate. I needed to check in with him to see if he needed something ordered, though she did say he sometimes brought his own lunch with him.

I took a deep breath and knocked on the door before sticking my head in. He was on the phone and held one finger up to signal me to give him a minute, so I poked my head back out and closed his door behind me.

"On the phone," I told his sister.

"He's always on the phone." She rolled her eyes.

The door opened and I jumped, feeling caught off guard.

"Kelsey," I felt like a melting puddle whenever he used my first name. Why couldn't he just stick to formalities? "Did you need something?"

"Oh, um, yeah, I just wanted to see if you needed me to order in lunch or if you would be going out today."

He smiled warmly like he really appreciated the thought, even though I was really just doing what Lily told me I should do.

"Hmmm, well, I hadn't thought about it yet." He checked his watch. "But yeah, I guess it's pushing that time already. I don't really have any plans today, so what are the two of you doing?"

Lily shrugged. "I'm supposed to meet Elise for lunch. You can join us, Kelsey, if you'd like."

"Oh no, thank you, but I wouldn't want to intrude. Besides, I packed a lunch figuring I'd take the time to decompress and let it all sink in. We went over a lot this morning. Just need to process it all."

"Well, if that's your polite way of ditching me," He genuinely looked disappointed and I had a strong urge to retract and make it right, "then I guess I'll just order in. You have enough on your plate for today already, Kelsey, so I'll just take care of it myself. But thanks."

Lily looked deep in thought as he closed the door and disappeared back into his office.

"Is he always so quiet and moody?" I couldn't help but ask.

"No. Something's up with him. I'll do my sisterly duties and harass him into telling me later. Now, are you sure you don't want to join us for lunch?"

"Not today, but thanks for the offer."

KYLE
Chapter 4

I knew I was pouting like a two-year-old, hiding in my office eating my lunch. I hadn't known the sting of rejection that would hit me when she turned down my offer to lunch. I placed a call to the cafeteria, asking for a bowl of the soup of the day. I suddenly wasn't in the mood to eat.

Pacing back and forth in my office, I tried to get a grip on myself. Yesterday when I gave her the job I had been so excited to find her that I hadn't really thought through what it would mean to work side by side with her when she refused to even acknowledge me in any way outside perfectly professional. Instead of soothing my wolf by, having her near, it made him more agitated, me too.

Last night when I sat at the edge the woods near her house and howled to her, I had expected her wolf to return in kind, but she had just stood there staring at me as if mesmerized before shuffling into her house. I had seen her through the window as she shed her clothes. I felt terrible watching as she walked from room to room, but I couldn't take my eyes off her. She was so beautiful and so natural. But seeing her unclothed made it even worse seeing her every time I left my office today.

I had decided that no matter what it took, I would somehow manage to get some curtains or blinds up in her windows. Just the thought of any other wolf strolling by and seeing her like that made my head throb and my eye twitch as I bit back the surge of anger. Nudity wasn't that big of a deal in the shifter world, yet I could not stand the thought of any other male seeing her like that.

Mine, I growled in unison with my wolf.

I wasn't sure how long I could stand working so closely with her and not having her. I couldn't just fire her, and I wouldn't admit to Elise that I had made a big mistake in hiring her, or admit why I couldn't work with Kelsey. It wasn't like all the other assistants I had managed to quickly fire. But I couldn't work with her when she continued to ignore me and our bond. It hurt too much.

I came up with a plan to work her so hard that she would quit on her own. Then maybe I could breathe again. Instantly the thought of not seeing her every day caused a stab of pain straight through my chest, but I brushed it aside. She had made it painfully clear she was not interested and I would have to learn to accept that.

After lunch, I called Kelsey into my office. I had her sit down and take dictation for two straight hours, then announced I needed the report before close of business and dismissed her. It had been wonderful and harder than I ever imagined having my mate so close and yet so distant.

As soon as she settled into typing, I called her in and asked her for five different financial reports I didn't really need but thought would help overwhelm her.

"Sure thing, Mr. Westin," she said with a smile that made my heart thump louder in my chest.

Ten minutes later, there was a quiet knock on my door.

"Come in," I said as I hit the button on my desk allowing whoever it was to hear beyond the barrier that kept my room safe from even the most sensitive wolf ears, wondering who it could be. No one ever knocked on my door, but when it opened, her scent flooded me and I knew it was Kelsey.

"Here are those reports you asked for, Mr. Westin." She looked me straight in the eye with a smirk as she set them on my desk and turned and walked away.

I was stunned. How had she gotten them together so quickly? My last assistant had taken nearly four days to find these exact same files. I knew because they were the same five files I had used to get rid of three other assistants I didn't find compatible.

And it did not go unnoticed how Kelsey had held my stare. My alpha power was strong. Not yet as strong as it would be when I took my rightful place as Pack Alpha when my father decided to step down, but even still, a little she-wolf such as Kelsey should not have been able to stand there and hold my gaze without cowering and showing submission. Her wolf should have demanded it, yet she had defiantly lifted her chin to me even.

If I couldn't smell her wolf, if I didn't feel the mating bond pull between us, I would swear Kelsey Adams was perfectly human. And yet, even humans felt enough of my power to back down and show submission.

A second odd thing occurred to me. My wolf didn't demand her respect. If anything, I felt as though he were bowing down to her instead of the other way around. I had no doubt my wolf would do absolutely anything for this woman.

I rubbed my eyes and shook my head. I was definitely losing it. I needed a break and had to get out of the office.

"Oh, Mr. Westin," Kelsey said as soon as I stepped out of my office, "I just emailed over the dictation you had asked for. Is there anything else you require this afternoon?"

I looked at the clock on the wall and noted it was only three o'clock. I had asked her to have them done by close of business knowing it would be near impossible. To say I was shocked was putting it mildly.

"Um, no, I'm just stepping out for a bit of fresh air." Even knowing I was trying to run away from her, I couldn't stop the words from tumbling from my mouth. "Would you like to join me, Ms. Adams?"

She fidgeted, looking nervous for a moment.

"Sure, let me grab a pen and notebook just in case."

Walking with her pen and notebook, she followed me out into the hallway and down the hall to the back door. I opened it and allowed her to step out ahead of me. That had been twice, and I wasn't sure why aside from knowing she was my mate. I couldn't stop staring at her tight butt and the way it made her skirt swish when she walked. Everything about her was mesmerizing and I noticed it all.

She looked around in awe at the back gardens. Everything about the Westin Foundation headquarters was designed to make wolves feel comfortable and confident. It was well known that we weren't exactly fond of being cooped up indoors, so as much of a feeling of the outdoors as possible was brought inside to help lift the burden for those of us stuck in an office much of the week.

From the smell of pine in the air fresheners, to the potted

trees, even the chosen warm colors of various shades of browns, greens, and blues throughout the building was designed specifically to help put our wolves at ease while we worked. The back gardens were no different. There were several of these oasis around the property with tables to work from on days where one just couldn't remain cooped up any longer.

I watched Kelsey as she took it all in. I saw her blush, but it didn't even register until she cleared her throat and shifted from foot to foot nervously. Oops, she had busted me checking her out. I didn't even bother to hide it or apologize.

She asked me a little about the company and my family, just making small talk, but her genuine interest soothed me, and her obvious affection already for both of my sisters filled me with warmth I didn't really understand. Just wanting to keep her talking, I divulged her of stories of me and my siblings growing up and loved the way she easily laughed along. If only every moment with Kelsey could be so enjoyable.

The second we set foot back into the office it was like flipping a switch. The small glimpse into this woman I had seen in the gardens was gone, replaced by the ever so professional ready to get back to work. I wondered if she had even realized she had dropped her guard for just a minute with me.

Shaking my head, I knew it was time to get back to work and carrying out Operation Get Her To Quit. I knew it would be best for the both of us. I didn't want this professional business front; I wanted to see her face light up and more of the carefree laugh she couldn't hold back as I told her stories, like the time Lily had climbed a tree so high she got scared and stuck. Of course, the story is much funnier knowing that wolves do not climb trees. It had taken the entire fire department half a day to coax her down low enough for them to reach her.

Yes, I wanted Kelsey Adams. She was my mate, and I could never turn my back on her or cause her harm, but I didn't need Kelsey Adams as my assistant. I needed her as my mate and something told me that as long as she worked for me, she wouldn't allow that to happen, but I couldn't fire her knowing it would upset her. Neither my wolf nor I could handle that, so the plan to work her till she gave up was on.

I couldn't help but be impressed. I tried to throw everything possible at her to push her away and she pushed back even harder every step of the way. Over her first week of work, no matter what I gave her, she was up to the task and exceeded my expectations. At some point, I stopped throwing useless work at her and started fully utilizing her skills and we quickly settled into a strong working routine.

I shouldn't have been so surprised the moment I realized that I couldn't live without Kelsey at the office. She was my mate after all, so finding her a perfect match, even if it was just work, should not have thrown me off, but it wasn't the plan, and I still worried she'd never see me as anything but her boss. The sting of her constant personal rejections continued but I seemed to have resigned myself to them already. I think if she didn't reject me, I'd be too shocked to deal with it.

"Hey big brother, you're coming tonight, right? Dad was not happy you skipped out on family dinner last week. You can't miss again tonight. You know Tuesday nights are Mom's nights, and Daddy doesn't take too kindly to a disappointed mate," Elise lectured me, walking into the office unannounced and dragging me from my thoughts.

"Hey E, have you forgotten how to knock?"

She snorted. "Since when do you expect anyone to knock?" She just stared at me then grinned. "Oh, except Kelsey. She spoiling you already giving you your privacy?" She laughed. "Well, don't get used to it. Rest of us have to keep that big head of yours from getting too carried away with your self-importance."

"What are you talking about? Just knock next time. Is that really so difficult?"

"Uh, yeah, it is. So, about dinner, you're going to be there, right?"

I had been so screwed up over Kelsey's first day of work last week that I had skipped out on Mom's mandatory Tuesday night dinner. I knew I couldn't get away with that again. Plus, I really needed to talk to my dad. I had heard some grumblings around the office about Kelsey's new position and how disgraceful it was to have her working for me. I knew there were plenty in the pack put off by her disrespect of territory lines and wanted her gone immediately. I couldn't allow that to happen.

I still didn't know why she continued to deny her wolf. Why

she still hadn't come to the Alpha House to present herself. And I needed the answers to these questions.

Elise cleared her throat. "Earth to Kyle. Have you heard a single word I've said?"

"Yeah, sorry, just a lot on my mind." I tried so hard not to look at the door, knowing she was just on the other side, and I knew the second Elise noticed it too. I sighed, "Yeah, I'll be at dinner tonight. Don't worry."

My sister backed off then. That never happened. I thought for sure she would grill me on Kelsey by now. Since Sara Winters, a lovely old lady who had worked for my dad my entire life and agreed to stay on for me when I transitioned into his former position as CEO of Westin Foundation, had decided to retire and spend her days watching over her grandpups instead, I had gone quickly through every assistant Elise had thrown my way. I knew she was curious and surprised to find the little lone-wolf who had strolled unannounced into our territory was actually working out. To be certain, I was just as surprised about it myself.

She gave me a kiss on my cheek before turning to leave. I should have known she wouldn't make it out without caving to her curiosity. With her hand on the door she turned back to me.

"Everything's working out with Kelsey?"

"Yeah, she's great." I tried to steel my voice to sound neutral.

She smiled genuinely. "I'm really glad to hear it, Kyle. I know there are a lot in the pack who think she should be run out of town, but Lily and I have really taken a liking to her and I truly do not believe she is a threat to us. I'm not sure why she insists on denying her wolf or not following pack protocol, but Kyle, I really think something happened to her. Something bad."

My wolf snarled and I had to bite my lip hard to keep it from escaping from me.

"What do you mean?"

She shrugged and came back to sit across from me.

"I don't know. She's opened up to Lily a little this week. Did you know her parents died when she was twelve? She wouldn't tell her how or what happened, but apparently, it was really bad, Kyle. Like majorly traumatic. I can feel her fear and stress heighten anytime it's brought up. And from the sounds of it, it was just her and her parents. She lost everything and lived in foster homes until she aged out of the system. Where was her pack, Kyle? How could they abandon a child like that? How could a wolf shifter survive all these years on her own? In foster care."

There were tears of true concern in her eyes and my wolf and I struggled between the need to comfort her and the need to run to our mate to shelter her from her past. I knew I couldn't go to Kelsey. She clearly wasn't ready, so I instead walked around my desk and pulled Elise into my arms.

"I won't let anything happen to her and she's not going anywhere. I promise. I'll discuss it with Dad tonight after dinner."

She nodded with damp eyes, and kissed my cheek again and turned to leave, for real this time. Before she closed the door behind her, I heard the concern in Kelsey's voice and knew she was trying to console my sister. That was just the type of person Kelsey Adams was. And clearly, she was a fighter and survivor too. My heart ached knowing she had been through something so terrible she couldn't even talk about it.

Dinner at Mom's was always entertaining. Just me, my dad, my mom, and my siblings. Aside from Elise and Lily there were our two brothers, Liam, Lily's twin, and Chase the baby of the family. It was the one night a week we set aside for just the seven of us. Every other night was devoted to the pack as was our responsibility.

After dinner, I didn't have to ask Dad if we could talk privately because he pulled me into his office before I could.

"So, I'm going to get right to the point because I know your mother whines when we spend too much time on family night discussing pack business, but son, you've put me in a bit of a bind here."

"What?" I was confused about what he was talking about. "What have I done?"

"Tell me about the little lone wolf you have apparently employed."

I know my face flushed. I couldn't help it. Even though I was planning to discuss the same with him, I was taken back that he brought it up.

"I understand she is quite beautiful." He smirked and a small growl escaped me before I could stop it.

I didn't like other men noticing or commenting on how beautiful my mate was, even though the reality was you'd have to be dead or swinging for the other team not to notice Kelsey Adams.

Dad stayed quiet and watched me with open curiosity after my little slip up, waiting for me to compose myself enough to speak.

"It wasn't my idea to hire her, Dad. I think Elise and Lily were too curious about her not to reach out. But honestly, she's the best admin I could ever hope for. I tried to push her away last week as I've done every other new hire they've thrown my way," I grinned sheepishly at the admission, even knowing my dad knew me well enough to know that had been the case, "and she just doesn't back down. Ever. She's strong and capable and super smart. I'm not sure I could possibly get by without her after only one week, so I'm really hoping you aren't suggesting running her out of town."

I watched my dad sigh heavily and lean back in his chair and pinch the bridge of his nose.

"Your sisters have made it clear they've already befriended the little wolf and now she's gotten to you too. You three are putting me in a very uncomfortable position. I cannot appear weak in front of the pack by allowing the blatant disrespect of a lone wolf strolling into town, settling in our territory and not even having the common courtesy to come to me."

"I know this puts you in a difficult position, Dad, but Elise and I have discussed and we really think something traumatic happened to her. She never recognizes her wolf in our presence. I mean not at all, Dad. I've even tried to push alpha command over her and nothing. If it wasn't for her smell, no one would ever suspect she was even a shifter. I've never seen anything like it, but there's more to her story than we know. I can feel it."

I knew that wasn't going to be enough to allow him to keep her here, so I pressed on. "She has shown no signs of aggression to anyone. She mostly keeps to herself, only ever venturing out for work or necessities like grocery shopping. From what little bit we do know about her, she is truly a lone wolf, an only child whose parents died when she was young. As far as we can tell, she has no one, Dad."

He looked surprised to hear that, and then a little angry about it. "What about her pack? She has to have a pack. Where are they and why weren't they protecting an innocent child?"

"I don't know, but I suspect she doesn't know or understand our ways. From working closely, with her I can tell you she is one of the most respectful people I know, insisting on calling me Mr. Westin at all times." I tried not to grumble out that last bit but I could see the questions it formed in my Dad's eyes.

"I'm not exactly sure what to do here, son. We are not in the business of showing weakness and allowing strange wolves to just waltz into our territory unannounced. I've let it go for weeks now but the pack is demanding something be done."

"Meet her. Meet her for yourself and then make the determination and I will try to accept whatever you decide is best for the pack."

"Try? Son, you've never questioned my decisions for the pack. What's going on? I feel as though there is something here you're not telling me. It really isn't like you to take to a stranger this way. What is it about this Kelsey Adams that has you even asking me to consider letting her stay in our territory?"

I shifted uncomfortably in my seat. I knew I had to tell him, but I hadn't admitted it to anyone except myself, and it was proving harder than a thought.

"Dad, I, uh, she, Jesus, I don't even know how to say it."

"Whatever it is son, just tell me."

I looked him in the eyes and held his gaze, even when my wolf wanted us to submit and lower ourselves to our alpha, I couldn't, he had to know the truth and the full importance of this.

"Kelsey Adams is my one true mate, Dad. She may not recognize it or even understand it yet. I can be patient and teach her our ways. I have to try, because I cannot lose her."

Nothing I had ever said or done in my entire life shocked him more than my revelation about Kelsey. As he tried to compose himself he started laughing, a full, deep, belly laugh that made me irritated.

"I'm glad this entertains you so," I scowled at him.

"Oh Kyle, you do understand the predicament you've put me and everyone else in here, right? And from the sounds of it you've got your hands full with this one without adding the mating craze." He shook his head and laughed again, "Every she-wolf within six packs has been sniffing around you for years, and a little lone she-wolf strolls into my territory and ends up being your one true mate. Priceless. The pack wants me to turn her out, but in light of this, you know I could never do that. The council will have to be told something at least. I assume you are okay with that?"

I hadn't really thought about it. "Um, yeah, if that's what has to happen. But please, Dad, explain to them the need to be discreet. Kelsey doesn't seem to know anything about our bond, or at least hasn't acted on it in any way. Heck, she's even turned down my human advances. I don't want to scare her away by her finding out too soon. Something tells me I'm gonna be tested to the max on patience with her."

"And lots and lots of cold showers in your future." He bellowed out another laugh. "But seriously, son, if she is your one true mate, you need to talk to her. If she truly doesn't understand our ways and customs, you need to explain them."

"I will," I assured him, "but please let me do this in my own way, in my own time. She's not like the other wolves we know."

Kelsey

Chapter 5

I sat on my back porch looking out at the woods and wondering where he was these last two nights. Ever since my very first day at Westin Foundation, each night when I arrived home the wolf had been standing watch and calling to my wolf. At first it had scared me half to death. I've always feared wolves, even before the attack, but there was something different about this one. He called to my wolf in a primal way. She begged to reach out to him and run with him, but I could never risk it.

Seeing him each night brought us comfort and a sense of security. It made me feel safe, even if my wolf was a little sad each time we saw him. The wolf was large, much larger than me in wolf form. He was a deep rich color of brown with startling hazel green eyes. There wasn't really anything scary about him and he never approached me, always just sat at the edge of the woods as if he were waiting for me to join him.

Sometimes I liked to imagine he was a werewolf like me. How awesome would that be? Then I remembered the monsters that created me and knew I could never even wish for that. So, then I'd think, would the wolves accept me as a wolf? Could I live full time in wolf form and find a home amongst them? I was not sure I could do that either, but I've always longed to be a part of something, have a family of my own, a real family. But then I would miss the Westin's so much. I've grown so close to them these last few years and I can't imagine my life without them in it. And I'm not talking just Lily and Elise.

I couldn't help myself from thinking of him. Kyle Westin. I couldn't believe I actually got to work with him side by side every day. There was something so dynamic about the man. He just drew me to him and made me want to do things entirely inappropriate for the office. I had a tough time even thinking straight when he was close by. His smell drove me wild, and more than once a week I was rushing home for a long cold shower. My body's reaction to him was unreal, like something you'd read about in an erotica book.

I sometimes caught him staring at me, and I had this feeling he felt the same, but then at other times I thought he barely noticed my existence. I've never had a boyfriend. Never even been kissed. Anything I've learned about that kind of stuff has come from books and I'm not sure how accurate those things really are.

My mind wandered to his family. I've been working for the Westin Foundation for nearly two years now. It's gone by fast, and yet it also felt like I'd been there forever, like life before I moved to San Marco was nothing more than a dream. I've never been happier and a lot of that was due to the Westins. I loved Lily and Elise like sisters. We ate lunch most days together, occasionally Kyle even invited himself along. We've gone out several times, but I'm not much for partying and hanging out in bars. I preferred my quiet life.

I remember once, shortly after I started working for Kyle, he took me to meet his father. Kyle's dad was quite intimidating, even more so than Kyle himself, yet he had the same carefree spirit of his daughters. I liked him immensely. He had asked me a lot of questions about my past that I hadn't been prepared for, but something about him set me at ease and I was able to answer them honestly. He was surprised and a little disgusted to hear I was an orphan with no family to care for me. But like I told him that day, that's just how life rolls sometimes and all you can do is pick yourself up and move on the best you can.

It hadn't been easy losing my parents at such an early age, and while I had told him they were murdered, I still couldn't bring myself to mention the details about the wolves who attacked us. Subconsciously, I caught myself rubbing my upper right thigh where I knew the ugly purple scars would forever be. It had taken the doctors eight rounds of skin grafts to close it back up and the skin around that area was still thin and ugly. I had to be careful not to

nick it or it would bleed easily. A constant ugly reminder of that terrible night and the terrible monster they had turned me in to.
I had lost more than my parents that night. I had lost my childhood and innocence, and I had lost my future all in one.

I could be very off about Kyle's feelings for me. Heck, I probably was. But it didn't really matter because no matter what, I could never ever let him know my secret, and we could never ever be together with that between us. Still, I longed for him to wrap his arms around me and hold me close. My body shivered just at the memory of the brush of his arm or him rubbing my shoulders after a long hard day. My body craved those little moments, but what did it matter when I could never let it go any further than that?

I looked back out towards the woods. Still no sign of the wolf. I couldn't help but worry about where he was. It wasn't like him to go missing like this. I sighed and stood up to let myself in. The familiar comfort and smell of my home washed over me in happy greeting, but my wolf was agitated more than usual. I couldn't remember the last time I had let her out for a good run, and thought maybe it was time I did.

In my mind, I could see her prancing for joy at the thought. So, I cracked the back door and quickly stripped, leaving my clothes in a pile on the floor and gave myself over to the change. I had barely hit the floor on all four paws when she was nosing the door open further and out, running at full speed towards the woods where the brown wolf usually stood.

When I reached the spot he normally stood guard, I sniffed the ground thoroughly, memorizing his scent. A feeling of familiarity swept over me and I was off and running again, this time heading deep into the woods. I followed the scent to the edge of clearing. My wolf jumped excitedly and howled before I could stop it from escaping. There was a cabin in the clearing and I didn't want to scare the people there and I was suddenly very afraid of what my wolf might do to the people inside.

It took more effort than I'd ever had to use to gain even a little control over my wolf side, but I had to do it and get us out of there. It had been a mistake to let her lose. It had been too long, and I prayed we wouldn't hurt anyone. I managed to turn us back around and head back into the woods, but not without a constant power struggle within.

My wolf finally laid down and whined. She whimpered like that often cooped up in the den when the brown wolf was outside. I sniffed the air and could smell his scent stronger than before, and it frightened and comforted me at the same time. I had to get us home and quick.

I managed to make us stand and started walking back towards my house, but we didn't get far before I felt eyes watching me. I turned quickly and the fur on my hackles stood up as I bit back a snarl. There was a new scent in the area that I didn't recognize, male and growing stronger, heading my way. Then another and another. An entire group of wolves were headed my way, and I instinctively knew it was too late to turn tail and run.

I backed up into the thick brush of the forest and laid low to the ground as they approached. I could see them clearly, four in all, and watched them sniff the air, knowing they had caught my scent and were looking for me. In two years, I had only ever seen the one brown wolf in the area, but I should have known. Wolves never ran alone, always in packs, well, except me, I thought ironically. Why did I think he would be like me?

I knew as soon as the first wolf scented my location. My back-end raised up and I snarled a low menacing sound his way. The others took notice and followed as they tried to surround me. Just as I started to pounce on the first wolf, I saw him. It was almost like a dream. That big brown wolf I had grown to love so much came seemingly out of nowhere and jumped over the first wolf to stand in front of me. His back was to me and he was growling and snapping his teeth at the others. I had been right all along. He was protecting me like my own personal guardian angel.

The first remained, even as the other three turned and ran off. The first growled back at my brown protector and started to make a lunge, but the brown wolf moved just in time and jumped on top of him, snarling and snapping his jaws. Leaping back, he started to come at him again, but the first wolf did the strangest thing. He looked right at me, then he stopped still and looked back at the brown wolf before lowering his head to the ground, then bared his neck to the large brown wolf who made a snorting sound and seemed to motion with his head for the wolf to leave. Their actions were almost human-like, and I was fascinated by it. Never once did I consider they too might be werewolves.

35

The large brown wolf turned toward me. I was surprised at just how much bigger he was than my own wolf. I kept my head lowered and averted looking directly into his eyes as I scooted out from my hiding place and stood before him. I dipped my head lower and bared my neck to him as I had seen the other wolf do. Something inside told me it was the right thing to do, that this wolf was something of importance. I couldn't begin to say how I knew it, I just did.

When I finally chanced a look, the wolf sat back on his haunches and quirked his head to the side studying me. Something about the motion reminded me of Kyle Westin and I laughed, but in wolf form it came out as a weird growly sounded that startled both of us. After the initial shock, I could have sworn the other wolf smiled. Can wolves smile? Surely, I must have imagined it.

I stayed mostly still as the wolf began circling and sniffing me. It irritated me feeling like I was being treated like a dog, and so I turned and huffed off, clearly surprising my self-appointed guardian. He snapped out, but I kept going. He growled, and it scared me, causing me to take off in a full sprint. It wasn't long before he had caught up to me, though, and the beast jumped on top of me, knocking me to the ground. I'm not sure if it surprised me or him more, but I pushed back and soon had him pinned to the ground on his back. His hazel eyes full of shock, but not of aggression. I no longer felt any threat from him.

He knocked me off balance and pinned me to the ground. I responded in kind before allowing him to stand as I began a slow trot back towards my home. He followed, keeping pace beside me. When he moved to brush the full length of his body against mine, a shockwave hit me. I felt a connection like I had never felt before. Like I belonged here with this beast. I had missed him while he was away and wondered why he had not come to see me the past two nights. I wished I could ask him. A part of me wanted to remain in wolf form forever, knowing he would keep me safe. I rubbed up against him and curled my head into his neck taking a deep breath and allowing his scent to wash over me. The wolf sat back and howled at the night sky. I had never seen anything more beautiful.

We spent the remainder of the night running and splashing in a narrow creek. I could not remember ever having so much fun in wolf or human form, but as the moon lay low and the sun began to rise, I knew I had to leave him. I had work in a few hours, and I would not be late.

I tore off at full speed giving him chase, heading for my house. We stopped at the edge of the woods and I sat back and howled. He responded the same, only when I moved to head towards the house, he remained at the edge of the woods. I prayed we'd be able to meet up again sometime soon.

Once inside the house, I wasn't sure what to do. I was still in wolf form and while I could change from human to wolf form with ease, I had never consciously changed from wolf back to human form. I had always stayed in wolf form until I fell asleep, waking in my naked human form. I looked up at the clock and knew I didn't have time for that. Pacing back and forth across my living floor, I began to panic.

I closed my eyes tight and thought of what I could possibly do while a strange, somewhat familiar ripple coursed through my body. I felt disoriented and cold. Opening my eyes, I realized I had shifted back to human form. I was naked, still on all fours on my living room floor.

I laughed out loud. "Well, that wasn't too bad," I announced to the empty room. Jumping up I ran for the shower and dressed as quickly as I could for the day. It was 8:01 when I sat down at my desk. Exhaustion nearly crippled me. Note to self: next time I decided to run with a wolf, do it on a weekend so I could sleep the next day.

I didn't really think Kyle would say anything about me being one minute late, even if he was used to me being at least a half hour early. I quickly started up my computer and ran to make coffee while it booted. God, I needed it if I were to survive the day.

With two fresh cups of coffee in hand, I headed for Kyle's office and knocked on the door. No answer. I set my coffee down on my desk and knocked a little harder. Still nothing, so I opened the door and peeked my head in. The lights were still off and there was no sign that Mr. Westin had been in so far that morning.

"Okay, well, I guess he won't even notice I was late."

"Why were you late?" Came a sweet voice I loved, but nearly gave me a heart attack.

"Don't sneak up on me like that, Lil. You nearly scared the daylights out of me."

She just laughed. "Did I really hear you say you were late this morning?"

"Yeah," I scowled. "I got here at eight oh one. Don't worry, I'll tell your brother as soon as he gets in."

The last thing I wanted to do was lose this job. I had just graduated a few months earlier with my business management degree and knew eventually I would move on, but I couldn't even think of it yet.

Kyle and Elise had taken me out to a fancy dinner the night of my graduation and told me how proud they were of me. It had been one of the best days of my life. Lily couldn't make it as she had already taken off to Europe to spend the summer with friends. I didn't envy her, though. I much preferred home to traveling, but I was thrilled when she returned just two weeks earlier.

"Eight oh one," she said in mocked horror, "surely he must fire you for such insubordination." She giggled. "I don't know anyone else besides you and Kyle who arrives before eight, Kels. I promise you it will be fine, though someone might actually believe you're human!"

Lily laughed. Little did she know just how much truth was in that statement.

"Who's human?" Came a deep voice behind me, causing me to jump for the second time that morning.

Kyle's eyes locked with mine and I couldn't have looked away if I'd wanted to. There was something so familiar in them, and I got the feeling he was waiting for me to say something. He looked like a man with a shared secret, only I had no idea what that secret was supposed to be.

"Mm-Hmm," Lily cleared her throat, dragging both our attention back to her. "Kelsey just might be human after all, big brother," she announced with authority and I couldn't stop the color from creeping up my neck and into my cheeks.

He laughed a deep bellowing laugh. "Yeah, fat chance of that." He winked at me and headed for his office.

"You're in too good of a mood to be strolling in this late. What's up with you?" I heard her ask as they entered his office and closed the door behind them. Even with my enhanced wolf hearing, I could never make out anything behind Kyle Westin's closed door, except when I knocked I could clearly hear him respond, and it drove me insane trying to figure out how he did it.

The day passed as any normal day, though Kyle seemed to grow grumpier as the day wore on. I had no idea what was up with him, but decided it was in my best interest to steer clear of him.

For the most part, I was pretty worthless throughout the day, surviving on caffeine alone. Over lunch, I chose to stay in and, pulling out a piece of paper, I began to sketch an image of the big brown wolf as he howled at the night sky. I added some trees behind him and knew it was a good representation.

Suddenly, I knew exactly what I wanted to do with it too.

The day couldn't end fast enough, and as soon as it did, I was racing for my car, leaving before Mr. Westin even, which was something I rarely ever allowed myself to do. Excitement had me speeding down the road and stopping in front of the Painted Dragon. I didn't hesitate, worried fear would set in and I'd chicken out.

A little chime above the door sounded when I entered.

"Just a minute," I heard a male voice call from somewhere in the back.

When he stepped in, looking enormous in the small doorway and covered from head to toe in tattoos with this black hair slicked back into a ponytail, I almost turned tail and ran, but I had made up my mind and this was something I had to do.

"Oh, it's you," he said, sounding confused.

"Uh, yeah, I guess. I'm sorry, have we met?" I asked him hesitantly.

His responding laugh set me at ease instead of fleeing for the door.

"No, I'm Cole Anderson, and you're Kelsey Adams. Everyone knows who you are. Everyone knows everything about everyone around here." He gave me a smirk and I felt more vulnerable than I had ever felt in my life. "So tell, what brings you into my humble abode today?"

"Well, it's a tattoo parlor, right? So I'll give you two guesses."

That caused a full laugh from him. "You've got spunk, I'll give you that, girl. For the mysterious little lone-wolf you appear to be, I sure didn't expect that. Come on in, and tell me what you have in mind."

"Now?" I said, suddenly feeling nervous and put off by his

wolf reference.

"Yeah, now, or do you have a better time in mind?"

"No, no this is great. I just didn't know you'd be able to take me back so soon."

"Nervous?"

"A little."

"First tattoo?"

"That obvious?"

He chuckled again. "Have a seat." He motioned me towards a chair that looked a lot like an old dentist chair, but the place seemed clean and I couldn't help but notice the wolf drawings on the walls in the lobby. If those were his, I needn't worry. His art was so much better than mine.

"So, what did you have in mind, and where?"

"Well, first I need to ask you a question."

"Okay, shoot."

"Um," I started nervously. It wasn't something I ever talked about and certainly never showed anyone.

"Can you cover scars with your tattoos?"

He frowned, "Scars? Yeah, no problem."

"Um, how about skin grafts?"

His eyes widened as he came to understand what I was asking.

"How bad and how long ago?"

"Bad, and it's been ten years."

"Let me see what we're talking about."

I hesitated.

"It's okay, Kelsey, there isn't too much I haven't seen in this line of work." His grin was meant to set me at ease, but it wasn't working this time.

"It's just, well, um, I've never actually showed anyone since I left the hospital. It's a little nerve wracking even considering this, but I'm so tired of being scared and having this ugliness as a constant reminder. I thought maybe a tattoo, something that makes me happy, would help?" I shrugged, feeling incredibly vulnerable.

"That's pretty normal, Kelsey, but I won't know what I'm dealing with until you show me, but most of the time scarred tissue and skin grafts can easily take the ink."

I nodded and slowly began to lift my skirt up, then stopped.

"Promise me you won't freak out or call me a monster." I was already fighting back tears.

He looked at me gently, understanding I had been through something very traumatic and spoke softly. "Nothing could make me think of you as a monster, and whatever it is, I promise I've seen worse."

I nodded, feeling only slightly better, and lifted my skirt the rest of the way tucking it into my panties so he could look at my entire right thigh.

I heard his breath catch and his eyes widen.

"What did this?"

"A wolf. It was a long time ago." I suddenly couldn't stop talking. Everything I'd been keeping inside of me burst forth to this one stranger. "I was twelve. Two of them attacked, killing my parents. I got away, but barely." I motioned to my leg for added emphasis. "It took eight rounds of skin grafts to get looking this good. But every time I see it, it reminds me of that awful night. I don't want that constant reminder, Cole."

"I'm guessing my lone-wolf comment earlier was a little uncalled for."

I snorted. I liked Cole Anderson immensely.

"Okay, well, did you have something in mind already or want to look at some books? If you want that fully covered it's gonna be something big and will take more than one session."

"Did you draw those wolves out in the lobby?"

"A wolf? You want a wolf to cover the scars left to you by a wolf?"

I grinned and nodded. "Not just any wolf though." I unfolded the paper in my pocket with the picture I had drawn of the big brown wolf and handed it to him. "I want this wolf."

Amusement flashed across his face. "This wolf? You're sure this is the wolf you want covering your body?"

"Absolutely. It has to be this wolf."

"Tell me why."

"My entire life I've been terrified of wolves, even before the attack." He seemed surprised to hear my admission. "This wolf, I've seen him in the woods behind my house. He's there almost every night, and there's just something about him. I don't know how to explain it, but I'm not afraid of him. He's big and should be terrifying, yet I'm not scared. I feel comfort knowing he's out there, kind of like he's protecting me. So yes, it has to be this wolf."

Cole looked extremely amused by my story.

"Okay, one more thing, did you draw this yourself?"

"Yes. I know you'll do a far better job."

"Uh-uh girl, this is amazing work. You ever want a part time job coming up with tattoo ideas, you just let me know. People pay a lot of money for designs this good. Maybe we could even cut the cost back some in exchange for a couple drawings. I really like this. Of course, the wolf would look a whole lot better being black." His grin was almost irresistible.

"Nope, it has to be brown, just like in the drawing."

"Okay, suit yourself."

It took five sessions to complete. Cole and I were well acquainted friends by the end of it. I gave him ten drawings in exchange and he refused to take any money from me. On the final fill in, he nicked one of the skin grafts, which started to bleed. He was quick to call in an antibiotic in case of infection and gave me stricter care orders. I was disappointed when he had to cover it. It was beautiful. So much better than I had imagined, and all the ugliness had disappeared.

KYLE
Chapter 6

I was continuing to stew over the fact that Kelsey was still ignoring me. We had worked side by side for two years, and every time she turned me down I felt the sting of rejection. Yet somehow, I knew the bond between us was strengthening. In the history of shifters, I had never heard of any mated pair taking this long to complete the bond. When she showed up in my woods in wolf form, I honestly thought, this is it. She's finally come for me. We ran and played and had the best night of my life.

Then later that same morning in the office, it was like she had no idea it had been me. How could she not know it was me? Rejection had never felt so bad as that morning.

Since then, I was quickly falling into a funk. Even my mother had commented on it at family dinner the night before. I knew I had to pull out of it lest it consume me.

A small knock on my door and I steeled myself for the scent that haunted me day and night. The scent I loathed and craved simultaneously.

When the door opened, I was assaulted by her smell combined with a coppery scent that shouldn't have entered with Kelsey. All the strength in the world couldn't have stopped me.

"Blood." I said, "Baby, you're hurt. Where? What's wrong?"

She looked at me in confusion.

"What are you talking about, Kyle? I'm fine."

In that moment, she said the one thing I had longed to hear, the only thing that could have jolted me from the compulsion to do anything in my power to protect my mate. She said my name. She

43

called me Kyle, and it had rolled off her tongue with ease. My wolf howled in appreciation, and I was vaguely aware that I had slipped up and called her "baby," yet she didn't seem to mind or notice.

Even that, as shocking as it was, couldn't stop the momentum propelling me towards my mate to ensure myself that she was okay.

I pulled her into my arms and hugged her closely to me. My hands roamed across her back and down her arms needing to touch her everywhere. The smell of blood was stronger, and I knew it was coming off of her. I held her chin in my hands and forced her to look at me.

"Baby, what's wrong? Where are you bleeding?"

She tried to push away, but I wouldn't allow her to reject me this time.

"There's nothing wrong. Wait," she thought momentarily, taking a step away from me and turning her back towards me. I saw her lift her skirt.

"Shit!" I heard her exclaim, marking the third most shocking event of the day, and it was barely 8:30 in the morning. Then she turned and ran out the door.

I followed her until I saw her running into the women's room. I tried to think what it could possibly be. She wasn't human so I knew she didn't get periods. She-wolves sometimes bled a little when they went into heat, but if Kelsey Adams was in heat, I'd know it, and so would every other male within six packs.

I had never felt so helpless, so I ran into Elise's office and grabbed her.

She shot away from her desk when she saw my face.

"What is it? What's wrong?"

I knew she had suspected for a long time that Kelsey meant more to me than I'd admitted, but I had never confirmed we were mates to anyone aside from my dad.

"It's Kelsey. Something's wrong. Blood. I smelled blood on her. She said she was okay, then cursed and ran for the bathroom. I don't know what to do Elise, and if you don't go check on her I'm going to barge in and find out for myself."

Elise laughed. "I knew there was more to you two than you were letting on."

"Nothing's going on E. I've told you that a million times. Now, go check on her."

I paced Kelsey's office for what seemed like an eternity before the girls came back laughing. They were seriously laughing and acting as though nothing had happened. I was immediately pissed, glaring at the two of them.

"It's nothing, Kyle. She's perfectly fine."

"Perfectly fine? Then why is she bleeding?" I asked Elise before turning to Kelsey. "Tell me what is wrong. I need to know you are okay."

Elise rolled her eyes as she turned to leave.

"He's like a dog with a bone." She jabbed at me. "Just show him Kels, and put him out of his misery." Then she winked at me and left our office space.

"Well?" I demanded.

She shocked the hell out of me when she grabbed my hand and headed for my office.

"Not out here."

Once in my office with the door closed, it took a whole lot of willpower not to just take her right there once and for all. She was mine, and it was all I could think about with her soft, small hand in mine.

"First," she demanded, "how did you know I was bleeding?"

"I smelled it. I told you that."

"No way. Normal humans do not smell blood."

I looked deep into her eyes. "There's nothing normal about me Kelsey, and I know you know that."

The confusion in her eyes took me by surprise. All this time I thought she was ignoring the obvious. She couldn't possibly be so clueless that she had no idea I was a wolf too. Could she?

Before I had a chance to think about that, she sat down and hiked her skirt up. All the way up. I could see her satin red panties, but she didn't seem to care.

"I don't know why I'm showing this, but Elise insisted I should."

I drew my eyes to the large bandage covering the entirety of her right thigh.

"A tattoo? You got a tattoo?"

She grinned happily. "Yes, and Cole nicked a part of my skin graft on the final fill in last night, so it's been bleeding off and on. It's fine, I swear. He has me on antibiotics to ward off any infections, but

I'm perfectly fine."

I doubted anything could have shocked me more.

"Cole Anderson did this to you?" All I really heard was Cole Anderson hurt my mate.

She rolled her eyes at what was probably a pretty intense look on my face.

"Look, Kyle," there it was again. Twice in one day she said my name. Two years of waiting and this was the closest to acknowledgment I'd gotten. "Mr. Westin." Kelsey said defiantly.

"Sorry. The smell of blood distracts me, and you, you called me Kyle, twice today." She blushed and shook her head. I squatted next to her and took her hands. "I much prefer it, you know."

Rolling her eyes again at me, she motioned for me to take a seat across from her. Not even bothering to lower her skirt back down.

"Do you want to hear this story or not? Elise already bullied it out of me, but I'd prefer you didn't hear this second hand. You've been really good to me, and I don't want to lose this job."

Her big brown eyes captivated me, and I simply nodded.

She took a deep breath. "When I was little, my parents and I moved around a lot. We finally settled into a small town, not much different than this one, when I was about ten. Two weeks after my twelfth birthday, two wolves attacked us. My parents were killed, and I barely got away. It was bad, Kyle. I was in and out of the hospital for months. It took eight skin grafts to cover the damage the wolf had done."

Fury filled me until I could barely see straight hearing her story, and I fought to control my breathing and not explode into my own wolf, demanding we protect our mate.

"Anyway, I was in and out of foster homes til I turned eighteen. My parents had left me a small trust fund, but it wasn't enough to cover four years of college if I wanted to live on my own too. I went for the first two years before taking a year to see some of the country. I knew I was home the moment I drove into San Marco, and when I found the little cottage for rent, I knew it was perfect. I re-enrolled online to finish my degree, as you know, and this job has helped me afford to stay here and live on my own. I can never thank you enough for taking a chance on an outsider like that. I know better than anyone around here how much you people hate outsiders.

But I have no complaints. I can't ever imagine living anywhere else, but, back to the scar. I've been scared of wolves my entire life, even before the attack."

I couldn't even comprehend what she was saying. How could a wolf shifter be afraid of wolves? I had once wondered if maybe she just had never made her first change, but I knew now, after having run with her, that that was not the case. How scared must she have been facing her first change all alone.

"Kyle, you're doing it again."

"I'm sorry. Please continue."

"Anyway, the scars were really ugly and a constant reminder of that terrible day. So, I decided to do something about it. It's taken a few weeks, but it's finally complete. It's not exactly something I had planned on showing anyone, but since you were freaked out about the blood, I thought I should tell you. I really am fine, though."

"Can I see it?" I asked with true curiosity over what picture Kelsey chose to erase those awful memories.

She nodded and slowly peeled back the fresh bandage covering most of her leg. I couldn't stop the gasp when I saw it. My heart nearly jumped to my throat staring at the vivid picture of myself in wolf form covering her beautiful leg. She had marked herself with me, and she didn't even seem to know it.

"Do you like it?" she asked hesitantly.

"Like it? It's beautiful, Kels," I said quietly, unable to stop staring. "Did Cole design this?"

"No, I drew it myself. I've actually done several designs for his shop already as he was so impressed with this one. Of course, he tried to convince me that the wolf would look better black, but this is my wolf and I wouldn't have had it any other way."

I almost chuckled, thinking of Cole's formidable black wolf. I'd punch him for it the next time I saw him.

"Why this one? Tell me why you chose this wolf and this pose."

She went quiet. Of course, I knew that night depicted on her body. The small creek in the background, the full moon in the night sky. I could even smell the pine on the breeze looking at it. It was the night we had run together, but something told me she would never confess that to me. I suddenly realized that I was going to have to present myself to her and explain some things before she truly understood anything. All this time I had thought she was ignoring things, but hearing her story, I realized she had no pack or anyone to show her what to do or explain our ways. I finally realized she honestly just didn't know she was living in wolf shifter territory, and so much seemed to become crystal clear with that realization.

"It's going to sound silly really, but I see this wolf almost every evening by my house. I've grown comfortable with him and like to imagine he's keeping watch over me. It makes me feel safe and secure knowing he's out there. He's truly as big as the tattoo depicts too, so by all rights, I should be terrified of him, but I'm not. By using his picture, I feel like I'm conquering my fears, facing the past, and ready to move forward, leaving all the ugly scars behind."

"Babe that's beautiful," I told her honestly, even knowing I slipped up again and she'd probably call me out on being inappropriate at work. I was thankful when she didn't.

"Thank you for not thinking I'm a freak. There's more I want to share with you, but I'm not sure how. I have secrets, Kyle. Secrets I've never confessed to anyone. Secrets that could hurt me and those I care about. Do you understand?"

Her confession was frightening me.

"I know you think you have feelings for me. But you can't. It's not safe for you. I'm not good enough for you no matter how much I wish I were."

She had tears in her eyes and was trying to make a quick exit. I grabbed her and pulled her onto my lap before she could escape and without thinking I kissed her.

Kelsey

Chapter 7

A part of me knew I shouldn't be kissing him back. I had tried to tell him, tried to warn him to stay away from me. I'm not even sure how we got to this point, but I had never felt such love.

At first his kiss was possessive, like he was consuming me and couldn't get enough. Then he softened and took his time, coaxing my mouth open. I was a little shocked at the invasion when his tongue slowly slipped past my lips, but the taste of him, combined with his scent surrounding me, was like pure ecstasy. It didn't take long for me to meet him stroke for stroke. I selfishly kissed him back with a wild abandon.

When I let out a soft moan against his mouth, he finally pulled back to stare into my eyes. I was entirely breathless. I had never felt something so exquisite and right.

My first kiss. I knew enough to know that was no ordinary first kiss. My entire body was tingling all over. He kissed like a man who knew his way around a woman, and the mere thought made my wolf surge to take control. I had to fight to reign it in and knew I had to put some distance quickly between me and Kyle Westin.

"I'm sorry," I said, knowing the tears were only seconds from falling again and I would be unable to stop them. "I can't do this."

The pain in his eyes nearly broke me, but I forced myself to get up and run.

"Kelsey!" I heard him yell after me.

I didn't stop or turn around, and I ran out of the office leaving everything behind. When Lily called to me from the lobby, I ignored her and kept running. I ran past the parking lot, cursing and kicking off my heels, and ran down the street. I needed to get home. I needed my den. I couldn't deal with the emotions that kiss had stirred within me. I had never wanted anything or anyone in my entire life, but I wanted Kyle Westin, and I knew I could never do that to him. I couldn't drag him into the living nightmare of my life.

I just kept running, not even noticing two men walking out of the woods next to the road until they were blocking the path in front of me. As my wolf went on full alarm I slowed up in my approach of them.

"What do we have here, Ted?" the larger man asked the shorter, stockier one. They both sniffed the air. I didn't think I imagined it this time. My wolf growled in my head, escaping from my mouth, but that only seemed to make them smile.

"Looks like we got a little lone wolf out here. Now, little she-wolf, what are you doing out here in the middle of nowhere? No car. No protector." He snarled back and barred his teeth.

I gasped! It couldn't be. I briefly wondered if these were the two werewolves that had killed my parents, even though the odds of it were insane. *How many things like me actually exist?* I had never stopped to think about it.

"Mike, don't. You know what the Alpha said. She's off limits."

"I heard 'em, but no one ever need know. This little bitch needs to learn a lesson or two on respecting the pack."

The man called Ted just shook his head.

"Pack Council's got their reasons for letting this bitch stay here in our territory. I ain't going against them, Mike. You know I'm already on suspension. What the hell am I gonna do if they find out and exile me from the pack? I can't chance it. Please don't do this."

Mike snarled back at him calling him a few choice words before he changed right in the middle of the road. His clothes flying off in all directions. I was facing down a real live werewolf. A small part of me rejoiced in the idea I was not alone. Mostly I feared for my life. I turned and took off running back towards the office.

The wolf was fast, but even in human form, I was faster. I felt certain I could outrun them and get back to safety, until I saw him up ahead, still yelling my name. *Oh no*, I had to get him away from here.

"Kelsey!" I heard Kyle yell.

"Go back, Kyle," I screamed as loud as I could. "Run!"

He did run. He ran straight for me. I could barely keep back the hysterics as my wolf threatened to change me at any second as we ran for our lives.

"No, Kyle, run. Kyle run!" I yelled over and over as he continued toward me.

When I was almost within arm's reach of him, I tried to grab for his hand, but it was too late. His eyes were already fixed on the wolf chasing me. A loud growl ripped through him, and I watched in stunned silence as he leaped and shifted in mid-air. His clothes lay in tattered shreds across the road in front of me.

I stopped and turned back to look. I expected a fight, but the wolf named Mike cowered quickly and whimpered in his presence. A shiver went through him and he was suddenly standing naked in the middle of the street. I was so shocked I couldn't stop staring.

"Aw, calm down man, we were just giving her a little fright. All in good fun." His smile as he looked my way made my whole body shudder, but it was nowhere as shocking as seeing my large brown wolf staring him down and knowing he was Kyle Westin.

Kyle was still growling at Mike and snapping his jaws as the man called Ted approached.

"I ain't had nothing to do with this, Kyle, I swear it!"

While they seemed distracted, I turned and ran.

Kyle's a werewolf. Kyle's a werewolf. Kyle's a werewolf. The verbiage was on instant replay in my head as I tried to make it sound real. Even seeing him change with my own eyes didn't stop the disbelief.

I had left my keys in the office, that's why I hadn't gotten into my car to begin with, and I ran straight there, grabbing my purse. On my exit, I literally plowed over Lily, knocking her to the ground.

"Kelsey, what's wrong?"

I needed to warn her. "Werewolves! Lily hide, quick, they're coming."

She was yelling at me to come back, but I couldn't listen. I was in full survival mode as I jumped in the car and nearly ran over Kyle and the two men as I tore out of the parking lot. I heard Kyle howl. It didn't sound as reassuring as usual, though it didn't really sound scary either, more sad, very very sad, and that sadness called to my wolf like never before.

I briefly noticed them all walking into the Westin Foundation like it was nothing, as I was speeding past. Kyle as a wolf, Mike completely naked, and Ted tagging along after them. I couldn't let myself think about what could happen to the people I worked with.

A part of me wondered if they were all in on it. Was I the only one that didn't know? Oh my gosh, Lily and Elise were Kyle's sisters. Were they werewolves too? Everything I knew about werewolves was evil, but I didn't think I was evil. I didn't think Lily or Elise had an evil bone in their bodies. And Kyle. Kyle had been good to me, both in human and wolf form.

In my mind, I understood these to be truths, but my history told me to run, to leave this area behind and survive. And I couldn't trust my heart. It was broken in a million pieces. Even though I knew I could never have Kyle, I cared a lot for him and had wished for so long things could be different. I never imagined he had been hiding something so big from me all this time. It was like all the lies of my life came crashing in on me.

I shut off my brain, and I shut off my heart, and I did the only thing I had ever known how to do. I turned the car towards my cottage and I ran into the house to grab my go-bag and I prepared to run. I prepared to survive. It was all I knew.

I was in my den trying to get the safe open with shaking hands when I heard tires screeching in my driveway.

Oh no! I thought I'd have enough time to grab and go. I was so scared. I cowered into the corner and when my wolf surged forward, I didn't fight it, and gave in to the shiver that went through my body. I then crouched low and backed into a hole and waited.

There was a knock on the front door and my wolf let out a low growl.

"Her car's still here, Kyle. She has to be here." I heard Elise say.

"Just check the door. Is it unlocked?" Lily said.

I heard the door knob turn and several pairs of feet entered my house. I couldn't tell just how many.

"Ugh, how does she live like this? There's so much air freshener I can't even tell if she's really here or not," Lily complained.

I knew wolf noses were super sensitive. It had taken me a long time to build up an immunity to the harsh smells of the air fresheners, but it was also an extra security measure that I knew helped cover my scent so any wolves passing by wouldn't suspect I was there.

"She's not here," Elise said.

"She has to be," Lily stated. "Look, her bag's still here."

"Kelsey!" Kyle started yelling through the house. I could hear his heavy footsteps as he paced back and forth. "Kelsey, where are you?"

My wolf started to whimper.

No you do not! I silently threatened.

I could feel him pulling my wolf towards him, and I struggled to stay in hiding.

My heart began racing as the basement door creaked open and footsteps began to slowly descend.

Growl at him! I silently demanded but the wolf in me wouldn't listen. Instead, I heard a light thumping and realized it was the wolf's tail happily wagging behind us. *Traitor!*

"Wow!" Kyle said aloud.

"What is it? What's down there?" Lily asked.

"Hold up, okay? She's down here. I can smell the fear rolling off her. Just give me a few minutes."

"Please tell her we're really worried about her and hurry it up."

"You hear that Kels? You got everyone concerned about you. I never meant to frighten you today, but I couldn't let Mike threaten you like that. I've made sure the others stay away. He broke a direct pack order and will be punished for it. I promise. I'd never let anyone hurt you."

He was quietly walking around my den. I should have felt violated. My den was a sacred place to me, but instead I felt... I'm not even sure how to put it into words. It was like for once in my life everything was righted, but that seemed all wrong. He was a monster, like the monsters that killed my parents and the one who changed me.

My wolf snorted and tried to move forward a little. It took a lot of willpower to keep us there.

"Kelsey, come here."

I felt this strange power wash over me that I didn't understand and my wolf whimpered as I fought to refuse the invisible leash trying to draw me out of hiding.

"Kelsey, come here," he said in a stronger voice.

The power emanating through the room became stronger, thicker, and harder to resist, but I stood my ground.

"Damn it, Kelsey, how are you doing that?"

"Doing what?"

I heard Kyle jump and knock something over as Elise entered my den. My wolf didn't like another female being there and began to growl loudly. I could feel my hackles rising.

"Shit! Elise, back upstairs, she's in wolf form."

That stopped me in my tracks. Pushing back against my wolf urges I surged to take control and felt the familiar ripple as I transformed, waiting for the nausea and dizziness to subside.

"You knew?" I demanded, crawling out of my now too small space. "You knew all this time and you never told me? Never even let on that you had any idea of what I am?"

The feeling of betrayal was so strong that I didn't even notice I was standing naked before them until Elise yanked my robe off its hook by the steps and brought it to me. She hesitated as if judging my stability.

"Thanks," I told her, letting her know it was okay. I wasn't mad at her right then, I was mad at him.

I watched him cringe as I turned my attention back to him.

"How could you? How could you not tell me, even after everything I told you today!"

I didn't want to cry in front of him, but I couldn't stop the tears. I had been alone all my life, and finding out that the only friends I'd ever had were monsters just like me was both a relief and a fear. I didn't know for sure that Elise and Lily were werewolves too, but I suspected as much.

"Why didn't you tell me?"

KYLE
Chapter 8

I have never cowered to anyone in my life, not even my father who is the only wolf in all of Westin Territory who out ranks me, but seeing the pain and betrayal in my mate's eyes had me ready to beg for forgiveness.

"Kelsey, let us explain, please." Lily was begging already.

Lily wasn't an alpha like me. I was born an alpha. Alpha females by birth were rare, and the Grand Council had a standing kill order out for any that were born. Alpha females were dangerous and too strong and too powerful to control. I didn't really agree with the Council on this. I couldn't imagine killing a young she-wolf showing extraordinary powers, but it had been done for generations. And luckily, it was an extremely rare occurrence. Better yet, it had never happened in the history of the Westin Pack.

"You?" she asked my sister breaking, my thoughts, "Are you, Lily? Are you a werewolf too?"

"We don't really like the term werewolf. We call ourselves wolf shifters, or just shifters."

"How? How did you all get like this? Did a werewolf come through and bite everyone?"

I couldn't help the stunned look on my face. Did she really believe the wolf that had killed her parents had turned her into a werewolf? I tried hard to think back through the little she had confided in me.

"Kels, we're not created from a wolf bite. We're born this way," Lily told her as calmly as she could.

I saw the disappointment and despair in Kelsey's eyes.

"Oh," she said quietly.

"Lily and Elise, excuse us. Kelsey and I have a lot to talk about."

I let some of my authority flow over them and saw Kelsey's eyes widen. So, she did feel it after all. I had always been lead to believe that alpha power was natural and that all wolves were born to it and born to recognize and respond to it, but since meeting Kelsey I had been second guessing that theory. Could it be that wolves were taught at such a young age about alpha powers that they never doubted it? Could it really be nurture and not nature? It went against everything I had ever been taught, but Kelsey wasn't raised in a pack and seemed immune to my powers.

With my sisters gone, I sat down on the floor, looking around and taking in my surroundings for the first time.

"This is amazing, Kelsey. I've wondered every day since you showed up in my office why you didn't come out to run. I waited for you. I called to you. This den is incredible. Is this what you use to keep your wolf side happy while cooped up inside?"

I could still smell her heightened stress levels, but they had eased a little with the girls' departure. I waited for her to respond, but all I got was a small nod of her head.

"Is it okay that I'm down here? Wolves are very territorial."

She shrugged. "She didn't like it when Elise came down. I had to change back to keep her from attacking." She looked ashamed. Didn't she know that was perfectly normal? "You don't seem to aggravate her, though."

I should hope not. Her wolf side had to know I was her mate even if she didn't seem to have any understanding of it.

"Will you sit and talk with me?"

She sighed and sat.

"You don't understand, Kyle, I'm not like you guys. I need to get away from here, far far away."

What in the world was she talking about?

"Babe, tell me why you think that."

"The werewolves, they are dangerous. If they find me, they'll kill me. My mother warned me to stay away from the wolves. I can't tell who's good and who's bad here. And I don't understand any of this. How can you be born this way? It doesn't make any sense!"

"So, tell me why you think you're some evil werewolf?

Cause I know you, Kels. There's nothing evil about you."

A tear slid down her cheek.

"I've never told anyone what happened that night."

"Can you trust me enough to tell me?"

She was quiet and I didn't think she was going to tell me. Then she surprised me by speaking.

"Two wolves came in the night. My father woke up and tried to hide my mother and me while he fought them off, but they were too fast, too strong for him, and they took him down before we could get away. I remember crying and wanting to scream for him, but my mother hushed me and wrapped me in her arms and dragged me out the back door. We almost made it to the woods behind our house when we heard them coming around the corner. They attacked my mother from behind. Her screams and the sight of all that blood gushing from her still haunt my dreams every single night. Something distracted them and they left for just a minute. She yelled for me run, but I couldn't just leave here lying there. I started to cry and she begged me to leave her, but I stayed. I didn't know what to do or where to go. She pushed herself up to sit with her back, raw from the attack, up against a tree. I know she must have been in pain, but all she cared about was me. I laid my head in her lap and she stroked my hair and begged me to leave. When we heard the wolves coming back, she got frantic and demanded I go. 'Kelsey, run. Run baby, and don't look back. Don't ever look back....' Those were her last words to me. I got up and started to run. One of the wolves chased me, but even then, I was fast, but I tripped and turned to face him, scrambling backwards. He lunged for me, snapping his jaws and clamping down on my leg. He took a big chunk of it and I screamed and kicked out, connecting with his nose. He howled and stumbled back. It was enough for me to get up and run. I ran and ran and never looked back. While running, I started feeling cold then my entire body started itching."

I couldn't believe what she was telling me. I knew what she was about to say. What she was describing. But how was that possible?

"I remember screaming, but I don't really remember it hurting. The next thing I knew I was on all fours, running even faster through the woods. I woke up the next morning, naked, lying next to a road. I was miles away from my house. I was in such shock and they said I lost so much blood that I blocked out a lot of the following days. I think they kept me heavily drugged while in the hospital. I had my first three skin grafts before I left the hospital. I was put in foster care, but even though I was young, I knew I could never let anyone know how they had turned me into a beast, a monster."

I reached out and gently wiped her tears away. I wanted to grab her and pull her into my arms and just hold her. But even that simple touch brought me a little peace. I didn't want to freak her out knowing how fragile she was in that moment, but I needed to feel her, to assure myself and my wolf that our mate was okay. I was thankful she did not shrink away from my touch.

"How old were you?"

"Twelve."

"Twelve? Jesus, Kelsey, I've never heard of any shifter changing that young, and all alone. I can't imagine how scared you must have been, and how lonely your world has been since then. But, baby, I can only imagine the stress of that night caused your wolf to come out sooner than it should to protect you. To the best of my knowledge, it's impossible to change someone with a bite the way movies and books depict. You're either born with a wolf or you're not. Most shifters don't change for the first time until somewhere between 18-20 years old, and it's not uncommon for it to be as late as about 25. For a long time, I wondered if maybe you were just late changing, but then your wolf showed in the woods, and I could tell in your eyes that it wasn't unfamiliar, like your first time."

"You knew it was me that night? How?"

"Kels, I'd know your scent anywhere. There's a lot about wolf shifters that you need to know about, and I promise you, you are a wolf shifter. There's a lot about pack life and protocol that you need to know too. It's going to be a lot to take in, and I don't want to stress you out or overwhelm you anymore than you already are." I remembered something that had bothered both me and my dad about her,

"Kelsey, do you know what pack you come from? Do you remember anything at all about them? It's the one thing that Dad and I have struggled with the most. Why would any pack allow such a young pup to go through life alone?"

"I don't even know what you mean when you say pack. You mean like a pack of dogs, a group of animals living together?"

"More or less, yeah, though most of us spend more time in our skin than in our fur. And I think of it more like a large close family who all live in the same general area and support each other," I smiled at her example, though, there was some truth in that too.

She shook her head. "I don't ever remember living with others. It was always just me, Mom, and Dad as far as I remember. I don't even remember ever having a babysitter or aunt or uncle. Nothing."

I frowned. How was that even possible? My wolf growled, and it escaped from me before I could stop it. Kelsey's eyes widened, but she didn't shift away from me, remaining within arm's reach.

"Sorry. It just makes me so angry to think about that happening to you. To think your pack just abandoned you like that. I could never do that to anyone, but especially not a young pup."

"I don't know how I could have ever lived with wolves, or wolf shifters, Kyle. I told you before I have always been terrified of wolves, even before the attack. You were the first and only wolf I haven't been scared of, aside from my own wolf of course. Why do you think that is?"

Because I'm your mate! I wanted so badly to blurt that out, but something told me this was not the time for that. She already had enough to take in and accept without adding that to it. So, I shrugged, unable to speak, and ran a nervous hand through my hair.

"Maybe we should let everything sink in for today and start going through all your questions tomorrow? I really think you need time to process all that's happened. I can't even imagine going through life thinking I was some fictional monster, only to discover there are plenty of others just like you. Somewhere out there you have a pack, and if you want to find them, Kels, I'll make that happen, but you have to know, you will always have a place in Westin Pack."

I couldn't explain to her just yet that she would not only have a place in my pack, but that, if she'd have me, she'd someday be the Pack Mother, the highest position possible for a she-wolf in the pack.

Kelsey

Chapter 9

I couldn't believe what he was telling me. Could it be true? I was having a tough time absorbing it all. There were others like me? I wasn't created, but I was born this way? When he talked about pack, he talked about family. I have a family? Where were they? Why didn't they come for me? The amount of questions bombarding me was overwhelming, and he was right in that I needed time to take it all in.

I had caught Kyle Westin staring at me so many times over our last two years working together. It had never seemed inappropriate or uncomfortable, and I always felt like he had just been waiting for me to do or say something. I shivered, thinking that's exactly what it was. He had known all along and never once alluded to anything. It shouldn't have hurt to think of it, but it did. I couldn't explain the stabbing pain in my heart when I thought about it. It felt like betrayal, yet I trusted him and believed what he said was true. I still didn't see how I could have been born a shifter and my parents never mentioned a word of it. They had to have known. Why wouldn't they have told me?

He was staring at me again. Waiting. Letting me sort through my thoughts and questions in my own time. I was grateful to him for it and as I thought about it, as I looked at him, a surge of something brushed through me. It felt like my wolf, but not like she was fighting for control or to get out. I had this uncontrollable urge to just reach out and touch him.

I know he saw my eyes go wide with shock. He gave me a slight little smirk of a grin like he knew exactly what I was thinking. I felt the urge brush through me again, and before I realized it, I had scooted closer to him. So, close. Our bodies brushed up against each other and my hand was out and headed for what? Him? His face? His body? I licked my lips at the thought just as it all came slamming into me.

What the hell was I doing? I jerked my hand back and made a move to scoot back, shocked and embarrassed at my actions. It had been like I was in a trance and couldn't control myself from reaching out to him for comfort.

He gave a small chuckle and reached out and grabbed my hand. He laid it against his cheek, and the slight stubble of the day's growth tickled my palm in a delicious way that I loved. I couldn't stop myself from stroking his cheek even while his large hand covered mine, holding it against him. And he looked. happy? It was as if my entire body relaxed into a puddle of goo at his touch and he looked as if he was having the same affect from mine.

"It's okay, babe, wolves crave touch and closeness. It is perfectly normal. Don't ever feel afraid to reach out and touch me. It will calm your wolf, as it does mine. Did you feel a peace wash over you at my touch?"

Oh, I felt something wash over me, but I'm not quite sure it was exactly peace. My heart was already racing just at his closeness, now I thought it may just jump out of my chest. But there was something searching in his eyes, like he needed me to confirm this for him. I nodded, even knowing I couldn't control the blush that was no doubt turning my face into a blotchy mess.

He let out a small breath I hadn't realized he was holding and smiled so big it was contagious, and I found myself returning it.

"Come here," he said. Not demanding, not quite asking, but I still got the feeling he was treading in new territory here too.

I gave a small yelp in surprise as he reached out and wrapped his arms around me and pulled me onto his lap cradling me like a small child.

My wolf stirred in excitement, though she made no attempt to take control. I could not remember ever feeling so content. Both my wolf and I were at complete peace, and my entire body calmed. Even my racing heart stilled as I soaked up the warmth surrounding me in Kyle Westin's embrace. I laid my head on his shoulder and turned towards his neck. Without realizing what I was doing, I took a deep breath, letting his scent envelope me. It was a scent I knew well, but there was something different about it this time, something I couldn't quite place. I felt him shudder lightly around me.

He turned and kissed the top of my head. My first instinct was to jolt and get away from him quickly, but I couldn't physically make myself do it. Instead, it was like this dam that had been holding back my deepest emotions for most of my life cracked, and with that small crack, everything broke free.

I was crying, borderline hysterical, the big ugly, full body sobbing cries. I should have been humiliated to do that in front of him, but I wasn't, and I couldn't have stopped it if I tried. He just held me, slightly rocking in a soothing pattern and telling me over and over that he was there and everything was going to be fine now, that he would never let anything bad happen to me again. No one had ever comforted me in a such a way outside of my parents, and I craved it.

At some point, he must have lulled me to sleep because the next thing I knew I woke up and couldn't remember where I was or what I was doing. I was in the in the most amazing cocoon imaginable. I felt safer than I'd ever felt in my entire life. I knew I was in my den before I even opened my eyes because I could smell my usual scents, but they were accompanied by a new smell. A masculine scent of pine and lemon that just smelled refreshingly like home combined with my usual den smells. I stretched and the palm of my hand rubbed against something firm, but comfortably inviting. A soft moan escaped as I turned and snuggled in closer. I sighed contentedly, opening my senses, surprised to hear a soft mumbling noise I couldn't quite place. With some concentration, the sound morphed into voices, and the hair on my body, even in human form, stood up.

"Shhh, you're waking her. Go away." A muffled rumble came much too close to my ear.

Suddenly, everything from the day came crashing back in on me. I jerked and sat up quickly. I moved fast, real fast, imagining they saw little more than a blur as I retreated into my favorite hidey hole in the den. I sniffed the air in alert confusion, and let out a low growl when I smelled intruding females in my territory.

"Oh my gosh! Did you see that?"

"No, where did she go?"

"I don't know. I've never seen someone move so quickly, especially in human form."

Human form, I thought? Oh right. I recognized the voices. Lily and Elise. My heart rate sped up in a panic before I remembered they knew now and they were all in on it too. The pain of that betrayal hit me like a ton of bricks.

"Back off, and get back upstairs. I told you she wasn't comfortable with you girls in her den."

"We're her friends, Kyle. You're an alpha, you're a bigger threat to her than we are."

"It's not like that. You know she-wolves are very territorial. You two couldn't even share a bedroom once you both came of age, and you're sisters."

"Yeah, yeah," Lily said, "But really, I'm worried about her, Kyle. Where did she go?"

I sighed as I crawled out on all fours, but still fully dressed and in human form.

"I'm here. I'm okay. Sorry. I think I dozed off and was just confused waking up with new scents and voices here. Just got spooked. I'm sorry."

I couldn't help feeling ashamed at how I'd reacted. Kyle made a move towards me but I held up my hands.

"Please, just give me a minute."

The hurt evident on his face at my words and actions felt like physical pain to me. It made no sense and my head was spinning as my new reality sunk in.

Taking a deep, cleansing breath, I nodded to him. "Okay, I'm okay now."

"You were so fast, Kels! I've never seen a shifter move so fast, especially in human form. Wow!" Lily sounded super excited and impressed. "Can I clock your speed in wolf form? I'm dying to know if you're faster than Kyle."

"He holds the fastest recorded speed in the Westin Pack," Elise filled me in. "And he's third fastest amongst all documented wolves throughout history," she proudly exclaimed.

I looked at Kyle, but he just kinda hung his head in slight embarrassment. It was clear how proud of him his sisters were, and it was kind of cute seeing him so humbled by them.

"So, what's the record stand at?"

"Sixty-seven miles per hour," Elise told me.

"And Kyle's at sixty-three last count," Lily was quick to add.

I looked at him, "Only sixty-three miles per hour?" I faked shock. "Bet I could take you."

He perked up and looked at me. One eye brow slightly raised higher than the other.

"You're on." I loved the mischievous glint in his eyes.

"Lesson one, Kelsey," Lily said with an exasperated sigh, "do not ever issue a challenge to another shifter that you aren't serious about, not even in jest. Man, you have so much to learn!"

"Kyle, back off, please," Elise said.

"No, I understand, lesson one is on, let's go," I told him lifting my chin to him in defiance.

"Ahhh! Kelsey! Lesson two, looking another wolf directly in the eyes and holding that stare is a direct challenge."

"But you said I already made the challenge and I said, OK, so what's the big deal?" I didn't understand what she was trying to say.

"It's more than that, Kels," Elise tried to more calmly clue me in, "Kyle is an alpha wolf, not just any alpha, he'll one day take over as Pack Alpha. He's not someone you can just stare down. The respectful thing is to avert your eyes at the very least. I can't even believe you can actually stand to hold his stare for that long. Your wolf should be screaming at you to look away."

"Look away? If Kyle stared back at me that hard, I'd be baring my neck in a heartbeat!"

"Baring your neck? What does that mean."

"Here, I'll demonstrate."

I watched as Lily walked down the stairs, suppressing the territorial demands of my wolf as she came to the bottom of the steps. Instead, I looked over to Kyle as he made eye contact with her. It was very brief before she dropped her head and averted her eyes, then turned her head to the right, exposing her neck to him.

"That's a full act of submission," Elise explained.

"The wolf in the woods did that." I said more to myself than anything remembering how I had copied them in wolf form.

"Try it," Lily encouraged.

I hesitated, and saw Kyle nod his head towards the stairs. I waited until she was back up, out of my den, before I walked over and attempted to mirror what Lily had done. But I knew he was staring at me still and I couldn't help but look. It was like I was drawn to his eyes and couldn't look away. I bared my neck and heard his slight intake of breath from the action, but his pupils dilated and I kept his stare.

"No, you're not supposed to be looking at him while you do it." Lily instructed.

I burst out laughing.

"I can't help it, I feel stupid. Why does he get to look at me and I can't look at him?"

"We have so much you need to learn before you're presented to Council," she pouted.

"It's okay, Kelsey, you're doing fine," Kyle assured me after having been quiet for quite some time.

"How about you? If you're the great alpha, do you ever have to bare your throat to anyone?"

"On formal occasions, I do to my father and members of the Grand Council when they travel here, but only for formality purposes," he informed me.

I really did have a lot to learn!

"And someday, we hope, to his mate, if there's anyone out there who can actually put up with him, and if he's ever lucky enough to actually find her," Lily piped in.

The look Kyle shot her to shut up did not go unnoticed by any of us. And I had to fight my wolf to maintain control. I didn't understand what they were talking about, but it clearly made my wolf very angry, and I had to bite my lip to keep from growling at her.

"Mate?" I couldn't resist asking when I felt some control coming back and noticed him pale a bit at the question, making me even more interested in the answer.

"You know, a mate, a...."

Kyle cut her off, "We have time to go over all that stuff another time." He flashed another look at Lily that clearly screamed, shut the hell up, but why?

Lily busted up laughing.

"Lil," Elise scolded, "clearly Kyle doesn't want to discuss

mating in front of Kelsey. Show some respect." Then she jabbed her sister with her elbow and winked down my way. "Don't worry, we'll fill you in on all the fun parts later."

They both laughed and averted their eyes as Kyle stomped up the stairs passed where they were perched.

"We racing or not?" he grumbled at the door.

KYLE
Chapter 10

I didn't wait for them to follow me as I left Kelsey's house and headed for the woods just beyond. I knew they would come, and I could feel her the moment she left her house. Not just smell her, but feel her. It was an entirely new sensation for me.

Something profound had seemed to happen when I touched her and held her. It was like she was already bonding with me, which I didn't know was even possible. I tried to shake it off. For two years, I had watched her and warned off everyone, taking pain staking patience to not show too much favoritism, and to equally warn off women and men so as not to alarm anyone to my intentions. But the intensity to claim her grew tenfold after finally having her in my arms. I knew I would have to work extra hard to keep myself in check where Kelsey Adam's was concerned.

For now, I would enjoy openly running with my little she-wolf, and God knew I needed the relief it would bring me. Stopping at the far back corner of her property, I turned and waited for the girls to join me. When Kelsey walked ahead of my sisters and stopped in front of me, close enough to be considered inside my personal space, I couldn't keep the smile off my face. My wolf rejoiced, and I thought I would change on the spot when she reached out and placed her hand on my chest and looked up into my eyes, elevating her stubborn chin a little higher than necessary to ask, "Okay, so what's the rules?"

I knew she could feel my heartbeat increase, they could all probably hear it, but I didn't care. Kelsey was touching me on her own accord. She needed me just as much, and the sensation of that knowledge was overwhelming me.

I noticed the brief look shared between my sisters and I knew the questions would come. That's just what sisters did. They were going to kill me when they learned she was my mate and I'd never said a word in all this time. My stubborn resolve to have her make the first acknowledgment had never in a million years considered she truly just didn't know anything about us. But she would, and I would be the one to teach her.

"What is the plan? Race to the office?" Elise guessed.

"Yup," I confirmed, not confident in what my voice would portray at Kelsey's closeness.

I loved when Kelsey's already big brown eyes grew bigger with amazement.

"I-I can't," she stuttered. "I don't know the way through the woods."

"You can't run through the woods and be timed, Kels, you need to stick to the roads. It's 5 miles from this point. Don't bother asking how we know," Lily giggled. "Elise will be at the one mile marker just on this side of town to calculate your first mile run. I'm calling Liam to the four-mile mark so we can get a true reading on your last mile, which is typically your fastest. Then I'll be at headquarters to get your five-mile run time and we can see what you're averaging per mile. I already know Kyle will run the full five miles in under five minutes. He's an easy sixty miles per hour on average, so you'll really have to run if you want to keep up with him."

Kelsey nodded, her back still to them and her hand still resting on my chest. She took a deep breath and I suspected she was breathing in my scent as I so often did hers, before turning to face them.

"What's the route?"

Elise quickly explained the exact path and made sure she knew it well. I, of course, already knew it like the back of my hand. Kelsey Adams wasn't the first wolf to challenge me in a speed race, albeit she was certainly the first she-wolf to ever attempt. I had run with her before and already knew she was fast, but I wasn't really worried and truth was, if anyone on this planet could outrun me, of course I would want it to be my mate. I wanted everything for her, so much it blew my mind.

Her nerves picked up slightly, changing her scent and bringing me back to the moment.

"What's wrong?"

"Are we running in, you know."

She was so cute, she couldn't even bring herself to say 'wolf'. It saddened me all she had been through, and I knew her life was going to change drastically from here on. I only hoped I could make it a better one for her.

"Wolf form, Kels, we're running in wolf form."

She seemed to struggle with that and her nerves increased still more.

"But, uh, but, won't the humans think it's weird seeing two wolves running down South Street?"

Lily snorted, holding back a laugh, "Sweetie, no one in San Marco will find it weird, I promise."

She hugged her in reassurance and I was taken back at the jealousy I felt watching, even knowing Lily was no threat to me and my mate.

"Kels, there really aren't any humans in San Marco. Honestly, not for nearly fifty miles of the place. Everyone here is Westin Pack. Now down at the factories, that's a different story, but up here, that remoteness that probably drew you in and made you comfortable here, that's all designed on purpose."

"Oh," she sighed. "What about the butcher at the grocery store in town?"

"Samson? Yeah, wolf."

"And Cole Anderson?"

"Wolf." Lily grinned and wagged her eyebrows, "Definitely all wolf there!"

I bit back the growl trying to unleash. Did she really just make a comment about another male to my mate? I took a deep breath. I needed to get a grip. Lily didn't know Kelsey was my mate, but if she made one more comment like that, I wasn't sure I'd be able to keep it a secret any longer. My wolf stirred and roared, remembering the tattoo on her thigh. It was me, she'd chosen to mark herself with me, but the thought that Cole's hands had been there on her, marking her body like that was difficult to think past. I had to get control of myself. I needed to run.

"You can head into the brush and change so you don't ruin

your clothes. I'll just be over there." I pointed in the direction I was heading even knowing the odd look my sisters were giving me.

I quickly stripped, leaving my clothes by a tree and changed into my wolf form. It didn't even begin to take the itch off as I knew Kelsey was nearby doing the same thing, and it was impossible not to picture her naked as I had secretly seen on far too many occasions and dreamed about on far too many other nights. Shaking my big furry head, I walked over to the girls.

"That was nice of you, big guy, giving her a little privacy like that. Probably don't want to scare her too quickly with the ways of the pack."

Then she proceeded to pet my head. Only Lily would ever dare and I shook my head and snorted in a light warning to back off. She just laughed and kept at it.

"Okay, I'm heading over now. Give me ten minutes to get everything lined up. Already called Liam and he's meeting me at headquarters. We'll three way Elise in when we get there. Shoot, we need someone to signal you to go. Let me see if Chase is available."

I felt Kelsey change and knew she was crouched in the woods, watching and waiting, unsure of exposing herself for what probably felt to her as the first time. I got up and walked over to lay beside her, nudging her with my nose. In some ways, I could express things to her in wolf form that I wouldn't dare in human form for fear I'd scare her away. But I also didn't think she fully understood her actions, even the ones in wolf form, that should have been natural instinct to her, but then again, maybe that's exactly what it was, I thought, as she nuzzled over next to me and laid her head across my paws, fully exposing her neck to me. I nuzzled into it, enjoying her natural scent. I couldn't help but give her a big sloppy wet lick across her face before jumping up and running over to my sister.

In wolf form, we could see fully and understand humans and shifters in human form, we just couldn't communicate vocally. Only mated pairs in wolf form could communicate in a sort of telepathic manner I didn't fully understand. It also wasn't something that just happened when mates first bonded. The bonding took time to fully develop, and talking telepathically was something only very committed, thoroughly bonded mates could do. I wondered if Kelsey and I would ever have that. I sure hoped so.

I noticed Chase had already arrived. He must have been close by because that was fast. I ran over and playfully lunged for him, laughing he rolled to the ground.

"Knock it off, Kyle. And mom says I'm just a big pup!"

Lily just shook her head, "Okay, I'm heading over to headquarters. Remember, don't say go till I give the word." She gave him a quick peck on the cheek. "I'll call as soon as I get there.

I noticed for the first time Elise was already gone and Kelsey was still in hiding. I walked over and nudged her, trying to encourage her to move. After a little prodding she finally did, but coming out into the open she hid behind me, trying to use my body as a shield. I let out something of a bark and tried to let my alpha power flow over her. It didn't seem to work, but did seem to calm her some at least.

I couldn't really make introductions in this form and I wasn't about to shift back and have her face me down in the buff with my brother standing there. But he seemed to catch on some.

"You must be the infamous, Kelsey Adams," he spoke softly and kindly so not to scare her.

He sat down on the ground in front of her and held out his hand for her to come to him. I watched curiously. Her small, blonde fur covered body hid entirely by my contrasting dark brown one and I mentally noted how similar our wolf colorings were to our human hair colors. Though, while she was quite tall in human form, her wolf seemed very small in comparison. I had been so excited the one time I had seen her wolf that I hadn't really noticed things like that.

Kelsey peeked her head around me and studied Chase, still patiently waiting with his outstretched hand. She slowly went to him and nudged it with her head, giving him permission to pet her. Chase jumped back in shock as a growl escaped me, just as my alpha powers sent out a massive punch I hadn't been aware was coming until too late. Holding his hands above his head he slowly stood up, clearly shocked by my behavior. Kelsey's wolf cocked her head to the side in curiosity.

"Shit, Kyle! I didn't know! I swear, I didn't know. Does Dad know? Is this why we've been protecting her and letting her stay here?"

I almost shifted just to shut him up, knowing she was listening to every word. Of course, he would immediately recognize my possessive actions for what they were. I shook my head side to side, trying to convey things to him I couldn't say at the moment, when the phone rang. I said a quick prayer he wouldn't mention it to our siblings. I needed to explain things to Kelsey before getting them all in a frenzy over the situation. Shaking my head no even harder, he nodded and signaled he understood. I could feel her stare on me and didn't need to look her way to know there would be plenty of questions later.

"Okay, well, you guys ready?" Chase asked, clearly over the shock and setting things aside.

I gave one nod of my head. Kelsey copied my actions and crouched low to the ground, almost lying down, but not quite. I was curious about her stance, but didn't have time to think about it, readying myself for a much-needed run.

"Alright, let's do this. All the way to headquarters. See you both there. Now, on your mark, get set, go!"

I launched forward and took off as a light-colored blur blew past me. *Holy shit, she's fast!* I couldn't help but be proud and awed at the same time, but my competitive drive kicked in, and I gave chase. There was no thrill greater that I had ever experienced than chasing my mate at full speed. As we approached the first mile where I knew Elise would be waiting, I had caught up and we were neck and neck. But she started to pull away as we came to the town limits and no matter how hard I pressed forward, I couldn't catch her.

Clearly word had gotten out, cause as we neared the town, I saw people lined up, watching and cheering us on. Kelsey faltered and slowed enough for me to catch up, and the roar of the gathering crowd grew as I passed her. That must have been enough for her to get her head back in the game because suddenly she was back by my side and pushing forward a full nose ahead of me as we rounded the third mile and headed down the long road that would lead us to headquarters.

I couldn't help but be massively impressed that she was still side by side with me, holding her own as we approached Liam at the four-mile mark. I chanced a quick glance at her the same time she looked at me. I could have sworn she smiled. She lowered her head and it was like her speed had suddenly doubled. I pushed on as fast as I could, but there was no way I could keep up. I was staring in awe and not paying full attention as we entered the headquarters

72

parking lot and spotted Lily waving for our attention to the side of the building. My foot caught on the speed bump as I swore in my head and went airborne. Two flips across the hard ground and I was back upright and gave it everything I had.

With my fall, Kelsey finished significantly ahead of me, but I knew she would have anyway. My legs were burning and my tongue was hanging as I gave everything I had into one final burst towards the finish. Kelsey was already well into the field behind the building, trying to slow her speed.

The crowd began gathering around us and I felt the panic rise in her. I knew they were expecting us to change back into human form and accept congratulations for her, and a whole lot of ribbing for me, but she wasn't ready for that. I got to her as quick as I could before she ran off, and nodded for her to follow me. She kept time, staying just off my right flank as I led her into the building and down into our office.

Elise was already there with the door open, signaling us in. I went straight to my office and quickly changed into human form and into the spare clothes I always kept there. When I came out, Kelsey was already dressed in an outfit I recognized as Elise's.

"Thank you," I mouthed to her.

She gave me a quick hug. "You're welcome," she whispered back.

I looked over at Kelsey, new emotions swelling within me at the cocky, knowing smile on her face.

"I took it easy on you, you know?"

I rolled my eyes. My pride could take the jokes that would knowingly follow, especially with the new pride handed to me in the form of my amazing mate, "Please, I threw it when I fell."

I saw her face fall into surprise and then morph into fury.

"You weren't even near me when you gritzed over that speed bump."

I shook my head as I started leading her out to the parking lot where I knew everyone awaited the final results. "You wish! I gave you that win. It was a sympathy win for your first time running with a real wolf."

Yeah, I knew I was full of shit, but she was too adorable all riled up and furious that I couldn't help myself.

"You are so full of it! If I hadn't checked up coming into

town, I'd have finished a full half mile ahead of you, slow poke."

We were suddenly within earshot of others and they began laughing their approval of her snide comments, which made her back off and drop her head in embarrassment.

"Why were there so many people standing around like they were waiting for us anyway?" she dropped her voice and asked cautiously.

"Kels, they've been waiting for two years for you to acknowledge your wolf too. People here are excited to really meet you. They want to know your story and they want to get to know you." *And they all really want to know why Dad and I protected you all this time*, but I didn't add that part.

Kelsey

Chapter 11

"Why? Why would any of them be waiting for me? Why would they even care?"

I had kept a low profile. I barely saw or spoke to anyone outside the office. How would they even know I existed? Up ahead, I saw people everywhere standing around the parking lot, waiting and watching for us. I didn't want to be the center of attention but I tried not to panic.

I tried to turn back, but Kyle was right there behind me, blocking the way. He took my hand and placed it on his chest.

"Look at me, Kelsey. Just at me," he said in a deep soothing tone.

I did, then remembered I wasn't supposed to.

"I'm not supposed to do that, Kyle. I don't want to screw up in front of everyone. There's so many people out there."

"I know, babe, but it's okay. Look at me, just this once."

I did as he said, and immediately felt the others begin to melt away in the distance.

"Okay, now just breathe. Feel my heart beat. I'm right here. I'm not going anywhere. This is important, babe, more than you know. I need you to be strong, smile, and just get through this, okay?"

I nodded, knowing there really wasn't anything he could ask that I wouldn't do, especially when he kept calling me babe. That was something new, and it made me tingly and giddy every time he did. I didn't think he really even realized he was saying it, but there was something possessive in the way he spoke it that both my wolf and I really liked.

"I'm right here beside you the whole way, but there's a lot of people ready to finally meet you."

I took another deep breath. He was too far away for his scent to fully envelope me, but I could feel the eyes behind us, and I didn't know if it would be okay to sniff him. I giggled a little at the thought. Kind of a hysterical, pathetic noise popped out in the process. And I laughed a little harder with the strange expression he gave me for it.

"What was that?" he asked and I knew he was trying to lighten the mood.

I nudged him. "Don't tease. I'm nervous."

"No one who can kick my butt in a race as badly as you just did should ever be nervous about anything." He grinned and started to walk off.

"Wait, so now you're admitting I kicked your butt fair and square?"

"That is something I will never admit."

"Kyle Westin, you did so admit it just now. I totally kicked your ass."

I didn't realize we were already outside until the ohhhh's and ahhhh's and laughter began joining in fully.

"Yeah, admit it, Kyle, you got wrecked by a woman!"

"I ain't ever seen nobody run faster than Kyle. Wonder what they clocked her at?"

"No way Kyle got beat by a girl. He let her win."

I knew that last one wasn't true, but I kept my mouth shut and my head down as I followed him through the small gathering as we headed toward his siblings. I had only met Chase and Liam a handful of times over the last two years and didn't really know them, but they were welcome familiar faces amongst the crowd.

Sneaking a look around, I realized I really did recognize more people than I imagined. Most of those here worked in headquarters and I even knew a lot of their names. Trying to reconcile them all as wolf shifters was a whole different thing, though. I stopped short, wishing I hadn't let that thought surface.

Wolves? All of them? How could it be? Mom always said to

steer clear of the wolves. She meant steer clear of these people before me. I needed to shift and run and get far, far away.

I started to move when I felt a warm hand on my lower back. I shivered and began to calm.

"You got this," he whispered, guiding me the remainder of the way to my friends.

"So? What's the final results?" he asked, feeling relaxed and confident beside me.

"Okay, y'all hush it up. Everyone quiet down for the results." Liam spoke up loudly, causing a hush across the crowd.

"First mile," Lily yelled so all could here, "Kyle and Kelsey were dead even at 65 seconds."

"Wow!"

"Oh my gosh!"

"Can you believe it?"

"Quiet down!" Liam yelled again.

"Kyle finished the 5 mile stretch in 4 minutes 37 seconds, beating his previous record of 4 minutes and 53 seconds."

Shouts of praise rang out across parking lot.

"Kelsey finished the 5 mile stretch in 4 minutes 11 seconds!"

Gasps came from everywhere as the crowd grew silent in shock.

"Kelsey was clocked at seventy-one miles per hour in her last mile. Kyle was just ahead of his fastest time at sixty-four miles per hour. We have some new records for the books!"

Cheers went up all around.

Seventy-one miles per hour? I couldn't believe it, and from the looks on many faces, neither could they. I knew I was fast, but that was well over what they told me was the fastest recorded time in history.

Several people began coming over and introducing themselves and congratulating me. It was awkward for me, and from what I could tell, for many of them too. Kyle was right, they did seem curious about me, but I couldn't understand why.

He was true to his word, though, and never left my side. As the group started dying down finally, I realized I was suddenly very very tired. How could it possibly still be the same day? The day I found out the truth about wolf shifters. The day I was suspecting would never end.

"You look tired, are you ready to head home?" Kyle whispered as I was saying goodbye to two of the other admins that I actually did know.

"YES!" I wanted to hug him just for suggesting it.

"Come on, let me grab the keys to one of the company cars and I'll drive you."

"Kyle? You can't miss dinner."

"It's fine, they'll understand."

"No, Elise is right, Kyle, you can't miss tonight. Daddy stopped me on the way out this morning to make sure I got you there. You have to make dinner tonight."

He ran a hand through his hair, clearly torn.

"Kelsey's been through a lot today. We can't just leave her now."

"It's okay, I can get myself home. Go. You guys have done plenty for one day, and I have a lot to think about."

"No, Kyle's right, Kels, we shouldn't leave you alone tonight. Come to dinner with us."

Kyle looked hopeful, but I couldn't possibly intrude.

"No, I can't do that. Tuesday's are your family time. Go. I'll be fine."

The look of disappointment on his face caused an ache in my heart. I wanted to reach out to him, make it right, whatever it took.

"I'm taking you home then."

"But." Lily and I said at the same time before looking at each other and laughing.

"Kelsey, it's fine if you want to join us." Lowering her voice, she whispered to me, "Don't worry, you won't be the only guest tonight." She grinned and winked at me, but I had no clue what she was talking about. "Come on," she said, hooking my arm and dragging me along despite my protest.

Kyle piled into Lily's small eco-friendly car leaving, me the front seat.

"I could have sat back there," I offered a little too late.

"Nah, it's fine," he assured me, though he looked scrunched up and uncomfortable.

"Do I really have to intrude on family night? Can't I just go home and take it all in? You guys have pretty much turned my world upside down already today."

"That's why we aren't about to just leave you alone tonight," he assured me.

Great. Just what I need. My overbearing boss who turns my knees to Jell-O with a simple look, refusing to let me out of his sight while I contemplate the new reality of him not only knowing and accepting my secret, but being just like me. It was just too much to process.

I couldn't deny I'd been attracted to Kyle Westin since I first laid eyes on him. I don't think I'd ever done anything to make those feelings known. I'd only ever been one hundred percent professional with him. I never once allowed myself to even consider him, or any other man, an option for me. How could I with the secret I kept for the last ten years?

Now, suddenly here he was. Everything I'd ever wanted ,right here seeing into my deepest, darkest secrets and not even flinching. It's more than I could ever have even allowed myself to think about. Plus, that kiss. Just thinking about it made my cheeks pink and my lips burn for more. I needed to get away, quickly. I was far too emotional, and what Kyle couldn't understand was that it wasn't coming to terms with who or what I was that had me a complete wreck. Yes, I had questions and confusion, but now that the knowledge had started to sink in, I realized it's just knowledge, some things about my heritage that I needed to know and understand. No, what had me completely freaking out was the man who just reached over and massaged my shoulder, somehow seeming to know the second I craved his touch. The man who refused to leave my side, yet didn't realize I forgot to breathe when he was that close to me.

I was thankful when we arrived at the big house I knew belonged to their parents. Both Elise and Lily still lived there too. I had never allowed myself to ask if Kyle lived at home or elsewhere.

Stumbling out of the car I tried to look at it from fresh eyes. I understood enough from what they'd told me throughout the day to know that their dad was Pack Alpha of the Westin Pack. I had met Jason Westin on several occasions, but never his wife. He had always seemed like a good person, though my brief passing of his wife around town had left me the impression that she was not happy with my being there and more than a little stand-offish. I had made it a point to steer clear of Mary Westin.

I didn't know what to expect walking into their home. As soon the door opened, their dad came over. He went straight to Kyle, not seeming to notice me at all and leaned in to speak softly to only him, but I was close enough to hear every word.

"I'm so sorry, son. It's all your mother's idea. Please just try to get through the night in a civilized manner. Remember, she doesn't know about…"

His words drifted off as his eyes met mine and grew large.

"Kelsey! What a surprise."

His panicking eyes flashed to Kyle's, then back to mine, and I think I held them just a fraction too long before I remembered what the girls told me, and I dropped my eyes and head quickly, feeling as though I were speaking to the floor.

"Hello, sir, it's nice to see you again."

I felt like a complete idiot. Who did that? I had never even really noticed it until they pointed it out.

Lily giggled a little at my attempt. Elise hugged me in support.

"You're doing great, Kels."

I sighed.

"Sorry, I'm trying, I really am."

Their father looked at each of us in confusion trying to understand what was going on.

"Sir, can I speak to you for a moment?" I asked before my nerves took over and I couldn't bring myself to do it. "Alone?"

"Uh, certainly, Kelsey. My office is right this way."

I saw him sweep a questioning look across his children ,and felt Kyle about to protest, but I looked him right in the eyes and shook my head no before turning and following the elder Mr. Westin into his office and closed the door behind me. My entire body was shaking with nervous energy.

"Please, take a seat, relax, Kelsey. Now tell me, what did you want to talk to me about? It sounded important."

"I don't know," I admitted. "I don't know much about anything apparently. From the pieces they have told me, I understand you are Pack Alpha of the Westin Pack."

He had visible shock on his face, though he quickly tried to mask it and simply nodded for me to continue instead.

"Your children, they've been wonderful to me." I knew I was

tearing up and also knew there was no way to get through it without crying. "There was an incident this morning, and well, I learned things I didn't know. Things I never dreamed of."

He still didn't say a word, so I continued to babble.

"They are trying to help me. Trying to explain things to me. Explain your ways and what I should and shouldn't be doing." I sighed realizing I was looking him straight in the eyes again and sadly lowered my gaze. "I'm screwing up a lot already, I'm sorry."

"Start from the beginning, child."

"Which beginning? My life as I knew it before today beginning, or what happened with Mike and Ted that started it all?"

"Mike and Ted? What the hell do they have to do with anything?"

"Well, I guess I should back up a little. There was first an incident in the office this morning. Anyway, I got upset and scared and I ran." I shrugged, knowing how pathetic I was, "It's just what I do. What I always do. It's the only way I know to survive, but as I was running for home, I ran into Mike and Ted."

He held up a hand for me to stop. "Back up some, what sort of incident at the office? Is it something I should be concerned with?"

I knew my face was on fire in brilliant shades of pinks and red. I took a deep breath, figuring it was best to just be honest with him.

"I got a tattoo. It was bleeding a little, Kyle apparently smelled it, he freaked out, we talked. I told him some things I had never told anyone before. It got pretty emotional. And he, he kissed me." I paused just in time to see the man attempt to hide the smile on his face, like he wasn't surprised at my admission at all.

"And how exactly did you react to that?"

"How do you think? I freaked out and ran for it. I was running home to pack my things and get the hell out of here when I ran into Mike and Ted. They were rambling on about some Council and command to leave me alone, but they didn't care, well Mike didn't. Ted tried to talk him down. Anyway, he shifted in front of me. I really freaked at that point!"

"Why is that, Kelsey? I mean, since we're getting things out in the open, we all know you're a shifter, so why go to such great lengths to deny it?"

I started crying, and Kyle burst through the door.

"Dad, that's enough."

"Out, Kyle, this doesn't concern you."

"Yes, it does, and you of all people know that."

"Son, out. Kelsey asked to talk, and we are only talking. You know I would never hurt her."

I felt a similar flow of what I knew now was alpha power, only stronger than anything I'd ever felt from Kyle. It not only gave me goosebumps but made me shiver just a little. I could see it made Kyle furious, but he turned and left the room without another word.

Jason Westin sat down and pinched the bridge of his nose in frustration. It was such a Kyle move it made me smile.

"I'm sorry about that, Ms. Adams, please go on. We can come back to my question later. Mike shifted in front of you?"

"Right, so I turned and ran back toward headquarters and when Kyle showed up I tried to wave him off. Mike was in wolf form and chasing after me, but instead of listening he changed too and they fought, but only for a minute."

"I really freaked out then and ran home to leave, but Kyle, Elise, and Lily showed up at my house before I could get packed and out the door. I tried to hide. I even shifted into wolf form but had to reign it back when Elise came into my den and my wolf saw her as a threat. And I guess that's why I wanted to talk to you. Kyle explained some things, so did the girls, but I know there's a lot more they aren't telling me yet, and that's okay, they gave me more than enough to take in."

I sighed, feeling a headache coming on from all that had happened in one day.

"No one's come right out and said anything, but I know you and Kyle have been protecting me from the pack. My mom told me to never trust a wolf, to steer clear and run far far away from any I came in contact with. I don't understand why she never told me the truth about what I am and I'll never know because she died a long time ago. But I know there are certain pack protocols. And while they didn't spell it out or say anything about it to me, I know how it felt when Lily and Elise came down into my den. My territory. They are my friends and I wanted to rip their throats out. For some reason, my wolf doesn't respond the same to Kyle, but she sees the girls as threats even when I know they aren't. And that got me thinking. This is your territory, sir." The tears were free flowing now. "Why didn't you attack me? Why didn't you make me leave? Why didn't you say anything? And I'm so sorry. I'm so very sorry. They tell me I'm not supposed to look you directly in the eye as it's a sign of disrespect. If that's disrespectful, I cannot even begin to imagine the level of disrespect it must be for a lone wolf like me to settle into pack territory without acknowledgment, but I swear to you, sir, I never meant any disrespect. I had no idea you people even existed, not like that, not shifters."

He came around the desk and pulled me to a stand and silently hugged me close. It wasn't the same as when Kyle had comforted me, but it was nice and reminded me of my own father. He let me just cry in his arms until the sobs subsided.

"You're right, Kelsey, I should have come to you. But at first, we were all so shocked with your arrival that we hesitated and waited for you to come to us. After a few weeks, and with you working at the Westin Foundation, it was clear to my children that something was wrong. They assured me you were no threat to us, and I know they were right. Kyle petitioned the Pack Council himself on your behalf to let you stay and leave you in peace. He's been watching over you, both against possible threats, such as Mike, and waiting for the time you were ready to open up about who you are. And who are you, Kelsey Adams? Where did you come from? I'll be honest, the curiosity of that has been what's kept you alive the most. Even after what, two years now? Even so the pack as a whole is still completely infatuated with the mysterious little lone she-wolf living amongst us who didn't seem to know she was a wolf at all."

I laughed, "Then I guess I at least did that much right."

"What do you mean, child?"

"I never wanted anyone to find out what I was. I..," I shook my head, "it doesn't matter the reasons or how silly they seem in hindsight, they were truly all I knew. Hide, run, don't let anyone close. Those are the rules I've lived by that have kept me alive. Now, I honestly don't know what to do!"

"What do you want to do, Kelsey?"

"I want to stay," I said without hesitation. "I want answers. I want to understand and to learn your ways. I'll understand if you ask me to leave, though. I've been a disgrace to your pack and to you. And even though I know Kyle is scared I'll run the second he turns his back, I fear he'll hope I will as today sinks in for him too."

He laughed at that. "I seriously doubt that would ever happen, but tell me what you mean."

"Well, for starters, I'm far more damaged than any of them realized. I'm not sure I can be fixed or fit into the pack, even if you'd have me. Plus, I don't think the pack will ever let Kyle live down what happened this afternoon. I didn't mean to embarrass him!"

Jason Westin laughed even harder, "Now this I must hear. What on earth could you have possibly done to embarrass my heir, little wolf?"

"I-I-I," trying to contain my stutter, I looked him directly in the eyes, "I challenged him, and then I kicked his ass in front of everyone, sir."

I lowered my head in shame as he let out a full belly laugh causing Kyle to run back into the office.

"Father," he growled.

"Simmer down pup, this little wolf tells me she challenged you and then embarrassed you by kicking your ass in front of everyone? Care to elaborate?"

I chanced a quick glance his way and found him smiling and proud, not looking embarrassed at all.

"I tripped!"

"Like hell," I said. "I won fair and square. I beat your best time even."

"Wait, wait, wait, clearly we're not talking about actually kicking his ass, so what are we talking about?"

"Racing," Kyle said, "Kelsey beat me in both the mile and five miles."

"What?" he boomed more surprised than angry. "What was her best mile clocked at?" They were no longer talking to me, but over me instead.

"Seventy-one miles per hour." Kyle sounded proud, like he had done it himself.

"Seventy-one? That's impossible!"

"Nah, my girl is super fast. Wish you could have been there to see it."

My heart felt like it was going to explode with happiness. I knew I had to reign it in. I didn't understand why his high praise made my pulse race with pride, but it did.

"Well that is certainly something I'd love to see for myself. Please let me know when the next race will be. I'm sure the pack will be talking about this for quite some time. Kelsey, you are welcome in my territory for as long as you like. Thank you, for coming to see me tonight. Now, if you'll excuse me, the wife doesn't appreciate work duties on family night. I assume you'll be joining us for dinner?"

I couldn't possibly, but something told me I wasn't getting out of it.

"No, thank you, I really don't wish to intrude. I think I've had enough to consider for one day, and I know how important family time is to you and your wife."

"Oh, nonsense. Besides, we already have company tonight, and it should prove quite entertaining." He winked at me and then guided me out of his office and down the hall to the kitchen with Kyle trailing behind.

KYLE
Chapter 12

Vanessa! I could smell her before we even entered the dining room. What the hell was she doing there?

I glared around the room, looking for the intruder, and saw my mom's face contort in confusion at seeing Kelsey walking in with Dad. I knew immediately it was her setup. She had made her desires to see me settle down with Vanessa very clear for several years now, long before Kelsey walked into my life. I shuddered to think of what a mistake that would have been.

True mates are a real thing in the shifter world, but as we've grown and spread out across the world, the chances of finding that one true mate have become rarer. Sort of like a prince stumbling across a long-lost princess and living happily ever after. That stuff just didn't happen in the real world. So, for several generations, shifters have been settling for compatible mates.

I knew Vanessa and I could be compatible mates, but after having met my one true mate, I knew settling was never an option for me. My parents were true mates, so I never really understood why my mother was so quick to find me a compatible mate. I mean, I got the whole wanting to see me settle down and the need for the next heir of the Westin Pack, but I was only now twenty-eight years old, and as far as I knew, Dad wasn't planning to step down anytime soon. Still, the moment I shifted for the first time at seventeen years of age, my mother had taken it upon herself to play matchmaker and see that I mated with a proper she-wolf to carry on the family legacy. I restrained a chuckle thinking of what she'd say when she found out Kelsey Adams was my one true mate.

"Hello, I'm Mary Westin," my mother said, rising to shake hands with what she undoubtedly perceived as an intruder into her home and family night.

"Kelsey Adams. It's nice to officially meet you," she said graciously.

My mom tried to hide the sneer. I knew she wasn't a fan of Kelsey's and had been vocal with Dad and me about running her out of Westin territory, but I also knew Mary Westin would never have been less than hospitable to any shifter in her home, especially one my father invited to join us.

"I invited Kelsey to join us for dinner, sweetie. I hope that's okay." My father offered, simultaneously giving warning for her to behave.

The look she shot back to him promised he'd be explaining himself later.

"Of course. Lily, why don't you grab an extra plate to set for our guest. Kelsey, I know you already know Kyle, and Lily and Elise from work. These are my other sons, Liam and Chase," she offered formally.

"Hi, thanks, we've met already."

"Oh," she sounded surprised by that news, "well, then this is Vanessa Relic, a dear friend of Kyle's."

My first instinct was to stare down my mother for her blatant intrusion into my life, but then curiosity had me turning to Kelsey instead as I felt a strange emotion ripple through her. Her body was tense and her smile painted on, but to the outside eye, I had no doubt she looked perfectly friendly and normal. I knew with all my being that there was nothing friendly about Kelsey Adams as she politely shook hands with Vanessa, never once dropping her stare. The direct contact only lasted a second as they were both distracted by Lily's return with the additional place setting, though I smiled, noting Vanessa looked away first.

There was an awkward silence across the table as we all sat down to eat. Mom had strategically placed me beside Vanessa, no surprise there, and had Lily sit Kelsey next to her, placing her directly across from me. I tried to send her an apologetic look as she looked back and forth between me and Vanessa.

"Mmm, this is really good, mom." I praised her perfectly cooked, juicy turkey with all the fixings. My mother always went above and beyond on Tuesday night family dinners. You'd think it was Thanksgiving every Tuesday in the Westin house.

"It really is, Mary, thank you so much for having me over," Vanessa said in a cheery voice complete with sugary sweet smile before turning her attention to Kelsey. "Kelsey, so tell me, what's it like working for Kyle?" Her laugh tinkled through the room as she laid her hand possessively on my forearm.

It took every bit of reserve not to push her away. *How dare she show such disrespect to my mate!* But I had to stay focused and remember, no one knew Kelsey was my mate because in the two years I had known her I had never made my intentions clear. I didn't want to paint an even bigger target on her back by doing something stupid, and that reminder kept me glued uncomfortably in my chair watching her closely from across the table.

To her credit, Kelsey kept a perfect composure, though I could clearly feel her frustrations and anger rolling off her. It was so strong, I wouldn't be surprised if the others noticed it too. Nex,t I felt a brush against my leg under the table and I couldn't wipe the grin from my face. I extended my leg feeling triumphant as my one true mate reached for me discreetly with her own leg. She rubbed her foot up and down my leg causing me to harden and thank God we were sitting down. Then she took a controlled deep breath before replying as my wolf howled in victory at one of the first signs that she truly did feel our connection too.

"Working with Kyle is a new adventure every day. Most of the time he's a complete pain in my ass, though," she replied so sweetly and innocently that I choked on the bite of corn I had just put in my mouth.

Looking around, all eyes were on me now, waiting to see how I'd react to that. I couldn't help but smile, and as soon as I did, the laughter and ribbing began. It was like a Kyle Westin roast for much of the remainder of the night. Even mom relaxed and added in several Kyle stories from my childhood that had left her with new grey hairs and tears of laughter in everyone's eyes. I was thankful for the change in atmosphere. Vanessa remained quiet by my side, looking a little defeated while Kelsey, my mate, shined and began to win over the remainder of my family whose hearts she hadn't already captured.

After dinner, Vanessa grabbed my hand and announced she

had to call it a night. I knew she was expecting me to walk her out, and my mother beamed in approval. I couldn't bring myself to look at Kelsey as I walked out hand and hand with another woman, feeling completely disgusted with myself.

"Look, Vanessa," I started the moment we were out of earshot of the others.

"Shhh," she said, silencing me with a kiss. She tried to deepen it, but I just couldn't. She pulled away looking a little hurt. "She's not one of us, Kyle. I saw how you looked at her. I know you want her, but it'll pass and I'll still be here. The pack will never accept her and you know it. You need a mate that will make you strong, not weak and pathetic."

I knew her words came out of fear. Too many people had assured her we were perfectly compatible mates meant to be together, but a part of what she said was also a true reality that I would have to come to terms with. The pack wasn't going to be happy about my mating an outsider, and not just any outsider, but the one that had disrespected territory lines for over two years and gotten away with it.

I kissed her cheek. "It was good to see you, Vanessa."

The look in her eye told me my words, that had meant to dismiss her, only renewed her hope. I knew I needed to talk to Kelsey, and soon. When others began to suspect my interest, every eligible she-wolf within three packs would be sniffing after her to check out the competition. It was why I had been so careful up until now.

Sighing, I headed back in to join my family. I stood at the door to the family room, just watching. Lily and Liam were at the card table deep in a game of chess. Chase and Elise wrestling for the remote as they argued over what to watch. And my dad and Kelsey laughing and talking together. My heart was full. But there was one important person still missing from this picture.

I made my way down the hall and into the kitchen to find mom washing dishes at the sink. I quickly grabbed the dish from her and a towel and dried and put it away. She smiled over at me, but looked tired.

"Are you okay, Mom?"

"Of course, I am. Just a little tired. And I'm sorry about tonight. I ran into Vanessa picking up some last minute groceries today and she had mentioned that she hadn't really seen or talked to you in months, so I just thought…"

I sighed. "I know, Mom, I know."

"No, watching you tonight and how uncomfortable you looked sitting next to her, I realized how wrong I've been to try and force a compatible mate on you. It isn't my decision to live with, it's yours. It doesn't really matter who I like, because I'm not the one that has to live with her the rest of my life. You are a grown man, proven to make good solid decisions and I promise to try and back off a little. You just promise me you won't shut out your options or waste your life pining for a true mate that you may never meet."

I grinned. "You found Dad, why would you think I would never find mine?"

She eyeballed me suspiciously. "Kyle Alexander Westin, are you trying to tell me you have found your one true mate?"

I grinned bigger. "I'm not saying a word."

With a peck on her head, I took her hand and pulled her out of the kitchen.

"Come on, the dishes will wait. It's family time."

She stiffened next to me when she saw Kelsey laughing at something my dad had said.

"Mom, please." I know my eyes were begging her to understand.

She gave me a sad look and shook her head okay.

"You're certain?"

I knew what she was asking and I knew I couldn't lie to her about it.

"I've never been more sure about anything."

"Does your father know?"

I nodded.

"That's why the two of you have been protecting her?"

I nodded again watching a tear drop down her cheek as she looked at Kelsey through new eyes.

"Why couldn't you just tell me?"

I ran my hand through my hair, searching for a way to explain.

"It's just complicated, Mom."

"She doesn't know, does she?"

I shrugged. "I see signs that she feels it too, but I don't think she understands what she's feeling."

"How is that even possible?"

"Mom, she's been on her own most of her life. She didn't even know what she was, let alone anything about our ways."

"Do the girls know?"

"They know about her, but not about, well, us. I've only ever told Dad, til now."

"We'll talk later. But you need to man up and talk to that girl."

I could feel her motherly instincts kicking in towards my mate and I knew that once she knew her story and got to know her, that my mother would stop at nothing to welcome her into our family. It's just the kind of person she was. And I suddenly knew, everything was going to be okay.

Kelsey

Chapter 13

I knew Kyle would beat me in the office. It had taken a lot to convince him I wasn't going to run last night. For a while I didn't think he was going to leave my house at all, but after much convincing, promising, and finally begging, he finally did. I felt him watching me through the night, though. I didn't really know how to explain it, but I would bet money he spent the night in wolf form guarding me. He really hadn't needed to bother. I was so emotionally and physically exhausted from the longest day of my life that I slept like a rock.

He on the other hand, looked exhausted and miserable. I wanted badly to make him feel better like he had comforted me so many times the day before. I walked in his office and straight into his little personal bubble, laying my hands flat against his chest. Anyone else I would have been mortified, but it just seemed so right with him.

"Good morning." I smiled up at him.

His appearance instantly changed. His dark, tired eyes brightened. The stress I smelled on him ceased, and I felt his body physically relax at my touch. He wrapped his arms around me and pulled our bodies flush. Before I knew what was happening he leaned down and brushed his lips lightly across mine. It was the briefest whisper of a kiss, making me long for so much more as he pulled back and placed his forehead against mine. I knew he was breathing in my scent, just as I leaned in to breathe his. I took in a good deep breath to center me before letting it out in a slow breeze against his neck that caused him to shudder in my arms.

When he pulled back this time, he was all smiles and looked ready to take on the world.

"Good morning," he finally said.

"I told you not to worry so much. I said I wasn't going to run and I'm not." I playfully pushed him back to put some distance between us, immediately feeling the loss, but determined to get to work and have something of a normal day.

I handed him a cup of fresh hot coffee I had picked up on my way in at the little cafe in town I knew he loved. It had been awkward and made me uneasy. I was used to the stares by now, but several people, or shifters, or whatever I was supposed to call them, actually spoke to me and Sally, the local barista, invited me out for drinks after work. I was too shocked to do anything but nod. No one except Lily and Elise had ever invited me to do anything.

I was still lost in thought when Kyle poked his head out of his office.

"Hey, lunch today in my office."

I noted it wasn't an actual question and I felt terrible for having let him down. The disappointment every time I told him no had not gone unnoticed and Lord knew I had done it a whole lot over the years we'd worked together.

"Sorry, Mr. Westin, but I have to say no." I could already see rejection written on his face and it hurt my heart, so I kept babbling. "I really am sorry. If I could get out of it I would, but Elise hit me up this morning on the way in and I promised her."

"Elise was in the office that early this morning?" He sounded skeptical and I had to laugh because it certainly didn't sound like his sister.

"Yeah, apparently you weren't the only one betting I'd flee in the night."

"How about tonight? We could grab dinner after work. There's some things I really want to talk to you about. It's kind of important."

I knew he could see my answer on my face before I even spoke, and knowing I was letting him down was killing me.

"How about a late dinner? I'm having drinks at The Crate after work."

"What? With who?" He sounded panicked and all I wanted to do was assure him.

"Sally, the barista at the cafe. The one with the really good coffee you love. I talked to her this morning when I picked yours up on my way in."

"Sally? You're having drinks with Sally Merchant?" Relief was evident in his voice.

"Yes. I don't expect we'll be that long. I can cook or meet you somewhere afterwards if it's important."

He shook his head, "No, I don't want you to have to rush home and cook and I don't want eyes and ears on us for this conversation. How about you just come by my place after you're done? I'll figure something out for dinner."

"Um, okay, sure."

His place? I couldn't help but feel a little nervous about being so alone with him. Then again, maybe he still lived at home like Elise and Lily. I had never really asked.

I noticed while I was freaking out, he had already retreated into his office. I picked up the phone and dialed his extension.

"Kyle Westin," he answered, probably not even having looked at the phone to know it was only me.

"Sorry, it's just me. Um, Kyle," it felt weird saying his first name here in the office, "where exactly do you live?"

He let out an unrestrained laugh and I noted, not for the first time, that my wolf ears could not hear him through the walls, only the receiver.

"I'll send you the address, Kels. You may be surprised to find that you do know where I live."

I could hear the smile in his voice as he hung up and I was certain now he did live at home, but a few minutes later when a new email popped into my account, I didn't recognize the address which thoroughly confused me.

I was still plugging it into my phone when a smell hit me causing a small growl to escape.

Vanessa Relic waltzed into my office like she owned the place heading straight for Kyle's office.

"Excuse me," I said, feeling irritated, "do you have an appointment?"

She laughed her tinkling, little girl laugh that grated on my

94

every last nerve at the dinner table the previous night. It had taken everything in my power not to pick up the knife next to my plate and hurl it at her head. But I smiled being the professional I was.

"Vanessa, right? Mr. Westin has a very busy schedule this morning and I don't see you on the list of appointments. Sorry."

If looks could kill I knew I'd be dead.

"Well call him. He'll see me anytime, anywhere."

She was goading me, trying to push my buttons. I could tell, but there was something in me that was not going to back down to this girl, and truth be told I didn't want to. But I picked up the phone and pushed for Kyle's extension.

He answered with a chuckle. "Check it out and realize you know the place already? Or at least your…"

"Mr. Westin, a Miss Vanessa Relic is here to see you. She doesn't have an appointment. I've warned her your schedule is tight this morning. Should she come back later or do you have a second?"

I heard him blow out a frustrated breath. "Yeah, okay, send her in."

What?!?!? I wanted to scream at him through the phone, and I must have let my carefully guarded face drop because she was smiling in triumph.

"Yes, sir," I steeled my voice while cursing under my breath. "You may go in," I told her sweetly.

She shot me an 'I-told-you-so' look that nearly had me coming across the desk to attack her. I took a few deep breaths as she closed the door behind her. No sense in trying to listen in. I knew I'd never hear through those walls. My blood was boiling and I had never wanted to kill, or at least very much harm, someone as badly as I wanted to with Vanessa Relic.

What kind of stupid name was that anyway? Relic? Was it even a real name?

I knew I was being petty, but I couldn't help it any more than I could control the insane jealousy pulsing through my veins.

I was worked up into almost a full blown anger by the time she finally opened the door and let herself out. Smirking in victory, she walked over to my desk.

"Kelsey, Kelsey, Kelsey, let me give you the 4-1-1. Kyle Westin is mine and there really isn't anything you can do or say to stop that, so you might as well just give up now. It's kind of cute really, in a pathetic kind of way, the secretary falling for the boss and all, but you're up against the big dogs now and you don't stand a chance."

She bared her teeth and growled at me. *She actually growled at me!*

I was out of my chair and on my feet in front of her before I knew what I was doing. My entire body was pulsing with energy I couldn't contain, and looking at her, all I saw was red until it was like something finally snapped within me and I smiled.

"No, Vanessa, I think you're the one that's scared right now and your intimidation tactics won't work on me because you have no clue who you are dealing with."

What the heck was I saying? I didn't even know who I was. But I couldn't stop the words from tumbling out. Kyle was mine. I tried to control the shock in that thought. Yet everything about it felt true and right.

I took another step closer to her and she went to bare her teeth at me again but was having a difficult time holding my stare. I lifted my chin a little higher, locking eyes with her and let out a small growl as something familiar surged through me and released.

"Now, get out of here."

I noted the wide eyes of shock followed by fear as she turned and ran from the office, nearly plowing over Elise. I shrugged my shoulders innocently, watching my friend run after her.

What had I done?

It was another two hours before Elise returned, ready for lunch. I needed to talk to her, needed to understand why I was feeling that way. Instead of heading for the cafeteria, I followed her down the hall and into her office. She had just recently been promoted to Vice President of Human Resources. It felt official, and for a moment, I feared maybe I was in trouble, but when we entered, I saw lunch was already awaiting us.

"The offices are sound proof, even from wolf ears, so we can talk freely from here."

I giggled nervously. "I'd always suspected as much."

She smiled back and I relaxed. "Lil's coming by later. She's just running late. We have a few things we just wanted to add in to yesterday's conversation, but probably best not said around the brother." She snorted like what she had said was funny. "First, I need to ask you something before Lily gets here."

I nodded, "Sure, anything."

"What happened with you and Vanessa earlier today?"

I sighed and sat down in a chair, feeling deflated.

"What did she tell you happened?"

"I need to hear your side first."

"I don't even know, E. She just kept pushing at me, telling me I wasn't good enough, I was wasting my time, she could see right through me, on and on until I just sorta snapped. I didn't touch her, if that's what you're thinking. And she growled at me first!"

"What exactly were you arguing about? That part was never clear talking to her."

I know my face was ten shades of red because she raised one eyebrow at me, becoming more curious.

"Kyle." I finally spit out.

To say she was shocked was an understatement. Then she laughed.

"Thanks, yeah, sure, go ahead, laugh it up. She thinks she has some kind of monopoly of him and was trying to threaten me away. Me! What have I ever done to her?"

Elise was still laughing and trying to get control of herself when she wheezed out, "Kyle? My brother? You were threatening her over my brother? I didn't even think you really liked him. I mean, yesterday I guess I might have wondered, but it seemed more one sided on his part than yours."

"What are you talking about?"

"Never mind. Look, you haven't, uh, how do I put this? You've never been intimate with Kyle, have you?"

I think I may have found several newly defined shades of red across my face.

"Define intimate. Like a kiss? I mean he held me yesterday. I fell asleep in his arms, that's kind of intimate, I guess."

"No, no, Kelsey, I'll just come out and ask. Have you had sex with Kyle?"

"WHAT?!?!? Of course not. Why would you even ask such a thing?"

Elise shrugged, grinning. "Honestly, Kels, it wouldn't be that shocking. He's crazy about you."

"You're insane, Elise, he's my boss, I couldn't possibly."

But oh yeah, I thought to myself, *I wanted to very possibly*. I brushed the thought aside as fast as it surfaced. This was insane.

"Okay, well, I was just asking because Vanessa is convinced you used alpha powers on her."

I laughed, "How would that even be possible? She-wolves don't have alpha powers. You know that."

She nodded, "That's why I asked about Kyle. It would be a really tiny possibility, but if you two had mated... which is more than just sex, but we'll get into that when Lily arrives … then you could, in theory, pull power from his alpha line. It's rare and usually only fully bonded mates can do it, but that would almost be better than the alternative."

She seemed to chew on that thought, but I didn't know what she was getting at.

"What alternative? What are you talking about?"

"I'm talking about the possibility that you could be an alpha she-wolf."

"I can't be. Kyle said they are very rare and killed as very young pups the moment their powers show."

"That's true, but there are some cases where people have tried to smuggle them away or hide their powers from the Grand Council."

"Seriously?"

"Yes. The most recent count I know was a set of triplets, identical she-wolves. They lived to be four and were supposedly the most adorable, most manipulative and powerful little she-wolves ever documented. Too much of a threat, so the Grand Council had them sentenced to death. The family tried to escape. The first was caught and killed immediately. The second was injured trying to rescue her sister, but the parents escaped with the third. It was several years before they were tracked down and killed too. But the point is, it's possible. What if that's why you had no pack? Why your parents told you to be scared of the wolves? And why you never knew what you truly were?"

"Elise, that's insane. I'm a nobody. There's nothing special or powerful about me. You know me."

"Maybe. Regardless, you can't mention this to anyone. I've already got Vanessa convinced she's headed to the looney bin, so just steer clear of her. I don't think she'll bother you again. You really freaked her out." I was about to address it, when the door flew open and Lily walked in. "We'll figure out the rest later. Not even Lily." She whispered to me, her eyes conveying the importance of it.

KYLE
Chapter 14

The Crate was the only bar in town. I couldn't stop her from going even if it unsettled my wolf. Sally Merchant was good people, and she was happily mated for nearly twenty years. She was a good friend to have and I couldn't dissuade Kelsey from that.

I hadn't seen her since the morning. I knew she was agitated and not happy about Vanessa's surprise visit. I only hoped that I was able to put a stop to her advances once and for all. My wolf had growled in warning when she tried to physically attack me right there on the couch in my office. How many times had I dreamed of claiming Kelsey there? I shuddered. That dream was officially ruined now.

I hadn't heard from Kelsey since I left the office. She assured me she was still coming but I found myself pacing back and forth wearing a path in my carpet as I impatiently waited. I was excited to have my mate in my territory for the first time. My home. Hopefully someday soon it would be our home, but I didn't want to rush things and scare her off.

I knew she was meeting Sally around five o'clock, so when seven-thirty rolled around and there was still no sign of her, I began to panic. By eight o'clock I was grabbing my keys and heading for the door when I saw car lights flash across my living room. My senses went on full alert. I swung my door open and immediately relaxed being greeted by her scent. That delicious scent that tormented me every day while bringing a peace and calm only her smell could produce.

"Hey," she said, stepping on the porch grinning. "You were

right, my wolf definitely knows this place. It's the cabin where I first came to when I let my wolf out to run that night, right?"

I smiled. She remembered. All I could do was nod. She looked happy and a tiny bit glassy eyed. I wondered just how many drinks she'd had. She didn't hesitate to stretch up and kiss my cheek before pushing past me into my house, ahead of me. I just shook my head. At least we hadn't explained that one to her yet.

"Did you have fun tonight?" I asked.

"I did! Sally's really nice, and Cole was there too. I hadn't seen him in a few days and we had a lot to catch up on. Did you know his wolf is almost solid black? That stinker tried to get me to put his wolf on my body."

I growled slightly before reigning it in. I didn't like hearing she had been with another male and I was finding it harder and harder to keep my feelings for her to myself.

She patted my arm like she was calming a small child. "Relax, only your wolf gets to mark up this body."

I could see the moment she realized what she was saying. She whipped around and caught my stare as her hand flew to her mouth and her face turned all splotchy in embarrassment. I couldn't help but laugh. She looked ridiculously cute.

I stepped closer to her, fascinated by a loose strand of hair that had escaped the ponytail she was wearing and I wiped it from her face and tucked it back behind her ear. I had meant to keep things light but the way she was looking at me wasn't helping.

"Only mine," I said in a voice deeper and huskier than my usual one.

Her pupils dilated in acknowledgement seconds before my lips crushed against hers. I'm not sure which of us it shocked more. I had sworn I wouldn't try anything with her, but when our lips touched it was a slight breath of hesitation before we both seemed to combust. Her mouth opened and she sighed this sexy moan right into my mouth and I was a goner. I wasted no time exploring every inch of her mouth and it was more glorious than anything I had ever imagined. She kissed me back full of passion and I had no doubt my mate desired me as much as I her

Her hands seemed to have a mind of their own as they unashamedly began exploring my body. She was driving me wild, and when her hands found their way under my shirt and she moaned, happily exploring every ridge across my abdomen with her hands, I knew it was stop things now or I would take exactly what I had wanted since the first moment I caught her scent, before I even laid eyes on my beautiful mate.

I tried to do the gentlemanly thing. I slowed our kisses and she responded in kind. It didn't stop the intensity between us, though. It only brought on a new kind of pleasure and I continued memorizing every crevice of her mouth, every motion that made her moan again. When I nibbled her bottom lip, I was rewarded as she wrapped her arms around me and pulled our bodies together. Every inch of her pressed against every inch of me and there was no hiding my desire for her as she rocked against me. I pulled back with a groan.

"Babe, what are you doing to me?" I asked in a voice I barely recognized, trying to catch my breath, and put a little distance between us.

I saw a panicked look in her eyes and realized too late she took it to mean she was doing something wrong. I wrapped my arms around her and pulled her in close, allowing myself full access to her neck as I nuzzled into it, kissing her and blowing my scent on her. I wanted everyone within ten packs to know this one was mine. Only mine.

"That was meant as a compliment."

I felt the tension that had quickly stiffened her, relax and I could feel her smile against my chest.

"Are you hungry?" I asked, slowly regaining my brain.

"Is that a loaded question?"

I laughed out loud at her unexpected response. Keeping my arm around her, I led her the rest of the way into my house, realizing we hadn't even managed to close the front door when our welcome frenzy began. I ran a hand through my hair in frustration at the thought of any wolf strolling by and seeing me and my mate in an intimate exchange. I knew I lived more remote than the others who all preferred to stay close by and live in groups, but still, the woods surrounding my home was often used for late night runs.

I felt a warm hand on my cheek as Kelsey angled my face to look down at her.

"Are you okay?"

Her brow was furrowed with worry. Worry for me, I

realized.

I smiled reassuringly. "Everything's perfect, and I did cook dinner if you are hungry.... for food." I added in jest and chuckled, enjoying her squirm in embarrassment.

She pouted. Her bottom lip, still swollen from my kisses, was clearing jutting out in an actual pout.

"I guess we can eat then." She sounded disappointed, then immediately back to her normal self. "Did you really cook?"

"Yup, I did. I'm not entirely helpless. You may even find I'm good for a few things."

"Oh, I've clearly already discovered one tonight."

She winked at me and I was floored by this new intimate, playful side of her. Who knew? She was always so formal and by the books at work. I loved it. I loved her. The realization almost knocked the breath out of me.

"So, what are we having?" She asked, unaware of my internal discovery.

"Um, chicken alfredo? I made it from scratch."

"Very impressive. And fortunately for you, I have very limited tastes in gourmet foods. And I'm a terrible cook. I know enough not to starve, but bouncing from one foster family or girls home to the next didn't exactly provide me with much in the way of domestic skills. So an unburnt box of mac and cheese would have impressed me just as much."

"Good thing for you then, I happen to be a great cook and a bit of a foodie, so get used to eating a whole lot better, babe."

She shied but smiled and I realized I had just alluded to us being something beyond today. Shit! I swore I wasn't going to scare her off. So far I'd managed two major screw ups in my plan.

"Okay, then, so impress me with your mad cooking skills."

I relaxed and dished out a sizable plate of pasta and chicken for both of us. A side of steamed lemon garlic broccoli and some garlic bread finished off the meal. I had bought a bottle of wine and there were grapes and various cheeses already awaiting us on the table. I filled her glass and took my seat when I was satisfied with my presentation.

"You know, you probably shouldn't be giving me anymore alcohol. I think I've already had more than I normally consume in a year tonight."

She seemed fine. Maybe a little looser and more playful than normal, but in a genuine way, not in a drunk way. I wondered again, just how many drinks did she have?

Mmmmm. Her moans of appraisal as she ate the meal I had prepared her jolted my attention back to her. The satisfied look of sheer pleasure on her face told me she more than liked it.

"Kyle, this is by far the best thing I have ever eaten in my life. Oh my gosh, it's delicious. You really cooked this all by yourself?"

"I swear it."

The way she was looking at me was going to quickly lead back to where we left off at the door. Not that I'd mind that, but I did need to talk to her and explain some things to her. Mostly I needed to explain about mating and what was going on between us. It wasn't fair to her that she didn't already know before we acted on it.

"So, how was The Crate tonight?"

She smirked at me. It was the sexiest look I'd ever seen on a woman and had me ready to pick her up and drag her off into my bedroom and finish what we had started.

"If I tell you, are you going to freak out and try to attack me again?"

I frowned, "No." I would never attack her. I wasn't even capable of hurting her.

"Damn, that's a shame."

I choked on the sip of wine I had just downed. I had certainly not expected that!

"Well, after work I drove over to The Crate and Sally wasn't there yet. I didn't really know what to do. I had never been in a bar before. No one has ever asked me out for drinks like that, so I had no clue what I was doing or where to sit or anything. Fortunately, Cole Anderson was there and it helped to see a familiar face. So I hung out with him and we caught up over drinks waiting for Sally to arrive. Apparently, everyone's talking about the big race. I had a few guys buy me a round as congratulations." She paused and frowned. "Sorry."

"I can take the heat of losing to a girl." I laughed.

"Oh, um, yeah, okay."

She was hesitating and I needed to know why, so I asked her.

No more beating about the bush with us now that things were coming out in the open. Mates aren't supposed to hide anything from each other and I wanted to know everything about her.

"It's just, I don't know. I'm not very good with this stuff so I could be way off mark here, but it's just that you seem to get a little, uh, upset, when I mention other guys."

Okay, she was definitely onboard with brutal honesty.

"Guess I haven't been keeping that in check as much as I thought I was."

"It's okay, you kind of flipped out the other day about the, uh, tattoo when you saw it and I can, I don't know how to explain it, but I can feel when you're unhappy about something. I don't always know what, but I know when something's bothering you and I just didn't want to upset you realizing I was talking about the guys in the bar buying me drinks."

"You feel my emotions?"

She nodded. All this time I thought she wasn't really feeling the connection and the call to mating, but maybe I was wrong.

"What else do you feel?"

She shrugged and I knew there was more.

"I know when you're watching me. I always know when you are in the woods in your wolf form guarding my house. Like last night. I knew you were there all night. I almost called you in just so you'd get some sleep. You were very restless last night."

I know I stared at her in shock. I really shouldn't be. I mean, I had noticed I was more and more in tune with her too, especially since our first kiss, so why wouldn't she reciprocate? But the enormity of what she was saying was still stunning. We hadn't even mated and yet what I had been feeling and what she was telling me sounded very much like what I had always been told about the bond between mates.

She sighed, "I'm not supposed to be feeling that, am I?"

I could see the disappointment on her face.

"No, not yet, it's too soon." The look she gave felt like pure rejection, like I'd just shamed her over what she'd told me and I had to make it right no matter how crazy it sounded. "Kelsey, we aren't supposed to feel each other on that level. Only bonded mates are supposed to be that aware of each other." I lifted her downcast head to face me. She wouldn't make eye contact and I missed looking into her beautiful brown eyes. "But I feel it too. I always know exactly what room you're in. I know when you're scared or stressed or disappointed with yourself or something someone's told you."

Her eyes flew to mine and we held each other's stare. Even as mates, we shouldn't be able to do that for this long either. I knew deep down that whatever this was between us was different, special.

She licked her lips and didn't break eye contact as she boldly asked, "So, you're my mate, right?"

I know I blushed. Guys aren't supposed to blush. I needed to pull it together.

"Uh, um, yeah, who told you about that?"

She giggled. "You're cute when you get flustered. Elise and Lily were cluing me in on a few things today that they didn't think you had any business discussing with me." She frowned. "They don't know, do they?"

I shook my head. "No, and I'm sorry you had to find out from them."

"From what they described, males in particular are extremely possessive and territorial. They can become aggressive when other males are near, and sometimes females, if they feel there's a threat, warranted or not. It's been two years, Kyle. How could you possibly control what they described all this time and never let on that you felt anything at all?"

She looked disappointed. I didn't know how to explain and I knew before I opened my mouth I was about to become a bumbling idiot.

"Kelsey, I just didn't know what to do. At first it was such a shock. Do you remember that first day we met? I could barely hold it together and couldn't get away from you fast enough. You didn't show any signs whatsoever that you felt anything at all, which made me angry and, well, hurt."

"Oh, I felt plenty. Too much. I considered running it freaked me out so much, but I love my little cottage and was determined to make it work. It wasn't easy, but I tried to maintain strict professionalism with you. I knew if I let it slip even a little there was no turning back, and," she chewed on her bottom lip, "well, one slip and look what happened."

He grinned. "Are you sorry? Cause Lord knows I'm not!"

She grinned back at me and shook her head no. My heart

nearly leapt from my chest. I took her hand and lovingly stroked it with my thumb as I had longed to do.

"Do you have any questions? About mating and stuff?"

She squirmed uncomfortably then sighed and shook her head yes.

"Everything we are feeling, you say we shouldn't be. What should I be feeling, Kyle?"

"There's nothing wrong with you, babe. You're worrying too much. Mating is perfectly natural. It's rare that one finds their one true mate, especially so young. We're lucky there."

"One true mate? They didn't mention anything about that. They said I could have several compatible mates."

I wanted to smack my sisters.

"That's true, you could have many compatible mates, but only ever one true mate. It's rare to find your one true mate, so for several generations shifters have just stopped waiting for it and settled for compatible mates instead." I wanted her to understand the impact of what I was saying, and for once I was grateful that she didn't turn away from my gaze. "I knew I could never settle for anyone less than my one true mate."

Kelsey

Chapter 15

What Elise and Lily had told me about mates was not the same thing as what I suspected Kyle was talking about. One true mate? Did he really mean that as it sounded, like I was the only mate for him and he for me?

Elise had described it much like normal human dating. A strong attraction, a getting to know you period, followed by sex to seal the bond. Though she was vague on that part, and we were rushed in our discussion and my limited lunch break. I knew wolves mated for life. Once I took a mate there would never be another for me. I was okay with that. I was even okay with thinking of Kyle Westin in the forever sense.

"What did you mean earlier about the bond between mates?"

"Only true mates can fully bond. It's a closeness of sorts, they can feel and sense each other more deeply than compatible mates."

I nodded, not knowing what to say or think about that. We were clearly already sensing and feeling each other, though according to what the girls told me we hadn't actually mated or bonded, we were just potential mates.

"I still don't really understand the whole mating thing. How does that differ from just dating, engagement, marriage sorta thing?"

He looked flustered again. God was he cute when he got like that. Several times through the evening he had caught himself raking his hand through his hair. It was quite mussed at this point. I wasn't used to seeing the calm, cool, collected Kyle Westin so frazzled. I liked that I was the one to loosen him up.

My thoughts drifted to earlier. I would have let him take me right there in the open doorway and not thought twice about it. I had never allowed myself to want a guy in that way. I didn't think it would ever be possible for me. Now that I knew otherwise, all I wanted was to be underneath Kyle Westin and whatever else this mating bond thingy he was trying to explain called for.

Crap, he was talking again and I missed it.

"Does that make sense?"

I stared at him blankly. "Didn't hear a word you said."

He looked at me like I was crazy and ran his fingers through his hair again. Hmmm, I loved when he did that, though I wished it were my hands.

He laughed and I blinked back to present.

"Sorry," I knew I was blushing.

"What were you thinking just then?"

I couldn't possibly tell him that. I shook my head.

"I told you already, true mates share everything. There's no secrets between them."

It was my turn to laugh. "We aren't off to a very good start then, are we?"

I didn't know why my tongue was so loose around him tonight. I had only a couple of drinks at the bar. Plus those three shots. Shoot, what did they call them again? Some sort of bombs? I didn't feel drunk, though. I felt relaxed, but then that make-out session alone was enough to cause that. Who knew kissing would feel like that?

I saw Kyle stand up and take the plates to the sink. I think maybe I was zoning out on him again. I got up and joined him at the sink. I took the dirty dishes from him and started washing them in the already filling soapy water side. I noticed he was just staring at me, but didn't move to stop me, so when I was done washing the first dish I handed it to him and moved the water to his side of the double sink. We worked side by side in silence and it was nice and comfortable and just felt right. I had never in my life just felt so completely right.

When the last dish was washed and dried and put away he turned to me. I could see in his eyes that he was more than ready for more of what we'd done earlier. I didn't want to feel nervous, but the nerves were definitely starting to sink in. The whole domestic thing we'd just done seemed quite intimate in an odd way.

"How about a tour of this place?"

He seemed okay with that. He talked me through each room as we made our way through the house. There was definitely a masculine vibe to the place. I could see small touches here and there that were not him and suspected it was Lily's doing, but overall everything was browns and greens and earthy tones and smelled of leather and pine and lemon and him. It was very comfortable. I hadn't really thought about it before hand but of course the tour had to end in the bedroom, and not just any bedroom, because there were four in his house, but his bedroom.

"So, this is my room," he said sounding just as nervous as I felt.

"It's nice," I said, walking around and testing the mattress, finding it firm but plush at the same time. Much like my mate, who I knew was staring at me without even looking to confirm it.

He stepped closer and soon his arms were rubbing down my shoulders like he couldn't stop himself. I knew that feeling too well. I should have been embarrassed by how forward I was with him earlier. I had never touched a man before and I was so mesmerized I just couldn't stop it.

I turned in his arms and when our eyes met, everything around us faded away. All I saw was him and this primal need rose up in me. It was terrifying and wonderful at the same time.

"I've never even kissed anyone but you," I blurted out.

I saw the lust flare in his eyes. I had no doubt he already knew that, or suspected it. but saying it aloud brought out a growl in him that turned my bones to mush. If he weren't holding me in his arms I swear, I'd be a puddle of goo on the floor.

"Mine," he said, smelling my hair and kissing the top of my head. It should have seemed weird, but we were wolves, smell and closeness were a part of who we were, and both my wolf and I strongly approved.

I looked him right in the eyes knowing I was about to be kissed, but not before responding, "Mine."

He growled again and descended on my mouth. The back of my legs were already pressed up against the bed and my arms wrapped around him to pull him close. Coming up for a quick breath of air, I more confidently proclaimed, "Mine."

That was like an open invitation because suddenly while his mouth continued kissing me senseless, his hands began exploring my body and the tingling sensation was almost more than I could handle. The build of desire in me grew quickly, even though we still remained fully clothed. He didn't slow his exploration, but he didn't move things further along until I couldn't stand it any longer and found my hands under his shirt again and pressing upwards. That shirt had to go.

My breath caught the first time I saw his hard body etched like a work of art. As he stepped back, allowing me to stare in wonder, I took the opportunity to shed my own shirt. His sharp intake of breath told me he liked what he saw.

Time seemed to lose consciousness after that. Clothing began piling up on the floor as his hands touched me, igniting a fire in places I didn't even know existed. I felt as though I were in a furnace about to combust from the added heat. The more he stroked and touched, the more I craved. I heard the moans and the sounds coming from within but I couldn't discern they were actually coming from me.

At some point, he had pulled me down on to the bed and when we finally made love it was the most intense moment of my life. As we escalated in our love, my body continued to ignite, bringing me further and further to an unknown cliff that I knew I would free fall over the brink. With our combined breaths growing more and more shallow, I clung to him. He nuzzled into my neck, as I did his, and just before we crested into the glorious unknown, I felt his vein pulsing in his neck and my teeth elongated. No one had to tell me what to do, I was acting on sheer instinct in the mist of our love making. I bit down onto his neck and seconds later felt the pinch on mine knowing he was doing the same. And we both let go and fell together.

As we lay still connected, sweating, with shallow breaths, my teeth retracted to normal. I felt him withdraw too and he licked my neck in the place he had bitten. I copied his actions then kissed the mark now evident on his skin. *My mark*, I thought. *Mine.*

He cradled me without a word as our breathing and heart rates slowly returned to normal.

"Stay with me tonight?" he asked.

Wrapped in his arms, there was nowhere I'd rather be.

"Ok," I whispered against his chest.

His arms tightened around me and I knew I had just made my mate very happy. My mate. Just thinking it made me smile. When Elise had said there was more to completing the mating than just sex, I wondered if maybe that was what she was talking about. I would ask Kyle later. I just wanted to enjoy being close to him.

Neither of us moved or spoke again until I shivered. I had come down off my high from our love making and felt the chill in the air. He separated and I immediately felt his absence.

"You're cold."

I nodded.

"Are you tired?"

"A little, yes, and then again no, not at all."

He smiled like he understood, then stood and reached for my hand. He had an up-to-no-good sort of little kid grin when he said, "Come. Run with me."

"Now?"

"Yes, now. Run with me."

"I can think of other ways to work off that extra energy," I told him in a sexy, seductive voice as I trailed a finger down his chest. I couldn't even believe that was me talking.

He grinned happily. "After, come, run with me."

"Okay, okay," I said standing and stretching. It never occurred to me to cover myself in front of him. Not even as he stood there checking me out from head to toe. "Well, come on," I urged him.

When we got on his back porch he changed. I followed. His wolf nudged up against mine and licked my face. Mine playfully jumped on him causing us both to tumble down the stairs. Getting up and shaking off, he motioned with his head towards the woods and took off running. I matched his pace in perfect synch running half a step behind him even knowing I could easily have taken him in another race.

As we came to a cliff overlooking the valley below he sat and turned his head up to the night sky. It was a full moon, the biggest and brightest I ever remembered. We both howled at it in perfect sync and harmony. It was a beautiful moment.

Once back home and shifted back to human form, we could talk again.

"Thank you," he said kissing me sweetly. "Are you okay?" He had worry in his voice and it gave me goosebumps.

"Why wouldn't I be okay?"

"Do you realize what we did tonight?"

"I can guess. Elise said something about sex and other stuff to seal the mated pair. She didn't elaborate." I stared at the mark I had left on his skin as his thumb lightly rubbed across his mark on me. "Is that the other stuff?"

He nodded solemnly.

"I'm sorry, I hadn't intended for it to happen so quickly. The intensity of it all just took me by surprise, and when I felt your fangs on my neck there was nothing I could do to stop myself from me marking you too."

"So that's it? I marked you, you marked me, we're now mated happily ever after?"

He laughed and kissed my marking, holding me tight. "Yeah, I'm afraid so. You're sorta stuck with me now."

I pulled back and looked at him. "Do you really think there's anyone else in this world I'd rather be stuck with? Cause there's not."

KYLE
Chapter 16

I couldn't believe what happened. Waking up with Kelsey in my arms was everything I'd dreamed it would be. I couldn't even describe the peace and comfort it brought me. I reached over and held her hand, wrapping her arm back around me and pulling her close. Our legs already entwined and tangled in the sheets. Her hair looked a mess, but her face glowed. She was beautiful and took my breath away. And I was the lucky guy who'd get to wake to this every day of my life. I didn't think anything or anyone could wipe the smile off my face, and looking at the clock I noted we were already late for work.

Grabbing the phone, I called Elise to let her know Kelsey and I would be late. When she didn't answer her cell, I called the house.

"Hello?" My father answered.

"Hey Dad, I'm looking for Elise, has she left the house yet? She's not answering her phone."

"No, she's still here."

"You sound stressed, is something wrong?"

I heard him take a deep breath and blow it out, "Nothing too concerning I hope."

"Dad, what's up?" I was focused and concerned now.

"Last night there was a shift in pack power."

"What do you mean? How is that even possible?"

"It's probably nothing, Son. I don't want to worry you. I just felt a shift in power, like I'd expect to feel when you finally step up, though not quite that severe. Perhaps like when you finally take a mate and begin funneling more power to you as next in line."

"That happens?" I had no idea.

"Yes, of course, but don't worry, I'm sure it's nothing and we'll discuss all of that later. Let me grab Elise for you."

Everything came crashing down around me. I had taken a mate. There was a power shift towards Kelsey and I in the pack. The Pack Council hadn't approved our mating and I knew there would be plenty displeased with my choice, even if it wasn't really a choice since she was my true mate.

The Challenge. I cringed at the thought. How many she-wolves would step up to challenge my mate? Kelsey had no fighting skills. She'd never been taught even basic survival skills. My stomach clenched in despair. What had I done?

"Hey, Kyle, what's up?" My sister's voice broke my thoughts.

"Did I wake you?"

"Shut up, I haven't had my coffee yet. What's up?"

"Just wanted to let you know that Kelsey and I won't be in the office today. I didn't want you guys to worry. If you could forward my calls to my cell, that would great."

"What's wrong with Kelsey? She never misses work. What's going on?"

"Nothing's wrong, E. We just have a few things to take care of outside of work today."

"What are you up to, Kyle? Please tell me it's not what I think it is?"

The woman was exasperating like a freaking dog with a bone, unwilling to let it go.

"Just drop it okay, it's personal."

"No, no, no. Kyle, please, no. Look, I know you like her. I've seen the way you look at her when you think no one's watching. And I'm your sister, I know you. Please don't act on it. You show any interest in her whatsoever and she's good as dead and you know it."

"Shit," I said, running a hand through my hair. "I can't talk about this now, E. Can you put Dad back on the phone?"

Without another word she handed the phone back over to our dad.

"Kyle, is everything okay?"

"It's going to be fine, Dad. It has to be," I said more to

myself than him. "Look, are you free this morning? We really need to talk."

"Sure, give me an hour."

"Thanks, Dad, see you in an hour."

As I hung up the phone, I was very aware Kelsey was fully awake and staring at me.

She sighed and it sounded so sad. I rolled back into bed and pulled her close. I wasn't about to let anything happen to her. Ever.

"Are we okay?" she asked awkwardly.

I looked down at her and smiled. "Never better."

I didn't mean to escalate the kiss I gave her, but the second our lips touched it was like a match bursting into flames. She was still naked in my bed from the night before and I knew I had to have her. Had to claim her once again and not just to calm my wolf, but for me. I needed her.

We didn't rush things this time. I took my time exploring every inch of her and learning what she liked and didn't. I was shocked when she started directing me with her words and telling me exactly what she wanted me to do to her. I had never had such a responsive partner in bed and she seemed to understand exactly what I needed and where I needed her to touch me, too. We moved in perfect sync and I thought my heart would explode when she fell apart in my arms and I followed her into oblivion.

It was nothing like it had been the night before. My body was still shaking from the intensity of it. And I knew Kelsey felt it too. I wiped a stray tear from her cheek and kissed her sweetly, not trusting myself to deepen it this time. I closed my eyes and breathed in her scent.

"That was beautiful. I had no idea it could be like that," I heard her say.

"I know, me too. No one's ever spoken to me like that before. No questioning what you wanted or how to please you. I loved it."

I nuzzled her neck and kissed my mark as I felt her stiffen in my arms.

"What? Wh-what are you talking about?" she stuttered as I knew she only did when she was really upset or nervous.

I looked at her in confusion.

"I wasn't talking during… that," she waved her hand over the two of us not able to say the words.

Why would she deny it? It had been incredible.

"Babe, I would never have known to…" I trailed my hand down her waist heading for what I knew now was her most sensitive spot when she nearly jumped out the bed.

Her face showed pure shock and embarrassment.

"I didn't tell you that," she insisted.

"How could he possibly have known that anyway?" I heard her clearly but watching her saw no signs of her lips moving.

"Kelsey?" I tested, thinking it instead of saying it aloud.

"What?" she answered aloud in frustration, but not able to bring herself to look me in the eyes.

I knew my eyes were nearly bugging out of my head. It was impossible! I knew my heart started racing, I couldn't stop the panic rising in me. This wasn't supposed to happen. I mean I had heard it could happen, especially between true mates, but not for many, many years, sometimes even many decades.

"Kyle, what's wrong?"

Now Kelsey was panicking too, most likely feeding off my elevated stress levels, but I couldn't calm them even for her. I was freaking out.

She rushed over to me and when her hands touched my chest a calm washed over me and I felt like I could breathe again.

"Thank you," I told her without speaking, testing the connection again.

"You're welcome," she said sighing against my chest.

"Big bad wolves chase little red riding hood," I told her through our bond just to make absolute sure she was hearing me.

She pulled away and looked up at me in confusion.

"What? That's not even funny, Kyle. You know I was terrified of the big bad wolf growing up." She smacked me for added emphasis.

"Um, Kels, there's something you need to know and try not to freak out like I just did, okay?"

She looked at me with worry in her eyes.

"I knew it was too good to be true. It's okay, I won't cry in front of him. Do not cry, Kelsey!" I heard her internal conversation loud and clear and I wanted to shake some sense into her.

"Damn it. Doesn't she know I'm not going anywhere? Why can't she understand I'm hers? Only hers!"

117

She was staring at me with a similar freaked out look that I was giving her a few minutes earlier. Oops, shouldn't have been talking to myself like that.

"Kelse,." I said aloud.

"I-I-I heard you. Your lips weren't moving, but I heard you!"

I gave her a half smile.

"I know, it's freaking me out too."

"THAT's how you knew? About that…" she waved towards the bed and I couldn't help but chuckle.

"I didn't know then, I swear, I just heard what you wanted and acted."

Her face was flaming red. I couldn't help but pull her into my arms and try to tell her it was okay.

"Better than okay. It was freaking awesome!" I thought.

Her wide eyes told me she heard me too. Oops.

"Why can I hear you in my head when you aren't talking?"

"I don't know," I told her honestly. "I mean, I've heard it can happen with bonded mates, but bonds take time, like years, decades even to fully establish to this point."

"You said we were starting to show signs of bonding before we, um, did what we did last night. That wasn't normal either, right?"

"True. Maybe that accelerated things? Babe, I have no idea. I'm just as freaked out as you, but it's going to be okay. May take a little getting used to. I feel like I have to monitor my thoughts already."

"Well, you're the one that said mates have no secrets," she grumbled, making me laugh.

"Yeah, truer than we thought, huh? And Kels," I made her look at me even knowing she was still embarrassed by everything happening. "I'm not going anywhere. You are mine. And I am yours and nothing can change that."

She sighed contentedly in my arms and pressed a kiss into my neck, reminding me of the mark she left on me. My mate. Nothing was better than that.

Kelsey

Chapter 17

Kyle explained that we needed to talk with his dad. Maybe he had an idea of what was going on. I hoped so. I was trying hard not to freak out over the mind reading thing. It was just too much. I had no idea mating would be like that. It was hard enough to deal with my own thoughts and feelings, now I felt like I was dealing with both of ours. I knew he felt the same. It was just so overwhelming.

We didn't pass anyone in the Westin house as we headed straight for his father's office. The door was shut and Kyle knocked before opening it. Her smell hit me like a flying brick and before I could stop myself I had moved Kyle behind me and stared down at Vanessa whose wild eyes looked everywhere but into my mine. I felt the surge of power release from me and saw Vanessa turn with wide, shocked eyes and kneel before me, baring her neck.

"Kelsey, I'm not here for Kyle, I promise, you made your point yesterday. You won't get a challenge from me."

I calmed at her words and felt the power withdrawal within me.

"Thank you. You may go," I dismissed her and watched as she left the room without a word.

Turning back to face Kyle and his dad I saw nothing but shock on his face. I sighed and dropped my head.

"I screwed up again, didn't I?" I asked Kyle through our connection.

He hugged me close, rubbing his hand down my back in reassurance.

"It's okay," he told me through our bond.

"Kelsey?" His father's attention was on me now as the shock on his face wore off.

"I'm sorry, Sir. She just makes me so angry that I can't control it."

"Kelsey, do you know what happened just now?"

I shook my head no. I could tell they were both shocked and maybe disappointed in me but I really didn't understand what I had done.

"Kyle, could you excuse us please, I'd like to talk to Kelsey alone."

"No, I'm sorry, Dad, but that's not going to happen."

His father raised one eyebrow higher than the other and glared at him curiously at his defiance.

"Excuse me?"

"Dad, we need to talk to you," his eyes were pleading with his father to understand, "together."

Jason Westin sat down hard.

"The power transference I felt last night. You didn't. Did you?"

Kyle sighed and raked his hand through his hair.

"Yes, we did."

Jason blew out a deep breath.

"Well, that explains that, but Kelsey, how were you able to pull alpha power that way? I've been in front of some of the most powerful alphas in history and I've never felt anything like that."

"I have a theory, Dad…"

He nodded for him to continue.

"Kelsey and I, we started bonding before we completed our mating."

I know I shouldn't have, but hearing him speak of our mating to his dad made me blush furiously.

"That's not possible."

"But Dad ."

"Kyle, it just isn't possible. I'm sure you had very strong feelings, but bonding takes time, years before even the very beginnings of it begin to blossom."

I heard Kyle swear in his head and knew his dad wasn't taking him serious.

"What are the signs of a bond, Mr. Westin? Perhaps feeling your mate's emotions? Knowing his exact location? How about hearing his every thought and being able to communicate telepathically?"

His eyes widened. "Yes, all of those things. It starts off mild and grows into what you are describing."

Anger flared in me. We were telling him this was happening and he wasn't believing any of it. Worse, he seemed to be listening to me more than Kyle.

"Mr. Westin, I get you may not believe me. I'm a nobody."

"You are not a nobody, babe." I heard Kyle's words in my head and turned to glare at him for distracting me mid-rant.

"But Kyle is your son. Why would he lie to you? You've groomed him his entire life to run this pack. I would think you would trust him with anything."

I felt a hand on my shoulder and I turned to look at Kyle.

"What?" I thought.

"Kels, I love that you are riled up and ready to come to my defense, but please," His eyes were pleading with me, *"I'm the alpha male here. It's my job to protect you, my mate. It is my honor to bear. Please don't take that from me."*

I nodded and took a step back, not cowering behind him but standing tall in support of him.

His father watched our silent transaction in awe.

"It's true, isn't it? You really have bonded, fully bonded, so quickly?"

I let Kyle nod and take control of the situation, but his father's eyes were immediately drawn to me.

"I understand now."

"What?" We both asked at the same time.

"I didn't feel it when we spoke the other day. Kelsey, did something happen aside from the obvious, to you this week?"

I looked at Kyle for approval before answering. He nodded and smiled, encouraging me on.

"Like what exactly?"

"It's really hard to tell. You were quite reserved and I felt no authority in you at our last meeting nor any time before. But now?

121

Now I feel power pouring off of you demanding attention and control. And what you did to Vanessa? Even as Pack Mother you shouldn't have that much power and authority. And she gave allegiance to you right here in my presence."

Kyle's sharp intake of breath told me that was a very bad thing.

I dropped my head in submission and didn't make eye contact when I spoke.

"Vanessa. She came to the office yesterday. She threatened me. Told me I could never have Kyle, that he was hers. It felt like something snapped inside me and I saw that she was afraid. My wolf rejoiced over it but I had felt bad when she stormed out of my office. I got angry when I saw her here just now. It felt... similar." I all but whispered.

"Please, sit down, both of you. This is very important and something we mustn't share with anyone. I mean anyone. Do you both hear me? If you were anyone else Kelsey I'd have you removed from my territory so fast your head would spin, but I could never do that to Kyle and I strongly feel you are no real threat to us, but if the Grand Council ever hears of your existence, it could mean war. They would stop at nothing to destroy you."

"Father!" Kyle started in, but I laid my hand on his arm to silence him.

"So, Elise's theory is right? I have no pack. The wolves that came for my parents were really after me, and I shouldn't exist because I should have died as a young pup because I'm a-a-a alpha she-wolf?"

"We will never speak of this again, do you hear me?"

I nodded.

"Both of you?"

Kyle looked like he was in shock but slowly nodded in agreement.

"What does this mean, Dad? What does it mean to the pack?"

I could hear him cursing himself for acting so brashly and not seeing what was in front of him. I couldn't console him. It was tearing me up inside that he was regretting our mating. I knew the moment he realized I was upset.

"Hey, it's okay. I promise you I don't regret a thing. You are my one true mate, nothing could have stopped it, no amount of knowledge in who or what you are would change what I feel. You are mine and I am yours. For better or worse, we'll get through it together."

His father smiled at the two of us as I fought back tears. "Good, because you are both going to have to be strong and help each other through this. Kelsey, I'm going to ask you to do something for me, just once. I need to know just how powerful you are."

"No Father, you can't."

"Kyle, it will be fine."

"No, Dad, you saw how quickly Vanessa gave allegiance. It's not worth chancing it. Let me. She's my mate."

"And as such you will willingly give her the world, including your full allegiance, as it should be. Someday, Kyle, I will step down as Pack Alpha and give my allegiance to you and to Kelsey as Pack Mother. Worst case, that happens a little sooner than expected."

"I don't understand what you're asking of me," Kelsey said.

"Babe, Dad's going to ask you to push your full power against his. It is a test of strength amongst alphas."

"And if I am as strong as he suspects?"

"My wolf could try and give our allegiance to you, however, there is a lot more to becoming Pack Alpha than that and I do not see you issuing a fight to the death to take my role."

I looked at him horrified. He couldn't possibly be serious!

He smirked seeing the horror on my face. "That's what I thought. Okay, let's do this."

"Now?"

"Now."

"What do I do?"

"In theory, you shouldn't have to do anything, your natural powers should take over much in the same way it did when you felt Vanessa was a threat."

"But I do not see you as a threat, Sir."

"No, perhaps not, but your wolf should not appreciate the dominance I'm about to invoke on you."

I gulped, not liking the sound of that.

"Rise and face me. You will hold my stare for as long as you possibly can. You will feel my full power directed at you and you are free to respond in kind."

I was terrified of what he was asking. I didn't know what to expect but Kyle smiled and encouraged me to continue.

I stood before him and met his stare. I had never had a problem with that, only dropping it out of courtesy as the girls had told me to do. I felt a tingling across my body that lightly stirred my wolf. She didn't like it, but it was tolerable. As the pressure increased, goosebumps came across my body. The tingling grew to the feel of pins and needles, like when you've sat in one position too long and your foot falls asleep. Tolerable. And I felt no release like I did with Vanessa.

"Kelsey, I need you to push back."

"I don't know how!"

I felt a surge come off him and it was uncomfortable and awkward, but I never dropped his stare or budged from my spot. I tried to conjure up something similar to throw back, but I didn't know how and I felt stupid standing there like that.

He eyed me suspiciously as one would a chess opponent. "Interesting."

He upped the dosage again, or at least that's what it felt like. I imagined my hackles were standing tall if I had been in wolf form and a small growl released from me but nothing in the way of power like before.

"You are strong, I'll give you that, but I feel no return power from you, only sheer defiance."

"I'm sorry, Sir, I don't know how to make it happen."

Next, he looked at Kyle and turned his focus to him. I saw Kyle's knees start to buckle under the strain.

"No!" I yelled and like a bolt of lightning my powers released in one swift punch aimed for Jason Westin. I saw the shock on his face when it hit him, knocking him over into the chair behind him and flipping him over and into the wall beyond. The wall was the only thing keeping the Pack Alpha on his feet. He waved a hand in the air acknowledging the end our experiment.

I immediately ran to Kyle whose knees had given out from under him and he was fighting to catch his breath like the air had been punched from him too.

"Kyle! Kyle, are you okay?"

I was terrified I had hurt him.

"I'm fine. I'm fine. Just need to sit for a minute. Can you help

Dad into a chair too?"

"Did you feel that, Son?"

"The drain just before she sent you flying across the room?"

"Yes. We're going to have to work on that. I'm not sure how she's doing it, but we need to find some way to control it. I've heard of she-wolves bonded to Pack Alphas able to pull pack power through their bond, but this. Wow! I've never felt something like that before."

"What? What did I do?" I was trying not to freak out.

"Babe, you not only used your power, you pulled Pack power, and a lot of it. Nearly knocked the breath out of me even though you were aiming for Dad. Basically, you crippled him of his power and power punched him with both yours and his at the same time."

He chuckled, sounding impressed.

I smacked him. "It's not funny! What if I had hurt you, either of you? It's too dangerous to be messing with!"

"No, I'm sorry, my dear, but the three of us are going to need to work on this for balance and control. Though I find it very interesting that your power is practically non-existent in you right now, only acting as a defense mechanism."

"A what?"

"Babe, he's saying your powers kick in only when you feel threatened. Vanessa was a threat to you. Dad turned his powers on me and you acted to protect me whether you realized it or not."

"Word ever gets out about you, and we're going to have a fight on our hands. We will need to train and work on controlling this. Do you understand, Kelsey?"

I nodded, still in shock.

"Not a word to anyone. This knowledge does not leave the three of us."

"Not even Mom? Or the Pack Council?"

"No one, Kyle. It's the best way to keep your mate safe. I can't promise the day won't come that I tell your mom, but for now, this stays between us. There are very real reasons and fears regarding alpha she-wolves. No one wants to kill young innocent pups but the power within you, it terrifies many. We will work to help you control this, but it absolutely stays between the three of us."

We all nodded solemnly in agreement.

Then he broke into a big grin. "She's going to make one heck of a Pack Mother and an even better mother to my grandpups someday."

I blushed at his supposed compliment as Kyle proudly put his arm around me and pulled me closer kissing my temple.

"Okay, well, enough of that for today. We have a few other important matters to discuss. First, I need you both to keep up a normal pretense. Not a peep about your mating to anyone. You continue to show no interest or favoritism towards each other. Are we clear?"

We both nodded and he continued.

"The last thing I need is challenges being issued or threats made causing you to unleash your power on another unsuspecting she-wolf."

I cringed at his accusation.

"Second, Kelsey, go back to work as usual today and tomorrow, too. Go home, keep to your normal routine." I heard Kyle growl next to me and his father sighed. "Go home, Kelsey, then you can change into wolf form and head to Kyle's but at least your car by all appearances will be at home where you would be expected to be."

"Okay, I can do that."

"Kyle?"

I could tell he wasn't happy with the situation, but he begrudgingly agreed.

"Next, cover your markings." This elicited a growl from both of us. "It's only until the pack meeting on Sunday, just a few days," he assured us. "Again, I can't have challenges being issued before the announcement."

"What announcement?"

This time Kyle spoke, "Our mating announcement will be made at the pack meeting. At that time the limitation for challenges will be given. It's typically four months."

"What do you mean by challenges?"

They both shared a look that I didn't like.

"When a new mating is announced," Mr. Westin began, "any unmated wolf has the right to challenge. It's a fight to the death. The announcement will go out to all unmated wolves within three packs, though word that Kyle has taken a mate could draw a crowd of potential challengers from even further away. You may not realize, but he has been the most eligible alpha for quite some time and there will be many displeased to find him off the market."

"I have to fight off these girls in death battles????" Where they crazy? I'd never fought anyone for anything in my life. I flee, not fight.

"Calm down, it's going to be okay, babe."

"Though those in our pack will think twice about challenging Kyle, we have had numerous requests for mating compatibility inquiries for you, Kelsey."

"Me? What?"

"She has no clue how sexy she is," Kyle proudly proclaimed.

I know I turned all ten shades of red once again.

"Two final things," his dad continued, ignoring his comment, "Kyle, I need you to attend the Pack Council meeting this afternoon. We'll discuss to what degree we share information with them, but most importantly we need to petition them to lower the challenge time. And finally, I'm afraid you're going to have to break the news to your mom."

KYLE
Chapter 18

I knew mom was going to be furious and excited at the same time. I had more or less told her Kelsey was my mate at family dinner, but in her mind, everything would have happened too quickly and a normal mating would have petitioned the Council before consummation. That was another thing the Pack Council wasn't going to be thrilled to find out. We'd broken protocol plain and simple. But I also knew that once my mother got to know my mate, she'd love her as much as I did.

Leaving my father's office, I took Kelsey by the hand, reassuringly brushing my thumb across the inside of her palm. I felt her shiver beside me and smiled, smelling a combination of nerves and arousal mixed with her usual scent. I loved knowing I had that effect on her. It made me stand a little taller and maybe even puff my chest out a little. I just couldn't help it.

"Mom!" I called out as we neared the kitchen, expecting to find her there.

"Kyle?" She returned as she entered the room and saw us. First fear flickered across her face as she demanded to know, "What's wrong? Why aren't you in the office? What's going on?"

Then I saw it in her eyes as she caught sight of our joined hands. Kelsey shifted uneasily next to me.

"Nothing's wrong, Mom. Everything's fine." I grinned looking over at my beautiful mate, "Everything's better than fine."

To say she was surprised would be a major understatement, but then she smiled, a true smile, not a forced friendly one for Kelsey's benefit.

"This is what you were trying to warn me of the other night at dinner isn't it? I'm sorry for being an old meddlesome wolf. I just want to see you settled down and happy, and if you think Kelsey can do that for you, then I'm behind you 100%."

She stepped forward and embraced Kelsey in a warm and welcoming hug as I struggled to pull my hand back in time.

I felt the change in the air the second she caught my smell mixed with my mate's. She gasped, pulling away quickly.

"Kyle, no! Tell me you didn't go behind the Council's back. Please tell me you two got permission first."

I raked a hand through my hair, fighting off the stream of questions Kelsey was pouring into my head. I leaned over and kissed my mom on the forehead. I was more than a head taller than her at this point in life, yet I still squirmed under her scrutiny.

"It's going to be fine, Mom. Dad and I are meeting with the Pack Council this afternoon. It's going to be okay, you'll see." I tried to assure her, hoping beyond hope I was right.

She nodded, "Nothing we can do about that now. And they'll come around, you're right." Then she turned her attention back to my mate, "Kelsey, how much training have you had?"

"Training for what?"

Mom shook her head at her answer. "Fighting."

Her eyes went wide with shock. "That wasn't a joke? I'm going to have to fight to the death? I've never been in a fight in my life. I wouldn't begin to know what to do."

My arms immediately went around her and pulled her close to comfort her.

"It's okay. You're a lot stronger than you know and there's a chance no one will challenge you."

"A really small chance," I thought then quickly apologized knowing she heard my thoughts.

Mom studied us curiously then dismissed it. There was no way she would suspect the strength of our bond.

"Okay, Kelsey, I need you to go to work. There'll be enough questions and comments regarding the both of you being out this morning, so for now, I need you to lay low and maintain your normal schedule. Right after work we need to meet up and start your training immediately." She pondered that, "I don't want it to look odd or disrupt your routine incase anyone is watching you.

"Do you think they are?" She was suddenly stiff in my arms.

"It's certainly a possibility, or will be once they get a whiff of you, so try to steer clear of people in general. And whatever you do, don't let anyone hug you."

"Lily and Elise are the only two that would dare come that close."

She nodded. "We'll have to let them in. They can help with your training. In fact, I'll call Elise and ask her to go home with you this afternoon. I don't think that would look too out of the ordinary. I know your good friends already. But where to practice unseen?" She was more or less talking to herself at that point.

"Kelsey's den is plenty big enough and private. If you run over, Mom, no one would suspect a thing. Her car would be in her driveway and by all appearances proceeding through life normally."

"Great idea."

"Is that okay with you, sweetheart?" Kyle asked, surprised by the flicker of unease in her eyes. "What's wrong, babe?"

"It's just last time Elise and Lily were in my den it was... hard," she sighed, embarrassed.

I kissed her temple. "That was my fault. With me not there, you'll likely be okay, especially now that we've bonded."

"Mated," his mother corrected. "Don't confuse the girl, son, there's a very big difference between mating and bonding. Though I suppose you are technically bonding mates at the moment, still, not bonded."

We both looked at her with guilt written all over our face.

"Do we tell her?" The small voice I loved asked in my head.

"Not unless she puts two and two together and all out asks. Don't lie to her, though."

Kelsey nodded her head that she understood.

Mom's eyes were huge like she couldn't believe what she was seeing right in front of her.

I sighed, *"Looks like we may be telling her after all."*

She smiled sheepishly, *"She's very intuitive."*

I snorted, *"I think all moms are."*

"So," I finally said aloud, "I think that'll be a good plan to start. You and the girls can get her training going and I'll be by tonight. We'll go for a run and head home."

"But I don't think we'll be getting much sleep," I told her

slyly through the bond, remembering how it felt to have her beneath me. My wolf practically howled in delight.

"Kyle," mom scolded me, "you know you shouldn't be around her. You can't take her back to your house. You need to keep your distance until it's all sorted. It's for the best."

"Mom, you know I can't do that."

"He's tried, even before the, uh, m-m-mating," Kelsey stuttered, clearly nervous. "He'll just spend the night in the woods and be completely miserable without sleep, and too grumpy to live with."

"Hey!"

"What? It's true. You're horrible to be around without your beauty sleep."

"Me? What about you? It was like waking the dead trying to get you up this morning."

"Maybe, but I'm going to sleep regardless. And besides, once I'm up, I'm up. You mope around like a zombie for half the day, snapping at everyone, when you aren't getting proper sleep."

I opened my mouth to protest then shut it knowing she was right.

My mother actually laughed out loud.

"My my my, this is going to be quite fun to sit back and watch the two of you. I always expected my boy to take a meek mate. Someone caring and nurturing and catering who would stroke his ego. You, my dear, I never even saw coming, but how he needs someone capable and strong enough to dish it back at him and keep that big head of his grounded."

After the plans were finalized, I dropped Kelsey off at the office. The story was that her car broke down and I was helping her get it repaired and would take much of the day to do it. It wasn't any surprise to anyone. I loved tinkering with cars and had skipped work on more than one occasion to do just that for others. It would also explain why her car was currently at my house and why Elise was taking her home. I'd see to it that her car was back home before they got there.

In the meantime, I quickly changed and headed back to my parent's house in preparation for the Pack Council meeting. A part of me was dreading the outcome of the meeting, but like my mom had said, what's done was done and nothing they could do or say would make me less mated at this point.

The Pack Council was comprised of seven men, including my dad. They were all older, except for Cole Anderson who was only a few years older than me. Ambrose, Saul, Mallick, Quinton, and Neil made up the remaining board members. No, they didn't have last names. Until about two decades ago when it became trendy and safer in the digital age, shifters rarely held last names outside of the pack name. As far as they were concerned, they were all Westins. But an entire town of Westins would look a little odd to the outside world. It never used to matter, but with credit cards, and electronic IRS forms and so on, it was determined necessary and most of my generation had begun choosing their own names for just such purposes. Sometimes it got a little weird, like one Miss Willow Flowers or Christine Canine. That one had nearly started a riot, but she'd batted her long dark lashes and flashed her perfect pearly white smile and the board had dropped it. It was hard to say no to Christine Canine when she set her mind to something. But whatever.

When I walked into the room, all eyes turned to me. I watched Saul take a deep breath and shake his head in disappointment.

"She better be worth it, Kyle."

I couldn't erase the grin on my face if I'd tried. "Oh, she is."

Cole chuckled. "You see the tattoo I gave her?"

A growl slipped out as I tried to control my jealousy that this wolf had touched my mate and marked her, even if it was with my picture.

"I take that as a yes. Tried to talk her into making it black, but she said she wouldn't have it any other way."

I couldn't help but grin a little sheepishly. I did love that Kelsey had chosen my wolf to adorn her body, even before she knew it was me.

Ambrose cleared his throat, "God, son, we can smell her all over you. You could have at least taken a shower before you came."

I know I blushed. They thought they were just smelling her scent on me, they hadn't figured out it was our combined scent they were smelling. Newly mated pairs shared the same scent much stronger than at any other time. It alerted other wolves to the fact that they were mated and potentially volatile in the early days post consummation.

"I take it this is why you're here today? Are you finally ready to take a mate, Kyle?" Neil asked solemnly.

"Gentleman," my father interrupted, "we have a bit of a sensitive situation here. And this is, as always, in complete confidence of the Council. As you know, Kyle has been quite vocal about allowing the lone she-wolf trespassing on our land to stay. Not just stay but left alone. Kelsey's been here for more than two years and has finally come forth and relayed her story to me. It's a hard one to hear, and my heart goes out to the girl, but Kyle's protection of her throughout this time has been entirely selfish in nature."

That got a few mumbles and whispers.

"That's not exactly news to any of us single wolves, sir. Kyle's marked his scent around her property and been in more than one scuffle over her."

I snorted, yeah, that's true, but then Dad and the rest of the Council had been entirely unaware of that, so I gave him a half-hearted glare thanking him for ratting me out. It just made him laugh again. He was certainly enjoying me being in the hot seat.

"Kyle, while you youngins may not be surprised by it, I can assure you there will be plenty of pack members upset that you've chosen this particular she-wolf. And she would need to be properly prepared for challenges before you dive in and do something crazy. As always, we, the Council, would like the opportunity to meet with her and trial her to verify she is indeed a compatible mate for you. In the meantime, we'd ask that she be reassigned to a new office and you keep your distance from each other. If you are certain, we'll move through the process as efficiently as possible."

Another growl escaped as my wolf grew agitated.

"I'm sorry Saul, but that will not be possible."

They certainly were not happy with my blatant defiance.

"Kelsey Adams is my mate. My one true mate. This is not a matter of compatibility."

Their disappointment quickly turned to shock.

"But you've been in her presence for over two years, Kyle. How is that even possible?"

"You should have known immediately."

"It's near impossible to find a true mate and not act on it. Two years, Kyle. I'm sorry but she cannot be your one true mate."

"Hush down, now and hear it out," my dad calmly spoke.

"Kyle came to me almost immediately upon meeting Ms. Adams. He did know immediately, but given her unique circumstances he chose not to act upon it. We considered telling you all, but as we were unsure of what to do with the girl, and Kyle was making no advances toward claiming her, I opted to keep this to myself."

"I thought she was denying it or that she couldn't feel our connection. I didn't know she was just even more stubborn than me."

That gained a snicker from most in attendance.

"Look, Kelsey wasn't raised in a pack. She didn't even know shifters were real. She grew up in the human world."

"A late bloomer then?" Mallick guessed.

"No sir." They all quieted down. "Kelsey changed for the first time when she was twelve years old. She was alone and running for her life after two wolves attacked and killed her parents in front of her and then attacked her. She honestly thought that since she was bitten and had no real knowledge of the shifter world, that she was a werewolf."

Grumbles began around the room at the thought. Anger over a young pup having no pack. Frustrations over the human portrayal of werewolves. And heartbroken for a little girl alone in the world going through change with no guidance.

"She's been running ever since, keeping this huge secret to herself all this time."

"Kyle, that's the craziest story I've ever heard!"

"No," Cole spoke up, "it makes sense. It fits with everything she shared with me too. The tattoo she got covers the damage done by the wolf. She confessed her fear of wolves and a little about why. It all makes sense, even hearing Kyle is her one true mate. The tattoo she drew herself and brought to me. Of course, I immediately recognized it as Kyle's wolf. Even tried to convince her to change it knowing the shit-storm something like that could cause, but she was adamant, it had to be his. Now it makes sense why. At the time, she simply told me it was the only wolf in her life she hadn't feared. I don't think she knew at the time why."

I smiled at him, slightly jealous that she had opened up to him like that, but trying to contain it. Cole Anderson was a good guy and I knew there was nothing between them.

"She didn't. She said she had felt something strong since day one but had fought against it knowing she could never allow anyone close enough to know her secret. And I had stubbornly been waiting for her and facing rejection after rejection anytime I attempted to reach out. Which is why I didn't come forward earlier with my feelings."

"A true mate?"

"This does change things."

"Kyle, if she is your one true mate, the Council will not intervene no matter who she is," Quinton assured me.

I smiled and let out a breath I didn't realize I was holding.

"Thank God, cause we've already consummated our mating." I blurted out.

"What?"

"Without notifying us first?"

"How could you?"

"Kyle, that's a blatant disrespect to the Council."

And so they got their two cents worth in and voiced their disappointment with me, but they couldn't knock the grin and happiness off my face for anything. The only thing I had heard loud and clear, no intervention. There would be no consequences for going against protocol. As mom had said, what's done was done.

"I'm sorry," I said, not really sorry. "Two years I waited for any signs of reciprocation. I could not control myself once I knew she felt our connection too."

"Speaking of connections. I think it is important to note that with the prolonged mating period of the two came a deeper connection faster than we are used to seeing in normal mated pairs."

What was he doing? Dad had said not to tell anyone about that, so why was he blabbing now.

"They can already sense each other's feelings and general locations, same as other mated pairs in the two to five year stage. I've never seen anything like it, though they have spent every day for the last two years together and I believe on some level their wolves began bonding even prior to the mating consummation. Because of this I would petition the Council to consider lowering the challenge time."

Murmurs and shocked whispers began again.

"Sir, it's Kyle we're talking about. She-wolves from at least three packs, possibly further, will wish for the opportunity to challenge. And as you know, we've already had several inquiries into compatibility for Kelsey. It is possible Kyle could face a few challenges himself from within the pack."

"I am well aware of all of that, Neil, but we also must take into consideration that challenges are only accepted in the first four months to ensure bonding has not begun already, and clearly in this case it has. Do you know what it would do to my son if his one true mate were to die in challenge?"

They all nodded solemnly.

"I'm sorry, Kyle," Ambrose started and I knew I wasn't going to be happy with what he was about to say, "but we can not wave the challenges. However, in light of the situation, I make the motion to lower it to only one month. With immediate notification, that is time for anyone to arrive and make their wishes known and we will accept challenges in any manner, not just in person. I think it has to be that way to keep peace amongst the packs and give opportunity to those seeking it."

The others nodded in agreement.

"I second that motion," Quinton piped in.

I rolled my neck, feeling the tension building. One month. Okay, we could handle one month.

"We must also ask that the two of you keep a distance from each other during this month to hopefully stall the bonding process you've already started. It's for the best, Kyle," Ambrose added.

"I'm sorry, sir, as I already told my father, that is not an option."

The older man sighed and nodded in acknowledgment.

"So, all that's left is to set a date of notification."

"The sooner the better, sir," I told them just wanting it all passed us. "Sunday. There's already a pack meeting being held. Announcements to the other packs can be emailed on Monday to expedite. The sooner this is all over, the better."

"That soon? You're certain the girl will be ready?"

"Kelsey may not have been raised in a pack, sir, but she's a fighter, she's super fast, and I have full confidence in my mate."

"Sunday it is then."

"Thank you." I stood and shook hands with each of them thanking them for their time before leaving.

The weight of the world seemed to be holding me down as I thought ahead to the next month. I was confident I could hold my own in any fight, and even more confident that few, if any, would dare to challenge me. But Kelsey? Could I just stand there and watch her fight to the death, for me?

Kelsey

Chapter 19

My biggest concern of the day was Elise and Lily. They had said don't let anyone get too close because they could smell Kyle's scent mixed with mine, but I was supposed to ride home with Elise, so did she know already? If not, surely, she would once in the car alone with me.

Lily had the bigger mouth of the two, though, and was more likely to pick it up in the office. So all afternoon I listened for the clacking of heels in the hallway, unable to concentrate on anything remotely considered work.

When I finally did hear the click-click-clicking of heels in the hallway, I immediately grabbed the phone and began talking into it. I motioned to it and waved Lily off. I knew it wouldn't keep her away, but it was the best I could do. Three times this occurred and each time stressed me out even more.

I decided to retreat into Kyle's office during the afternoon break. Lying down on his couch, surrounded by his smell helped calm me a little. When Lily barged into his office with that 'ah-ha, I found you' look on her face, I cursed myself for not thinking of locking the doors.

"Hey, Kels, what's wrong?"

"Headache," I lied, not bothering to get up from my sprawled out position on the couch. Maybe she'd think I was sick and stay away.

"I take it big brother isn't coming in today?"

I immediately sat up, realizing how out of character it must look with me being in his office so intimately. I hadn't even thought about it until now.

"Sorry, I just needed to lie down for a few minutes. And no, I don't think he's coming in today. He's, uh, fixing my car," I tried to hold to our cover story, but I felt like she saw right through it.

She sat down across the office from me, "It's fine, Kels, I'm not gonna rat you out to the bossman and doubt he'd care anyway. Lay down, relax. You look more stressed than usual. Is it because of everything we told you?"

"What?"

"You know, everything that happened the other day. It had to be a lot to take in."

"Was it really just the other day? God, it feels like a lifetime ago already," I said, throwing my arm over my face to blot out the light. I really didn't have a headache, but we had stayed up entirely too late and with the added stress of talking to his parents, I was beyond exhausted.

"So, you're okay with everything?"

"Yeah, yeah, I'm a big girl, I can handle it. I feel a bit stupid after knowing it all, but I'll be fine."

"So, I was in the tattoo parlor yesterday checking out Cole's new designs after seeing the fabulous job he did on yours, and he was going on and on about how amazing you are and how he loved your work. What exactly was going on during those fill in sessions?"

She made it sound so clandestine that I actually snorted when I laughed.

"Oh yeah, Lily, me and Cole Anderson, that's it, right?" I laughed, "You're insane!"

"I don't know, Cole's really cute. Kyle would say he's too old for me, but then I don't think he'll ever approve of anyone for me, and certainly not Liam. Liam would freak out if he heard me talking about a guy, any guy."

"So, you like Cole?"

"No, I was asking if YOU like Cole. He'd be a great match for you, you know."

I felt him before I heard the door open in the middle of Lily's rant. I could feel the waves of anger and possession wash over him and I shuddered.

139

"Um, Lil, shut up!"

"What? Come on, don't tell me you don't think he's hot. Everyone knows he's hot. Heck he knows he's hot."

The tension grew around me. How could she not feel it too?

"He's not hot, and I'm taken, so please stop!" I shrieked as Kyle walked fully into the room to assess the situation with a scowl.

I was horrified. My mate had just walked in on me talking about another man with his sister. Albeit, she was doing all the talking, but still.

"Kyle, close the damn door, quick," she demanded of him. "Girl, you've been holding out on me?" She looked a little hurt. "Who? When? How?"

I sighed, "Ten years I kept my mouth shut. I can keep a secret, even from friends. What is wrong with me?"

Kyle laughed which made me angry, but this time he spoke through our bond so his sister couldn't hear. *"Babe, for 10 years you had a secret you were terrified of anyone knowing. This time, you'd rather not have a secret at all and scream it from the rooftops for all to hear. Am I wrong?"*

"Probably not," I grumbled.

"Probably not, what??" Lily demanded. "Come on, tell me about your mystery man."

I sat up quickly, realizing how wrong this all was and we were supposed to be keeping up normal appearances. I smiled brightly and smoothed down my skirt sitting straight and more businesslike.

"My sincere apologies, Mr. Westin. I had a slight headache and came to lie down. I thought you weren't coming into the office today or I never would have… I'm so sorry, please forgive me." I stood and started walking to the door. "Is there anything I can get you, Mr. Westin?"

He shook his head. "Go lay down, Kelsey, and knock it off with the Mr. Westin crap." He smacked my butt as I passed causing me to yelp, then giggle even knowing I was blushing furiously.

"You two looked awful cozy when I walked in. What the hell are you doing in here?"

"Hiding from your sisters. Didn't think you were coming in today."

I finally looked at him and clearly saw what I figured, he not only didn't mind me being there, but seeing me comfortably sprawled out across his couch when he had walked in his office had pleased him.

"Doesn't look like you're doing a very good job."

I pouted, *"Forgot to lock the door. Didn't think she'd look for me here."*

"Hello, I'm right here! What is going on?"

"Don't tell her," He told me in my head with a smirk.

"You're terrible and I already blurted out I'm taken, she's never going to drop that." I responded, glaring at him.

"Yeah but she probably thinks it's Cole Anderson," I heard him growl out the name and I laughed.

"Lily, let me be very clear," I spoke aloud to her but staring into Kyle's eyes while I said it, "I have not, nor will I ever be interested in Cole Anderson."

"Your loss. Seriously, cause that wolf is hot for you, girl. And well, he's just plain hot, period. So who's this guy you're talking of, or did you just want me to stop trying to set you up with Cole so I can live vicariously through you? Because seriously, girl, you are gorgeous and every available male within five packs is going to want a piece of you."

Kyle growled so aggressively that Lily cowered and turned to him with wide eyes.

"Stop, Lil, just stop."

I couldn't help but grin at him. He was raking his hand through his hair in frustration and came to sit on the couch next to me. I immediately leaned into him not even caring about our audience anymore. My mate was jealous and upset and I had to calm him. Pressing the side of my body against his and leaning my head on his shoulder, I placed a hand on his thigh and gently rubbed to soothe him.

He wrapped his arms around me, took a deep breath into my hair, then kissed the top of my head as I felt him begin to relax.

He looked right at Lily and said, "Lil, Kelsey's taken, stop trying to fix her up."

As the initial shock wore off, I saw sheer happiness light her up.

"Are you serious? Oh, please tell me you aren't yanking my chain? Kyle Alexander Westin, are you trying to claim Kelsey as your mate?"

"Already claimed," I volunteered.

He laughed, "You weren't supposed to tell her that part."

"That part? You guys told me not to tell anyone anything. I've been faking phone calls and meetings and hiding from her and Elise all afternoon and you walk in and freak out over an innocent conversation and blurt everything out."

Lily pouted, "You've really been trying to blow me off all day?"

"I'm sorry, Lil, there's just so much going on and it's just making my head spin. Of course I wanted to tell you. Your mom said not to tell anyone till a formal announcement was made. I'm sorry."

I wasn't thinking when I stood and walked to her. leaning down to hug and reassure her.

"Oh. My. Gosh! Oh my gosh! You, you, you, smell like him." She jumped and ran to her brother and took a big whiff as he sat there just grinning. I wanted to punch him so bad. "And you, you smell just like her! Oh my gosh! You mated already?!?!? Clearly Mom and Dad know already. Does the Council know? Did you even get permission? How the heck did this happen? I mean, I knew you were crushing on her, but Kyle!" She smacked him. "She barely even knows what mating is. So, did you just have sex and didn't shower off each other's scent or, no, it's too strong for that. Holy crap, what did you do??"

Kyle was holding his side laughing at her. I was horrified. She ran over and picked up his phone pounding on the buttons.

"Elise, get over here to Kyle's office. Right. Now."

It was only a moment before Elise burst through the door slamming it behind her.

"What's wrong? What's going on?" She was breathless and looked terrified.

I had sat back down next to Kyle on the couch, leaning forward with my hands covering my face in humiliation. He was casually rubbing my back and I could feel the perm-a-grin on his face when he spoke.

"Nothing's wrong, E. Lily's just being overly dramatic."

"Overly dramatic? Overly dramatic! Elise, he mated Kelsey!"

I dared to sneak a peek at her. Elise was grinning. I knew my face was probably various shades of purple and pink and not just red.

"It's about damn time!"

"What? You knew about this?"

"Well, come on Lil, it doesn't take a genius to know Kyle's been protecting her for two years against the pack. That he stares at her like a lost puppy every time she turns her head."

I whipped my head around at him.

"You do?" I asked through the bond.

He didn't deny it or show any embarrassment about it, just shrugged his shoulders at me.

"I mean, I suspected pretty early on, then thought maybe it was my imagination when he never acted on it. Guess you were just waiting on her, then, huh?"

"Yup. And like I told the Council this morning, after two years of rejections and denying my feelings, the second she showed interest, I was a goner." He winked at me.

"Yikes, what did the Council say?"

I know he could feel me tense. I had been wondering the same thing all morning. He rubbed my back reassuringly and spoke directly to me, even though Elise had asked the question.

"Compatibility tests are foregone when it is a true mate situation. As such, they would not have intervened or stopped it had I notified them ahead of time, and therefore no repercussions would be issued over our mating without prior approval."

"Awe, you think she's your one true mate?" Lily sighed.

"Oh, I know she is. I've always known she was."

I nodded, "Yeah, I didn't even know what a one true mate was, but I knew from the start too. It's why I insisted on only calling him Mr. Westin and keeping everything one hundred percent professional."

They both laughed.

"God, did you drive him nuts with that!" Lily confessed.

I felt like, after the initial shock of it all, that the girls accepted me with open arms. It felt good and right.

"Okay, well, it's quitting time. I only came back to see you for a few minutes before they whisk you away. Mom has forbidden me from showing up during your training. She thinks my presence in your den with the girls around had more to do with your territorial aggressions than them actually being there. I guess we'll see if that theory holds true."

"Training? Mom's going to train her?"

"Yeah, E's taking her home and mom was going to explain things then. Guess now she doesn't have to."

"When will the announcement be made?"

"Sunday at the monthly pack meeting."

"Sunday! That doesn't leave much time for training."

"No, but my girl's gonna do just fine. You'll see." He turned to me and kissed me sweetly. I couldn't help but blush with his sisters right there gawking over us. "I'll be nearby. Let me know when you guys are through and we'll head home, okay?"

A warm happy feeling enveloped me when he spoke of home, and I nodded.

"Okay, okay, let's go. We'll take good care of her, big brother."

"I know." He said, full of confidence.

"Lil, you coming too?"

"Are you kidding? I wouldn't miss it for the world!"

Mary was right, my wolf didn't mind the girls in the den when Kyle wasn't there. She also suspected that the aggression would be lessened now that we were properly mated, but we weren't going to risk training to test the theory. I only had a few days to learn the skills of fighting that other she-wolves were taught from birth.

She was happy to see the level of control I had over my wolf. I was able to shift easily now from human to wolf and wolf to human form. They already knew I was fast, but while defensively I was thought to be lethal, I had no offensive aggression whatsoever.

After three grueling days of training and learning basic techniques for defense and offense, Sunday arrived. I knew the likelihood of a challenge being issued on the spot was slim to none, so I'd have a few more days, maybe even weeks to continue training before I actually had to fight.

I hadn't slept a wink the night before, tossing and turning and stressing over the day's events. I would do just about anything to keep Kyle in my life. But could I kill for it? Would I be able to sink my jaws into the neck of another and hold her there until her life ended? That was what they were trying to teach me and the best strategy for attack. Did I really have it in me to do that? I mean, if someone was threatening my mate, my friends, my family, I have no doubt I would kill without thought, but to kill just because another she-wolf was interested in him? It seemed so barbaric, and I just hoped that when the time came I could push past my reservations and do what was necessary.

KYLE
Chapter 20

Waking up with my mate in my arms each morning meant the world to me. I had barely seen Kelsey since she began training. She came home late and exhausted. I understood the importance of it, and greatly appreciated what my mother and sisters were doing for her, but I could not wait for the next month to pass and we could finally start our lives together.

This would be the day, the day we would share with the pack the truth about our mating. The day my mate could be threatened with challenges. I knew she was strong enough to handle herself, even with the little training given, but I still worried, and everything inside me demanded I protect her.

At the meeting, Kelsey was asked to stand up front shortly after Dad called everyone to order. There were lots of whispered murmurs and surprised faces to see it. Even though after our race word had spread, the fact that an outsider was invited to a pack meeting said a lot.

"Please settle down, settle down," Dad called to order. "I think just about everyone present knows Kelsey Adams. She has come forward to speak to me and ask the Council to join the Westin Pack." He paused to allow the shock of the news to settle down.

"Why now?"

"How can we accept when she's been trespassing on our territory for so long?"

"What's her story?"

So few knew Kelsey's story even still. It had been kept under wraps, and I wasn't happy that Dad was about to share with the pack, even knowing it was necessary.

"Settle down. There will be time later to answer all your questions, and for each of you to get to know Kelsey a little better tonight at the pack meal. Right now, I just want to share a quick story of a little girl left alone in the world at the age of twelve. A wolf shifter who watched her parents die before her eyes. Who changed that same night after being bitten. Who knew nothing of our ways of life. This is Kelsey's background. It is a sad and terribly painful one, and I hope you will all respect the fact that the Council has taken things into consideration and knows her full story, tragic as it is. She is still learning our ways. I know many of you were shocked and disappointed over the last two years she has invaded our territory. I ask you to please understand, she truly did not know what she was doing. I hope you will support and welcome her to this pack. No wolf should ever be alone, but especially not a young pup with no training, no guidance, living alone in the human world while hiding such an enormous secret."

The room was silent. A few of the women had tears in their eyes. I knew no one would object.

"Now, I'd also like to open the floor to hear any objections."

Not a peep was heard, not even a whisper.

"Okay, Kelsey, welcome to the Westin Pack!"

"Thank you," she said softly.

There was a round of applause. Kelsey's nerves had increased steadily through Dad's speech and even more so with being put on the spot. I could smell it in the air, acutely aware of her. And I knew that others would perceive it as fear. My mate was not comfortable being on the stage and did not know how to curb her scent yet. It took everything in my power not to rise and go to her, to shield her from the prying eyes and whispers from the curious. It wasn't any of their damn business anyway.

Feeling more and more agitated only seemed to heighten Kelsey's nerves. I had to calm down. I knew she was responding to me responding to her. It wasn't a good combination, especially in front of the entire pack. My dad glared at me and I felt a slight pressure as his alpha power washed over me to try and calm me which only pissed me off more. I couldn't stop from glaring back and saw him sigh in resignation.

"Okay, while Kelsey's already up here, uncomfortably up

here, as I'm sure you can all smell." The room chuckled as a whole. "We might as well get this over with. First, I urge you all, please do not mistake Kelsey's uncomfortable nervous energy, being put on the spot in front of you all with weakness. I cannot stress this enough. I have tested her myself and she is strong and not as easy prey as she may appear. Please do not underestimate her."

Both of our stress levels elevated further, and I had no doubt everyone in the room was feeling it. The idea of them seeing my mate as weak prey did not sit well with me, and I knew my dad realized his mistake the moment he insinuated it.

"Jesus," he muttered under his breath, then turned to speak softly to Kelsey. "You have to calm down, Kelsey. No one will here will hesitate to challenge you with the level of fear you're producing."

"It's not fear. I just don't like standing up here with everyone staring at me," she pleaded. "And Kyle isn't helping. He's freaking out."

"Just a little longer, hang in there," he said sympathetically, while turning to glare at me, but at this point I knew I wasn't controlling my emotions at all and just making the situation worse.

"Okay," he spoke back to the group, "let's just rip the Bandaid off. Kelsey Adams has taken a mate within our pack. Many of you will not be thrilled with the match, but it is important to note that this is her one true mate."

I could feel the aggression rising as she-wolves all around prepared themselves for the challenge before the announcement was even made. I couldn't stand to just sit there any longer. I started to get up, and Cole Anderson, sitting next to me, quickly yanked me back. I let out a low growl his way.

"Jesus, just come up here. Please everyone just tone it down a bit. The emotions, stress, and aggression in this room are not helping the situation." He looked at me and nodded, "Just come on up and calm yourself and your mate so we can just get through this."

He didn't have to tell me twice. In a flash, I was on stage and comforting Kelsey. My wolf immediately calmed, and in response so did Kelsey's as she touched me. I didn't immediately register the shock and anger flooding the room. I didn't really care. My mate had been suffering and I had to protect her first.

"Settle down, settle down. There's no easy way to say it,

Kyle has taken Kelsey as a mate. As his one true mate, he did not need the approval of the Council, though he did seek it.

Yeah, it may have been after the fact, but saving face and setting an example was too important for the Council.

"Yes, you heard me, his one true mate! As such, I again urge you not to underestimate her and think fully through the potential consequences of challenging her. That said, challenges will begin immediately. However, due to other extenuating circumstances, that we will not be sharing at this time, the challenge period has been lowered to only one month's time." Protests immediately set in. My father simply raised his hand until the room had quieted again. "I understand your frustration, just trust me in that this was not an easy decision for the Council, but a necessary one. Notices went out to the nearest five packs this morning. Kelsey has been made aware of the challenge process and is ready to accept what may come."

She stood stoically beside me showing no more fear, and nodded, glancing around the room, making eye contact with several of the she-wolves showing potential for challenges. No doubt my mother had schooled her on that.

"Now, any further pack news is clearly a moot point tonight. I will adjourn early. Kelsey and Kyle will remain up-front and you are free to come forward to show your support or opposition."

He quickly adjourned the meeting and motioned for us to join him down on the floor in front of the stage.

"Well, that went splendidly," he whispered, sarcastically.

"Like ripping off a Bandaid!" Kelsey smiled, using his earlier words.

"You look so much more relaxed, my dear, are you okay?"

"Never better. I got this, Sir."

Her confidence astounded me. She had no idea how her nerves had made her look weak in front of the entire pack. I knew it was largely my fault too, but I also suspected when she said she had it, she meant it. She was steeled and ready to except her place in my pack, by my side. The pride my wolf and I equally felt was indescribable.

A line throughout the room formed quickly as people readily came forward. Sally Merchant was the first to come through and wish us both well. I was grateful for a familiar face. Many gave their congratulations and bared their neck to both me and my mate in acceptance. Some only to me, and a few of the males, only to her. I wasn't too concerned, and thought they'd likely reconsider their odds against me later.

When Vanessa Relic came forward the entire room went still, waiting on bated breath. There was no doubt in anyone's mind that she would be the first challenge to Kelsey. She had never been discreet about her interest in me. She came up and hugged me. I heard the low rumble from Kelsey beside me and saw Vanessa roll her eyes at my mate.

Vanessa congratulated me, lowered her head and bared her neck to me formally. Then she turned to Kelsey.

"Simmer down. I've already told you I will not challenge you for him. I would never go against a true mate. I am sorry for how I behaved before and truly hope maybe we can even be friends someday."

Kelsey hesitantly smiled and nodded to her.

Then loud gasps sounded as Vanessa lowered her head and bared her neck to Kelsey. I stood by proudly, unable to stay neutral and keep the smile from my face. Vanessa smiled at us both. Affectionately squeezed her arm, and gave her some encouragement.

"You got this, Kelsey. Just remember, no matter what happens, he's worth it. And if you need any help preparing for challenges, just give me a call."

This time it was Kelsey's turn to be shocked, but she also looked thankful. Whispers had turned to full out talking by the end of their transaction.

At the end of the night, ten men had not given consent and needed to be noted as potential challengers. I wasn't overly concerned with any of them. After Vanessa's submission, only three she-wolves dared not to submit to my mate. The most notable of them was Christine Canine. She was tenacious with a mean streak in her, and I knew she could hold her own in a challenge. Vanessa volunteered to talk to her and try to warn her off for me. I was thankful for her help.

With the news out and the shock waning, the pack meal took on a festive feel. Many were surprisingly supportive, not just of Kelsey's intro into the pack, but also of our mating. I was shocked at how much concern, particularly from the older wolves, my pack had over my continued bachelorhood. They were especially thrilled that I had not just chosen a mate, but indeed found my one true mate.

"How can she possibly be his true mate? It's ridiculous. They've known each other for years. That's not something that just suddenly reveals itself. Shouldn't they have known immediately." Christine vocalized, close enough to draw my attention.

I couldn't stop myself from responding.

"You really think I haven't known for the last two years? There were extenuating circumstances, Christine. Do not confuse my lack of action for a lack of awareness. She is my one true mate."

I could feel the air grow thick around Kelsey and expected a growl to escape, fearing it would only encourage Christine further towards challenge, but Vanessa of all people jumped in to save the day.

"Keep it calm, girl. Don't let her get to you. Do not show weakness. I know you, and I know what you're capable of. Let her dig her own grave."

The last part was said just loud enough to ensure Christine's attention. And although Kelsey had not managed to control growling around Vanessa since the moment they met, she breathed and relaxed and took her words to heart, no longer sensing her as a threat to us.

Kelsey

Chapter 21

Vanessa Relic. Who would have thought I'd be so grateful for her? My wolf was agitated in the close proximity to so many shifters, especially with potential threats against my mate. I wasn't so much concerned for me, or the three she-wolves that did not acknowledge and support my mating to Kyle. I knew they were potential threats for challenge, but I was far more concerned for Kyle as there were a lot more males that did not give consent.

Christine Canine. She could be a problem. I could feel she would be a tough competitor, but I knew I was stronger. She may have been trained longer, but she was not a born alpha she-wolf. I knew from the brief discussion with Kyle and his dad that it was something I needed to control and hide.

Still hiding. I had thought maybe I could have a normal life. Finding out that Kyle and the others in San Marco were just like me was like a dream come true, and then yet another curse and more secrets. Why did I have to be different even amongst equal monsters? Life just didn't seem to want to give me a break. The stories of the young girls being hunted and killed were giving me nightmares, though, I didn't want to admit them, even to Kyle. I did everything I could in my waking hours to keep my fears about it from him.

I knew Vanessa had felt my alpha powers. She was accepting them and had been gracious not to mention them outright, though she had hinted on several occasions now. What would happen if I slipped up and released that power on Christine? What if the pack found out and demanded I be turned over to the Grand Council? Those thoughts terrified me. Yet without my alpha powers, I was weak against the likes of Christine and other she-wolves who may challenge me. My only relief was that I had thus far managed to keep everything from Kyle's mom and sisters. Well, I knew Elise, and maybe even Lily, suspected because they knew what I had done to Vanessa, but they were good to never mention it, and if I was using it as an unfair advantage in fighting, I think they would point it out to me.

The line had been long and seemingly endless meeting person after person. I was exhausted by the time we moved to the dining area for pack dinner. Kyle never left my side and we took the first table with two available seats to settle into for dinner. I was relieved to be seated between Kyle and Cole Anderson, though I did not know anyone else sitting at our table.

"Hi, I'm Morgan and this is my mate Franny." The man sitting directly across from Kyle introduced and I vaguely remembered them coming through the introduction line earlier.

"Don't worry, Kelsey, we can only imagine how overwhelming all this is for you. No one expects you'll remember everyone's name after one quick introduction." Said his mate sincerely.

I laughed, "Thank God for that! I'll be lucky if I remember my own name by the time this night's over."

The entire table laughed along with me and it felt like a lot of the tension eased.

"We're the Stranges, Dan and my mate Melinda."

"Leo Tripp."

"Sandy Mason."

"And I'm Leslie Matthews." The last of our table introduced themselves.

"It's really nice to meet you all." I said, and I meant it.

"You did good tonight, Kels, though, I think we need to work on your scent control." Cole shook his head and laughed. "I'm kind of shocked you have so few potential challengers after the nerves you were producing in there, though I will tell you, I thought a few times I was going to have to physically hold Kyle down from joining you on stage before he was called."

"It wasn't that bad," Sandy tried to assure me.

Leslie laughed, "Yes, yes it was. I'm sorry but I'll admit I was more than a little shocked to hear you were mated to Kyle. Kyle? This little shy nervous she-wolf? But watching you stand by his side, it was an entirely different picture."

"Don't judge her off that as a first impression." Kyle laughed, "I'm sorry, I shouldn't have been in the room. I know Dad was right when he suggested it, but of course I wouldn't hear of it. I know I made things a thousand times worse. Cole's not kidding when he said he was going to have to hold me down. It was hard watching her up on that stage so exposed to everyone. And I may be able to disguise my scent, but every time my anxiety rose, she felt it and increased her nerves tenfold." He even blushed and hung his head sheepishly. It was the cutest thing I think I had ever seen.

"I didn't even know we could disguise our scent. Someone needs to teach me that trick."

The whole table laughed along with that, easing the tension of Kyle's confession, which raised a few eyebrows, but not one commented on it.

"It's not easy, but it is possible with practice, restraint, and determination." Dan clued me in.

"Oh, she's up to the challenge for sure." Cole sounded proud in his assessment. "I've never met a female quite so assertive, especially when she sets her mind to something."

Kyle softly growled at him and I elbowed him. "He's just trying to goad you. Stop letting him." Then I turned to Cole, "And you, behave." I shook my head at the two of them causing Leslie and Sandy to start giggling.

"So, I take it you know Cole pretty well then? I mean I know you work at Westin Foundation with Kyle, but even their word is you tend to keep to yourself and haven't made many friends. Why is that?" Leo asked, but didn't sound judgmental when he did.

Kyle started to speak for me, but I stopped him and knew it was my time to step up. This was going to be my pack. These people were going to be my responsibility as future Pack Mother. It was time to start acting like I was up for the job.

"I can imagine it's difficult to understand, and in hindsight I know how stupid it sounds, but I genuinely didn't know there was anyone like me, like us, out there. Or I guess that's not entirely true, I did know werewolves, or wolf shifters as I know now you prefer to be called, existed, I just feared them my entire life. I watched two wolves kill my parents. I changed that same night for the first time. I thought," I couldn't stop my cheeks from changing colors with how stupid I knew I sounded, "I thought I was a monster, that those wolves had turned me into this monster. I didn't know anything about our kind."

"That's a pretty big secret to grow up with," Melinda said, her voice filled with sympathy.

I nodded, "Yeah, it was. I couldn't trust anyone. Ever. So, I got used to being alone and avoiding people as much as possible. I didn't mean to come off as nervous or weak up on stage tonight. You just have to understand that my entire life I've worked so hard to be invisible that it's more than a little intimidating being shoved in the spotlight now."

When I looked up, Franny and Leslie both had tears in their eyes, and the others nodded in understanding.

"You poor thing. I just can't even imagine. And weak? Who among us could handle such a life? You must be the strongest shifter I've ever had the privilege of meeting to withstand such trauma so graciously." Sandy stood and came over and hugged me close. My wolf sighed in contentment.

"Thanks," I said trying not to let my voice crack.

Leo cleared his throat, "Life will be very different for you now, Kelsey."

"Oh, it already is. You have no idea. It's a bit overwhelming at times, but I've never been happier."

He smiled at that. "So, I'm curious. How did you meet Mr. Anderson?"

"Don't be silly, Leo, he's on Council, of course she's met all the Council already."

"True, but actually, aside from Elise and Lily, Cole was my first friend here. It was pretty recent, but still. He did a tattoo for me and I've done a few designs for his shop since then."

"Oh do tell," Melinda asked sounding scandalous. "What's your tattoo?"

Cole laughed, "You don't want to know."

I blushed. "I didn't know! Still, I am so glad you did not convince me to make it black." I elbowed him in the gut trying to wipe the smirk off his face.

"Black?" Melinda persisted.

I closed my eyes and tried to push my embarrassment aside. "It's a wolf, okay? My tattoo is a wolf. It was before I knew any of this."

"Not just any wolf." Cole laughed and I glared at him.

"It's me!" Kyle announced proudly. "Her tattoo is a large picture of me in wolf form. She knew my wolf because I stalked her regularly in wolf form for the last two years."

I looked at him and knew my mouth was open in shock at his admittance.

"What? I'm not too proud to admit it. I stalked her every night, guarding her house, and hoping and waiting for her to come out and join me."

"The story she told me," Cole added, "after giving me a brief description of what she'd been through as a child with her parents' death and a lifelong fear of wolves, was that she had this guardian wolf that watched over her house and for the first time in her life she wasn't afraid. What no one's mentioned today, and maybe I'm out of line for pointing this out, is that she too was attacked that night. She was bitten badly and it caused severe damage to her leg. So much so that even though her wolf was called forward at a ridiculously young age, it wasn't enough to fully heal her. The tattoo she wanted and drew herself was designed to cover the damage done. It's quite beautiful if I do say so myself."

Kyle growled softly and glared at him for mentioning it. I just rolled my eyes at the two of them.

"So, there you have it. It took many weeks to complete the tattoo and I've been drawing ideas since, so yeah, that's how I got to know Cole. I just found out that he's on the Council. Well, just found out there even was a Council."

That cleared the air and made the table chuckle. I suddenly noticed the surrounding tables leaning in closer trying to listen in.

"Wait? Black? Cole, you tried to convince her to change it to a black wolf?" Cole grinned sheepishly and nodded as Kyle glared at him. "Kelsey, do you know that Cole's wolf is black?"

I laughed, "I didn't then, but I do now. Kyle wasn't exactly happy to hear that and I had no clue why. I just knew it could only be my guardian wolf. No other. And a black wolf certainly wouldn't do."

Cole shrugged looking smug, like he'd tried, what more could he have done.

I looked at Kyle and he grinned and leaned in and kissed me sweetly to the awe's and eye dabbing of those surrounding us.

"That's so romantic," Sandy sighed.

We were amongst the last to leave for the night and many others had come by to talk to us and introduce themselves further. I was never going to remember them all, but it was nice of them to go out of their way to make me feel welcome.

Alone at last, I cuddled up to Kyle's side in our bed.

"So, how did you think it went?

"Rough start, but you had them eating out of your hand by the end of the night."

"I did not."

"You did too. And Cole's ribbing and retelling of your tattoo I think melted everyone within earshot."

"You guys are never going to let me live that tattoo down are you?"

He peeled back the covers and pulled my nightgown up to my waist. Carefully he started tracing and really examining my tattoo. He frowned, feeling the rough ridges and skin grafts it was designed to hide. He leaned down and kissed the damaged area.

"Does it hurt?"

"No, not anymore."

"I hate that you went through all that. It kills me that I wasn't there to protect you."

"Kyle, I was twelve. There's nothing you could have done, but you're here now and more than I ever hoped or dreamed for."

I couldn't read the expression in his eyes, but I felt the emotion and passion behind it when he kissed me. When we made love that night I cried, overcome with emotions. It was nothing like previous, his love poured over me and there were no coherent words even through our bond as we moved as one. I had wondered before if I would be capable of taking another life to guarantee my position in the pack and at this man's side. It was then that I knew there was nothing I wouldn't do for Kyle or to be with him. I didn't know it was even possible to love someone so much.

"I love you," I told him for the first time meaning every

word.

KYLE
Chapter 22

Two weeks ago, my life aligned to perfection as far as I was concerned. Kelsey was officially made pack. Our mating was announced and she told me she loved me. I'm not sure how I got so damn lucky. Finding your true mate is difficult enough, but it isn't always the smoothest transition. Yes, as shifters we strive to find our one true mate, but one of the reasons people settle for compatible mates is because the clashing of true mates occurs far too often.

It's not easy when fate intervenes. True mates are often extremely passionate, but not always for each other. Many rebel against their fate. Passion can be negative as much as positive. Fighting and resentment has been known to occur with true mates. I have never questioned Kelsey as my true mate. My initial resentments only occurred against her constant rejections. Even then I never resented her. If I were being honest I have loved Kelsey Adams since the moment I laid eyes on her. To have her love reciprocated is beyond all expectations. I felt like the luckiest man alive.

Kelsey and I fell into an easy routine. It wasn't that we always agreed, but after working closely for two years we already knew how to communicate and resolve differences without arguing or causing hurt feelings. So, as she slowly moved into my house and began turning it into a true home, everything just fell into place naturally. My only fear was that everything was going too smoothly. I was waiting for this nearly perfect life we were creating to crumble and crash and burn.

For two weeks, no one had issued a challenge. We'd had a

few visitors from other packs and I knew a large group of people from three different packs would be coming in over the weekend. I didn't want to be nervous, but I knew getting through the entire month without one or both of us being challenged would truly be a miracle and too much to ask for.

Kelsey's position as future Pack Mother of the Westin Pack made her an easy target for challenges. I was more than a little shocked that someone hadn't already stepped up and issued her a challenge. I wasn't as surprised that no one from within my pack had challenged me, though I thought the chances of someone from outside the pack was highly likely. The Westin Pack was one of the biggest and strongest in existence and anyone who challenged and defeated me would stand to take over as next in line as Pack Alpha. It was a unique position that put me in potentially grave danger.

Earlier in the day I had a meeting with Cole Anderson. It had not gone unnoticed by me that he had not given his consent to my mating of Kelsey and I confronted him on it. After much discussion, I was both relieved and pissed by his thinking. He had told me that he would not challenge me directly, but that he would not consent on the chance that I was challenged and defeated. He made it very clear that he would challenge my victor for Kelsey to keep the Westin Alpha in pack. I couldn't argue his thinking, but the thought of him and Kelsey together was driving me nuts and making it hard to focus on anything.

A knock at the door jolted me out of my thoughts.

"Mr. Westin?" Kelsey peeked her head in. I grinned and shook my head at her determination to keep everything normal and professional at work. "Your father is here to see you."

Dad? A feeling of dread immediately settled into my gut. We didn't have plans that I could think of, which meant he had to be there for pack business, or worse to give me a heads up on an upcoming challenge.

"It's okay, send him back." I told her trying to keep my thoughts to myself and not share my feelings through the bond, but the second I thought that she started laughing and walked in and closed the door behind her.

"Kyle Alexander Westin, you've been ranting and stressing since Cole Anderson left here, and now you try to hide your thoughts and worries? Silly boy, don't you realize you can't keep anything from me? This sound proof office of yours isn't sound proof enough for our bond."

"Shit," I said under my breath. "Babe, I didn't want to worry you..."

"No, save it, mister. We're in this together. I'm just as worried about challenges as you are and I know exactly what's at stake. Stop trying to protect me. You can't protect me from this anymore than I can protect you. It sucks, but come on."

I rose and went to her immediately pulling her tightly against my chest and breathing in her scent.

"I'm sorry. I know this is stressful enough. I just didn't want to worry you further."

It dawned on me that we were alone in my office and she was letting me hold her. Kelsey was quite strict about what was and was not appropriate during business hours. My thoughts immediately flashed to a fantasy I'd had of taking her over my desk pretty much since she walked into my life and my wolf howled in my head in approval.

I knew I had broadcast the image loud and clear when she pulled away and smacked me.

"What?" I tried to suppress a grin on my face.

"Your father is in the next room!"

I shrugged and tried to pull her back into my arms, but she brushed me off, back to her utmost professional exterior, even though I knew damn well she liked the idea as much as I did. That thought had me grinning like a love-sick fool as she ran from the room and my father entered.

He put up a hand immediately, "I don't care to know what put that stupid look on your face."

I burst out laughing feeling better than I had in days.

"What can I do for you, Dad?"

"I wish I were coming with news that would keep you this happy, son, I truly do."

I sobered immediately.

"What's happened?"

"I did get word that no-one from the Longhorn or Collier Packs that visited over the weekend will be challenging. But, this coming weekend we have visitors arriving from Maxwell, Kyton, and the Alaskan Packs."

"Well, that's good news on Longhorn and Collier, two down three to go. I fully expected the other three packs would be sending potential challengers this weekend, so that's not much of a shock."

"I'm afraid there's more."

"What? Who?"

"As word has spread that you are up for challenge, Kyle, the Virginian Pack, Central Pack of New York City, the Irish Clan, and the Bulgarians have all sent formal requests. They were quite put off to hear of the shortened challenge period, but assured me each of their challengers would arrive within the week. I'm sorry."

I took a deep breath and held it for a second before exhaling.

"Okay, well we knew the possibility was there and there's hope that like the Longhorn and Collier Packs, no challenges will come from it."

He didn't look too optimistic about it, but I needed to hold on to the hope of something.

"Is Kelsey ready?"

I shrugged. "Mom seems to think so. Elise and Lily are singing her praise and she's started working out with Vanessa some too, but I just don't know. I haven't been able to bring myself to watch her fight. I hate that I've put her in this position."

"She's strong, Kyle, with her own advantages, but we need to be especially cautious that she does not let her little secret out, especially with the Bulgarians coming into town."

"I understand, and I'll talk to her."

He sighed, "There's one last thing, Kyle. It has been noted just how close the two of you are becoming and it has been requested that you not live together for the remainder of the challenge period."

My hands balled in fists and I held back a growl, "Is that a request or a command, Sir?"

"I'm sorry, Son. It's a command."

"You know we can't do that."

"You'll see her everyday here in the office. We will not request she be reassigned. But at night, she needs to sleep at the cottage or you need to move into the main house for now. I'm sorry, it's not negotiable. Your combined scent has upset several potential challengers and it grows stronger every day. I know we initially dismissed this, but Kyle, I'm worried."

"But Dad, you know, I can't do that. I need her."

"I know, Son, that's what worries me. What would happen if your bond somehow completed before the month's end? What then? What happens if Kelsey doesn't survive a challenge? I can't risk losing you to that because I sat back and let the bond grow too far. No, the Council discussed thoroughly last night and it is a unanimous decision. I will speak to Kelsey on my way out. This is how it must be. No further physical contact between the two of you. Is that understood?"

He let his alpha powers flow over me as I gritted my teeth and tried to fight it. "Understood, Sir," I snapped.

He nodded resolutely and left me to my own thoughts, fears, and worries.

Two weeks, it's only for two weeks. I can do this. I chanted those words to myself over and over trying to make them true, but how was I going to survive without my mate for two whole weeks? I hadn't dared tell father that I suspected his concerns were already a reality. The only sign of a full bonded pair I hadn't yet seen was feeling each other's physical pain, but I could feel her emotional pain loud and clear, and I knew when my dad told her the news. It was like a punch straight to my heart.

I wanted to run to her. I wanted to comfort her, but that was exactly what I wasn't supposed to do. So instead I paced my office feeling like I was trapped in a cage. My wolf wasn't taking too kindly to the feeling either. I needed to leave. I needed to run.

When I felt the absence of Kelsey's presence, I left the office and headed for the woods at the rear of the building. I undressed and changed quickly, taking off at a full sprint, my wolf caught a scent and headed west towards the river. I slowed in approach, crouching low, and wondering what he was hunting. Then I finally smelled it too. It was so strong, and my wolf sat back and howled, demanding attention.

Kelsey. Her small blonde wolf sat staring out into the water and turned at our howl. I'm so used to being consumed by her scent, that until I was practically on top of her, I had no idea what my wolf was hunting, or that he was hunting our mate.

She approached hesitantly with her head lowered to me. I hated to see her like that. She was every bit the alpha I was, but right then she just looked broken.

163

We had never successfully communicated through our bond in wolf form, but I reached out and tried anyway feeling the connection had grown over the last few days. I was right.

"Kelsey, are you okay?" I asked her, and watched as her head shot up, and her eyes bugged out in shock. My wolf did a little dance of joy at the recognition.

"Kyle? How is this possible? I thought we couldn't communicate in wolf form."

"Only fully bonded mates can as far as I know."

Her wolf shook its head in horror, looking far too human.

"No, don't say that. Please don't say that. Your dad told me what that could mean. We can't be fully bonded."

"I don't know, babe. If not fully, it's close. I've felt every sign I've ever heard but one so far."

"That's good then, right? One means there's still hope."

"Hope for what, babe?"

"Hope that if I don't survive this challenge that I'm not killing you too in the process!"

I knew if she were in human form she'd be crying right now. My wolf went to her and rubbed against her soft fur, trying to comfort our mate.

"Has it not even occurred to you that I wouldn't want to live without you? That I'd prefer to die with you?"

"Don't say that!"

"Kelsey, wolves mate for life. This tradition of challenges is ridiculous, because you are my mate, and even if I were forced to take another, my wolf and I would never fully accept her. No one could ever replace you. We're too far gone and I wouldn't want it any other way."

She sat back and with her nose to the sky howled a sad, mournful song. My wolf joined in immediately to create a haunting sound I had never heard before, but felt it straight through my core.

When she turned, without a thought, and walked back to the office complex, I simply followed, knowing I'd follow her anywhere. For a brief moment, I thought maybe we should just leave. She was used to being alone and as long as she was by my side I felt like I could survive anything.

I watched as she shifted and stood before me in naked beauty, but with a scowl on her face.

"Don't even think like that, Kyle! This is our pack. It's our home. We aren't leaving."

She dressed quickly and ran back into the office, nearly knocking Elise over in the process. I hadn't even heard my sister's presence I was so consumed with Kelsey. I knew from the surprise on her face that she had seen enough to know.

I shifted back to human form. "Do you mind?" I spat out at her as she turned and gave me time to change. It wasn't like she hadn't seen me naked before. Nudity was normal in a wolf pack and modesty was practically unheard of, but seeing the look on her face made me feel naked in an entirely different way.

She wasn't leaving. I had hoped snapping at her would cause her to stomp off, but not this time.

"How long?" She asked softly.

I sighed, knowing what she was asking, but determined to play dumb. "How long what, E?"

She looked at me, shooting daggers right into my eyes. "How long has it been since the bond started?"

I shrugged. I honestly didn't know.

"She was talking to you when she shifted like you were in the middle of a conversation, but Kyle, that's not possible."

I just stared at her as tears welled up in her eyes.

"Kyle, swear to me that's not possible!"

"I don't know what to tell you Elise, but you have to keep your theories to yourself. Are we clear?"

"No, no, no. I'm not keeping this quiet, everyone needs to know. If you are communicating through a bond in wolf form, Kyle, then there's a very real possibility that your bond is fully formed. You could both die! I can't just let that happen."

"It's fine E." I hugged her, feeling my sister on the verge of a complete meltdown. "Everything's going to be fine. You'll see. Maybe no one will even challenge us."

"She didn't tell you?"

I stiffened with my sister in my arms. "Tell me what?"

"Christine gave her a formal challenge this morning. The challenge is to take place tonight."

"WHAT?!??!" I growled out, trying to get control on my emotions, and trying to keep my surging wolf from changing and going after Christine Canine for threatening our mate.

165

Kelsey

Chapter 23

I knew the second Kyle found out about my challenge. I was thankful to be back at my desk because the intensity of his emotions nearly knocked me over, and I had to sit down or fall over. I knew he wouldn't be happy, but I wasn't prepared for the sheer anger, nor the fear that swept us both.

I had known for weeks, basically since the start of my training, that Christine would likely be my biggest challenger from within Westin Pack and as such had been drilled and prepped not just in offensive fighting skills, but also in her weaknesses. Mary had discussed several other potential challengers she was aware of from outside our pack as well. I was ready for this, or at least as ready as I'd ever be. My biggest fear was that my alpha powers would escape.

Jason had initially said that we would need to work hard on controlling my power, but so far focus had been on me learning how to actually fight. I had controlled it from escaping at the pack meeting when Christine had tried to bait me, but there was a lot of distraction, support, and nerves that day. I hadn't truly been tested since I had nearly knocked out Jason and Kyle testing my powers. It terrified me.

I was so consumed with thinking about it that I didn't even hear Kyle enter the office.

"Ms. Adams, can I speak with you in my office, please?"

"Ms. Adams?" I thought and heard him chuckle.

"Infuriating, isn't it?" he said evilly through our bond.

I glared at him as I entered, and as soon as the door was shut, he wrapped me in his arms and held me close. I was shaking all over as I let the threat of the challenge and everything that could go wrong sink in, fueled by his own thoughts, concerns, and fears he was loudly projecting.

"Why didn't you tell me?"

I shrugged against him.

"I had no idea you were so worried about your powers. You've been doing so good."

I looked back at him at first confused, and then realized I hadn't locked down my thoughts earlier. I had been getting good at shutting him out of my thoughts. I left enough that I didn't think he fully realized. It felt so wrong to do it, and I was constantly biting back the guilt, but I didn't want him to know how weak I really was. Now knowing that I could kill him with one screw up had me so scared I couldn't keep that wall up between us.

"It's going to be okay. You're going to be fine. You can do this. I know you can. You are not weak. You are the strongest woman I know. Not to mention the fastest."

He pulled me back, forcing me to look up at him as he smiled down with love shining through his eyes.

"I meant it when I told you I never want to live without you. We don't know for sure that our bond is strong enough to kill the other if anything happens to one of us, but I know for me, I would want to die regardless, because I couldn't stand living in a world where you didn't exist."

"Stop saying things like that. It's not helping, Kyle. I don't want you to die. I certainly don't want to be responsible for that. And I don't want to die, but I don't want to kill anyone either, not even Christine Canine, as obnoxious as she is and as much as she annoys me. I hate being put in this position, but I promise you I won't give up. I know she will fight to the death and I will be forced to do the same. I just hate it. All of it."

He soothed me, stroking my back and kissing me all over. As he made his way to my mouth I remembered what his dad had said.

"Kyle, we can't. You promised him. And if there's any chance at all that the bond isn't fully sealed, then it needs to stay that way until these challenges are over."

"Kels, you can't be serious. You're going up for a challenge tonight. And you're going to need me when it's over. Or at least I know I'm going to need you tonight."

I sighed. He was so sure I could win this, but at what cost?

"Would it be okay if I went to see your dad this afternoon?" I decided to change the subject.

"Yeah, sure, of course. What's up?"

"He had said he'd help me learn to contain my powers, but we haven't really spent any time on that and I'm scared they could unleash during the challenge. I just wanted to discuss it with him, see if he has any advice to offer."

"I think that's a good idea. Want me to come with you?"

I felt his hope, then his disappointment, as I started shaking my head no.

"He was serious this morning about keeping a distance. I think you showing up with me would be disrespectful of that."

He nodded and kissed my temple. "You're a very wise woman, mate."

I suspected he knew how it warmed me and made me all tingly every time he called me mate, and if he hadn't before, he did now that I had thought of it.

"My mate." He grinned, holding my gaze. "My perfect, beautiful, strong, courageous mate. Mine."

He kissed me hard, nearly taking my breath away.

"You're going to do great tonight."

"Will you be there? Watching?"

"Yes, it is a requirement. Just as you will have to stand by and watch when my challengers come. Honestly I think that may be harder than the actual challenges themselves."

"Says you, who gets to stand by and cheer me on."

He chuckled. "Actually, I'm not allowed to show favoritism during the challenge. Lucky for us, you'll still hear me loud and clear even if I look impartial to everyone else." He tapped on my forehead for added affect signaling our bond.

I was glad I had opened up to Kyle and let him soothe some of my fears. I felt a thousand times lighter and more resolute in what I had to do.

I left work shortly after that and headed to the Westin family home. Mary greeted me at the door and told me her husband was in a meeting, but that I was free to wait. We talked casually at first, neither of us wanting to mention the night's challenge. Finally, she cracked first.

"Are you ready for tonight? Any last questions or things you want to work on??"

I shook my head. "No, but thank you. You and the girls have been wonderful. I hope I make you proud tonight."

"Oh sweetheart," she moved next to me on the couch and hugged me close to her in the way only a mother could, "we couldn't be prouder of you. You're stepping up and fighting for my son. It's an honor as much of a curse. You'll see."

"B-b-but, why does she have to die for me to live?"

"That, dear, is up to you."

"Wh-wh-what?" I stuttered, as I often did when nervous or upset.

"You have the right to step aside and let her keep her life, but do not do so unless you are one hundred percent, without a doubt certain, she has conceded and you are the clear victor."

"B-b-but I thought that was a sign of extreme weakness and that I couldn't afford to be weak, especially on my first challenge, as there would certainly be more following."

"There's some truth to that. But you listen to me, Kelsey. I don't care what others tell you. Tonight, you are being forced into our most barbaric tradition. And at the end of the night, you have to be able to walk away and live with what happens."

"Or I'm dead and it won't matter," I said humorlessly.

"Don't talk like that. I've prepared you well. You're stronger than you give yourself credit. You'll see. Christine is no match for you. So, in the end you need to do what you have to do."

I heard a gasp behind us and turned to see Franny and Morgan coming out of Jason Westin's office. I had met them at the pack meeting and knew they were good people. Franny's face immediately screwed up and tears fell from her eyes.

Mary nodded solemnly as Morgan physically led her away.

"What was that all about?"

"That was Franny and..."

"I know who they are, they were at my table at the pack dinner. They seemed like really nice people, but I felt like they were shooting daggers at me just now."

"I'm sorry, Kelsey. Franny and Morgan are Christine's

parents. They are very distraught over her challenging you."

"Those are her parents? I-I-I hadn't really thought about things like that. I hadn't thought about how many others I could destroy tonight. Family's still a new concept to me. All I have is Kyle. I've never had anyone else."

"You have far more than just Kyle, Kelsey." She hugged me tight.

Jason cleared his throat. "Is everything okay?" he asked, looking surprised to see me.

"Kyle said it would be okay if I left early to discuss a few things with you, sir." I said, respectfully averting my eyes.

He shook his head in frustration.

"I just asked my boss and tried to leave it at that. I promise. We're trying to do as you asked, but this has nothing to do with that. I just had a couple things I wanted to talk to you about before tonight, sir."

"Very well, come on into my office."

Mary got up and followed me as far as her husband stood. "What did you do, Mr. Westin?"

I saw the grown man cringe before his wife. It was kind of cute and he didn't seem so magnanimous. I politely left them and walked into his office, but with the door open and my wolf hearing, I could hear every word spoken. I wondered why they didn't use their bond, surely they could do that, right?

"What did you do, Jason?"

"We can't discuss it here. Come into my office or leave it be."

They were both rigid and stoic walking in and closing the door behind them. I could only assume the room was sound proofed like those in the Westin Foundation.

"Well?" She demanded.

"I've asked Kyle and Kelsey to separate for the duration of the challenge period."

"Why? You of all people know how much harder it will make things for the both of them."

"There are things you don't know. Things I haven't shared with you that make it absolutely necessary. I will not lose my son!"

I think they forgot I was in the room and I shrunk into the chair desperately wishing for invisibility. He was concerned I wasn't

One True Mate

going to win tonight.

"What do I not know?"

"They've already begun to bond, Mary."

"You'd have to be blind not to see signs of that, Jason."

He nodded. "The Council has noticed as well. But I fear for him, for the both of them. Their mating is too new for this to be taking place so quickly. What if the bond seals before the challenge period ends? Then what? We risk losing them both? Can you live with that? Because I can't. A few weeks of stress apart is worth it. Plus, they work together every day, so it's not like they will be completely cut off from each other."

"Kelsey," Mary turned her attention to me and I saw the regret in Jason's face as he realized I was in the room. "Tell me about your bond."

I first looked at Jason who nodded permission to speak.

"What do you want to know, ma'am?"

"Do you sense Kyle when he is near?"

"Yes ma'am."

"Can you tell where he is right now?"

"Yes ma'am. He's pacing his office at the moment trying not to freak out. He only heard of the challenge just before I left to come over here.

"Well, that's a pretty good guess then. But how can you be sure."

I shrugged. "I just know. He's pacing back and forth and every now and then he stops and stares out the window." I concentrated harder, then blushed. "Nope, sorry, he's actually going to the bathroom."

She picked up the phone and called him. He didn't pick up. A full minute later the phone rang.

"Hey Mom, what's up?"

"Kyle, this is very important, but tell me, what were you doing just then when I called you."

"Mom? What's this about?"

"Kyle, just answer your mother's question." His dad demanded through the speaker phone.

"Well, I was going to the bathroom if you must know, why?"

I couldn't hide the grin of satisfaction on my face and shrugged innocently when they both looked my way.

171

"Thank you." She hung up on him. He immediately called back, but they did not pick up.

"That's a great distance for such accuracy."

"You see my concern now?"

"Kelsey, can you feel Kyle's emotions? Like, you know when he's in a bad mood or when he's happy?"

"Yes, of course."

"When he's not in front of you or within smelling range?"

"You mean like how infuriated he is right now and how he's trying to talk himself out of jumping in the car and coming over here? Yes."

"Kelsey, you asked last time about telepathic communication. Can you talk to Kyle through your bond?"

I hesitated, then nodded.

"For how long?"

I bit my lower lip, not wanting to answer. I first reached out to Kyle through our bond.

"Kyle, your parents are quizzing me on our bond, should I answer them?"

"You're safe with them, Kels. Answer whatever they ask. I'm on my way."

I looked back to them both staring at me, waiting.

"We first noticed it the morning after we completed our mating."

Mary had to sit down from the shock. "How is that possible Jason?"

"I don't know. Kelsey, were you just talking to him through the bond?"

I stared at the floor wanting to be anywhere else but there.

"Yes. He's on his way over now."

They shared a look.

"You can talk to him from this distance?"

I looked confused. "Distance doesn't seem to have an impact at all. Should it?"

I was more curious than anything now, but they didn't answer.

"How about in wolf form. Can you communicate in wolf form?"

I didn't want to answer that. A part of me felt our bond was sacred, and sharing this information was harder than I thought it would be, but I slowly nodded.

"That just started as far as I know."

Mary closed her eyes. "Physical pain. If I were to punch you, would he feel it?"

I looked at her strange and laughed. "I don't think so. I've never tried that, but I didn't think that was even possible."

They didn't seem to think the possibility was that funny.

"Wait, you mean at tonight's battle, whatever happens, he may physically feel it all too?"

"From the sounds of the strength of your bond it's a possibility and eventuality and what I'm hoping to prevent prior to the end of the challenge period."

"Because if that happens it's a sign our bond has sealed and if I die, so will he," I whispered.

Mary had tears in her eyes. "That's not going to happen, do you hear me?"

Jason consoled his mate but finally asked me, "Kelsey, why did you come by to see me this afternoon."

I glanced at Mary who's back was toward me and shook my head no while trying to discreetly explain, "I have some concerns about tonight's fight. Stuff you, uh, said you might could help me handle better?"

I saw him stiffen and nod, "Mary, will you excuse us for a bit? There's a few things Kelsey and I need to discuss in private.

"Not a chance." She said as her chin jutted out in complete obstinate. "I'm her trainer and I need to know everything to properly prepare her for tonight."

"This doesn't concern..."

"Jason Westin, don't you think I know exactly when you're lying to me."

He sighed just as the door to his office opened unannounced and Kyle stormed in.

KYLE
Chapter 24

I wasn't sure why my parents were grilling Kelsey over our bond, but I damned well was going to find out.

I saw my dad sigh in frustration, and look at Kelsey who shrugged and said, "I told you he was coming."

"What's going on here?" I demanded.

"Close the door at least, will you." I could see my dad was breaking down, but I didn't know why or what this was about. I closed the door and went straight to my mate. She immediately touched me and I felt a sense of peace and could finally breathe again.

"I thought you were coming to, uh," I looked around noticing Mom was in the room. To my knowledge, she didn't know about Kelsey being an alpha she-wolf. "to ask for some tips on tonight."

"Okay, what is it I don't know. Someone better speak up right now."

I looked at my dad and tried to understand what his intentions were and how much we should tell her, but while we were trying to communicate the extent of truth we should share, Kelsey started blurting everything out.

"We think the reason I have no recollections of pack, why my parents and I were attacked by wolves, and why we were in hiding to begin with. Why my parents were adamant I steer clear of wolves and should fear them is because I'm an alpha she-wolf."

Dad and I waited in shock with bated breath for mom to react.

"That's the big secret?" She looked back and forth between

us. "You don't think I can't feel her power? You don't think Elise isn't convinced she's the long lost triplet and the story of the third's death was false? She's been obsessively looking into it for weeks."

Then she turned to Kelsey. "Sweetheart," I couldn't help but grin for the affection Mom was showing my mate. "You remember when we were going through the breathing exercises, and how to clear your mind?" Kelsey nodded. "Those are focus techniques to keep your powers in check. I would never coach a wolf in the amount of control we've practiced. A normal training would have been to let go of your human side and give fully into your wolf. I didn't train you that way so that you would maintain control and not allow your alpha side to escape in full. Sure, some may, but you're strong enough to control that power."

Tears streamed down Kelsey's face and it took everything in my power not to scoop her up and take her far, far away. It was even harder to control my urges as she pushed me away and hugged my mother close.

"Thank you. I've been so scared about this."

"About what, child?"

"About losing control during the fight tonight and everyone finding out what I am. About you and the girls finding out and thinking I'm some sort of dangerous freak that should be sentenced to death. And..."

"Shhh, shhh, we'll have none of that. You have a battle to prepare for, and as a Westin, you are above such self-pity. Everything's going to be just fine tonight, you'll see."

As if sensing my unease, Mom pulled my mate away and pressed her into my arms. I sent a silent thank you to her as I just enjoyed the closeness of having her in my arms.

"Kelsey, do you want to test your powers before tonight?"

She looked at him in shock with big eyes. "I thought we were never to try that again."

"If it will make you feel better about heading into tonight, we can give it a try."

She shook her head. "No. I trust Mary, and if she says I'm strong enough to handle it, then I know I am. I just have one favor to ask, though."

"Anything." I said, but she wasn't looking at me, she was looking at my father.

"I need you to keep Kyle separated from the other wolves. Family only near him, not even Council. Please. I am not confident I can control anything if he is threatened or if another she-wolf even speaks to him during the challenge."

My father laughed. "Done. In fact, with your previous aggression towards the girls, I will set it up so that only Kyle and I are in the staging area for tonight's challenge."

"Thank you," she said, and nuzzled up against me. With a deep breath, I knew she was taking in my scent, and the physical and emotional responses it triggered, made me shiver in delight.

"I have one request, sir," I said formally.

He frowned like he knew what I was going to ask and nodded.

I suspected he was answering yes to my unspoken question, but I wanted to be very clear. "After the challenge tonight, I want to take Kelsey home. She'll need time to heal and recover from the challenge and you know she will only fully do so with me there.

"I know I know," he resigned. "Kelsey is yours for the night. I will not interfere and neither will the Council."

Shortly after that I had to say goodbye. Kelsey stayed with my parents while I returned to the office. It wasn't like I was going to get anything accomplished. There was too much on the line tonight with her first challenge. How could they expect me to focus on anything else?

Sure, I knew what was going to happen would happen and me pacing back and forth wearing a path across the carpet of my office wasn't going to help anything, but I wasn't used to being a man that couldn't control things. And I really didn't like it.

A knock on the door distracted me.

"Kyle." Lily poked her head in, "um, you have a visitor."

"Who is it?"

"It's Christine."

Great. The last person I wanted to see today.

"What does she want?"

I watched Lily shrug. "How should I know?"

I ran my hand through my hair in frustration. If Kelsey was there she'd have gotten exactly what she was there for before interrupting me. Not that I was doing anything but worrying, but Lily couldn't have known that.

176

"Just send her in."

"Christine, come on in," Lily exaggerated as she held the door wide and motioned her in.

Christine Canine walked in looking around my office and seeming to take everything in. As she twirled around slowly no doubt trying to give me a full view of herself in the process, ending her rotation back towards the door.

"You can go now. Shut the door on your way out."

Lily looked at me and nodded as she stomped out slamming the door behind her.

"That wasn't necessary, you know."

"What?" She asked in a voice of pure sugar.

I shook my head, "What do you want Christine?"

"I wanted to come by and say hi and check out my mate's office." She looked at me waiting for a reaction, but I bit back the growl at her insinuation and just glared at her. "Besides," she continued, seeing she wasn't getting a rise out of me, "I think it's only fair that we spend a little time together. We haven't really done that in years, Kyle. Sure, I know we'll have plenty of time later, but I wanted to make sure this challenge is worth it and looking around this place, I'd say it definitely is."

"I assure you, it is not."

"Kyle, come on. I'm about to fight to the death for you." I saw her soften and a glimpse of the Christine I had grown up with, before she turned complete bitch, seemed to shine through. She shrugged, looking young and not so fearless suddenly. "There was a time you would have expected and even wanted this from me, Kyle. What happened?"

"You changed, Chris. I changed. We grew up. We grew apart. It happens."

"When we were kids we were so certain we would be true mates. Do you remember?"

I smiled. "I do. I remember how disappointed we both were when you turned eighteen and there were still no mating signs."

"Yeah, me too. I was devastated, yet I still always knew we were meant to be together."

"Chris, we've barely spoken in years. You've moved on. I've moved on. Why bring all this up now?"

"I know I've been a bitch to you. I was so hurt that there were no mating signs and even more so that you didn't fight for us, Kyle. We were still compatible mates. You know that."

"Christine, you know I could never settle for a compatible mate. You of all people know that."

"But how can you be so sure Kelsey is your true mate? I mean, come on, she's a trespassing little bitch who should have been run off our land the second she tried to settle here."

"And if it had been anyone else I would have done just that, but Chris, she IS my one true mate."

"I just can't believe that. She's been squatting on our land for over two years and suddenly you have this grand epiphany?"

"She's been squatting on our land for two years because she's my true mate. I wasn't going to let her get away, Chris. I'm begging you, don't do this tonight."

I knew the second the words were out of my mouth that they were a giant mistake. If I could kick my own ass for saying them, I would. I watched helplessly as I spurred her hurt and determination to have me. I had inadvertently solidified the challenge for her.

"This is happening, Kyle, and you're going to have to just get used to having me around. Kelsey hasn't been properly trained. She's still learning our ways and probably doesn't even have a clue what to expect from tonight. I'm the stronger, more knowledgeable and better trained wolf here. I'm the better mate for you and I don't care what mother nature has to say about it. You'll see. I'll be a good wife and mate for you."

She slinked over and kissed me before I knew what was happening. My wolf wanted to attack at the intrusion and it took every effort to hold back from doing just that.

"I'll be seeing you tonight," she said as she moved away as quickly as she had attacked. At the door, she turned back to me. "Don't worry Kyle. I'm not heartless. I won't toy with her and she'll suffer as little as possible. I promise."

The sound of the door closing hit me like a ton of bricks with the reality of my situation. I could lose Kelsey tonight. I knew a part of me would be sad to watch Christine die, but I could stomach that loss far better than the alternative.

I closed up my office unable to spend another second cooped up indoors. Lily, who had promised Kelsey she'd fill in for her while she was out for the afternoon, didn't question me or make a single snarky sister comment I would have expected. Somehow her silence made the sincerity of the situation even more real.

Shifting into my wolf form, I spent the remainder of the evening running through the woods. I knew we were seeking our mate, but I purposefully steered us clear of her house. Kelsey and I had our moment earlier to say our goodbyes. I had left demanding she not say the word despite knowing that's what it was. To hear her say goodbye would have felt like she was giving up, that she didn't think she could win, and I needed her desperately to fight with all she had.

"I'm not giving up. I'll never give up on you, Kyle, even if it means fighting to the death."

My wolf howled in the air hearing our mate's words. I knew Kelsey had shifted back to human form and as her thoughts became muffled, still there, just unreadable, but this sudden knowledge that I could feel her while she was in human form and me in my fur made me happier than I knew possible. If anything happened to her, I knew I could not carry on in life. Even if the bond didn't kill me, I'd find a way to join her in death. Resolute in my decision I shifted back realizing I was at my own front porch. I showered and changed and headed off on foot to the outdoor pack circle.

Dad was waiting for me below the council pavilion. We shook hands and he led me up the stairs. I had never stood on the council pavilion. Only the Council, and during challenges, the mate of the challenged wolf stood on the pavilion. I would have been happy to never set foot up here if it meant keeping Kelsey alive, but I couldn't think like that and I fought against our bond to keep my thoughts to myself. Dad had been true to his word and only he and I were in the pavilion. I looked out across the great circle as the surrounding seats filled.

I knew Kelsey was close, and I desperately needed to see her.

Kelsey

Chapter 25

We were expected to walk out in human form. There would be some formal ceremony or at least words spoken. I'd have to shake hands with Christine, something about humanizing the process more. Then I'd have to shift in front of everyone. I wasn't about to stand there naked in front of the entire pack, so I decided to wear an old outfit that I didn't mind shredding to pieces. I gathered that wasn't entirely normal, but it would have to do. My shifts had strengthened and were now instantaneous. Maybe it would shock her enough for a small advantage.

I had been a nervous wreck all day, but more so since Kyle and I said our goodbyes. I couldn't let myself believe it might be the last time I got to touch him. Sadness washed over me as I gave myself a pep talk, trying to just get through it all.

I was as ready as I was going to be. Mary had stayed with me through the afternoon up until the point she delivered me to the small wooden room at the back of what I knew was the pack circle. Basically, it was an outdoor arena where they held pack meetings sometimes and where formal ceremonies, including challenges were held. This room was like the waiting room and I knew it would open directly into the floor of the arena.

I didn't like the little room. It felt like a cage and made my wolf stir.

"It won't be long, Kels. Deep breaths and try to relax. No need to get worked up right now. Save your frustrations for the

challenge."

I sighed relaxing just a bit at my mate's words. Kyle always knew exactly what I needed to hear and I was so thankful that he was not blocked from me as I knew he would be during the actual fight. A fight to the death seemed ridiculous and barbaric to me, especially in this day and age, but that's what I'd have to do if I wanted to live and wanted to protect my mate. And I would do absolutely anything necessary to keep Kyle.

I heard the chuckle through the bond before he spoke to me again. *"You keep that thought with you, babe, and you're going to do just fine."*

I was laughing when the door in front of me opened at last. I stood still allowing my eyes to adjust to the bright light outside the dark waiting room. Then I stepped forward feeling lighter and not as scared as I should be. I ignored the presence of another wolf to my right as I stepped forward to the middle of the arena as Mary had taught me. I remembered to hold my head high and as my eyes scanned the stands for Kyle, I couldn't stop the beaming smile on my face when I finally saw him. He winked at me and I momentarily forgot where I was.

When Jason's voice boomed out across the circle, reality set back in. I was Kelsey Adams. I was a born alpha she-wolf. My mate was Kyle Westin. I would do whatever it took to protect myself and my mate. Nothing else mattered. I took a deep breath and I smelled her. Christine Canine. My challenger. A threat to my bond. A threat to me and a threat to my mate. I smelled a slight fear mixed with her scent. It was enough to energize my wolf. I didn't hold back the guttural growl that escaped me and rejoiced in her heightened scent of fear.

"Christine, do you on this day challenge Kelsey in the mating challenge rights for the mating of Kyle Westin?"

I saw Kyle shake his head no, then from my peripheral vision saw and even felt the determination and hurt as her chin raised a little higher solidifying her resolve.

"I do." She said loudly.

I felt an excitement grow in the air.

"So it shall be. Kelsey. Christine. Please face each other." We did as he asked. "Shake hands in acknowledgment and acceptance of the challenge." We did, then turned back to face Jason as I refused to meet her eyes, not yet at least. "You will not shift until I tell you to, do you understand?" We both nodded as he addressed the crowd. "Mating is a sacred event amongst our kind. And strong mates make strong packs. Kyle and Kelsey have chosen to mate and as it is written, any single she-wolf may challenge her for her mate and her place in the pack. Christine has done just that. This is a fight to the death. There are no rules and there is to be absolutely no assistance or disruptions to the challenge fight. Is that understood?"

"Yes, Pack Alpha," a booming, unified voice responded from the pack.

"Kelsey and Christine please move to the designated circles." I followed his order and moved to a circle on my far left and she moved to the far right. It put some distance between us to allow time for the change. "Prepare to shift." Christine stripped leaving her clothes in a pile at her feet and standing naked before the crowd. I chose to remain in my clothes daring them to make me remove them. I saw Jason Westin raise an eye at me and I nodded slightly. "Okay, well, face each other please." We did so and this time I looked right at her with just enough authority to make her shake as she fought to maintain eye contact. "Let the battle begin." There was a chorus of howls surrounding us.

I didn't hesitate and shifted in midair like an explosion of fur as I lunged towards her. I caught the panic in her eye as she shifted much slower, but managed to fully shift before I was upon her. She crouched low and we began circling each other. I lunged forward and tried to gauge her reaction and speed. I knew I was faster than her, but distance speed was not the same as combat speed in close proximity.

I felt the shift in her as she gave herself over to her wolf and I suddenly understood what Mary had meant when she told me she had trained me differently from the others. I felt no human presence before me, only animal, and my wolf wanted nothing more than to follow her lead and take full control, but I was stronger and knew we'd be better off together.

I watched Christine's black wolf circle me as easy prey. She was quite large next to my small blonde wolf. I knew my size made me look like easy prey. Let her believe that for now. She lunged at me and I easily side stepped away from her. We did this for quite awhile, just circling and testing each other. She'd lunge, I'd move. I'd lunge, she'd move.

I watched and waited for the time to make my move. She lunged to the left and so did I slamming right into her. I heard the gasp from the crowd and tried to push it out of my mind. Her wolf was pinned and snarling and snapping at me. I growled and she settled slightly, but my mistake came as I took that as a sign of submission. It wasn't. She pushed up and forward, knocking me off my guard. I stumbled backwards and she continued with her momentum and in seconds had me pinned on my back. I flailed my paws, kicking out at her, to no avail. She clamped down on my shoulder, missing my neck by mere inches. I howled out in pain.

She continued, relentlessly attacking and I was on the defense just trying to protect my neck and block her bites. I had been so certain of this battle. So, confident in my ability to fight and here I was letting her get the upper hand. I considered giving fully into my wolf, but I knew I couldn't. I was as good as dead if that happened, even if I did win. I had to think. I had to remember what Mary and the girls had taught me. Focus on my training and most importantly I had to get away from Christine and clear my head for an attack.

I let my body go slack. I felt Kyle's fear and stress rise at the same time Christine's dwindled. Cocky little thing she was. But I used that to my benefit as she began an early celebration instead of using the advantage to go in for the kill. It didn't take much to knock her off guard and get back to my feet then. She growled at me, but I was already off and sprinting at full speed. There really wasn't anywhere to run, but I had some energy I needed to burn off or my alpha powers were going to explode, so I ran along the side of the arena as fast as I could, just running in circles. At first, she made attempts to snap at me as I passed her, but eventually she retreated to the middle of the arena and just watched and waited.

When I felt a little more in control of myself I turned and ran right at her, full force. She didn't know what was coming. I leapt on her back and she managed to throw me off. Teeth were bared, jaws snapping, as we equally attacked each other. I was getting good at reading her moves, but she switched it up and went low when I thought she'd go high. She bit down on my right upper leg. The same spot that was thin and balding in wolf form and covered in skin grafts in human form. She locked her jaws and I felt the blood gushing from me.

My wolf howled in fury and turned even while she was still locked onto my leg and bit down on her exposed neck. I clamped down hard and when she didn't ease up on my leg I bit even harder. I felt the skin beneath her fur break and tasted her blood as it trickled into my mouth. I snarled and snorted but I never let go. I felt her grip ease up on my leg and eventually release. I continued to hold on, shaking my head back and forth and growling. Blood was coating the back of my throat and suddenly, without the personal threat to me, I couldn't do it. I eased my teeth back slowly and tried to look into her eyes. I could feel her life slipping away and I sobbed.

I let go and sat back on my hind legs and howled. It wasn't a howl of victory, it was a howl of sorrow and not a single other sound could be heard. I knew I didn't have much time. I quickly shifted back to human form, no longer caring that I was naked before the pack.

"Medic!" I yelled, spitting out fur and blood that did not belong to me. "Medic!" I called again and saw the doors open and a team rush in. They ran right to me, immediately assessing the injury to my leg. "Not me! Her! You have to help her."

They stared at me for only a moment before rushing to her side. I knew everyone thought she was dead, but I knew there was still life in her. A life worth saving.

I stood trying to ignore the pain searing through me. "Alpha," I called out to the pavilion above as the surrounding murmurs came to a screeching halt. "I understand this was to be a fight to the death, but Christine is not my enemy. She is pack. She is family. And she deserves to live. I have seen too much evil and violence in the world to end her life unnecessarily. Do not mistake this for weakness as it was fully within my grasp to kill her. But every pack member is precious and necessary and a life should not so easily be extinguished, but cherished." I bowed my head and bared my throat to him.

"I do not believe anyone will contest the victor of this challenge. The restraint you have shown is unheard of and the grace and mercy you've bestowed on her is a sign of true leadership. We will do all we can to save her life."

"Thank you."

The roar of the crowd and applause that followed was

startling, and I was suddenly very aware of my nakedness as I turned and limped quickly to the little room off the arena that I had started the evening in. Once behind closed doors, I collapsed against the wall and slid to the floor sobbing. I had almost taken a life and I would have to live with that knowledge.

KYLE
Chapter 26

Lily was rushing to the door of the waiting room where I knew Kelsey was crying. I cut her off before she could make it there.

"Hey! Give me that back," she complained, as I grabbed Kelsey's duffle from her.

"Give her some space, Lil. I'll take it to her." I didn't leave room for argument as I closed the space between me and the woman I loved, shutting out the world behind us with the slam of the door. I saw Kelsey jump at the noise and met watery brown eyes. I dropped to my knees and scooped her up into my arms.

"I-I-I almost killed her out there."

I couldn't help the chuckle. "That's my girl!" She punched me in the arm, but nuzzled her head against my chest. I sighed. "You had me scared for a minute there, baby. I wasn't sure I'd ever get to hold you like this again."

"Not a chance," she said, sounding more assured than ever.

We sat like that in silence for a long while, just holding each other. I could sense that most of the pack had retreated for the night, no longer waiting around to issue congratulations. There were only a few stragglers still waiting when we finally ventured out.

Kelsey's eyes were a little red and puffy. It looked obvious she had been crying. Not one person commented or made a sound, but as one the group dropped to one knee and bared their necks to my mate. The sight nearly made my chest explode in pride, and for the first time in my life I felt Alpha power freely flowing from me, and not just me, but from us, and not in the forceful way to push my will on others as I had used in the past, but a different kind of power, the kind necessary for respect and strength as a leader of a pack. The kind I had only ever seen come from my father and mother.

As she motioned for them to rise and they followed her command, there was some commotion at the back of the small group that had gathered and I strained to take a closer look. I knew visitors from other packs were already arriving and had come in to see Kelsey's first challenge. I knew they could make trouble even though they were given strict warnings against it on their arrival. My instincts screamed to protect my mate, but as the crowd parted, a small slight woman broke from the pack practically tackling Kelsey. My hackles stood up and I was in mid growl when I realized who it was.

"Thank you, thank you. I don't know how I can ever thank you enough for not killing my daughter," Franny, Christine's mother, said hugging on to Kelsey for dear life. "You will forever have our full allegiance for this act of kindness and mercy."

I rubbed Kelsey's lower back, feeling how close she was to breaking down again. She just nodded, and when the two broke apart, sharing a look I didn't fully understand, I began the slow process of escorting her away from the circle and towards the parking lot. I couldn't get her home fast enough.

Once safely in the car I allowed myself time to let the previous few minutes sink in. If it had been any other wolf being granted allegiance and respect at the level Kelsey was just given, the Alpha and the Council would have been furious. I wondered if those present even realized what they were doing. Her place as the future Pack Mother would allow it without contestation, but if any other wolves were around outside of Westin Pack, they certainly got a big awakening tonight and may just reconsider challenging my mate. Kelsey already had the full pack behind her and she didn't even know it.

I heard her sigh in the seat next to me as our home started to come into view. I reached over and took her hand. "What's wrong, Kels?"

"Do you think I'll ever do anything right or normal? I mean it was a death challenge and I couldn't even get that right. Do you worry it will make me look weak in the eyes of the other she-wolves?"

"Are you kidding? Did you not see the respect you were

187

given by our pack after the challenge?"

She sighed again. "Yes, and I'm assuming that wasn't normal either."

I chuckled. "No, not exactly, but it wasn't a bad thing. We have been recognized by a large chunk of our pack as future leaders with uncontested and full willing support. Any outside wolves present tonight would have seen that and recognized the strength and power that comes with it. I mean, couldn't you feel it flowing freely between us?"

"Is that what that was? That tingly sensation? I didn't know. It didn't feel like my usual power."

"Because it wasn't. It was our power and a sign that our bond is further strengthening."

"What?" she sounded panicked. "Did you? Did you feel anything when she bit my leg?"

"Only a mild sensation, babe, nothing that would have hurt or killed me." I had forgotten all about her leg. We hadn't even had the medics look at it. I knew I needed to call one in immediately. *How much pain was she still in?*

"Not much, but it does probably need to be looked at," she replied, hearing my thoughts.

After settling her in on the couch with a hot cup of tea, I called over to Mallick. His son, Micah, was the best doctor we had in town and I knew he was temporarily living back home with his parents during some home repairs at his place. I wanted to ensure he was the one that came out to check on my mate.

"Hello?"

"Mallick, it's Kyle. Is Micah at home? I need him to come by and look at Kelsey's leg. She sent the medics off to help Christine without a second thought to herself. Is he available?"

"Kelsey's with you?" I heard the disappointed sound in his voice.

"I know, I know. Dad's already talked to both of us about the Council's concerns, but he also promised I could keep her with me as she heals tonight. Just tonight." I sighed hating even thinking it.

There was some hushed muffled talking on the other end.

"Kyle? Hey, it's Micah. I'll be over in ten."

"Thanks, man."

Hanging up the phone I went back to the living room to

check on Kelsey. She was a little pale but otherwise looked nearly unaffected. But I knew better.

"How are you doing?"

She shrugged. "I'm okay I guess. Drained. Exhausted."

"Well, that's to be expected." I tried to lighten the mood. "Can I take a look at that leg?"

She nodded and stood to remove the sweatpants she had dressed in after the challenge. As soon as she shifted I smelled the blood. I wasn't sure how I had missed it earlier, probably just too concerned with her, but it was suddenly assaulting my senses.

She saw the panic in my eyes. "Please don't freak out on me. I was bound to get a little beat up out there, right?" I didn't say anything and she blurted out, "It's better than being dead at least!"

That made me chuckle and shake my head at her. I ran and grabbed a clean rag from the kitchen and wetted it before returning to her. I carefully cleaned the streak of blood running down her leg, starting at her ankle and working my way up. Just passed her knee I came to the first source. I dabbed around trying to mop up the blood without causing her further pain. She winced, but didn't pull away.

Frowning she looked down at the mess. "Cole's gonna have to fix it when it heals."

I small growl escaped me.

She laughed. "What do you have against Cole Anderson?"

I smiled sheepishly up at her. "Nothing."

"Riiiight!"

"No seriously, I like Cole. He's a great guy. I just don't particularly enjoy thinking of any other man's hands on you, or anyone marking you in any way. I know it's silly, and I really have nothing against him and the tattoo is beautiful. I just can't help it sometimes."

She smiled back at me. "I like that it makes you a little jealous."

"You do, do you?"

"Yes," she sighed. "Sometimes I worry that it's really just the bond that keeps you around. Like we didn't really have a choice in the matter. And I know we've sorta talked about this before, but it still gets me sometimes. Then you go all dominant and jealous and I have no doubts you're all mine."

"That's one way to look at it I guess." I laughed.

Micah knocked on the door and I yelled to him that it was open. Not knowing if he and Kelsey had ever met I made quick introductions and explained what I had found of her injuries, before moving to the couch to sit next to her and allow him to examine her.

Micah rolled his eyes. "Switch sides."

"What?"

"Kyle, I need to be on the side closest to the injury, so move it."

I growled before I could stop myself. Kelsey giggled and Micah rolled his eyes. "Bonding males, sheesh! Don't worry, I've dealt with more than my fair share in this business." Then he winked at my girl and I nearly lost it.

"Well, then stop egging him on." Kelsey scolded in good humor.

She winced, then moaned as he examined the injury, and it took every ounce of self-control to keep seated and not attack him.

"Ow!" Kelsey finally said and I was on my feet growling trying to get between the two of them. It was like I really, truly couldn't control myself.

"Not him, you idiot. You were crushing my hand. Calm down or go take a cold shower or something while he finishes."

My chin dropped to my chest in despair. My instincts to protect her were almost too much to bare.

"It's okay, I've had my look. And I told you I'm used to overbearing alphas, half delirious with protective instincts when their mates are hurt. And I've heard you two are particularly close already, so I'm not surprised to see it at all. Calm down, Kyle. I'm not going to touch her again."

"But you didn't even bandage it," Kelsey questioned as I tried to calm myself and lowered back to the seat next to her. I tugged her close to my side and breathed in deep to ground myself once again. She was safe. She was injured, but she would heal.

Micah was studying us closely. "Dad's been really, really worried about you, you know. He's asked me some pretty crazy questions about the bonding process, medically speaking of course. I wasn't sure where he was coming from, but I can see it clearly now. How long have the two of you been mated, seriously?"

"Seriously, I went to Council the very next day and that weekend the announcement was made at the Pack Meeting." I assured him.

"I've never heard of a couple bonding so quickly. I mean ever." He contemplated that for a moment. "How long did you know each other before mating?"

"Two years," we both said at that same time, laughing.

"And how often in those two years did you see each other."

"Every day." I told him honestly.

"Interesting. Now, I'm sure your father and the Council advised you not to tell anyone about the severity of your bond, but please remember, I'm a doctor and sworn to patient confidentiality which I take very seriously. Would you guys tell me about it?"

Should we? Is it safe? Kelsey asked through our bond.

I trust him completely, Kels.

She nodded. "Ok then, if you trust him that much," she said to me aloud, before turning to him, "What do you want to know?"

His mouth hung open. "You were communicating through the bond just now?"

We both nodded.

"How long have you been able to do that?"

"Since the morning after we mated." Kelsey said matter-of-factly.

"What else?" He said. "Can you feel each other's presence? Know where the other is?"

"Yes, and distance has no impact on that, though Jason said it should."

"What do you mean by that? Like if he were at the office right now you could tell me exactly where and what he was doing?"

"Yes. We can also talk to each at the same distance."

"Amazing!"

"How about in wolf form?"

"Yeah, that started recently," I added, "but it's still a little fuzzy when one of us is in skin and the other fur. Like it's there, but you're hearing things underwater or something."

"Yes," Kelsey chimed in, "that's exactly how I'd describe it too."

"When she got that injury tonight, did you feel it, Kyle?"

I hesitated. "Yes. But it was just a dull feeling. I didn't feel the full impact of the pain."

"So that part of the bond hasn't completed yet at least. Cause

191

you know that's what the Council is concerned about, right?"

"Yeah, we get it."

Kelsey yawned and I noticed how exhausted she looked suddenly.

"Okay, we can talk some more later. I didn't bandage your leg, because you will heal better in wolf form. If you change for me, I'll patch it up as needed and honestly by morning you'll likely be good as new. And if not, then Kyle will give me a call to come back over for another look. Okay?"

"Okay." She said softly. "Do you think it could have done any damage to my skin grafts?"

He shook his head. "Not likely, but if it's not fully healed tomorrow we'll take a look, okay?"

"Okay."

"In the meantime, I'm going to leave these antibiotics and some pain killers. You may want to take both before you change."

She nodded as I ran to get her a glass of water. Downing the pills and the water she excused herself returning quickly in wolf form. She was still limping badly on the injured leg. Doc got to work cleaning and bandaging it as I sat behind her rubbing her head and talking softly to her. She was fast asleep on the floor of my living room before he finished.

After saying goodbye, I carefully picked her up and headed for our bedroom. She'd fuss over the hair on the bed later, but for tonight I couldn't care. I quickly changed into wolf form too and snuggled in, curled around her small wolf in full protection. We awoke in the same position the next morning only in our skin and completely naked. My body responded to the morning closeness, but I headed off to the bathroom without waking her knowing there was only a cold shower in my future.

Kelsey

Chapter 27

Kyle and I were keeping a distance since the morning I awoke after my only challenge thus far. It was at the Pack Council's insistence, and with only a week left in the challenge period we were doing our best to behave. Still, I missed him and couldn't wait to get in the office each morning where I at least got to see him.

He had been so busy in meetings and entertaining the foreign wolves, arriving in greater numbers every day, so that I only caught him in passing. It was beginning to feel a bit like the circus came to town and I knew the locals were not happy.

I still had a slight limp from the challenge, but for the most part I had healed quickly. Micah assured me the limp and the pain would not last forever and he checked it every day to ensure I continued to heal.

The night I had gone to the Crate with Sally for drinks after work, Lily had met us there. There had been a table of foreign wolves that had given me the creeps. I'd guessed they were from the Bulgarian pack based on their heavy accents.

One thing I learned quickly was that the Westin Pack had my back. When one of the foreigners had tried to speak to me, it nearly caused a fight to break out, but I had felt safe, protected, like I belonged for the first time in my life. This was my pack and no one was taking them from me.

Three packs had already come and gone, declining to make any challenges. The last of them congratulated me on my victory upon their exit. Five packs still remained, though. No one could ever remember such a turnout in all of shifter history.

I had learned one truth about it all. Yes, word had gotten around about the lone wolf trespassing in the Westin territory and being allowed to live that caused enough interest to bring others there, but most importantly, Kyle had a huge target on his back. Me being a worthy mate after my victory only seemed to fuel this. All other she-wolves remaining in the Westin Pack had since conceded and their loyalty given to me was starting to attract some unwanted interest my way.

In the shifter world, not just within the Westin Pack, Kyle was a pretty big deal. I had learned that the Westin Pack was the largest and most thriving pack known, and as future Alpha his position in the pack was highly sought after. Seeing our unity after my victory of Christine, the remaining wolves of Westin had also given their allegiance. That included everyone in the pack, except Cole Anderson.

When things had died down at the Crate, Cole had come to sit with me and my friends, much to Lily's delight. After a few shots of tequila, my tongue had loosened enough to challenge him on it.

As I sat looking around my office, remembering the discussion of the night before, my whole body shook.

"Look, it's meant as no disrespect I assure you. I'm 100% in support of you and Kyle. BUT," my stomach churned remembering his words, "if something, God forbids, happens to Kyle, I will challenge his victor for you and keep Westin with Westin."

The conviction in his eyes would haunt me every night until the stupid challenge period was passed. There was absolutely no doubt in my mind that Cole would destroy anyone if needed, even someone powerful enough to defeat Kyle. Another shiver went through me at the notion.

The ringing of the phone distracted my thoughts.

"Kyle Westin's office."

I paused, waiting to take the message I was sure was coming. Instead I was met with a deep husky laugh that warmed my body through to my bones.

"Do you even look at caller id?"

I frowned and looked down seeing Kyle's office line on the display. I shot a look at the clock on the wall. It was only 7:30am.

"When did you get in?"

"Early. And why are you taking business calls before 8am?"

I sighed and rubbed my forehead. "Sorry, didn't even realize the time."

I felt a wave of worry before the door to his office clicked open with the phone still at his ear.

"What's wrong?"

I laughed. "Why do you assume something's wrong?"

"You're in even earlier than usual."

I tried to protest, but he continued.

"You haven't even made coffee. You look exhausted."

I tried again to interject.

"And you are distracted. It's not like you to lose track of time."

"Are you done?" I asked, turning my back to him as I made my way to the coffee pot. He nodded at me and just watched and waited. Once the sound of brewing met my ears I turned back to him.

"I was out late at the Crate. I have a bit of a headache from it," I said, thinking, but not admitting aloud, I may have been a little drunk still too. He snorted and I knew he heard that thought through our bond. "I don't sleep well without you and I'm stressed about the upcoming challenges. I wasn't sleeping anyway so came in early. I'll be fine after a couple pots of coffee."

I knew I was whining but didn't care. What was the point in hiding it when he already knew and felt every second of worry I had anyway. He pulled me into his arms and I flinched, my eyes flying to the open door.

"Kyle, we can't. The Council. We promised."

"Right now, my mate needs me. I don't give a shit about what the Council has to say about it."

His embrace tightened around me and I relaxed against his chest, breathing in his scent, and feeling the stress fade away.

"Thanks," I whispered as the gurgling noises of coffee stopped, silencing the room and the aroma drew me from his arms in desperate need of caffeine.

"Grab an extra cup for me and meet me in my office."

It felt kind of clandestine knowing how much the Council had been stressing the importance of us staying away from each other. I giggled thinking about it. If he didn't care, I didn't care. But when I walked into the office, closing the door behind me, I wasn't greeted in any way to be considered clandestine. Instead he was seated at his desk already talking on the phone and motioned for me to sit while he reached for his coffee.

"Yeah…Uh-huh... I understand… Dad, it is what it is... We knew this was a possibility, really an inevitability… It'll be fine… Yeah, just two more weeks."

As he hung up the phone I could feel the stress wash over him. Whatever his dad had called about wasn't good news. I quickly got up from my seat and launched myself around his desk plopping ungracefully in his lap. It made him smile and stop mid stroke as he mussed his hair like he did when worried.

"What…" He silenced me with a kiss. I indulged him for a few before pulling back and giving him a stern look. "What's happened?"

"I don't want to talk about it. I just want to hold you."

"You can hold me, but you're going to talk. Don't make me invade your brain to figure it out." We had both gotten good about not constantly invading each other's mind. My cheeks pinked as my mind headed for the gutter thinking of a few of the many thoughts I had managed to keep from him.

Oops. I knew he had heard my thoughts. His grin grew wider.

"I like what's on your mind a whole lot more." He said nuzzling into my neck and taking a moment to breath my scent in deeply there. Oh, what that did to me was unexplainable in words.

"Not getting off the hook that easy. What did your dad want, Kyle?"

"Nothing I didn't already know or wasn't expecting at least."

The challenge! My stomach rose in my throat as the crippling sick fear threatened to take over.

"Hey, hey, don't. None of that. I'm going to be fine."

"How many?" I whispered.

"Three," he sighed.

"THREE?!?!" I shrieked.

"It's okay." He continued to soothe me.

"Who?"

"It's not Cole Anderson if that's what you're asking." He

196

teased trying to lighten the mood and I punched him hard in the arm, but it only earned me a small laugh in retaliation.

"I know about Cole. He explained himself last night and why he wasn't going to concede to our mating until challenges are over. Now, who?"

"Patrick O'Connell from the Irish Clan is in route. His Alpha called in the challenge ahead of his arrival to ensure his chance. I'm not surprised at all by it. Patrick is the third son of the Irish Alpha. His second son successfully won a mating challenge against an alpha heir somewhere down in South America. Doesn't matter to him who you are, just that his son takes my place as pack alpha here. With six sons, he's systematically strengthening his pack in this way."

I nodded. "Who else?"

"Matt Snyder of New York City Central Pack. I honestly think he has the hots for you." He laughed, twirling my hair in his fingers. "Cause seriously, I see no real challenge in him. I'm not sure if it should be a mercy killing, or if I should spare his life as you did Christine's."

"Don't joke. If he was willing to challenge you, he must think he has a chance, so do not underestimate him. Who's the third."

"Andon of the Bulgarians."

My breath caught. *Not him! Please, anyone but him!*

"You know him?"

"No, but I know who he is." I shuddered remembering the small giant with the hard glare from the Crate the night before. "He was at the Crate last night. There were a few scuffles with the Bulgarians and the Westins. Cole told me who he was but I don't think he knew about the challenge at the time. That guy gives me the creeps, Kyle."

"Come here," he said, pulling me back close to his chest and rubbing his hands across my shoulders to comfort me. "Nothing's going to happen to me, babe. I got this. I just need you to have a little faith in me."

I pulled away and stared at him in shock. Did he really believe I didn't think he could survive a challenge? "Kyle, I have full faith in you. You are the strongest, best wolf shifter in the world. Please don't mistake my fear of the challenges as my lack of faith in you." I felt terrible knowing now that's how he was feeling and vowed to give him only my best, most confident thoughts going forward.

"Sometimes it's hard to differentiate the two."

"I'm know. I'm sorry. The mere thought of someone like Andon taking your place disgusts me, but I know you aren't going to let that happen. Not my wolf." I smiled at him with confidence and fixed his hair back into its normal perfect place. "How soon?"

"I don't know yet."

"They moved quickly once Christine issued me her challenge."

"I know, I suspect I'll hear something more later this morning."

"They won't stack them all in one day, would they?" I asked horrified at the thought.

"No, I'm guaranteed a day's break between each fight. Guessing the delayed announcement is due to scheduling. We'll hear something soon though, I'm certain."

At some point, we moved to the small couch in his office and spent the day snuggled up and talking through our fears, concerns, and future. By lunch time, his sisters were on the hunt wondering what was wrong. A soft knock on the office door was followed by a head peeking through.

"Found her!" Lily announced, as she and Elise descended upon us.

"Close the door." Kyle said gruffly, making no motion to move from the cozy position we were in.

"Awe, you guys look so cute. The Council will freak if they see you together. What are you thinking?"

"Kyle was issued three challenges today." I said, and it was all that needed to be said. Shock, fear, and anger all flashed across each of their faces. "We're waiting to hear the schedule."

"Screw the Council and their stupid concerns," Elise said wiping a tear from her eye.

Kyle grinned, "Yeah, that's pretty much our thoughts this morning too." He paused awkwardly. "Well, did you at least bring lunch with you? I'm starving!"

Lily disappeared returning sometime later with a feast for the four of us. The atmosphere was lighter, even with the heavy layer of concern wrapped around us. We laughed and joked and I fell in love with them all just a little bit more.

When the phone rang, we all stared in shock and denial, but on the third ring, Kyle finally made his way over to answer.

"Kyle Westin... yes... yes... okay... no... okay, I'll see you in an hour. Thanks."

The lightheartedness of our lunch was over as a stone wall went up in my mate as he prepared for battle. "Seven o'clock tonight, against the kid from New York Central." We all nodded somberly.

KYLE
Chapter 28

The second I opened the door to my dad's office, I could hear angry raised voices.

"What do you want me to do, Morris? The kid issued the challenge. For me to deny, or Kyle to refuse it, would make him guaranteed victor by default. My son is not losing his one true mate just to spare some idiot pup."

Morris slammed his fist down on my father's desk. "Dammit. He just barely came of age, Jason."

My father sighed, "I understand the position you're in, but I don't know how to help. I've talked to the pup too. I can see he isn't ready. Hell, anyone can. That pup doesn't have an ounce of alpha in him and he chooses to go against Kyle? It doesn't make sense."

Morris chuckled a sad little sound, "His father was my second. Died in an attack just last year. Pup's always been a runt out to prove himself, but apparently, your Kelsey ran into him the other day and was kind to him." Morris rolled his eyes. "She's all that boy talked about since. Bad case of puppy love there."

I smiled. Who could blame the pup for that?

"Morris," I interrupted, "look, I don't want to fight this pup, but I'm not about to just hand him my mate either. Look, I'll do what I can to spare his life, but I can only do so much in there. I will defend myself. If he persists in attacking there's nothing I can do. I won't pull back just to save him, but if he concedes I will spare him, and if it is in my power to save him once I'm declared victor, I will. But that's as much as I can give you."

The older wolf bowed his head to me in gratitude. "That is

more than I deserved to ask of you, Kyle. Thank you."

I nodded back to him. He shook hands with Dad and left.

"You showed much grace and diplomacy just then, son." He smiled proudly. "You will make a fine Pack Alpha someday."

"Not someday too soon I hope." I joked, embarrassed by his high praise.

"Are you ready for tonight?"

I shrugged. "Ready as I'll ever be, I suppose."

He nodded. "How about Kelsey? Does she know yet?"

"Yes. I was having lunch with her and the girls," I added when he eyed me suspiciously, "when you called."

"How's she holding up with everything?"

"Good, I think. I think she's more concerned with my challenges than fearing anymore against her."

Dad smiled, "Yes, that sounds about right and as it should. She's a fine mate for you, Kyle. In all of this craziness I'm not sure I've actually said that, but I like Kelsey immensely. Your combined powers will make you strong and keep the pack safe, but you must never let your guard down and show them."

I understood the gravity in his subtle warning.

"Uh, thanks. Hey, you called me here, was there something you needed?"

"Oh, I think you're good. Was just going to discuss tonight's challenge. See if you had any questions or concerns and warn you about the pup you're up against."

"Yeah, this sucks. I won't lie and say I'm not happy about an easy challenge, especially with O'Connell and Andon later this week, but I don't want to hurt this kid either."

"I know, Son, but the law's the law and the Grand Council's law surrounding challenge are very specific and not negotiable."

I left Dad's house with that thought heavy on my mind. Without even considering where I was headed I found myself walking back into work. To her.

I stood there outside the door into my office suite, just staring at her. She was so beautiful. I carefully closed our connection through the bond, as we both had learned to do, for a bit of privacy and just watched her. My mate. The most precious person in my life and I would do absolutely anything for her.

As she stood and walked to the filing cabinet I admired her

slender long legs that seemed to go on for miles before reaching the bottom of the skirt that fit to her backside like a glove. She was professional in the office and this was no different in a charcoal gray women's suit. If only she knew what those short skirts of her suits did to me. I was admiring her behind, lost in thought when she shook her butt a little too noticeably.

"You gonna stand there staring all day?"

I think I may have blushed a little. Busted ogling my mate.

"Not if you plan on staying in that position much longer."

She yelped and whipped around quickly, her eyes wide and red creeping up her neck. It was the cutest thing I'd ever seen. I wanted desperately to go to her, but instead headed for my office. Holding the door open I motioned for her to enter.

"You know when you do that bond shutting down thing right now with everything going on that it just freaks me out thinking something's wrong." She scolded. "Lucky for you I smelled you long before you decided to camp outside my door."

I turned her to face me. "You talk too much." I said before crushing my lips to hers. She sighed against me, and the stress of the day melted away and I just held her.

"You ready for tonight?" She asked breaking our perfect silence.

"Yeah. I don't like it, but I'm ready. You don't need to worry about anything tonight."

"Do I get to go home with you like I did after my challenge?"

"I don't think the Council will approve that, especially with the slaughter they've setup, but if I need you, I'll let you know and to hell with them."

She nodded. "You're going to try and spare him?"

"I don't exactly want to kill him. Kels, he's little more than a pup and determined to see this through. Can't fault him the puppy love he has for you, but still."

"What?" she demanded.

I chuckled. "Yeah, the other challengers, they're out for pack position, but this kid fancies himself in love with you."

I laughed harder at the incredulous look on her face. I knew her touch and a few stolen kisses would see me through the day. Much too soon we said goodbye, I mean, see you later because

Kelsey refused to say goodbye before a challenge for fear of jinxing it, and headed straight for the pack circle.

I decided to hide out in the room behind the arena. It was dark and quiet and I knew I had two hours to go before anyone would begin to show. Placing my earbuds in my ears I cranked up some old 80's metal and got lost in the beat. It was freeing as I gave myself over to the music and blocked everything else from my mind.

I don't know how long I had been sitting there, but when Metallica's 'For Whom the Bell Tolls' began to play, it was like a beacon calling to me and I could no longer sit still. Running in place, pushups, sit-ups, whatever I could physically do in the cramped space I began to do and when AC/DC's 'Back in Black' started up, I was ready to explode into my wolf form. Never had I been so pumped and ready.

I didn't hear the roar of the crowd's arrival, or the call for introductions over the loud music cranking in my ears. I was in a full on dance, head banging and sweat already dripping from my forehead when the door opened.

I didn't stop the song, but let it fuel and propel me forward and towards the center of the arena. My arms were pumping in the air and I had never been more ready for anything than this challenge. As the song began its closure, the deafening roar of the crowd grew louder than my music. I turned and waved to my pack and even blew my girl a kiss, much to the dismay of the Council, as my father desperately tried to reign in the noise.

As I removed my headphones, smiling, I was greeted by loud boos as young Matt Snyder entered the arena. He looked small and scared, but the pup was scrappy, raising his arms, begging them to continue and fueling himself off the negativity towards him. I knew immediately this was a kid who'd fight til his dying breath giving, 200% and refuse to back down. The thought immediately sobered my post musical high.

It took a few minutes longer before Dad was able to calm the crowd down and begin the formal ceremonial start to the challenge and giving the pup one last chance to pull out, which of course he refused.

When Dad called the challenge to order, I shook hands with Matt and we both moved to our designated side of the arena and stripped to prepare to shift. I heard a little growl in the back of my mind coming through the bond, and couldn't wipe the smile from my face. Not having been raised around shifters, Kelsey still didn't understand how nudity really wasn't a big deal, but a part of me liked her jealous streak at others seeing me that way.

The signal was given and I quickly shifted and stalked toward the pup as he took his sweet time shifting into his wolf. I tried not to roll my wolf eyes. In the time it took him to shift, I could have ended the entire fight, but I waited for him to at least change.

When he finally changed, I saw the ugliest, scrawniest pup I'd ever laid eyes on. Some sort of white colored wolf with black and brown and grey spots in weird shapes. I felt even more sorry for the kid. Not allowing my wolf to take full control, I held back to see what he'd do. He pounced around erratically. No rhythm or rhyme whatsoever. I waited until he finally approached. I wanted this to be quick and over already.

I tried to find a pattern to his movements where there were none. That was perhaps his best advantage and he was driving me, crazy circling me without any forward movement. What was he waiting for? I finally lunged toward him and he sprang in the air like a scared cat and landed on my back immediately clawing and biting at anything he could, which ended up being mostly air. When he finally landed a swipe across the back of my neck that made contact I roared back and shook hard throwing him off of me. He landed with a thud hard on the ground. I heard a bone break, but he was already trying to get back up.

Not wanting this to last any longer than necessary, I quickly attacked and put my teeth to his neck, but did not bare down. I let me alpha powers flow over him to submit, and I felt him still beneath me, but I made the mistake of thinking that was submission and was about to ask my Alpha to call the challenge to my victory when the kid started to fight back the moment I stopped my powers. My teeth were still close to his neck, but he thrashed and kicked out. I tried desperately not to bite down hard enough to seriously hurt him, but enough to let him know I wasn't kidding around. Still, he fought until he finally reared up with every ounce of strength he had, right into my mouth. I knew the second my sharp canines pierced him and I tasted his blood as my wolf growled in victory trying to take full control of us. The kid went deathly still this time. I released my grip and sat back to watch and see if he would get back up, but there was too much blood lost and I knew we were on borrowed time to save him.

My wolf sat back and howled in the air. My father stood and nodded, acknowledging my victory. I quickly changed and called for the medics. My eyes caught Morris' with a sad, but honest apology. He nodded to me and mouthed thank you. I didn't know why he was thanking me. I wasn't sure the kid would survive his injuries, but at least there was still enough life in him for the medics to whisk him away in attempt.

I was angry with myself for letting it happen. This was no victory as far as I was concerned. It was an all out slaughter, and I hated myself for it. I couldn't even look Kelsey's way, though my mate was screaming in my head to shake it off. We both knew I had bigger challenges coming and I couldn't afford to beat myself up over this one. The important thing was, I won, and Kelsey was another challenge down from safety because of it. That's all that mattered and I had to force myself to concentrate only on that.

I went back to the small room at the back of the arena and just sat down on the ground letting the emotions wash over me. They changed to something positive flowing over me and I wasn't sure why until the door opened and Kelsey walked in.

"You can't do that, you know that. Someone else could feel it." I said, knowing she was sending positive alpha power to wash over me.

She shrugged. "I'm getting good at controlling it and you need it right now. Stop wallowing and get up."

I did so and watched her eyes widen and sweep over me as she realized I hadn't bothered to dress yet. A grin spread across my face as I felt her heat up inside and out. My mate wanted me as badly as I needed her.

"Come home with me."

"You know I can't. Your dad said it was okay to see you and allow our wolves to settle with the knowledge that you are ok, but that was it."

I grinned and stalked closer to her. She blushed and backed up until her back hit the wall.

"Kyle, there are people still out there waiting for you. We can't."

"I guess you better keep quiet for once then," I challenged as my lips met hers with all the frustrations and fears of the week. The last night we had been together she had been injured and I had spent it caring for her. It had been far too long since we had last really been together. The Council had planned it that way, I knew, and I knew their reasons, but I didn't care.

I didn't think she was going to submit to me, but when she did, I couldn't have stopped myself if I had wanted to. And I did not want to. I needed my mate in every sense of the word. I slowed only long enough to be careful with her clothing, even though I wanted to just rip it from her body. This wasn't the careful caressing we were used to, this was all pent up want and desire mingled with fear pouring through us and I felt like she was the air I needed to breathe and I couldn't get close enough to her. It was fast and furious as I pressed her body against the wall and we both took and gave with equal urgency. I felt sated for the first time in far too many days, even if it was over much too quickly.

Breathless and panting, I softened my grip on her and when her legs unwrapped from around my waist, I lowered her to the ground. I kissed her softer this time and pulled her to me, just holding her a minute, basking in the afterglow.

She shook her head against my chest. "There's still a lot of people out there waiting for you." *And I'm probably going to die of embarrassment when you open that door, so you won't have to worry about your other challenges anyway*, she half teased.

I laughed and reached down to gather her clothes, tossing them back to her, but I watched and didn't move to dress myself until she was fully clothed.

Worth a million challenges, babe!

She let me exit first and held back a few minutes as the crowd erupted and congratulations began. Then she tried to sneak out and melt into the crowd. Fat chance of that. I grabbed her hand and pulled her arm around my waist. This was our pack and this was my mate, their future Pack Mother and we would not hide our love. Though she was stiff, and a tad uncomfortable, she humored me.

Cole Anderson shot me a knowing look and shook his head laughing. "One down, two to go. And because of the number of challenges you've been issued, and the shortened challenge period, word has gone out that challenges will only be accepted for another seventy-two hours. After that it's closed to allow time to schedule before your challenge period ends. There's some alphas not real happy about it, but you two have the Pack Council so worried that they want this over as quickly as possible. We'll know in the next few days exactly what you two are facing."

Kelsey brightened next to me. "Really? No more challenges can be made after that?"

"That's right."

I felt her relief flood me. It made me happy to see my mate so happy.

We headed over the Crate, a public place we could spend time together and celebrate, though I still didn't feel there was much to celebrate. Kelsey and I stayed for quite awhile before we said our goodbyes. The Council was watching us closely and I was told in no uncertain terms that we were to have no further physical contact. Yeah, I'd heard that one before too. But I did try to behave and my wolf only growled slightly when Cole escorted Kelsey home instead of me. I didn't like going home alone. It felt too empty without her, so I instead went to Mom and Dad's and crashed in my old room for the night.

I slept in late, though I had planned to get to the office early to see Kelsey as soon as possible. When I finally did wake, there was a flurry of excitement through the house. Not the good kind of excitement. Several skirmishes had broken out through the night between the Westin Pack and several of the visiting packs, particularly the New York Central Pack though Morris was already busy disciplining his wolves and preparing for departure, the Irish Clan which had just arrived with Patrick O'Connell, and of course the Bulgarians.

I was told before my second cup of coffee that I would be battling O'Connell that night. I had questioned the decision as it was unheard of to have back to back challenges like that, but in light of the lack of injury from the previous challenge, the Westin Council was certain I would be up to it and the sooner the challenges were over, the better, as far as they were concerned.

I didn't have time to properly stress over the day's challenge before duty called and I was off to discipline and understand exactly what was happening.

Amidst a day of excuses and stories of he said, she said, that were enough to give anyone a headache, I was able to sneak off for a whole ten minutes to catch Kelsey on the tail end of her lunch. It was long enough for me to at least see her, kiss her, and have her wish me well before I was off and running again. Dad was equally busy as there had been so many problems uprising through the night. The day was gone in a flash with little resolved aside from a few slaps on the wrist and some extra security details issued.

Patrick had asked to meet with me prior to the night's challenge, but with everything going on, I was unable to meet his demand. Now I sat, once again, in the room I was coming to think of as a cage awaiting my second challenge. Unlike Matt Snyder, who I was sorry to hear did not survive the night, Patrick O'Connell was a worthy challenger. Not just that, but I had always known him to be a good man. I did not look forward to this battle, yet I knew I would do anything to keep Kelsey. Because of his position and power in his own right, I also could not afford to spare Patrick's life and that weighed heavily on me.

The rallying noise in the arena had grown so loud that although I could feel Kelsey's arrival, I was unable to even hear past the noise to reach out to her through our bond. In fact, it was so loud that someone had to come and motion for me to enter when the time for challenge finally came.

As I entered the arena, a roar rose up surrounding me. I saw O'Connell enter as well and nodded my acknowledgment to him. He looked upset and off. I could smell worry wafting off him and knew that would play well to my advantage. I couldn't think of him as my once childhood friend, only as my enemy and I would be victorious over him.

Don't get cocky there, hairball. I need you to stay focused. O'Connell is quick and well skilled. Elise and I watched him prepare earlier today. Your sister left visibly shaken, but even I could tell he is a solid fighter. Not as good as you, of course, but please keep your head straight and stay focused. My mate encouraged me through our bond. My eyes met her and the noise seemed to disappear. I smiled, gave her a wink and nodded.

I got this, babe, I assured her watching her nod back.

Once again only she and my father sat in the upper deck area. Should her powers try to escape he was ready to help her reign it in. She had done well during my battle with Matt, but he was hardly a real threat to me. This would be a true test to her as well as me.

O'Connell made his way to meet me in the center of the arena as my father began the slow process of quieting the crowd.

"I told you we needed to talk before this battle," he said quickly.

"I'm sorry, there were a few uprisings in the pack that had to be addressed. And honestly Patrick, what does it matter now?"

"It matters to me!" He said, looking upset. "I have to know, Kyle, is it true?"

"Is what true?"

"Kelsey, is she your one true mate."

I stopped and stared at him, curious of his sudden questions. "Yes, of course she is. You know me. Would I ever willingly battle for anyone less?"

He sighed and slammed his fist into his thigh in frustrations. "You're certain?"

"Two hundred percent."

"I know this is an unorthodox request, and I truly wish you had made time before now, but may I approach your mate? I just have to know?"

"Now?"

"Yes of course now, when else could it possibly be?"

"What do you want?"

"I need her close enough to smell her."

"Have you lost your mind?"

"Look, I only arrived this morning. I haven't had time to even properly meet her and I do not wish to risk my life without knowing for sure."

"Knowing what for sure, you're not making any sense."

"If she could ever possibly be my mate!" He screamed just as the crowd began to die down. Dad had begun to speak, and I knew we were running out of time.

"Father," I yelled up at him. "a momentary delay, please."

Kels, I need you to come down to the arena door. I told her trying to stay calm. I had no clue what was going on in Patrick's head.

Now? She demanded.

Yes, now. It's apparently important. Just come.

I watched as she whispered something to my father and made her way down. All eyes were on her. Patrick turned to stare at me after she had disappeared from our view.

"How?"

"How what, now?"

"Kyle, are you bonded to her? You only asked your father for a moment's delay, yet she's on her way down here, isn't she?"

"Yes, as you requested." I said, trying curb my irritation with him. What was he up to?

"But you didn't actually ask her to come down here."

"Yes. I did." I said before realizing what he was talking about.

His eyes widened as I made my silent confession unknowingly and I cursed under my breath.

"You're already bonded? How? How long?"

"It doesn't matter."

"Of course it matters, Kyle. It matters to me."

"Why? I mean let's be real here. It's not my mate you want, it's my pack position."

He shook his head, "No, that's what my father wants."

I felt the truth in his words and bit back my anger.

Kelsey opened the door and walked out. I politely introduced them.

"Hello Kelsey. May I, smell you?" He hesitated slightly, and even blushed a little.

She looked at me seeking permission first. I nodded and she stepped closer to him. He stared at my mark on her neck before leaning in and taking a deep whiff. She was supposed to keep it covered during the challenge period, but I knew she wore that shirt on purpose today to show it off. He stood back looking almost sad.

"This morning, you came to watch me fight."

She nodded. "Yes I did."

"You cannot be her though. My apologies. I knew, I just had to be certain." He smiled sweetly at her. "You may return now." He told her, pointing up to where my dad still stood looking sullen and confused.

"Okay," she said, slowly dragging out the words, but turning to make her way back.

He watched her leave before turning back to me. My wolf was ready to rip him into shreds. If he was making an attempt at a distraction to throw me off his game, he was about to realize his plan was backfiring badly. I had never been so pumped to fight in my life. I could already smell the stench of his death in the air.

He clapped a hand onto the back of my shoulder in a too friendly gesture as we made our way back to the center of the arena.

"She's a beautiful woman. Any wolf would be lucky to have her." By this point I was only seeing red and could barely hear Kelsey's small voice in my head trying to soothe and calm me before this battle. "You are a very lucky man, Kyle."

I looked at him like he had gone mad, but he just continued to ramble.

"Earlier when your mate came to watch me, I felt her," he said in almost a whisper. My fists balled at my sides and he shook his head, "Not Kelsey, HER, my one true mate. She's here, Kyle, and now that I have her scent I'll stop at nothing to find her. I believe she arrived with Kelsey, or around the same time, but I can't be certain as there were so many in attendance. I think she's definitely from your pack though. Will you allow me to stay and track her? Let's face it my da's not going to let me come home after this."

"What are you talking about? You're not making any sense."

He actually held up one finger my way before turning towards my father again. Did he have a death wish? I was already pissed enough with his outrageous request. Kelsey was back by my dad's side, and all eyes were on us when he spoke again.

"Alpha of the Westin Pack," he formally said, loud enough for all to hear, "my apologies for the delay. As you know I only arrived this morning with the challenge blindly bid on my behalf. I only wished to meet your lovely future Pack Mother in person." I let out a growl, but he continued on like it was nothing. "Upon doing so, I regrettably must request your approval to renege my challenge at this time. It is clear to me that Kelsey is Kyle's one true mate, and I will not come between them."

The roar of loud whispers and a few cries of outrage were deafening. It took my father some time to get them settled, and I nearly doubled over as bile rose up in my mouth at the suddenness of his words. He was reneging. I wouldn't have to fight him. I would not have to kill my friend to keep my mate.

"You're serious?" I asked him. "This isn't some sort of sick prank of yours to throw me off my game going into challenge?"

"Kyle, we've known each other a long time. We've had our

211

differences certainly, but I've always considered you a friend. My request stands. May I stay in Westin territory in search of my own true mate?"

I stood tall and grasped his forearm as he did mine in the formal manner of which his pack greeted respect. "Aye, you may." I told him as the biggest smile lit my face. He closed his other arm around me in a brutal hug that I returned. "Thank you."

My father was still waving for quiet.

"You are certain of this, Patrick O'Connell of the Irish Clan?"

Without a word, Patrick dropped to one knee, bowed his head then exposed his neck to me. When I nodded he jumped up.

"I've never been more certain of anything, sir."

"Then so shall it be."

With that the noise grew again and it didn't take long before the door to the arena cracked open and Kelsey ran across to us, launching herself into my arms. I caught her midair and her legs easily wrapped around my waist as she kissed me for all to see. I knew we'd catch some hell for it, but I didn't care and it certainly didn't seem to bother Patrick who was grinning almost as widely as I was. Setting her back on her feet she hugged close to me fitting perfectly into my side and we both turned to the man who had given such grace to us.

"Patrick, you are welcome in Westin territory anytime, and for as long as you would like. In fact, if I'm honest, Kelsey has very little left at her place. We'll move out her remaining things and she can stay with Mom and Dad until the challenge period has ended and you are welcome to her house for the duration of your stay." She nudged me and quirked an eyebrow up at me. I just winked at her.

Not like you need the place anymore anyway. I reminded her.

"Don't get cocky, Kyle. Andon is not going to be so gracious and you know it."

"I have two days left to prepare, it will all work out."

"And really, it's fine," Kelsey rambled. "I so rarely use it anyway, might as well give it up." She blushed all over realizing her admittance.

Patrick laughed, a genuine full belly laugh. "Fear not, your secret is safe with me."

"This place it going to be insane tonight. How about we all

lie low. Drinks back at our place?" Kelsey elbowed me at the insinuation regardless of the truth in it. It was our home.

"Yes, I think that would be wise."

"I'll see if the girls want to join us and we'll meet you at home," she caught herself that time and blushed deeper. "I mean at your house.

Kelsey

Chapter 29

I swung by the Alpha's house to see if Lily and Elise wanted to join us as they had already left the arena. Lily was game for it, but Elise still seemed off. She said she wasn't feeling well and would just stay in, but something told me there was more to it than that. I was worried about my friend.

Still, there was much to celebrate, so I pushed my concerns aside and Lily and I sped off to Kyle's house to meet the boys. The entire way she was babbling about how cute Patrick was and how sweet it was for him to drop the challenge. That girl had more crushes than I would ever keep up with.

It was fun getting to know Patrick O'Connell. He had an easy nature and was quite animated when he talked and that accent of his just drew me in. Okay, not just me, I noticed, seeing the dreamy eyed glaze on Lily's face. I'm pretty sure that boy could have been reciting the phone book and the look wouldn't have changed.

Snuggled up to Kyle on the couch with my feet propped up on the coffee table and a few drinks to the wind, life was really great for that brief moment. We all eventually crashed right there in the living room and waking up in his arms just felt righter than anything in the last week had.

But, all good things must come to a crashing halt. With the 72 hour warning having been issued, we all knew it was only a matter of time. And I knew when the phone rang, stirring the others back to life that it wasn't going to be good.

"Hey," I heard Kyle say. "What?" He ran his hand through his already ruffled morning hair. "Jesus, Dad. Are you kidding me?" There was a pause and I tried to listen in and gain some knowledge both with my ears and through the bond, but nothing. "Yeah, okay. Yes," he said a little louder and full of frustration. "I understand, Dad." He sighed, "It is what it is. We'll do what we have to.... okay, bye."

"It's bad isn't it?" I asked softly.

He looked around at the audience before us and I knew he didn't want to talk in front of them, but I had to know.

"Spill it, Kyle. I'm a big girl. I can handle it."

He played with my hand almost absentmindedly and couldn't look me in the eyes. "First," he began slowly, "since I didn't fight last night, Andon's challenge was moved up to tonight." He paused and let that sink in. "You have three potential challengers, Kels. And I have a potential for another five. All of them put in their request for consideration and extension, meaning they haven't formally issued the challenges, but have been granted the right to do so for the remaining challenge period despite the 72 hour warning issued."

"What the hell? Kyle that would be eight challenges for you. EIGHT?!?" Lily screeched with barely controlled hysterics.

"Lil, I can't think of that right now. I have to concentrate on just surviving the Andon challenge tonight."

I hugged him, trying to hold back tears. I wasn't scared for myself. Something freed in me during the Christine challenge and I no longer had any doubt in my capabilities. But back to back challenges against Kyle were causing a lot of stress on both of us.

"Do you want me to help prepare you for your battle against Andon?" Patrick offered.

Kyle nodded, "That would be nice. I could use a solid sparring partner this afternoon. But for the remainder of this morning I do not wish to discuss or think about challenges any further. How about pancakes?" He winked at me and I knew he was just trying to put up a good front.

Still, I played along. "Only if you have bacon to go with them."

"You drive a tough bargain, mate."

We kept the remaining morning to a light banter, but there was a falseness to it, an evil lingered over us all. And when it was time for Kyle to begin preparations for the evening, he and I said our see ya laters. Never goodbye! And he and Patrick left in reverent silence.

Lily wasn't about to leave me alone feeding off my fears, so I was dragged to the Alpha house with her to waste the afternoon. I almost wished it were a work day so I'd at least have something to occupy my time.

We found Elise sitting in the living room staring at a magazine but really just looking lost in thought.

"E, you okay?"

"Yeah, are you feeling better?" I added.

She looked up. "Um, yeah, I'm fine. What are you two doing here?"

"Wasting time," we said in unison. "Jinx." We giggled. "Double jinx!"

"You heard about Kyle's next challenge, right?"

"You mean against Andon? Did they set a date?"

I sucked in a sharp breath as Lily rubbed my shoulders in loving comfort.

"It's tonight, E. Since he didn't actually fight last night, the Council bumped it up to tonight."

Elise started crying. "I'm sorry. I don't know what's come over me lately. I just feel so off and out of it. I don't know how to explain it. I should have been there with you guys last night. I didn't know he'd have to fight today."

I smelled something strange waft through the house, and my shoulders stiffened. I knew my hackles would be standing tall if I were in my fur. It was a foreign smell. No, a foreign wolf. Jason Westin poked his head in and I was briefly confused.

"Ah, good, Kelsey, just the gal I was looking for. I'm afraid, you have a visitor."

I let out a low growl of warning when Andon appeared behind my Alpha.

"Kelsey, you won't be alone with him, but as a challenger and therefore a potential mate to you, he has the right to request your audience. Don't worry, I'll be with you the entire time."

I know my eyes begged and pleaded for him not to make me do it. But there was no getting out of it as I was escorted past my enemy and into Jason's office. Andon entered and closed the door behind him. I had to fight to maintain control of my powers as I suddenly felt caged in with this man.

He eyed me suspiciously, and my eyes never left his. I knew he was an alpha in his own right, but when he tried to power play me I simply held my ground and bit back the release of my own alpha powers.

"There is much spirit and stubbornness in you, little one." He said in an accent so thick I could barely discern he was speaking English. "But fear not, for I am quite powerful and need a strong she-wolf to stand by my side. You will take some breaking in, but I am confident you will do nicely." He gave me an eerie smile of sorts that sent shivers through my body and as I was about to show him just how powerful he wasn't, Jason stepped in and intervened.

"That is enough, Andon. You will not upset the girl any further. You have met her, now I must ask you leave my home."

I felt the wall of alpha power against alpha power and gave a small boost to Jason's thinking they wouldn't notice. The quirk of an eyebrow from Andon made me momentarily fear I had been wrong in that assumption.

"You intrigue me greatly, little wolf. I shall have more of you tonight, after my victory."

He turned on his heels and exited as Jason physically held me back from attacking him.

"Kelsey," he demanded, pouring his power over me. Even though I knew I was stronger and could take him, I respected him too much to ever use my powers on him again, so I settled. "You know you can't afford to lose control like that. Especially with the likes of the Bulgarians. I don't know if he felt your additional power as I tried to make it appear I was pushing mine stronger against him, but please, do not intercede again."

"I am sorry, Alpha." I said formally, baring my neck to him.

He hesitated briefly before pulling me into his arms in the biggest fatherly hug I could ever remember in my life. I embraced him back, only withdrawing when Mary entered the room to check on us, ranting over the rudeness of the Bulgarian.

The Westins kept me close by their sides, and I was struck by how much they had become family to me. It wasn't just me and Kyle. I had a mom, and a dad, and sisters and brothers. My life mattered to them and theirs to me. Chase and Liam took on a particularly protective role that day, even going so far as to escorting me to the pavilion above the arena where I would stand and wait and watch.

The Council had decided not to stand with us there once again, but it wasn't just me and Jason this time. I was surrounded by my family. I was surrounded by love. It felt good and terrified me all at the same time as it signified the true importance of this challenge.

I'm here, my mate. Be strong, and fight hard. I paused. *Cause there's no way I'm waking up to that dog breath every morning.*

He laughed and then growled. *Did that dog come near you today?*

Only formally and your father would not allow him alone with me. It was fine. Just, just kill him quickly. I nearly spat out the words in my head and I felt the truth of them strengthen Kyle.

Things moved fast after that. Jason called the contenders out. The formalities were given. And they stripped and waited for the signal to shift. Unlike Matt Snyder who took forever and a day to shift during his challenge, Andon wasted no time and was stalking towards Kyle as he shifted. His wolf was big and powerful looking. Bigger even than Kyle's. But bigger didn't always mean better. I quickly noted he wasn't as quick and that he was slower on his left side than his right when he attacked. I wished I could communicate with Kyle to give him the heads up.

Heard ya loud and clear, babe! An excited voice came through our bond.

I gasped a little in shock, but Andon had snapped close to one of Kyle's legs at that exact instant so no one thought anything suspicious of it.

Stay to his left. I don't think his peripheral vision is very strong on that side. He's going to try and force you to his right though. I directed him.

Okay, okay, I got this, now let me fight already.

I laughed wanting desperately to cheer him on for all to see and hear but knowing it wasn't allowed during the challenges for me to show favoritism. I started to cheer in my head instead, but then I didn't want to distract him so I tried to just send calming vibes through our bond or nothing at all. This was such a new development I didn't know what to make of it or what to do.

I stood there helplessly watching as Andon jabbed at him and he jabbed back. Kyle got a few good bites in and Andon was bleeding now, his fur caked in blood down his left hind leg, but he fought on, perhaps more violently seemingly angered by the bite.

Kyle kept pursuit. He smelled blood and I felt his wolf dominate control. His alpha powers flowed freely demanding the other wolf submit to him. But Andon was an alpha in his own right and fought back with his own powers. It was unlike either of the previous challenges I had fought or observed.

When Kyle got the upper hand, and began making advances on him, I squealed in my head in excitement. The energy and the rush of the victory in sight was contagious and our entire pack was on its feet cheering him on, but he faltered when I squealed. I hadn't meant to distract him. It was the last thing I ever wanted, but it was just enough for Andon to take advantage and suddenly he had Kyle pinned on his back snapping his massive jaws at him.

Jason Westin's hand was on my arm and I knew it wasn't good. He was worried and prepared to whisk me away before my powers set free on all who attended. I was having to fight back to reign in my control as I watched in utter disbelief.

Andon chomped down hard on Kyle's right front paw that was protecting his neck, and in that moment, I felt every ounce of pain my mate was suffering and I held my arm close to my chest, dropping to my knees, and screamed out in pain. I saw blood flowing from my right hand and the pain continued as I screamed. I was vaguely aware that all cheers had stopped and all eyes turned towards me.

Kelsey, I heard Kyle scream through our bond.

I couldn't respond, too shocked by the pain and blood, but I heard a large growl and felt my powers being pulled from me as Kyle channeled everything we both had in a full on attack of Andon. Jason dropped to his knees gasping at the same instant. Kyle's power, my power, and the pack's power combined crippling Andon in the flash of eye as Kyle sank his teeth into his neck. I tasted his blood and fur in my mouth, spitting and gagging on the invisible taste of it, and felt the snap of his neck despite being nowhere near him.

The second the wolf's life extinguished, Kyle changed and ran straight for me, screaming my name both through the bond and aloud. The others parted ways and watched in solemn shock as he reached my side. My entire body was shaking uncontrollably.

"Move back," I heard a voice demand. "Give her some space. Kelsey, breathe, come on honey, just breathe for me." A familiar voice I couldn't quite place encouraged me.

"Dude, I thought you said things hadn't escalated this far." I finally recognized Micah's voice as he scolded Kyle.

"It hadn't. I mean, seriously, we were telling you the truth. This is entirely new. I swear." He rambled. "Just promise me she's going to be okay."

Micah started to lift me, but Kyle growled aggressively.

"Okay, okay," he said backing up with his hands raised in retreat. "Jesus, Kyle, you're fueling the full Westin Pack power now, you gotta calm down, man. You carry her. She's mostly just in shock. Her hand is already healing at the same pace as yours and since you were in wolf form, that's accelerated. Your adrenaline is so hyped, I doubt you're feeling a thing right now."

Kyle reached down and carefully picked me up. "I got you, baby. You're safe now. Nothing's going to happen to you." Kyle crooned reassuringly in a soft lulling voice and I fought the darkness threatening to overtake me. Just before my eyes closed, I saw three faces sternly watching the scene from a distance. Who were they? I wondered.

When I came to, I was tucked snuggly into bed. My bed. Mine and Kyle's. I was home. I deeply inhaled the familiarity of our combined scents. The air was tainted with that of other wolves. Opening myself to my wolf hearing I heard low mumbled voices from down the hall.

Kyle? I tried to reach out through our bond and immediately heard footsteps running down the hall.

"She's awake," I heard him tell someone just before opening the door to our bedroom. "Hey sleepyhead. You had me really worried. How do you feel?"

I began to sit up, expecting my head to throb and my hand to ache, but nothing. Hmm. Okay, so I sat up all the way and shrugged. "I feel fine." I examined my hand. Not even a scratch. "Look, all healed too."

Kyle smiled and held his out to show me, "Mine too."

I yawned and stretched. My head was a little foggy.

"Doc gave you a sedative to help you sleep, but you took to

it a little too well."

"What do you mean?"

"Kels, you've been out for two days."

"What?" I exclaimed sitting up quickly. "Two days?"

"Yeah, babe, you had me terrified. The whole family's been here off and on keeping me from panicking. Are you sure you feel okay?"

I did a quick self-assessment. "Yeah, I feel fine, perfectly normal." And then tears started flooding my eyes and I jumped out of bed and threw myself into his arms. "I thought I'd lost you. I was so scared."

A soothing but strong hand rubbed my back reassuringly, easing the tension and fears as I cried in his arms.

"It's okay, I'm here."

"This is real, right? If not, I don't even care, as long as I can feel your arms around me."

He chuckled. "It's real and I'm here."

A throat cleared behind us before I even had a chance to kiss him.

"Hello, Kelsey," Micah said. "Can I run a few tests on you, just precautionary."

I looked up at Kyle and he nodded and smiled reassuringly.

"Okay," I said, taking his hand and dragging him to the bed with me. I sat down but didn't let go. No way was Kyle getting away from me anytime soon. I didn't give a damn what the Council had to say about it either.

Micah was quick with his questions and basic checkup, or so that's what they told me it was. Since my stay in the hospital at age twelve I had successfully avoided doctors for fear they'd be able to tell I was different. This was an odd and slightly embarrassing process I only had vague memories of from my past. Kyle stayed by my side the entire time.

When the exam was done, Micah asked if he could run some bond tests and after consulting with Kyle, we agreed.

Okay, we'll start off with some basics. He took out a pen and wrote something on his notepad and showed it to Kyle, though I couldn't see it.

"Kelsey, what number did I just show Kyle?"

One thousand and twenty-one. Kyle told me through our

bond.

"One thousand and twenty-one." I repeated aloud.

"Good, now Kelsey," he said, flashing the notepad my way.

I'm sexy and I know it. I snorted ,relaying the message Micah had written

"Yeah you are!" Kyle exclaimed and Micah knew his message had been received without further confirmation.

"Great, now Kyle, shift for me."

He did without further prompting. Then he flashed the notepad to his wolf.

Micah's a dick and I'm not repeating that one. He said sullenly.

"Um, apparently, he wasn't happy with what you wrote. He said you're a dick and he's not repeating it."

Micah laughed so hard a tear escaped his eye. "Okay, switch."

I didn't want to strip in front of Micah, but looking down at my favorite pajamas, I didn't want to ruin them either. So, I scooted behind the bed and stripped and changed in record time. Kyle had changed back to his skin and sat gloriously naked, without a care. Part of me envied that about him. I knew I'd always be self-conscious.

Micah flashed another card to Kyle.

Now he's just being an ass. I heard him say loud and clear. It was so surreal, the first time I'd ever heard Kyle clearly when we both weren't either in human or wolf form. *He wants you to howl once then turn three times in a circle.*

I did as instructed, and suddenly Kyle was by my side nudging his muzzle into my neck. This time Micah pushed the big wolf aside, earning himself a small growl, before showing me the message.

He wants us to run into the living room and jump on Lily. This is so dumb. I know I rolled my eyes, and it probably looked ridiculously human, despite my animal shape, but we did as we were told, and after hearing Lil scream in surprise, we were called back and told we could return to human form

"Okay, now that the fun is over, let's get down to the important test." He had us both sit side by side on the bed and he took out something that looked like a tiny tomahawk, only plastic, and he hit it against Kyle's knee. Without warning my leg shot up in the air in synch with his. He repeated a few other similar tests before pricking my finger with a needle and causing it to bleed. Kyle held his hand up and stared in wonder as his same finger bled too.

"Not exactly anything we didn't suspect, but man, this is insane, you guys. And I'm overriding anything the Council says and quarantining you both till the full challenge period has ended. This pack is not risking the loss of you both. Your bond is sealed. Challenges are over. I've already discussed security with your dad. You'll have round the clock guards surrounding the house on all sides. The Bulgarians are already causing a bit of stink saying your dramatics were faked to give Kyle the upper hand to defeat Andon. The Grand Council has been called in to assess. It's not pretty, guys, but it'll all blow over soon."

KYLE
Chapter 30

I couldn't stop pacing the room and every few minutes I had to touch Kelsey just to keep myself grounded. Calling on Micah's medical assessment, my father shutdown the mating challenges and ordered all foreign wolves from our territory. I still couldn't believe it. It was too much.

Currently he was in his office arguing with the Grand Council over it. People still didn't know the full truth of Kelsey's powers, not even Micah, and everyone was so distracted by her screams and collapse during my last challenge with Andon from Bulgaria, that they didn't seem to suspect anything either despite the fact that I was a hundred times more powerful in his defeat than I should have been. Still the strength in our bond was enough to spread gossip quickly.

I cringed, haunted by her screams of pain and fear when Andon had attacked me at the challenge. My power, combined with hers, and even pulled through the pack line I'm told, had given me the force and willpower needed to defeat him. I could never imagine the fierce protectiveness that had overpowered me knowing my mate was in pain. And the two days I watched her lay there, still and unmoving, afterwards made my stomach roll just thinking of it. I thought I had lost her. It was the scariest moment of my life. I walked over and brushed a hand across her shoulders as I passed her in my pacing. It calmed me and I needed to touch her for affirmation that she was truly okay.

It was still unclear when the Grand Council had arrived exactly. My dad hadn't even mentioned them to me and I was furious because of it. All I knew was that they were here now and they were watching us.

My greatest fear was that the Bulgarians would cause enough trouble to instigate a formal inquiry into my mate's background. I had already heard from several sources that they were screaming foul play in the defeat of Andon.

Pack Councils vary in numbers based on the size and needs and politics of the pack. Westin Pack has seven council members overseeing pack needs. But the Grand Council only ever had five. And once on the Grand Council you were there until death. It was a lifetime commitment. They released all ties to their original pack, including their mates and pups. The thought behind it was that they have absolutely no loyalties aside from the greater good of the wolf shifter world.

Of course, that's how things were supposed to work. You often found Grand Council members to be extremely old and wise, but they were still fallible beings as well with self-motives and were not above corruption. In order to overthrow a Grand Council ninety percent of the established packs must join together to make it happen. Since packs were very territorial and rarely agreed on anything, this had only happened once in all of known wolf history.

The current Grand Council is comprised of Cedric, Omar, Titus, Victor, and Callum. Callum came to them on curious terms having been initiated far younger than his counterparts and without having taken a mate previously. The other four surpassed their mates in life making them more ideal for the positions. Then again, this council had issued more than its fair share of questionable laws and verdicts. I didn't trust them with the safety of my mate and though we hadn't discussed it, I knew Kelsey was aware of the bags packed and stored under our bed in case we found cause to flee for her safety.

"Titus, you know me, there is nothing underhanded going on here. I have told the Grand Council, we do not understand why their bond grew so quickly or why it began to forge prior to their actual consummation. They fought it for over two years. Clearly their wolves did not believe that time to be rejection." Jason's voice boomed from the front hallway outside his office.

"I hear what you are saying, Jason, but it doesn't make sense. We understand and witnessed with our own eyes the extent of their bond at the challenge. The Grand Council will support you in terminating any further mating challenges for either of them. However," I held my breath waiting to hear the bad news I felt in my bones was coming, "the Bulgarians are demanding a full inquiry into the female. Stories have floated around that she was a lone wolf permitted to live in Westin Territory and even protected by your own Council despite blatant disregard for you and your pack. It is unclear exactly what the special circumstances were around that situation, but we do intend to get to the bottom of it. There will be a full inquiry. I am sorry. There is nothing I can do to stop it."

My heart lurched into my throat. The Bulgarians were going to pursue this because I killed Andon. Going after my mate was nothing more than revenge, but there was no way for them to know the skeletons they were about to find in her closet by such an inquiry. What if they were able to verify her heritage? What if someone remembered her and her family? What would happen when they discovered she was an alpha female who escaped from her childhood death sentence and was raised without a pack, fearing all wolves?

I couldn't take that chance. I looked around the great room, watching my siblings interact with my beautiful mate. They fully accepted her even knowing what she was. They would fight to the death to protect her, but could I allow them to do that? No. I knew I couldn't. Our best chance of survival would be to go off-grid until this all blew over.

But, Kyle, that'll just make us look all the more suspicious. Kelsey's sweet voice answered in my head.

I should have known she was listening in on all my thoughts. She looked so peaceful and deep in conversation with my brother Liam that I honestly thought she had been spared overhearing Dad's conversation.

Kels, I can't sit around and wait for them to come for you, for us, because once they know what you are, they will have no choice but to come for us. I don't see how we can win this.

Our pack in strong. We are strong. And our family is worth fighting for. If I die, you will too. I will never allow that to happen. You felt our combined power. The strength of it. We are powerful together, and I say we stand and fight. I did nothing wrong. I'm not a threat to anyone except those threatening our pack. And can you honestly tell me that even if you and I ran, that they wouldn't take it out on them? We have to stay and protect them. It's what we were born to do, together.

I walked over to where she sat on the couch and dropped to my knees before her. I laid my head in her lap and nodded. She stroked my hair lovingly. I just wanted to throw up.

"Ok, if that's what you want. We'll stay and fight."

"Huh?" The moment was broken by Liam. "Uh, what's going on here? I feel like I missed something. Is everything ok?"

"No," Kelsey said, "but it will be. It has to be."

When Titus left, Dad called me into his office.

"Liam, she doesn't leave your sight, understood?"

"Uh, yeah, got it big bro. I'll guard her with my life."

"Okay, spill it, what is going on? That felt really intense, and I know you two were doing that bonding mind trick thingy again," I heard Liam demand as I walked away, and her twinkle of laughter in response, softened the rock that was pressing down on my chest making it difficult to breath.

Dad closed the door behind me when I entered so we could talk in private.

"Kamen, the Bulgarian Pack Alpha, is insisting on an inquiry to the challenge. He was so certain that Andon would defeat you, that he is in disbelief of the turn of events. Many rumors are floating around as to what happened."

I gritted my teeth, "Like what?"

"Well, for starters, that Kelsey was faking pain to draw his attention away and give you the break needed to end him."

"That's absurd, her hand was bleeding."

"I know, son, I was there for the front row seat to it all, remember? And it is also being said that I collapsed under your alpha power during the challenge. This is causing quite an uproar with allegations that you and Kelsey have assumed leadership in the pack." He cleared his throat, "And there a rumor going around that she is a, well, a witch."

"What?!?!?"

"I know it's absurd, but if that rumor doesn't end soon it will lead to a full investigation into her past. Before the killings of female alphas began, they were often called witches. Women of magical powers over other wolves. We need to take this rumor serious and stop it at all costs. Do you understand?"

"Yes sir."

"You have your bags packed should they come for her?"

"Yes, but she isn't going to run, Dad. She's become very protective of this family and this pack and she is adamant that we can not leave everyone to face the wake of this alone."

"Kyle, I'm not going to lose you over this. If it comes down to a fight, I need you to take your mate and leave. They come after her, they come after you."

They come after you, they come after this entire pack. No one will back down from this. I heard her warn me and I knew she was speaking truth.

"Kelsey believes the pack will rise to protect us if it comes to that."

My father sighed looking far older than he had even one day earlier. "You know they will, but we're talking a potential war here, Kyle."

"I think we need to bring in the Pack Council and formally fill them in. If they agree with Kelsey, then we need to hold an emergency pack meeting to prepare our wolves. If they do not, when the time comes I will grab her and go despite her protests. They will not kill my mate without first killing me."

Dad nodded in agreement and made a few quick phone calls. Within an hour, the full Pack Council was assembled in his office and Kelsey joined me as we filled them in on what we knew of her past and confirmed to their shock and horror that she was indeed a female alpha.

"This will go to war amongst the packs when they discover what she is, and I do not think Kamen will back down until he has all the answers, including this," Ambrose spoke up first.

"Yes, but she is pack. Have you not seen the response of the pack to her presence? She has allegiance of many already. They will fight for her. I have no doubt in that," Quinton spoke, generally the quietest of the bunch which caused the others to subdue.

"I move to tell the pack. Hold a special pack meeting and discuss this with them as a whole. If they fear what she is and the outcome of that news getting out, then Kyle is prepared to take her and run," Kelsey started to protest but I shook my head and she submitted as Cole continued, "But, if they are willing to stand in support of her, then I say we prepare to fight. This is our future Alpha and Pack Mother we are talking about here. Kyle will die by her side if we do not. We can not allow that to happen."

Heads nodded around the room and the issue was settled. We would move forward with talking to the pack. It was a risk, especially since Kelsey's alpha powers had not yet come to light. Still we all felt we were on borrowed time with that and needed to proactively stay ahead of the Grand Council and whatever packs aligned to take her.

The emergency pack meeting was called for that very night. Because of the severity in the nature and because, despite my father's insistence for the visiting packs to clear out, with the Grand Council's presence in Westin Territory, there were still more unwanted ears potentially listening in than desired, so the meeting was being held in the sub-basement of the pack house which was fully shielded from prying eyes and ears, same as the offices in Westin Foundation and my father's office in our family home. The room was much smaller though so wolves were brought in in groups of thirty by alphabetical order.

It was a good plan also in that the numbers were small enough not to draw too much attention to the outsiders and should the pack not accept Kelsey's power and position, we would not be ganged up on by the entirety of the pack at once. I honestly didn't think that would happen, but had to be prepared for the possibility. Because of this, I strategically placed Kelsey near the emergency exit that only a handful of people knew existed and even fewer knew where the escape tunnels exited. I would do anything to protect her, even against those I cared about.

When the first group arrived, I was an aggressive nervous mess. It was my mate that had to calm me and she chose to speak up on her own behalf. I was equally humbled and grumbled over it. On the one hand I wanted to take the lead and properly introduce her, but on the other hand, I wanted to keep her secret safe and protected. I was a mess. She was right to take the lead.

"Hello," she greeted everyone equally. I knew the other wolves felt my unease and it stirred their own, but she smiled and welcomed everyone and almost knew each of their names. I wondered when that had happened.

"Please take a seat, this won't take long." She said with

authority. "Most of you know my story by now. But there is a part of it that was held back to protect you all as much as me, but circumstances are changing quickly and a pack joint decision needs to be made immediately."

There were murmurs of confusion around the room, but my father nodded and raised his hand asking them all to settle and hear her out.

"I know you all are fully aware of the rumors that Kyle and I have fully bonded. I know you saw the scene I caused at the challenge. That was not faked, our bond has sealed."

Again a few concerned whispers.

"We don't know why this happened so quickly, but there are a few theories, and unfortunately it was enough to stir questions and a formal inquiry to the Grand Council forced through the Bulgarians who are angry over Andon's defeat."

She paused again and let that sink in.

"I've always told you the truth. I do not know where I come from, or what pack I may have once belonged to. I do not know for sure why my parents chose to raise me away from a pack, or why they told me to fear wolves, and never mentioned what I truly am. I'll likely never have these answers, however, with Kyle and Jason's help we do have a theory. And there's no easy way to say this, so here goes, I am a natural born alpha female."

She hesitated and waited for reactions, but there was complete silence.

"We believe this is why my parents acted as they did. We believe they were trying to save my life. It is also suspected that this may be why Kyle and I bonded as quickly as we did. And this is something we fear could come out in the Grand Council's inquiry into me."

I was taken back by the fierce grumbles that followed in that. My dad again raised a hand to silence them as I began mentally preparing to protect and remove my mate.

"You all know the implications of what she is saying." Cole Anderson spoke up. "If they find out what she really is, they will no doubt order her death, and with that comes the death of Kyle too. We are certain of this. Micah has examined their bond and there is no doubt here. You all know what's at stake. We are risking the loss of both our future Alpha and Pack Mother if this comes to light. Kyle is prepared to run and live in exile to keep her alive, in which case we will still lose our future Alpha and Pack Mother."

That brought up a fury of angry voices.

Leo Tripp stood amongst the crowd and raised his hand. "What does the Pack Council propose?"

"We are not proposing anything right now," Saul assured them only to be received by angrier voices. "We are giving you this knowledge and as a pack will decide what is best for all."

Leo smiled, "In that case, there's no discussion far as I'm concerned. Kelsey is pack and we protect our own." He turned directly to Kelsey. "I will fight till my dying breath to protect you, future Pack Mother." Then he kneeled before all and bared his neck to her in allegiance. Many others dropped to their knees pledging allegiance with him, but not all.

Sally Merchant stood and raised her hand. "Kelsey, you know I love you and appreciate our friendship, but I have to know," turning towards her Alpha, "Alpha, is she a threat or danger to us? There is a reason female alphas are sentenced to death. They are too powerful. Have her powers even been tested? Are we certain she is what she says?"

"Oh, we're certain," Vanessa Relic spoke up. "Trust me, being on her wrong side isn't exactly fun." That earned a few chuckles. "But a danger, no, not to us at least. I don't know this for sure, but having been on the receiving end of her powers, I would say they are defensive and protective in nature. I do not believe she was even aware she had them when I goaded her over Kyle causing a surprising jolt to surface."

Kelsey smiled and laughed, "I am truly sorry. I didn't even know I could do that at the time, Vanessa. I have learned to control them since. Honestly we believe they were entirely dormant until you provoked me." That earned her many laughs and nods or approval. They all knew how aggressive Vanessa had been to claim me.

"To answer your question, Sally, yes, I have tested Kelsey's powers myself and she is very strong. But no, I do not feel she is a danger to our pack. If anything, she is a danger to anyone seeking to harm our pack. She is also able to combine powers with Kyle and both can easily pull pack power on their own now. Powerful? Strong? Most definitely. But a risk to us. No."

She seemed pleased with his answer and turned back to Kelsey who laid a soft hand on my arm and stepped forward. I hadn't even realized I had taken up position in front of her readying myself for anything coming our way. I didn't like her exposing herself as she stepped forward, but I felt like it was about to be a profound moment and bit back my natural urge to protect her.

"Kelsey, can you push your power out for all to feel?"

"I can, but please do not ask me too. I do not wish to demand allegiance from anyone. I am asking if you will stand up for me, and for Kyle, should the threat arise against us."

"I will." Sally said without hesitation and the remaining in the room dropped to their knees with her.

"I'd still like to feel your power, Kelsey. Are you controlled enough to make it present without being demanding?"

I understood what she was asking. She wanted to know how much control Kelsey had on it. My mate nodded.

"I am still learning, but I know there are different types of alpha power. There is the quick and absolute power of defense, which, I sincerely regret Vanessa having to have faced. I had to learn to control it during the challenges and honestly it was easier to do battling Christine, than to have to watch Kyle suffer at the hands of another and not protect him. There is also the power of demand which the Alpha gives with a command or order. If I told you, Sally Merchant, to rise now, you would do so." As proof the heat of her power propelled forward but only to Sally who stood and dropped her gaze to the floor unable to look at her. "There is also the power of love, acceptance, and commitment. I discovered this mutually with Kyle after the allegiances granted me at the end of my challenge with Christine." The room suddenly flooded with warmth and happiness as she let her power flow easily from her.

I stepped up next to her and taking her hand released my own power to join hers. She looked at me and smiled warmly. Combined it had a very calming effect on every person in the room. I knew when she cut it off and I did the same. The others began to rise and stir and murmurs were heard throughout.

"Thank you for your demonstration, you are indeed powerful, but controlled and I would never believe you a danger to our pack." Sally confirmed unnecessarily. "I will stand with you should the need arise, even against the Grand Council."

A census of consent was taken and all agreed they were ready and willing to fight for her, for us, for pack.

Group after group came and went with the same results and a unanimous decision was made. I knew Kelsey was wearing down, exhausted from the day's events, both emotionally and physically and excused us as soon as the last completed. I had never been prouder to be a Westin than I was that night.

Kelsey

Chapter 31

A knock at the door jolted me awake. I looked at the digital alarm clock on the nightstand next to Kyle's side of the bed. Two twenty-six am. We had barely laid down. The urgent knock sounded again and I shook Kyle but he was dead to the world. Out like a light and snoring loudly. I stumbled out of bed and down the hall to the sound of more urgent knocking.

When I opened the door five men stood before me.

"Kelsey Adams. We have been issued a formal inquiry for background check. Are you aware of who we are?"

I nodded, "Yes, you're the Grand Council members."

"That is correct, and we mean you no harm."

"Mean me no harm? Then why are you knocking down my door in the middle of the night?"

"We assure you, we want no problems," the short one I knew was Omar, spoke up. "We only want this over quickly without issues and concerns escalated from your pack."

I nodded. It sounded reasonable even if didn't sit well with me.

Kyle? Kyle wake up, and get out here! I screamed into our bond.

"What is it you want from me?" I asked hesitantly allowing them in and motioning for them to sit.

"We just have a few questions to ask and a little blood sample to take."

"Blood? Why?"

"Do you know Kamen of the Bulgarian Pack?"

"I've heard the name."

"Well, the Bulgarians have brought up some concerns regarding the strength of your bond to Kyle Westin."

"I understand they are upset because he beat their challenger in battle."

"There's some truth to that which is why we're trying to keep a low profile and get through this as quickly as possible."

Another, with dark hair and a slight foreign accent spoke next. "Seems there was some hype around here these last few years about you. A little lone wolf squatting in Westin Territory. It should have come as no shock to anyone to find you mated to Kyle Westin giving the fact that you remain alive today. You are aware that no other wolf would have been granted such a privilege?"

"I'm aware now. I wasn't at the time. As I am sure you have already heard my story. Is it confirmation you seek? Yes, I was a little girl when my parents died in an attack. I was bitten trying to escape. I turned that night for the first time. I thought I was a monster. Laugh all you want, but I had no one and knew nothing of wolf shifters. I drifted in and out of foster homes until I aged out and have kept a low profile ever since. It was sheer luck that I stumbled into this territory and learned what I am."

Kyle, wake up, I need you! I begged to him.

"Should I have my Pack Alpha present for this?" I saw a shared look between them and knew they had hoped I wouldn't ask.

"There's really no reason to bother him in the middle of the night like this. I think we have our confirmation, just a quick finger prick and we'll be on our way."

One of them held me down by my shoulders with force as the other reached for my hand.

Ow, what the? Babe, where are you? What's going on? I finally heard Kyle.

I don't know what they want, they're hurting me. I cried back.

It was then that I heard a noise from the bedroom and a loud menacing growl came through the house the same time a flash of brown fur jumped on the man behind me holding me down. I heard him scream out in pain.

"Quickly, get her blood," Omar insisted to the one holding

the needle above my finger, but Kyle was fast and he was angry.

What do they want? Why are they here?

I don't really know.

Why didn't you wake me?

In the midst of all the chaos I know I glared at him for that comment. *Don't you think I tried?*

Get behind me, I'll hold them off and get to the bottom of this.

"Enough!" The demand came from the largest of the men. Cedric, I think his name was. His demand was punched with more alpha power than I had ever felt. My initial reaction was to stand my ground and refuse to back down to him.

Kneel. Kneel now, Kelsey. Don't confirm their suspicions.

Against every ounce of fiber in my body I complied to my mate's plea and submitted as would be expected of me.

"Kyle, change." Cedric ordered.

"What is the meaning of this, Cedric?" Kyle demanded. "You barge into my home and attack my mate in the middle of the night? Is this how the Grand Council operates now?"

The man sighed, "My sincere apologies, Kyle. We were just trying to get to the bottom of things without drawing any attention which is in the best interest of us all."

"Physically assaulting my mate is in no one's best interest," he growled out.

"I can see we were mistaken in our methods. A simple drop of blood and we'll be on our way."

"Why? Why do you want her blood?"

"A lineage test." Omar spoke. "That is all. Kamen has requested a lineage test to see if it can be determined to which pack Kelsey's family derived from. Nothing more."

"It does not matter to anyone in Westin Pack where she derived, she is Westin now. Period."

"This will all end with a simple finger prick, Kyle. Please do not be unreasonable."

"One drop of blood, and then this is all over? You'll leave?" I asked.

Kyle glared at me. *Do not do it, Kelsey.*

Why? Kyle why?

He didn't respond and I submitted to the testing only

realizing in hindsight that they distracted me before I could fully heed the warning. And with my blood in hand they left as they had said they would.

"What have you done? I told you not to give it to them."

"Why wouldn't I? I just wanted them gone." I was still freaked out and shaking from the encounter with the Grand Council and now my home felt violated too.

"Because now, they have their proof," he whispered.

"What?!?!"

"Your alpha line will run strong through your blood."

"Why did you let me do it then?"

"Kels, they silenced me. I tried to tell you, but you wouldn't listen."

"Silenced you?"

"Yes, they are very powerful Alphas, they can even silence a bond. We need to call my dad and prepare our pack. Once they know what you are, they will come after us. It's only a matter of when now."

I began sobbing. What had I done? How could I have been so stupid? But how could I possibly have known they could tell all that from a drop of blood? Our pack would be forced into war and it would be all my fault. What could I do now? Run? It's what's always kept me alive. I would run, on my own. They wouldn't hurt Kyle if I weren't here, would they?

"Babe, stop thinking like that. You aren't running away. Not without me. And apparently not without the entire pack from the sounds of things last night. We are strong together. They will not defeat us. And to answer your question, no. If you ran they would simply kill me knowing it would also kill you, remember."

"They wouldn't dare! Would they?"

"It's possible. But we aren't going to find out. You hear me?"

He pulled me close to his body, still warm and naked from his transition from wolf. I clung to him, taking in as much of his scent as I physically could breathe in while fighting back hysterics.

"It's going to be okay, Kels, but I have to call and warn Dad. They came at us in the middle of the night while we were most vulnerable. They will not hesitate to do that again."

It took several phone calls, but within the hour the entire Pack Council and a few other notable wolves from the Westin Pack filled our living room and dining room areas. Each had been informed on what the Grand Council had done and were furious. Strategies and ideas were flying all around from each of them.

Elise hugged me tight and kept telling me it was going to be okay.

"Maybe they won't find anything out from your blood and it'll all blow over," Lily encouraged with little faith.

Jason had the phone glued to his ear making calls to allies outside the pack. He called in every favor possible as he set up alliances.

"Collier, Longhorn, and Central Pack of New York are onboard. They are each sending an elite team of representatives to stand and fight with us should it come to it. Alaska and the Virginians are staying neutral for the time being. They want to see what, if anything, arises before choosing a side. And unfortunately, Dermot, Patrick's father, is still a bit miffed over his refusal to fight in the challenges, but not enough to go against his son either. Since Patrick has allied with us, the Irish Clan will neither fight against or for us."

"How many packs are there anyway?" I asked aloud. The room went quiet as all eyes glued on me.

"Well, my dear, there are many packs around the world, but only eleven that we know of big enough to cause a war."

"The Grand Council recognizes fifty-seven packs worldwide, last I heard confirmed," Cole Anderson added.

I couldn't believe there could possibly be that many wolf shifters in the world.

"The Westin Pack is amongst the largest in numbers, Kelsey. Some of the recognized packs could have as few as four members." Cole added seeming to read my mind. "The top eleven packs each have more than five hundred shifters and comprise the majority of known wolf shifters in the world."

"So, Collier, Longhorn, Central, Alaska, Virginia, and the Irish Clan are all part of the top eleven too?"

"Yes," Kyle joined in. "We have four confirmed, including our pack, willing to fight if it comes to it and three more currently staying neutral. That still leaves four packs that could potentially ally against us. But hopefully that will bring an even match, or best we have the slight advantage because of the size of our pack and the fact that they will have to bring the fight to us."

"No pack will risk their entirety on a battle such as that. We will have the numbers." Jason confirmed stoically. "Let's just all pray it doesn't come down to it."

By that evening, Collier and Longhorn representatives had already arrived and Central was only a few hours out. We had more than filled our home and decided to move everyone to the pack house. Mary and several of the she-wolves were busy preparing meals. I stopped by the kitchen to offer my help and was immediately shooed out, but not before giving her a quick hug and thanks. I smiled at Sally Merchant who reached out and squeezed my hand as I made my exit.

There was a knock at the main door as I passed through the foyer heading for the community room where everyone was currently sprawled out in deep conversations. I knew that was odd because pack members wouldn't knock. I hesitantly opened the door only to be greeted by all five of the Grand Council wide eyed and maybe even a little fearful.

"Kelsey," Omar began, "we humbly ask to speak with your Pack Council."

Kyle, they're here. I screamed through the bond trying not to show an outward response.

A low growl of warning sounded off to my left coming from the direction of the community room and growing louder in approach. I wasn't scared though, I would recognize that growl anywhere. Relief washed over me.

"Kyle," his father said with enough authority to calm him and piss him off a little. "Please, calm yourself. The Grand Council means no harm entering our halls. Isn't that correct?" He demanded more than questioned.

"We need to talk, Jason."

He sighed and invited them in. All five seemed oddly uneasy.

"Alone," Omar said. "This is a private conversation."

"You entered my son's house in the middle of the night," he accused. "You stole blood from our future Pack Mother. I can only assume you wish to discuss the results of such actions. There is nothing you will say that will not be taken back to my pack, so please, speak freely."

Man, Jason sounded pissed, and as scary as the Grand Council was, I could have sworn each of them squirmed slightly under his accusations.

"I agree, our methods were perhaps out of line. But Jason, the results are not something we wish to broadcast publicly for fear of the outrage and fear that could result."

Cole stepped up as Kyle's arm possessively tightened around me.

"Kelsey is an Alpha Female, hidden by her parents from the executioners and shouldn't be alive today." He said frankly.

Their eyes grew wide and their faces reddened in anger.

"You knew? And yet you harbored her all this time?" He paused and looked around at the Westin Pack Council in shock. "Jason, do you realize the predicament you have put us all in? Do you realize how dangerous this all is?"

"Kelsey Adams is no danger to us, nor you. And I know this to be true because I have tested her powers personally, and if even an ounce of that strength showed up in your little test then you know that she willingly gave it because otherwise there would be absolutely nothing you could do to stop her. Yes, I agree, she is powerful, even more so than you realize now that her bond has sealed with Kyle's. I do not say that as a threat, I say that for you to consider that with so much power, how is she able to control it? Afterall, isn't that the real reason the Old Council placed a death sentence on children like her? Because females are too emotionally unstable to actually control the power? That is what the old books say, and I dare challenge you to test her level of control. It is unlike anything I have ever seen."

The Grand Council was furious. You could see it all over their faces.

"The penalty for harboring such an atrocity against nature, is death. You have just willingly admitted that you and your Council have done just that. And now you make threat against your Grand Council?"

"I've made no such threats, Titus. Do not put words into my mouth. I have simply invited you to test her for yourself and see that she is no threat to you."

I hated that they were speaking about me as if I weren't standing right there.

"Jason, there's more to it," Callum spoke softly. "I'm afraid the Bulgarians were the ones to raise the alarm and demand inquiry. We honestly took the sample of her blood only to try and identify her pack line. Nothing more. So forgive us, as we are all in shock over this discovery even if you do not seem to be."

"And was it?" I asked softly. "Was my pack line discovered?"

He looked at me sadly and nodded. "I'm afraid it will not bring you peace. Quite the opposite actually. May we sit?"

I started to shake. I didn't like the sudden softness of his voice. I could deal better with the fury and outrage than whatever this was.

"Kelsey, how much do you remember of your childhood?"

I looked to Kyle, then to Jason. Both nodded their heads encouraging me to tell my story. They already knew what I was, so what harm could possibly come of it now?

I took a deep breath and launched into the story of my childhood, what little I remembered and the dreadful night of my parents' murder, how I got away, how I changed that night, and a little about how I survived afterwards prior to coming to San Marco.

They were quiet for a few moments after I completed my story. I wasn't sure what to do or say. They just sort of looked at each other knowingly.

"Kelsey," Victor began slowly. "We were able to not only determine your pack line, but we are 100% positive we know your identity. We have not shared this information with Kamen yet, but he will insist on hearing it and he will explode when he finds out."

I took a sharp breath and felt Kyle's arm wrap around my waist. He was standing just behind me. I was grateful for his presence.

"Perhaps we should take this in private if you wish to know your history. If not, Jason, as Pack Alpha, you will most assuredly need the information."

"Here is fine. Kyle and I made a conscious decision not to keep anymore secret from our pack. From our family," I corrected myself.

Elise squeezed my hand and held it tight. The rest of our Westin family closed in behind us. The remaining six Pack Council members moved closer just to my left. And then I felt and saw my pack circle us all, or at least those that were present at the time.

I couldn't keep the smile off my face. "You say you have info about my pack, my Family, but truthfully, I know exactly who I am, who may family is, and what pack I belong to. I am Kelsey Adams. You are surrounded by my family and I am proudly a member and future Pack Mother of the Westin Pack."

Cheers went up all around and I could see the unease cross each of the Grand Council's faces. Giving them all time to settle down, I held up my hand as I had seen Jason do in several pack meetings to quiet the group. "However," I said, "if you have information about my parents and my history, I would like to hear it."

You could practically hear a pin drop it was so quiet as all ears tuned in for the story. Callum attempted to protest, but I dismissed the thought. "No. My pack deserves to hear this as much as anyone. They have every bit the stake in this as I do." It was true too. They had decided to fight for me. They would be laying their lives on the line if it came to that. I would not keep this from them.

"Very well," Victor continued, "Your parents were Adelina and Dragomir of the Bulgarian Pack."

A collective intake of breath could be heard. The Bulgarians? I didn't think I wanted to hear anymore.

"I remember you as a small child. You and your sisters were perhaps the most adorable little pups I had ever laid eyes on. Each of you different, yet combined even as young as age four you were lethal."

"Oh my god, she's the lost triplet." Elise said under her breath as she squeezed my hand harder.

"That's correct," Victor confirmed. "Your name was Elena. You sisters were Lidiya and Mila. You were the youngest of the three, quiet, shy, always within arm's reach of your mother. Mila was loud and a bit of a diva from the second you were all born. She loved the attention. Lidiya always chased behind her trying to keep up. But by four all three of you had come into powers. The little witch girls they called you. Mila liked to show off her power and shortly before your fifth birthday learned that she could combine her power with Lidiya's and bend people to her will. Your parents were good people and they tried to control her, but there was no controlling Mila. Kamen had fought off making the decision, but the time came when she was just too powerful and too dangerous to the pack and called for the death of all three. They came for Mila first."

"Lidy went after her," I continued with tears running down my face. I could see the story unfold like a nightmare before my very eyes. "Papa told me to stay with mama, but I tried to go after them. I knew I was stronger than the two of them combined. I was the only one that could keep Mila in line, but I didn't like to use my power. Mama said it scared people and I needed to hide it. I tried to run after them. I wanted to save them, but mama grabbed me and we left. I could hear their screams in my head and knew the moment they had died. We had been able to communicate telepathically, much like the bond Kyle and I have. I told Lidiya to run away and save herself, but she wouldn't listen. Papa couldn't stop it either. Mama took me far away. It was a long trip and later papa met up with us." I looked up the Grand Council. "I remember now." I whispered. "My name was changed to Kelsey Elena Adams when we came to the United States. They left Elena in my name as a reminder so I would never forget who I was."

Kyle's arm tightened around me and I felt him push a calming feeling of love through our bond. Elise squeezed my hand and Lily hugged me around my other arm.

"What happens next?" Chase asked.

"When Kamen finds out she's Bulgarian, he will come for her. He will not be happy to find she lived. All the Bulgarians remember the strength she and her sisters had as just little girls. He will either sentence her to death, or try to use her to gain more protection for his own benefit."

"We will not allow that to happen," Chase stepped forward and said in a menacing tone. Growls throughout the room began and I saw Victor's eyes widened.

I had never seen this side of fun loving, crazy baby Chase, the youngest of the Westin kids. His determination made my heart swell with love for my family. And they were my family, more so than my own had ever been. I was accepted without question or fear and the realization of that was making it hard to keep my emotions in check.

They love you too, Kels. Kyle told me through our bond. *But not as much as I do.* I could see the smirk on his face in my mind.

"You do what you must, Victor, but hear me now." Jason

said with the utmost authority. "Westin Pack has unanimously decided to stand and fight should it come to it. Kelsey will not leave my territory, nor is Kamen or any of his Bulgarians welcome here. To come for her will break territory alliances and end the peace we have all thrived under for the last seventy-five years. Cedric, you are old enough to remember the days before peace. Consider what will happen, carefully. Because Kelsey is Westin and Westin Pack is in our right to protect our own against all enemies."

Cedric sighed. "We will make it known and pray it does not come down to it, but acknowledge that it is in your right to do so. We only ask that this stay between Westin and the Bulgarians. We do not wish to see an all out war."

"It is too late for that," Kyle spoke this time. "We have made our alliances already. I will not take any chances regarding my mate. You be sure to let Kamen know that he wants her that badly, he does so facing a full war. One he will not win."

KYLE
Chapter 32

For three weeks, patrols had been upped on ten hour rotations around the clock. Our perimeters were run regularly by our best trackers in search of any signs of intruders. Collier, Longhorn and Central had made good on their promise and I had an extra thirty-seven battle ready wolves at my disposal.

As for Westin Pack, all in San Marco began immediately training. All wolves abroad were called home indefinitely to begin their training as well. It wasn't that Westin was soft. All wolves were trained to fight, but peace amongst the packs had left us weaker than we should have been. Most fighting skills were taught in preparation of the mating challenges, which, yes, was a fight to the death, but it was also one on one combat. What we were potentially facing would be very different.

There were still many older wolves who remembered the ways before peace and they were called in to properly prepare the others. At first everyone went all in with an excitement even as they set about preparing for war. But as the days went on, turning into weeks, the excitement began to wane. I couldn't afford for even one of them to be complacent so I pushed and urged them to keep up their training, keep their ears up, their noses to the ground, and always be on alert. Still life was slowly returning to normal, just with a little extra in patrols and awareness.

I couldn't sleep, always worrying. Kelsey fussed at me that was exactly what Kamen would want. He needed to wait us out and weaken us and allow our pack to become complacent once again. I knew she was right, but what I heard was 'if we drop our guard, he'll attack with the advantage.'

It was late, or rather early in the morning hours. Kelsey was lightly snoring next to me as I once again laid wide awake, contemplating every potential attack and any weaknesses we may have. When my phone buzzed quietly beside me on silent, so as not to wake my mate, I startled.

"Hello."

"Kyle, It's Leo. Look I don't want to worry you needlessly, but Ted was making a run of the north pass and he's nearly an hour overdue on return."

I shot up out of bed and immediately began dressing.

"Leo, sound the alarm."

"Look Kyle, we've had three false alarms already, and this is Ted we're talking about, are you sure about this?"

"I don't give a shit if this is a false alarm or not. Sound the alarm. Full alert until Ted is found."

As I hung up I saw Kelsey was up and staring at me with wide eyes. I went to her and kissed her forehead hugging her close to my chest. "Go back to sleep, babe. It's probably just a false alarm."

"No, I'm up now and I won't sleep without you anyway. Let me come with you."

I nodded praying it really was another false alarm. Then as she began to get dressed I called Patrick O'Connell.

"Hey man, already got the alert." He answered before I could even speak or ask. "Got a few guys from Collier and two from Longhorn on their way over now, along with Cole. We'll head up to the north pass and see what we can find. Keep this line as open as possible, okay?"

"Thanks Pat. It really means a lot to me having you here."

"Don't go getting all sappy with me. I'll touch base every fifteen minutes till we find him just as we rehearsed."

Hanging up the phone I immediately set the timer for fifteen minutes. I knew once I got busy I would otherwise lose track of time. Then I made one more phone call to my dad and was pleased to find him not only awake, but in full action. We had had three false alarms already, two just in the last week, so hearing everyone taking it seriously gave me a calm and strength I didn't realize I was missing.

With Kelsey ready, we strolled out hand in hand as if there wasn't a care in the world. But not ten yards off our back deck, I smelled them on the wind. Immediately I called it in, and raised the alert to battle mode.

They're here. I told Kelsey through our bond.

I know. I can smell them. They are north about a hundred yards and closing in. I watched as she took a deep breath. *Kyle, I know that smell. It's Kamen. He's here. He's not alone, but he's here. I don't know how I know it, but I know it's him. And this is going to sound crazy, but I think I smell my mother too.*

Kelsey, shift and run. I told her as I grabbed my phone and quickly texted Dad that it was not an alarm. *Run to Dad's. I'll be right behind you.*

Come on, they're headed this way. Quick Kyle!

One thing I was certain. The wolves who turned and started to give chase were never going to catch my mate and they weren't going to catch me. We were too fast for them, but they had to know now that we were on to them. I could feel the distance growing between us. Kelsey was quite some ways ahead of me. She got to the house a good five minutes before me and even though she was not talking to me, I could feel her and understand that she was confirming my text and getting everyone in position.

"This is what we've been training for. Everyone at the ready. They are coming and they are coming fast." I announced to all present when I entered my father's house.

"How many?" my dad asked.

"I'm not sure, but it felt like a lot. Kelsey smelled Kamen. Would he really come all this way for her himself?"

"Titus seemed to think he was more than a little obsessed over this, so yeah, I believe it's possible."

The house phone rang and I quickly picked it up.

"Kyle."

"Hey man, we found Ted," Cole said solemnly. "He's dead. Looks like a large group came through the north pass."

"Damn it. Okay, come on back, and prepare your team. I'm already at Dad's. Kelsey and I almost ran into them near our house. We need to organize the teams, just as we practiced. They never should have gotten this close."

"I'm sorry. The guys were starting to get a little lax. You were right to keep on us."

"No time for that now, Cole. It's go time."

As I hung up the phone, Liam came into the room. "All the women and children are accounted for and safe inside the pack house. All but, Kelsey."

"What?" I asked, furious.

"I'm sorry, Kyle, she refused to leave."

"And I'm not going to either. They are here for me. I fight side by side with you. Period. There's not time or room for discussion. I can hold my own, Kyle."

"Babe, I know you can." I went to her and hugged her. "That doesn't mean I don't hate that you're going to though."

She laughed in my arms. "Thank you for not forcing me out. I couldn't stand to sit in there and not have any idea what was going on out here."

"I would keep you updated every step of the way." I tried, hopeful she'd reconsider even though I knew otherwise.

"Kyle, Dad says they are heading this way. There's about 75 of them and they are moving quickly but in a dense pack. Staying together and all," Chase told me. "He wants to meet them at the break in the woods, head on."

"Okay, let's roll out. Tell Cole and Ambrose's teams to come in from behind. And Quinton and Mallick's teams to the left and right. We'll surround them. Only 75? We've got them outnumbered by a lot. Do not lessen the guards at any of the passes. We need immediate intel if more are on their way. And I strongly suspect they are."

Only seventy-five? I heard the small voice squeak in my head.

I turned to Kelsey. "For an attack on a pack as big and strong as Westin, seventy-five is a suicide mission."

She nodded in understanding.

I rubbed my hands up and down her arms, needing to calm my wolf and watching her visibly relax too. I leaned forward so that our foreheads touched and I breathed her scent in allowing it to wash over me.

Not wanting to share the moment, I spoke through our bond. *Babe, I know you are strong and powerful, but every instinct in my being says to lock you up and keep you safe.*

I felt her stiffen.

I'm not going to stop you. I understand you need to do this, but I don't have to like it. Please remember I'm an alpha too and it's my job to protect my mate. It is my only job that truly matters. Please stay behind me tonight. Let me take the lead and if things get too heated out there and I say run, you turn tail and run and don't look back. I promise I'll be right behind you.

I held my breath, awaiting her response. I was fighting against my nature trying hard to give her what she needed. After what seemed like an eternity she slowly nodded. I kissed her forehead, flooded in relief.

With that we were on the move again. My brothers each had a unit assembled. I nodded and they took off leading their units as we had planned. Kelsey and I joined Dad's unit. She stayed just behind me to the left. I didn't think she could possibly understand how much it meant to me. I tried to tamper the happiness resonating through me. After all, we were headed to war.

We knew the exact location of interception and did not expend any energy getting there as our unit purposefully walked on to face the enemy in our territory. Just as Kamen and his pack of wolves came into view at a full sprint heading straight for us, so did Chase and Liam's units flanking them from our right and left.

The trespassers checked up and came to a halt. I knew exactly which wolf was the alpha and saw him signal to his pack before changing to stand as a man before us.

"Jason of the Westin Pack, we mean no harm to you or your wolves. We only want the girl lost to us. She must return to her pack."

My father shifted and turned to scold me with his stare as a growl erupted from me.

"As you well know, the girl has bonded with my son. And she has officially joined Westin Pack. As their bond is complete, I can assure you that every member of my pack is prepared to fight to the death for their future Pack Alpha and Pack Mother."

Howls erupted all around us, and many from much farther away responded in kind. The Bulgarian wolves growled in return. Kamen's face scrunched up in a snarl, baring his teeth even while in human form.

"Do not fool yourself, Jason, I have come to take back what is mine. This abomination defeated death once and she will not do so again. My condolences for your son, but what must be done, must be done. Make no mistake, they will die the death she should have died alongside her sisters nearly twenty years ago, and each of my men here are committed to see this through."

Kamen then raised his head and gave a strange grunting, howling, sort of sound I had never heard but if I had been in my skin knew would cause goosebumps. The sound reverberated throughout the woods and off in the distance. He then grinned the most evil grin I had ever seen.

"Surely you didn't think me foolish enough to come with such a small pack. Did you?"

I was so focused on him as he finished his speech and quickly shifted to wolf to begin his attack, that I did not feel Kelsey's power stirring until it was wrapped with mine. I chanced a quick look back expecting to see fear in my mate's eyes, but only saw resolve. Her focus alone was lethal and her eyes were locked on to her prey.

Kamen sprinted towards my father without even giving him time to shift. He snapped hard at his neck missing by only inches as he bit into his shoulder. Dad let out a howl of pain that jolted the Westin pack into action. I felt Kelsey moving, stalking slowly towards them. I didn't bother trying to reach out through our bond, she was fully open to me. No thoughts remaining, only emotions and I knew she had given herself fully to her wolf.

We moved in sync towards her one goal. I tried not to let my wolf over power me too. Seeing our mate in her most primitive state made it more difficult than ever, but I needed to think and protect her. Movement to my right had me turning just in time to see a large grey wolf leap for attack. I side stepped and came back abruptly as he landed in the spot I had been just seconds before. I threw my entire weight into him and quickly latched on to his neck ripping his throat out as quickly and efficiently as possible.

I turned back to Kelsey and found her crouched, still watching and biding her time, but I also felt she was obeying and waiting on me. I quickly joined her taking the lead once more. And as she rose and followed off my left hindquarters, my wolf jumped a few extra steps jubilantly even in the midst of such danger. I didn't dare look around any further than immediate threats to my mate. I had faith in my pack and knew they would do what needed to be done. My job was to protect Kelsey, and that meant killing the man that so blatantly threatened our lives.

A large female wolf lunged towards Kelsey. My heart started pumping as adrenaline fueled me. My mate was in danger. I roared in anger and felt my own alpha powers rising to their full power. I was nearly blinded by the power and surprised by the strength that coursed through my body. Jumping over my mate I met her predator head on. The she-wolf never even saw me coming. I wasted no time sinking my teeth into her until her body withered in my mouth. With a jerk of my head I sent her dead body flying into a group of wrestling wolves.

Not waiting to see the aftermath or the surprised faces of those I'd interrupted, I quickly turned back to Kelsey. Her power was growing, as was mine. I was nearly blinded by the enormity of it. She no longer walked behind me, but side by side we made our way to where Kamen and my father fought. Blood was everywhere and I could not tell who it was coming from. I knew from the earlier howl that my dad had been injured but had no clue to what extent. In that moment, it didn't matter.

Kelsey stopped just before them but I did not. I leapt onto the back of the alpha wolf and let my claws sink in. He yelped and tried to throw me off. Someone from behind took a swipe at me and I felt the sting of an open cut then heard a gurgling sound. The world was spinning in Kamen's attempt to thrash in circles to disarm me, but I closed my eyes and held on tight.

Suddenly it was like I could see through Kelsey's eyes. The world was distorted in greys tinged with red. She was in a fury. The next thing I realized was that the fighting surrounding us had momentarily stopped. Kelsey made a lunge for Kamen causing an abrupt stop to his flailing. I felt his power shifting beneath my paws and knew he was about to change.

The most sacred shifter law was never to kill in human form, or another shifter in human form. Most packs extend that to humans entirely. It was something I held firmly to. It was a sign of our humanity. A sign that we weren't the monsters Hollywood portrayed us as.

Kels, he's going to shift! I yelled through our bond.

Instantly she sprang into action biting his neck, but just missing his carotid artery. I lashed on to the other side of his neck. Our mouths snapping open and closed over his neck in close proximity as we fought to end him. Kamen wasn't alpha of the Bulgarians without reason and he wasn't about to go down without a fight. We had weakened him to the point he would not be able to change, but he was still alive.

He thrashed about once more, and this time my paws met slick blood coated fur and I couldn't maintain my grip. I hit the ground with a thud and went sprawling from the momentum. This left Kelsey to face Kamen alone. I quickly recovered and raced to rejoin the fight. Two large Bulgarian wolves tried to block my path. I didn't have time for them. I faked left and skirted off to their right. They were big but they didn't seem too bright. I saw Liam's wolf jump in to intercede as I raced back to my mate.

They were in a standoff with Kelsey staring down at Kamen's injured body lying on the ground and I joined her by her side, taking her lead when every instinct in me screamed to finish him. A female wolf sat beside him licking his wounds and I knew it must be his mate, Nadya. He growled and snapped at her as he struggled to his feet. Nothing but pure anger showed in his eyes. There was no signs remaining of humanity and I knew, if he was going to die, he was going to do everything in his power to see that Kelsey went with him.

In a last attempt, he threw the she-wolf off him and jumped right towards Kelsey and me. Neither of us moved and a strange power unlike anything I had ever known surrounded us in a bubble. It was so constricting I was surprised you couldn't visibly see it.

Kamen felt the power before he reached us, the shock on his face evident. The pull of this new power was too strong and I couldn't hold on any longer. In a haze, blurring the world around me, I gave in to my wolf side.

Suddenly everything was crystal clear. It was so surreal, like watching things happen from above. I was emotionally detached, yet emotions and instinct were all I was moving on. I watched Kelsey rear up on her hindlegs in attack and I went low at the same time. It was like our movements were orchestrated as we moved as one. I was only vaguely aware of Kamen, but I knew every snap, every bite, every scratch Kelsey gave. Our bubble of power seemed to hold some sort of protection to us both. I saw Kamen kick out but I was moving before his leg ever reached me. Same seemed to go for Kelsey too, as she dodged every swipe or bite that came her way.

As Kamen made the deadly mistake of leaving his neck unprotected, I watched Kelsey go in for the kill, but something clicked inside her. I could feel it, and I swore I could see it happen even. She pulled back before she completed the kill. That was my sign to act. My jaws clamped down on his neck and with a quick pop I snapped it in two.

The howls surrounding us and the soft tongue of my mate across my fur shocked me back to reality. I sat back on my hindlegs and raised my nose to the sky. The howl I let out was the most powerful I'd ever had and it felt like a release went through me when Kelsey joined me in my victory song. It was immediately answered back with a new strength I had never felt before.

As I breathed in my mate's scent, knowing she was okay and the threat to her life laid lifeless at our feet, I calmed and allowed myself to shift back to human form. I knew I would not be able to assess the situation while in wolf form. It had been too emotional and strange and had me a bit unbalanced. Kelsey followed my example and stood proudly by my side. I tried to keep the grin off my face knowing how she felt about public nudity and realizing everyone was staring at us.

Fights were still broken out around us, but they all began to settle in confusion at seeing us. The Westins stopped fighting and began to group behind Kelsey and I. The Bulgarians stood before us in confusion.

"Bulgarian Pack, your Alpha is dead. You have six hours to collect your dead and remove yourselves from Westin territory, or face the same demise as your Alpha."

There were whispers of shock behind me, and growls from the Bulgarians before me.

Is it over? The sweet voice I loved sounded so quiet and uneasy.

I turned and hugged her close. It was then I took a real look around. I was shocked by the amount of bodies and blood surrounding us. A heavy weight began to settle on my heart and my eyes frantically began scanning the area taking inventory.

My entire body went still as a saw several men hovered around a large brown and black wolf lying still on the ground.

"Dad!" I screamed releasing Kelsey and running to the wolf. The men surrounding him parted for me. I dropped to my knees next

253

to him and began inspecting the damage. The first thing I noticed was that he was breathing. I couldn't let relief wash over me though, because he wasn't moving. "Where's Micah?"

"Your dad refused to let him fight. He was too big a commodity he had said. He stayed back with the she-wolves." Leo Tripp informed me.

"Radio!" I yelled.

Chase ran over. He froze when he saw who I was tending too. "Dad?" He whispered. I grabbed the radio, ignoring him.

"Kyle to base."

"Kyle!" Lily replied half hysterical. "What's going on? Mom collapsed and is unresponsive."

"It's Dad, Lily, we need Micah out here ASAP!"

Lily must have accidentally kept her finger on the button because I could hear the commotion in the background as she relayed my message. Then it briefly went silent.

"Kyle? Is it over?" My other sister asked.

"Yeah, E. I think so. Kamen and his mate are dead. I have no idea the extent of damage. I need you to send Micah and then take the list and do a full unit check in."

"Micah's already on his way."

I sighed in relief.

Kelsey sat next to me. She was staring at my Dad. There was a strange look on her face and she kept staring at her hands, flexing and fisting them.

I watched as whatever was going on in her head that had her so concerned in her internal battle began to resolve. I was concerned that I couldn't hear her thoughts, but was so fascinated, sensing an important moment that I didn't even reach for her in our bond.

Kelsey laid her hands on my father. He moved slightly and let out a soft moan. I went to stop her, but a strange woman halted me.

"Don't. Let her. She can help him."

I looked back at Kelsey who was still lost in some sort of trance. Fear pricked me. She laid her hands on my father again. I fought not to stop her. A warmth similar to the tangible power I felt during the battle enveloped me. Dad moaned loudly.

It's not enough, he's really injured, Kyle. I finally heard her in my head. *I need your power.* She said like an epiphany.

I laid my hand on her shoulder and she shuddered. I didn't know what she was doing but now that I had felt her and no longer felt the disconnect between us, I implicitly trusted her. I opened myself fully to her and felt the pull of my power through our bond. It was a strange and new sensation. She had twice before pulled power from our bond, but it had been a quick pull. This was very different.

I stared at my mate in awe. The moans she had been inflicting from Dad began to subside. The energy buzzing between us stopped and Kelsey collapsed across my father.

"She's ok," the strange Bulgarian woman assured me.

There was some commotion as Micah ran up to the scene. I eased Kelsey off my dad and gently rested her head in my lap. The Bulgarian didn't seem to have any personal boundaries as she sat close to me and leaned in, lovingly stroking my mate's hair. I was so confused by the situation, yet nothing in me or my wolf felt any threat what-so-ever.

"Who are you?" Vaguely aware that my father was talking to Micah.

The woman smiled at me. "Kyle of Westin Pack, I am Raina, Elena's aunt. Adelina was my sister."

She continued stroking Kelsey's hair and clearly had no plans to move or leave despite the threat I had issued. I looked around quickly as memories consumed me and saw no other Bulgarians in the area.

"They've left. I do hope you will consider extending the window for me. I would hate to miss out on this chance to know my niece. I mean look at her. She's beautiful. Look at her miracles." She pointed to my father.

"Dad!" I looked him over quickly. He was pale but he was sitting and talking clearly to Micah.

"I don't know how it's possible, Kyle. I can see the full extent of his injuries, but it is like they are months old. What happened?"

"It was Elena," her aunt informed him. "It was always suspected but never confirmed before Adelina and Dragomir vanished with the girl. There were originally three. Identical triplets. They were the most beautiful babes you'd ever seen. Mila had the power of the elements and she was manipulative and caused storms that would rattle buildings with her temper tantrums. Lidiya had the power of healing. And Elena, well, she was the most feared of all.

Her alpha powers came in at such a young age. She was two the first time she brought Kamen to his knees. People would pledge their allegiance to her just walking in her presence. But she was a good girl and only ever used her powers to protect her sisters, otherwise you'd never know she had them. I always said with that restraint at such a young age she'd learn to control them. After a particularly bad tantrum from Mila, Kamen ordered the girls be put to death. They grabbed Mila first. Lidiya with the powers of healing came to her rescue and tried to heal the girl. Upon finding her dead and not just injured she went into a full rage greater even than the likes of Mila and it was speculated that she inherited her sister's power upon her death. That is why Kamen to this day feared Elena so badly."

"You think Kelsey inherited both of her sisters' powers? I've never even heard of shifters with extra abilities like that."

"Oh yes, child. Special abilities have always been among the shifters. They are rare, but they are real. Many call them witches. And three young witches in one pack was far more than we could handle."

"I've only ever met one witch," my father spoke in a ragged voice. "Seems your mate, my son, is far more rare and special than even we thought."

"Kamen is dead father. The Bulgarians are fleeing and any remaining will be escorted out or killed upon my command." I grimaced admitting my over-step of authority to him.

Kelsey stirred in my lap and lazily opened her eyes as if she were waking from a deep sleep.

"Wh-wh-what happened?" She stuttered.

"It's a long story, Kels. Why don't we get you home and we can tell you all about it." I told her aloud then added to her alone, *Just know you are safe, and loved, and cherished. Oh, and you have an aunt who'd like to get to know you, but mostly know that together we're going to be okay.* My mind drifted to all the ways I planned to make it more than okay the second we were alone again. I smiled and winked at her knowing she'd heard my thoughts and enjoyed watching the color creep into her cheeks and I felt her love wrap around me like a warm blanket and I knew we were going to be more than okay.

"Help me up, Micah." Dad said, "And come along you two. Your mother has been screaming in my head since the moment she awoke. That woman won't let me have even a second of peace till she's truly convinced I'm okay." Shaking his head and smiling down at us he added, "Just wait, son, a lifetime as mates is a long time, but when it's your one true mate, it's worth every second."

Kelsey

EPILOGUE

Nearly 8 weeks have passed since the battle with the Bulgarians. It was hard to believe as it just flew by. My Aunt Raina was granted permission to stay with the Westin Pack for as long as I needed her. I have learned so much about my family, sisters, and most especially my powers. It's been more than a little overwhelming dealing with all the new possibilities, but Kyle and I have been working hard on how to channel them for the security of our pack.

Speaking of Kyle, it turned out, he inadvertently transferred power to us during the battle while his dad was incapacitated. Jason is doing okay. The injuries he sustained fighting Kamen had been expedited in healing, but were so extensive that even months later he was still recovering. Because of this, there was no challenge to the cessation of power. Micah said there was no way Jason would have survived without my powers. Honestly, knowing that, has helped me a ton with accepting my gifts. I shuddered to think of what we would do without Jason and Mary. They may no longer be Pack Alpha and Pack Mother, but to me they were now and forever Mom and Dad.

Kyle and I were officially made Pack Alpha and Pack Mother about a week after the big battle. As if discovering you have crazy new witchy powers you inherited from your dead sisters wasn't enough. Though, if I'm honest, I've never felt more in control of my life and more settled and assured in who I am than in my new role as Pack Mother. It's like I was born to do this and I finally had the family I had longed for. Life was good.

I walked into the office, where we both still worked even knowing we would need to transfer duties soon, allowing Liam to step up and take over for Kyle, and then I would step down and into full-time Pack Mother duties once their transition was complete and a replacement for me found. I saw Elise's door was shut. It seemed it was always shut these days. Kyle was constantly worrying about her. It was like everything just changed in an instant and she wouldn't talk about it with anyone. I sighed but needing to talk to her I knocked softly on the door.

"Enter," she said, not even looking up from her work as I walked in. When she finally did I was happy to see a genuine smile. "Kelsey, hey, is something wrong?"

I laughed, "Does there need to be for me to stop in and say hello?"

"No, of course not. As long as my brother didn't send you here to harass me." She rolled her eyes.

"He's just worried about you, but no. He doesn't know I'm here. I sorta need your help with something."

That seemed to cheer her up. I knew she hated being asked what was wrong, so I was determined to just pretend like everything was normal and not question at all why she was locking herself away from family and friends, never venturing out into the town of San Marco anymore, and working ungodly hours, day and night. Today, none of it matter and I knew she'd talk about it when she was good and ready.

"So, what's up then? I can tell there's something you definitely want to talk about."

I gave her a sly grin and handed her the gift bag I'd been carrying with me, trying to decide what to do with its contents.

"Um, here. You're the first person I've shown this to, and honestly I'm terrified and ecstatic and," I started to tear up feeling overwhelmed. "Anyway, you know Kyle better than just about anyone. I need help figuring out how to tell him."

She peeked into the bag and her eyes went wide and immediately started misting over as she pulled out the positive pregnancy test I had taken that morning. She just held it, staring, and crying with a huge smile on her face before jumping up from her seat and rounding the table to embrace me in the biggest hug I'd ever received.

"I'm the first person you've told?"

I nodded unable to speak. My emotions had been running rampant for several days.

"Kels, I'm so honored. I can't believe it, I'm going to be an aunt!"

I just kept nodding.

"How the hell have you kept this from Kyle?"

I laughed, "It's not easy. I've had to shut down our bond link entirely and he's freaking out because of it."

"Good, make him sweat. He's been driving me insane and totally deserves it."

"Tonight's family dinner night. Should I just announce it then? Should I just tell him? Do you think he'll want to keep the news to ourselves till I'm further along? I've never even held a baby before. All the girls homes I was placed in were for older girls, we never had babies. I don't know anything about babies, Elise. What am I going to do?"

She hugged me tighter and laughed. "Relax girl. Just breathe. You are a natural Pack Mother which means you're going to be a phenomenal mom to my little niece or nephew. Now, on to the real dilemma. Kyle's been driving me insane for weeks. I say let him sweat it out and announce it at dinner. Or maybe take him to Dad's office, er, Kyle's office? That's going to take awhile to get used to! But maybe take him in there and let him know and then you can announce it together?"

I nodded like a fool again. "Okay, yeah, I like that plan. But E," I looked at her seriously trying not to be complete freaked out with nerves, "what if he's not happy about it? I mean we've never talked about having kids. I have no idea how he'll react to this."

"Trust me, you have nothing to worry about. Just do me a favor, keep a lock on your bond and torture him for the remainder of the day!" She grinned evilly and for the first time in months I truly saw the real Elise and was suddenly glad I had come to her first.

Ignoring Kyle throughout the remainder of the day had proven more difficult than I had thought and I knew it would be hard. When dinnertime came, I couldn't even look at him. I was so nervous and he looked terrified. We said pleasant hellos to everyone and he asked to speak with me in private. I chanced a glance at Elise who grinned and nodded in silent support.

Behind closed doors in what was now Kyle's office I watched my strong mate melt before my eyes.

"I'm so sorry babe. I don't know what I did, but please just tell me and I'll fix it. Please don't keep shutting me out. Whatever it is, I promise you I'll make it better."

My eyes teared up and I laughed walking straight into his arms and hugging him tight. I opened our bond but purposefully kept my mind blank. I was overwhelmed with our combined emotions and started crying uncontrollably. I suspected this new sensation was going to be sticking around for the duration of this pregnancy.

"I'm sorry. I wanted to surprise you, not terrify you. I-I-I mean, I'm a bit terrified and excited and nervous and..."

He silenced me with a kiss that I felt radiate through my entire body all the way down to my toes. Knowing his entire family was waiting just down the hall, I didn't encourage him further, so when the kiss ended I stepped back out of his reach and took a deep breath before handing him the gift bag I had shown Elise just that morning, only now it contained a few baby items I had added in, including a little onesie that said "My Dad Rocks" with a guitar on it.

Kyle pulled out each item setting it on his desk until he finally pulled out the pregnancy stick. I held my breath waiting for some sort of reaction. I tried to reach through the bond, but he had locked me out. My heart flopped into my stomach and I thought I was going to be sick. This wasn't at all how I thought this would go.

He plopped down into the chair behind his desk, and clasping his hands behind his neck, he lowered his head between his knees, like the entire world was spinning out of control around him. With a deep breath, he finally spoke. "This is real?"

"Y-y-yes," a squeaked out in a stutter preparing to apologize.

"Not some sort of sick joke, you're serious? You're pregnant?"

He still wasn't looking at me.

"I'd never joke about something like this, Kyle." I said softly and sadly prepared myself for the apology speech I had planned should he not be happy about the news. "Look, I know we've never talked..."

He cut me off as his head shot up and his face was practically glowing with the biggest grin I'd ever seen. He let down the wall between our bond and immediately emotions washed over me. Happiness. Joy. Love. And I knew everything was going to be okay.

He picked me up and swung me through the air as I laughed with tears streaming down my face. He kissed me sweetly before dropping to his knees and kissing my belly over and over.

"I love you. You hear that, in there? And I love your beautiful mother too."

As we rejoined the others, Elise silenced everyone. She was beaming. Kyle looked at me and back at his sister. *You told Elise first?*

Who do you think convinced me to keep it from you and torture you all day? I playfully grinned and winked at my gorgeous mate who looked happier than I ever imagined possible.

He chuckled, *Thank you, it's good to see my sister again.*

"Mom, Kyle's doing that mind thing with Kelsey again." Chase whined.

"Kyle, no bonding talk during family dinner. You know the rules." His mother scolded him like a small child.

Jason laughed, "Share it with the family or sit down and let's eat already."

"We're having a baby!" He blurted out to all our family as cheers erupted throughout the room.

Dear Reader,

Thank you for taking the time to read One True Mate: a Westin Pack Novel. This is my first self-published project. I greatly appreciate the support and truly hope you enjoyed the book.

If you liked Kyle and Kelsey's story, just wait! There's plenty more of them both to come in Elise and Patrick's story, book 2 in the Westin Pack Series coming Fall 2017. Keep reading for a sneak peek of Fighting Destiny: a Westin Pack Novel.

For further information on my books, events, and life in general, I can be found online here:

Website: www.julietrettel.com

Facebook: http://www.facebook.com/authorjulietrettel

Instagram: http://www.instagram.com/julie.trettel

Twitter: http://www.twitter.com/julietrettel

Goodreads:
https://www.goodreads.com/author/show/14703924.Julie_Trettel

Amazon: https://www.amazon.com/Julie-Trettel/e/B018HS9GXS/

With love and thanks,
Julie Trettel

Julie Trettel

SNEAK PEEK

Fighting Destiny: A Westin Pack Novel

Coming Fall 2017

.

Elise
Chapter 1

I smacked the alarm clock with a groan. Who got up at that ungodly hour? For the last two and a half months that answer would be me. And why? Because the one person in this world I didn't want to see had come to town, and he wasn't leaving.

His auburn hair stuck out like a beacon anywhere I went. And like the coward I was, I hid every time. A part of me longed to look into his eyes and feel that final spark of recognition. What color were his eyes? I had wondered about that too often and immediately scolded myself.

Patrick O'Connell would give up and go home, eventually. He had only come here to kill my brother in that ridiculous mating ritual and take his one true mate. No doubt he hadn't smelled me coming until it was almost too late.

I was out with my sister, Lily, and my brother's mate, Kelsey, to scout out Kyle's latest challenger during the mating challenges. See, once a newly mated pair is announced there's a challenge period where an eligible wolf can issue a battle to the death for those mating rites.

Kyle and Kelsey's period was shortened due to extenuated circumstances. Basically, Kelsey's a super powerful she-wolf witch with all kinds of awesome powers that caused them to bond faster than should be possible. I had totally called it, but even still they had to endure a month of absolute terror through the challenges.

Sure, Kyle, being Alpha of our pack made his position much more sought after, but my position in the pack made me only slightly less desirable, and I didn't have any super powers to lessen the challenge period. Four months. That's what I'd have to endure if I took a mate. Four months of hell. I couldn't do it.

Currently Kelsey's expecting their first child. If it's a boy, some of the pressure will come off me. As second oldest to my parents, should I take a mate, that would put the line of succession to him until, and unless, Kyle heirs a son. It's such a mess. My plan all along has been to just not take a mate until that happens, but then Patrick showed up and he won't go away.

Anyway, back to my story. Lily, Kelsey and I went to scout out the Irish challenger that had just arrived. As we got close, my whole body started tingling almost like I needed to shift to my wolf form, and then, I smelled him. It was the most delicious thing I'd ever smelled and it called to me. I saw the tall, strong man with the auburn hair from behind and he stiffened his shoulders and sniffed the air. I knew immediately, like some blaring neon sign pointing and exclaiming, 'this is your one true mate'. Of course, I did the only sane thing possible. I faked a headache, and ran home with my tail between my legs, scared half to death.

Since that moment, I had done everything in my power to avoid one Patrick O'Connell. San Marco, the town my pack inhabits is not an extremely big place. Everyone knows everyone, and everyone knows everyone's business. It's both a blessing and a curse.

So, of course I knew Patrick had gotten whiff of his one true mate, and had no plans to leave without her, or rather me. He had even reneged his challenge against Kyle for Kelsey, telling my brother there was no way he could do that after he'd smelled me. My now sap of a brother thought it was pretty romantic and actually gave him clemency in Westin territory, and put him up in Kelsey's old cottage on the edge of town after she'd moved in with him.

I couldn't even run through my favorite woods anymore for fear of running into him. My theory was that there had to be more than just his smell, but I knew if I saw his eyes I'd be a goner. So, avoidance it had to be.

My alarm sounded again, interrupting my thoughts. I turned it off instead of hitting the snooze button again, and reluctantly got up, pulling on my robe and heading for the bathroom.

Four A.M., that was my new routine. Up at four meant in the office by five ,where I could hide out with little to no chance of crossing paths with him. I brought my lunch and ate in my office alone every day. It was what I needed to do to survive.

Yes, I knew my family was worried sick about me. Some days I even agreed they should be. It had become almost a sick obsession – avoid Patrick O'Connell at all costs. But the alternative made me physically ill. Not him. Not meeting him, but I knew from everything I'd compulsively found out about him these past few months, that I'd likely fall head over heels for him. It wasn't that that scared me. It was the challenges. It was the thought of losing him. I'd rather just not have him at all.

I was twenty-five years old. I was a strong, independent woman. I was a wolf-shifter from one of the strongest blood lines in shifter history. I didn't need a man.

I grabbed a strawberry pop-tart from the pantry on my way out, trying to be quiet and not wake anyone. I was not a morning person, but you had to do what you had to do.

At 5:01. I unlocked the door to my office and sighed in relief at the safety I now associated with the room. The Westin Foundation was a private company used to legally and gainfully employ wolf-shifters and keep up appearances of a normal community in the eyes of the humans. It didn't hurt that it was extremely profitable, and gave the Westin Pack a much plusher living than any other pack.

I had recently been promoted to VP of Human Resources and I loved my job. Part of what I loved most was the interactions with people. I was very much a people person. But lately my focus was on paperwork and it hadn't gone unnoticed. I was asked if anything was wrong, or if I wanted to talk about it, on a daily basis. They meant well, but I could never confess what a coward I was. Kyle had even called me in for two disciplinary chats, now formally on my record. I still couldn't believe it. Who was I? I wasn't sure I even knew anymore.

It had been a quiet morning, but by lunchtime I was fighting a massive headache and considered going home. A knock on my door sounded, making the pain worsen. I considered ignoring it, but the banging just continued.

"What?" I snapped, opening the door.

"Is that anyway to welcome your sisters?" Lily, my little sister, asked, with Kelsey in tow.

"Sorry, headache. This really isn't a good time." I tried to close the door, but she just stuck her foot in the way, and I knew they weren't going to leave peacefullly.

"What?" I asked, a little snappier than I meant, as they barged passed me. "Please come on in." I said under my breath, and not in a polite way.

"Don't mind if we do," Lily said, as Kelsey fished an aspirin out of her purse and handed to me.

"Thanks," I said, genuinely feeling like a tool for taking out my frustrations on them.

"Sit down" Kelsey said, motioning to the sofa in a corner of the room. Something told me she meant business, and that I wasn't going to like it. "Shall I start or you?' she asked my sister.

"Oh, I got this," Lily said, with a wicked grin. "Elise, it's been over two months of the sulking, hiding, hermit crap. We've tried to be understanding and give you your space." I snorted at her. "I said 'tried'! Anyway, enough is enough. You don't want to talk about whatever happened to you. Fine. But E, you're really scaring us."

"Kyle's convinced you were raped and ready to start interrogating every wolf in San Marco to get to the bottom of it." Kelsey said, matter-of-factly.

"What? Raped? He can't be serious. Nothing happened to me. I appreciate the concern, but honestly, I'm just busy with a lot on my mind."

"Bullshit," Lily challenged.

"It's just some personal stuff I'm dealing with, but I'm fine."

"You're not fine. There's nothing fine about you waking up at 4 A.M. and sneaking into the office. You are less of a morning person then I am. There's nothing fine about locking yourself away from everyone, whether here in your office, or at home in your room. If you had a smile on your face, even once, I'd think you were having an illicit affair you didn't want anyone to know about, but E, you look completely miserable, and it scares us."

I sighed. I was going to have to stop being such a coward and start facing things. I certainly never intended to upset or scare anyone.

"I'm fine. I promise. How about we head to lunch? I don't want you guys to worry about me."

"If it's the new position at work, Kyle will hire another assistant to help with your workload." Kelsey offered, fishing out reasons for my behavior.

"No, I'm fine. I can handle it." Oh God, they thought I couldn't handle my job now? This was getting bad. I'd just have to prove to them that everything was just fine.

"I hear the Crate is serving lunch. How about we go there?" Lily suggested. I knew she was really hoping to see Cole Anderson who's tattoo parlor was only a few doors down, and who Lily had been crushing on forever.

"Sure," I said. Of course, I didn't want to go, but I had to get some of the heat off my back and just prayed Patrick O'Connell was no where in the area.

Planting my best fake smile, I grabbed my bag and we headed for the door. Maybe lunch out with the girls wouldn't be so bad.

As we entered the Crate, I couldn't help but sniff the air and look around. No sign of Patrick. I tried to breathe a sigh of relief, but if I were being honest, I was a little disappointed by it too.

The Crate was really a bar and a bit of a dive., but it was a popular hangout in San Marco. Dark paneling covered the walls matching the dark wood floors. A bar with stools for seating ran along the back wall. To the right was a small stage, mostly used for karaoke night, but occasionally a group of local kids would attempt to start up a band and they'd play there some nights. The current hot group in town was my youngest brother, Chase's band. They really were pretty good, too.

We headed off to the left towards the booths that ran along that wall. There were also several tables that sat in the middle of the room and at night they were often pushed aside to clear a small dance floor. The place may be a little dark, but it was always clean and when Jesse, who owned the bar, had decided to open for lunch it had become a popular eatery too.

"Hey Misty," Lily waved to the pretty blond waitress who was as much a staple of the crate as Jesse himself.

"Hey ladies. Elise," she said, surprised but happy to see me, "we've missed you. How have you been?"

Fake smile in place, realizing that gossip and concern had surpassed just my family. "I'm good, just really busy. How are you?"

We chatted for a few and she took our orders before flitting off to the next table. Misty had always reminded me of a hummingbird the way she moved throughout the room. I couldn't help but smile, genuinely smile, and realized it had been a long time since I'd done much of that. It felt good.

"So, Kels, how are you feeling?"

I didn't miss the shared look she gave Lily with my change in character.

"Overall not too bad. It's still early. A little nausea in the mornings and a constant hunger, and I get overly emotional easily which drives me nuts, but overall, I can't really complain. Micah thinks I'm about ten weeks along, but that seems farther than I thought. I go for my first ultrasound next week, so we'll see."

"Ok, if you're listening to Kyle you'd think she's about to pop second, always fussing over her. It's cute and annoying." Lily rolled her eyes. "Who knew that big strong wolf of a brother of ours would be such a kitten over his mate? It's hysterical."

Kelsey glared what I'd deem the 'mom eyes' at Lily. "Lil, don't harass him. This is new for both of us and he's just nervous. I am too. We're going to be parents. I can't even believe it."

I looked at her and said sincerely, "You two are going to be the best parents any kid could ask for."

I hadn't meant them to, but my words started a flood from Kelsey's eyes. It made us all laugh.

"I'm sorry. I just get so emotional!"

Conversation the rest of the meal was light and friendly. They weren't on my case anymore and I was relaxed and actually enjoying our time together. Excusing myself, I headed for the bathroom. Staring at the mirror I was surprised to see me staring back. Not the empty hollow, scared coward I'd gotten used to seeing, but me. And I looked happy and alive again. I vowed to try to open up a little more and not let a certain wolf continue to drive me into darkness.

As I stepped out of the bathroom I smelled him. Patrick was there. I was certain of it. My palms started sweating and my heart began pounding in my chest. I peeked around the corner, out into the dining hall and sure enough, there he stood with my brother at my table talking to my sisters. I watched him for a moment as he talked effortless and laughed with my family, but something in his posture was tight and I found him looking around the room like he was searching for someone. Then it dawned on me. He's looking for me. He knows I'm here.

I flagged Misty over and asked her to tell the girls that my headache had returned and I had gone home to rest. She looked at me with concern, but said she would. Like the chicken I was, I let myself out of the back door and fled once again from the man who haunted my thoughts day and night.

Patrick
Chapter 2

The moment I entered the Crate my body warmed and relaxed. Her scent was everywhere. It was the strongest I'd smelled my mystery woman, my mate, since that very first day, warming up before my challenge with Kyle Westin. I had reneged on the challenge and it had cost me everything.

I was so grateful to Kyle and all the Westins for taking me in, and allowing me to stay in their territory. Liam and Chase had become staples at my place. They hung out there all the time, and it was great. I had a lot of brothers, five of them actually, but our father raised us in competition. His dream was to be the strongest, most powerful alpha in history. His plan was to keep Colin, my oldest brother, close to him, groomed to take over the pack someday. Then as other packs' firstborns began to mate we would each in turn challenge and defeat, essentially taking over that pack in alliance and dedication to him.

My brother Finn had done exactly as planned, challenging and defeating the alpha of a small pack in the Amazon. He seemed happy enough in life. So, when Kyle Westin mated, I was next in line. I had no choice in the matter, and my father had sent my challenge ahead of sending me. I was prepared to do as I had been raised, to fulfill my father's dream. As alpha of the prestigious Westin Pack, I would have been top son in my father's eyes. It was all I had ever wanted, and while a very small part of me regretted it being Kyle, who had been a friend to me through our college days, still I knew what I had to do and was prepared to do so. Until I got one whiff of the woman that would change my life forever.

It had been a rash decision on my part to pull out of the

challenges. I did not discuss with my father. I knew what he would have said. 'True mates made for weak males'. But knowing she was there, I hadn't been able to think straight. My entire focus had shifted to her and I didn't even know what she looked like, but her smell was like a drop of rain amidst a drought, and even through my frustrations over her elusiveness, I could not find it in me to regret the decision.

I had given up everything for her. My father had disowned me, furious over the situation and calling me a fool, telling me I had thrown my life away for a little bitch. The man I had worshiped my entire life had turned his back on me. I was forbidden to return to the Clan and it hurt. A lot. I could only hold on to the hope that she was truly worth it all. If only I could find her.

To say I was frustrated was an understatement. She was everywhere and yet I had never once laid eyes on her in the months I had been in San Marco. Every time I got close, she slipped away. After nearly three months I could only assume that she was deliberately avoiding me. But why? Finding a true mate was everything to a wolf. Our very core sought out that one person that would complete us, and while culturally our society had shifted away from the disappointment of never finding one's true mate, to settling for a compatible mate, it was still every wolf's desire to find that closeness and bond with a mate. I had never known how badly I wanted, no needed it.

There was no way that my mate did not recognize me equally as I had her. I just didn't believe that was even possible. So, every time I got close and she faded away on me, I responded in rejection and it was awful.

I knew the moment she had left the building and even though a part of me realized my friend was asking if I were okay, I ignored him and turned, running for the door, only to see a small dark car pull out amidst a cloud of dust. She was running from me. There was no mistaking it this time, and the physical pain that knowledge caused was staggering. Fighting the primal need to change and give chase was the hardest thing I had ever done.

"Are you okay? Dude, what's wrong?" Chase jumped from his truck and ran over to check on me. Liam was quickly by his side.

"Patrick? What's wrong?" his brother asked.

I just shook my head, trying to clear it as much as push them

277

away.

"I'm fine," I said, rubbing the empty hole in my heart she had once again left behind.

"You sure? You don't look so hot, man." Chase assured me.

"I said I'm fine." I snapped, turning to walk back into the Crate.

Kyle was grinning and his face fell when he looked at me. "Dammit, she eluded you again?"

I sighed, trying not to let the full extent of my frustration show even knowing that if there was anyone on this planet who understood, it was Kyle Westin. His mate had worked side by side with him for more than two years before ever showing a sign of mating. Daily rejection was his life, but even knowing he got it, I didn't want to share my pain with him. So, I just shrugged. "Safe to say she isn't ready for me to find her."

"What do you mean?" Lily asked.

"Every time Patrick gets close to his mate, she disappears on him." Kyle informed them.

A shared look between the girls didn't go unnoticed.

"What do you know about it?" I demanded.

"Nothing." Lily said like I was crazy and I felt crazy.

"I'm gonna head on," I told Kyle.

He sighed, no doubt feeling my frustrations and nodded.

"Call me if you want to talk. This one put me through absolute hell, but I can honestly say I'd go back and do it all over again. She's worth it, I promise." He grinned lovingly down at his beautiful mate.

"How about some Call of Duty to take your mind off things?" Chase offered.

"I will yea." I said sarcastically before changing my tone. "Sounds great," I replied, still with little enthusiasm. I really didn't want the company just then, but I couldn't tell the kid no. He meant well.

Kyle ended up blowing off the day to hang with us too. All my frustrations and anger were geared toward kicking three Westins' butts. After awhile I started to relax and even enjoy just hanging out with my friends, who had grown to mean more to me than my own brothers. These three men were truly everything I had wished my brothers had been. They were so close and loving. They actually cared for each other and respected one another. A simple video game such as that would have led to blood shed amongst my brothers, but while they were competitive with me and each other, there was no animosity. Whoever won, won and they congratulated each other and ribbed the losers.

I counted myself lucky to be a part of it, even in a small way. Why couldn't my mate have been their lovely sister, Lily? She was a little wild and still a little young in many ways I had noticed, but she was also sweet and fun. She was craic through and through. But mostly she would have made me a Westin. I sighed, wondering where that thought had come from. It wasn't that I had a bad family and I loved my clan. But it was just hard not to notice the differences there. I truly envied the close relationship the four Westin siblings had.

"Oh slam! Yes! You suck!" Chase yelled, jumping up suddenly and shaking me from my thoughts. As if on autopilot I raised my hand as he slapped his against mine. I hadn't even been paying attention to the game we were playing, but knew from my partner's enthusiasm we had just kicked some butt.

"Alright, alright," Kyle said. "I've got to get back to the office. Tomorrow is the Winter Solstice run, but Friday night you're on for a rematch, and Liam and I won't go so easy on you guys this time."

"Yeah, yeah, big words there suit boy. No way will you two ever take me and Patrick."

I laughed despite my melancholy mood. Chase could talk some shit. You had to love him.

"You're running with us tomorrow, right?" Liam asked me.

I sighed. I had always loved the Winter Solstice run. The longest night of the year. It was the best, but it was a pack thing.

"Wish I could, but that's a pack thing. It wouldn't be right."

"Don't be ridiculous, Patrick. Of course you are welcome to run with us. As long as you are staying in Westin territory, as far as I'm concern you're honorary Westin. Now I'm sure some would take exception to you showing up for a pack meeting, but I can't imagine anyone will care about the run." His face transitioned into a rather evil grin. "Plus, all pack members are required to run tomorrow. No exceptions. If your mate is truly Westin, she'll be there."

I didn't know how to feel about what he said. My mate would

279

be there. She couldn't just run away from me. Well, not exactly anyway. I realized there were a lot of wolves in the Westin pack. I'm not sure anyone but Kyle probably knew for certain just how many, but a lot. In wolf form I knew with certainty that I would hone in on her quickly, despite the large number.

"We'll start with a pack meal at the pack house and then we run. Hope you'll seriously consider joining us, for dinner and the run." Kyle added.

I nodded. "Sure, yea. I will. Thanks."

Nervous excitement caused goosebumps on my arms. Tomorrow night I was going to find her.

"Another round?" Liam asked after Kyle left.

We spent the rest of the evening wasting away in video games. Don't get me wrong, I loved playing and hanging with the guys, but I wanted some time alone to both sulk at the earlier rejection and to relish in the knowledge that I would see her in less than twenty-four hours.

"Do you have anything to eat around here?" Chase asked as his stomach grumbled.

"There's some crisps in the press," I told him.

"There's some what in the where?" he asked.

I just shook my head and walked into the kitchen to grab the bag of Lay's from the cabinet next to the fridge. I threw it next to him and sat back down.

"Chips. These are called chips," he informed me.

I rolled my eyes at him. "We will agree to disagree on that."

We continued to play for several more hours.

"Last round. I'm wrecked. Gunna call it." I informed them halfway through our current game. It was half eight at night. I was done.

"Ohhh, you suck. You suck." Liam teased, less obnoxiously than his younger brother at the close of our final game.

I shook my head at them, suddenly sad that none of my brothers would ever tease me in such a manner. The Westin's were truly a great family and they treated their pack fairly and with respect. Like they treated each other. Like family.

I had been around a lot of other packs. My father had seen to it that my brothers and I knew everyone in pack leadership for nearly every pack. We had been sent out to the best camps, schools, and eventually colleges for that purpose alone. Where other future alphas went, so did we, and we all knew that one day we would battle to take one of the lives and live that life with their mate. Having smelled my one true mate and knowing she was out there, it felt like the fear just thinking about it.

I couldn't afford to love this pack. I couldn't afford to fit in. Life just didn't work that way. My father was pissed, yea. But I had to believe he'd get over it and accept me back to the pack when the time came. As much as I liked the Westins, it was customary for a male wolf to find his mate and bring her back to his pack, not follow her to another pack. That could be perceived as a sign of weakness, and after the mess I had made with the challenges for Kelsey, I didn't need any more ammo pointing towards weakness.

No, I would find my mate and take her home. I sighed looking around the cottage I had grown to love. So why did it sometimes feel like I was finally home?

Made in the USA
Columbia, SC
15 October 2020